# The Unicorn Chronicles

Book One: Into the Land of the Unicorns
Book Two: Song of the Wanderer

## Bruce Coville

SCHOLASTIC INC.
New York Toronto London Auckland Sydney
Mexico City New Delhi Hong Kong Buenos Aires

*Into the Land of the Unicorns*, ISBN 0-439-10838-1, copyright © 1994 by Bruce Coville.

*Song of the Wanderer*, ISBN 0-590-45954-6, copyright © 1999 by Bruce Coville.
Book design by David Caplan.

All rights reserved. Published by Scholastic Inc. SCHOLASTIC and associated logos
are trademarks and/or registered trademarks of Scholastic Inc.

12 11 10 9 8 7 6 5 4 3 2                                   6 7 8 9 10/0

Printed in the U.S.A.                                   23

This edition created exclusively for Barnes & Noble, Inc.

2005 Barnes & Noble Books

ISBN 0-7607-6481-6

First compilation printing, March 2005

# Into the Land of the Unicorns

For Cara

# 1

# THE HUNTER

ramma, is that man following us?"

Cara's grandmother glanced over her shoulder, toward the library. When she turned back, her face was twisted in a look that Cara had never seen before. Tightening her grip on the girl's hand, the old woman began to walk faster.

Cara felt a sudden knot in her stomach. She had expected Grandmother Morris to say, "Don't be silly, child!" — as she usually did when Cara expressed some unlikely fear. She certainly hadn't expected her to act as if she took that fear seriously.

Stretching her legs to keep up, Cara asked, "Where are we going?" She tried not to whine.

"I'm not sure," muttered Grandmother Morris.

"Are we in danger?"

"Yes."

Cara's stomach grew even tighter. "How do you know?"

"Hush, child! I don't have breath to waste on talking."

Clutching her new library books, Cara bumped against bundles and packages as they scurried through the crowds of last-minute shoppers. A light snow had started to fall a little while ago, and it had had just enough time to cover the bright holiday decorations, making everything look crisp and white. Though it was hard to imagine any harm coming to them in this time of good cheer and fellowship, her grandmother's fear was unmistakable — unmistakable, and catching.

"In here," said Grandmother Morris suddenly, pulling Cara's arm to steer her to the right. They went down a narrow street — little more than an alley, really — and turned in through the side entrance of St. Christopher's.

Cara knew the church well. They had come here often with Simon, her grandmother's gentleman friend.

The building was dark and quiet inside. Grandmother Morris led the way to a pew near the back of the sanctuary, where they huddled together while the old woman caught her breath.

"I don't think he saw us come in," said Cara softly. The statement had more of hope than reality in it.

She actually had no idea whether their pursuer had seen them enter.

After a moment, Grandmother Morris removed a chain from around her neck. "Put this on," she said, handing it to Cara.

Cara's eyes widened. "Your special?" she asked. This was almost more frightening than the problem of the man who was following them. Grandmother Morris's "special," as Cara had always referred to the locket that dangled from the chain, had been off-limits for as long as she could remember. Despite the times she had coveted the gold and crystal amulet, she could barely bring herself to take it from her grandmother's hand. She felt accepting it would somehow confirm that the world was twisting out of shape.

"Take it," said her grandmother sternly. "Put it on. You may need it before this is over."

"Before what is over?"

"No time to talk," hissed her grandmother. *"Take it!"*

Trying not to make a sound, Cara placed her books on the pew. Then, reluctantly, she closed her hand over the bauble. Her fingers began to tingle.

Beneath the amulet's crystal lid lay a tightly coiled strand of white hair. "It came from a unicorn's mane," her grandmother had told her when she was little, and Cara had believed her until sometime around second grade, when she finally understood that unicorns were imaginary.

3

"What will I need it for?" she asked as she slipped the chain over her head.

Grandmother Morris leaned forward and rubbed her brow with her fingertips. "Do you think I'm crazy?" she whispered.

Cara felt another twinge of fear. *What kind of question is that?* she wondered. Before she could decide how to answer, they heard a step in the hall, followed by the creak — ever so slight — of a door swinging open. It was the same door, Cara was sure, that they themselves had come through when they entered the sanctuary.

Silence.

Was their hunter standing there, waiting for them?

To Cara's astonishment, her grandmother slid to the floor, ducking her head so that it was hidden by the pew in front of her. She tugged at Cara to indicate she should do the same. When Cara had joined her, the old woman began to move toward the center aisle of the church. Cara followed. The pews were too close together for them to drop to their knees and crawl. They moved instead by a sort of scooting method, until they came to the end of the pew. Then her grandmother did drop to her hands and knees.

No sound yet from the open door where their pursuer stood waiting. And no chance for Cara to question her grandmother as to what was going on.

When they reached the back of the church, they huddled together behind the last pew. Six or seven feet ahead of them loomed a pair of large wooden doors, impossible to open without drawing the attention of the pursuer. Cara stared at them the way a traveler in the desert might stare at an unclimbable glass wall behind which lay a pool of clear water.

They waited.

No sound from the front of the church. Was the man still there? Or had he closed the door so silently they hadn't heard and gone on to search elsewhere? How long would they have to stay like this? *Who was he, anyway?*

Cara trembled and tried not to cry as the questions and the fear swept through her. Raising her hand to her neck, she clutched the special. The feel of it brought back an old memory, something she could glimpse only in tatters and fragments. It was from just before she had lost her parents. She had been two, maybe three, years old, and very ill. Her grandmother had stayed by her bed for many hours. When she had finally been forced by another emergency to leave, she had acceded to Cara's pleading and left the amulet behind.

It was the first and only time Cara had had the special to herself. She had clutched it tightly as she drifted in and out of fever dreams. And in that time, as she tossed and moaned on the bed, something had come to her. She remembered only a glimpse of white and a sense of peace. Then something had touched her, a touch that was fierce and hard, both hot and cold at once. In that moment the fever had broken.

That was all that remained to her of a memory that had tugged and teased in the years that followed, slowly fading from the surface, yet never leaving altogether.

As she grew older, she told herself that it had been a hallucination, a side effect of the fever. Yet whenever she thought of the incident, she had a sense of something altogether unearthly having brushed her life. At times she had even longed to be ill again, in the hope that she might once more experience the strange mystery of that night. She could certainly use a little magic right now. . . .

She blinked. How long had she been sitting here, lost in memories? With some discomfort she realized that her leg was going to sleep beneath her.

Grandmother Morris leaned close. In a voice so soft that Cara could barely hear it, even though the old woman's lips were brushing against her ear, she whispered, "We have to get out of here. We're going to crawl to those doors as silently as we can. I will push one open. You go through first. Be ready to run if I give the word."

Cara nodded. Hoping that her sleeping leg wouldn't betray her, she tipped herself forward and began to crawl. The beating of her heart seemed to pound in her ears, the sound so loud she wondered that it alone did not alert their pursuer.

Grandmother Morris was close behind her.

And what of the man who was stalking them? Was

6

he still here — or had he given up, leaving them to fear nothing but shadows?

The smooth floor was cold beneath Cara's hands. The door was warmer and carved with designs that her fingertips couldn't quite decipher.

"Be ready," whispered Grandmother Morris. Kneeling beside Cara, she began to push on the door.

Cara wedged her way into the opening, scarcely daring to breathe. She was halfway across the threshold when her grandmother cried, "Run, Cara! *Run!*"

Springing to her feet, Cara bolted for the next set of doors, the ones leading to the outside. She grabbed the handles, then cried out in despair.

The doors were locked.

# 2

# LEAP OF FAITH

ara turned, frantic with fear.

"This way," cried Grandmother Morris, grabbing her hand.

They hurried through a small door at the side of the foyer. Inside, a set of narrow stairs spiraled up in a tight curve. Turning, Grandmother Morris shot the bolt in an old-fashioned latch. They started upward.

They had gone about ten steps when Cara heard someone slam into the door. The hunter! He slammed into it again, and she realized he was not just venting his anger; he was trying to break it down.

She didn't need her grandmother's urging to move faster. Heart pounding, she climbed as fast as she could, spiraling up into the darkness, ignoring the prickling of the pins and needles that tingled along her leg.

They came to a small landing. Cara heard a click as a dim light came on overhead. Her grandmother was leaning against the wall, one hand still on the light switch, the other pushing back loose strands of her long gray hair.

A thick rope ran through the center of the room, entering through a hole in the ceiling, leaving through a hole in the floor.

Another crash below. This time they could hear wood splintering. The door was not yet down, but it was clear that it was not going to last much longer.

"Do you have the amulet?" asked her grandmother.

Cara nodded.

"Good. Hold fast to it, and listen to me. I am going to ring the bell. It may bring help, but we can't be sure that it will come in time to save the amulet."

*The amulet?* thought Cara. *What about us?*

"Here is what you must do," continued her grandmother. "Climb to the top of the tower. The roof is flat, with a low wall surrounding it. Count the tolling of the bell. On the twelfth stroke, press the amulet tight to your chest and whisper, 'Luster, bring me home.' Then . . ." The old woman faltered, closed her eyes. Across her face moved a strange mixture of fear and longing, joy and loss.

Cara shivered again, with a new kind of fear, unlike that brought on by the pursuer.

"And then . . . ?" she prompted.

Her grandmother flinched at the sound of another crash from below. Turning to Cara, she looked her full in the eyes. "Then," she whispered, "you must jump."

Cara stared at her grandmother in disbelief. The question the old woman had asked in the sanctuary — *"Do you think I'm crazy?"* — took on a new and terrifying meaning. Before she could think of what to say, they heard another crash from below.

"That door won't last much longer," whispered Grandmother Morris. "He must not find the amulet. Climb, Cara, for your life, and for more than you can imagine. I have been there, my love, and it is wonderful. Do not be afraid. Hold the special. Count the chimes. Throw yourself to the wind, and this I promise: You *will* see unicorns."

"But . . ."

Another crash from below.

"Climb!" urged her grandmother, flinging herself on to the rope and pulling it down with all the weight of her slender body. "Climb! The amulet must not fall into his hands!"

"Who *is* he?" asked Cara.

The look of pain and sorrow that lanced through her grandmother's eyes was heartstopping. The old woman shook her head, as if driving away some unwelcome thought. "There's no time for talk," she replied, shouting to be heard above the tolling of the bell. Suddenly the rope surged up, pulling her with it, lifting her feet from the floor. "Remember," she cried, "you must jump on the twelfth chime of the bell! Don't lose track! Now go. *Go!*"

Cara turned and ran.

Another chime. And then her grandmother's voice, calling one last request: "Cara! Find the Old One. Tell her . . . tell her, 'The Wanderer is weary.' "

What Cara heard after that might have been a sob, but it was lost in the third toll of the bell, and she could not be certain.

Three strokes already. Cara ran faster, fearing she might not reach the top of the tower before the twelfth chime. At the thought, her footsteps faltered. She was running as if she actually intended to jump.

Did she?

*Could* she?

Hand on the rail, she spiraled up through the darkness, counting off the fourth and fifth chimes.

And their pursuer — was he running up the stairs now, too? Running toward Grandmother Morris? What if he caught her before she could toll the bell the twelfth time? *What then?*

She was breathing in great gasps. The back of her legs felt as if they were on fire. She heard the sixth chime — or was it the seventh? No, it was the sixth; it had to be the sixth. She mustn't lose count!

Her free hand, the one not on the rail, clutched the amulet hanging from her neck. It felt warm. She opened her fingers. To her astonishment, the amulet was starting to glow.

The seventh chime. *Seventh? It had to be the seventh, not the eighth.*

The glow of the amulet grew brighter. She loosened her grip on it and light flowed from between her fingers, bright enough to light her way as she scurried up the worn, wooden stairs, spiraling, spiraling toward the top of the tower.

At the eighth toll of the bell — she was sure it was the eighth — she came to a ladder. As she stepped on the first rung, she heard a scuffle break out below her, cries of anger from her grandmother and from a deep male voice. She wanted to turn back, to help, but her grandmother's urgent instructions had been to keep the amulet away from the man.

Clambering up the ladder, she pushed with all her might at the trapdoor on the top.

It wouldn't budge.

For a terrified moment she thought she would be trapped. But a sudden cry of pain from her grandmother filled her with such rage that without realizing what she was doing she flung the door open.

Footsteps from below. He was coming after her! And what of Grandmother Morris? What had he done to her?

The bell tolled again. Cara smiled grimly. Whatever had happened, her grandmother still had the strength to work the rope. Cara couldn't let the old woman down now.

She scrambled onto the roof of the tower, then

12

stopped as a heavy male voice called from below, "Wait! Cara Diana, wait!"

Terror froze her limbs. She had heard that voice before. Where? *Where?*

A cold wind whipped around her. The snow had turned from flakes to icy chips that stung her cheeks. She stumbled to the edge of the roof. Her senses reeled as she saw the white-covered world spread out beneath her.

The tenth chime sounded.

Again her grandmother's question, "Do you think I'm crazy?" caromed through her brain. The old woman *had* to be crazy, telling her to throw herself from the tower. Yet the amulet, casting its fierce glow through the storm, said otherwise, said there was magic afoot.

The next chime — the eleventh? — sounded as she climbed onto the chest-high wall that circled the roof.

Far below her, tiny dots were racing to get out of the storm. Were any of them racing to the church, racing to help her and her grandmother?

She braced herself, ready to jump — or at least try — at the twelfth chime.

Silence.

Fear clutched her heart. Had she miscounted? Had she missed the moment? If she jumped now would she simply fall to her death? Racked by confusion, she tottered on the wall, staring at the world so far below. Cold fear wound its way through her body.

A sound behind her. The pursuer had made it to the top of the stairs. Then the bell tolled once more, the twelfth and final time, and ahead of her a ball of light blossomed in the sky, its color the same spring green as the light flowing from between her fingers.

Clutching the amulet, Cara whispered, "Luster, bring me home!"

"Wait!" cried the man.

Snow whirled around her. The wind whipped through her hair. Leaning forward, Cara threw herself from the tower.

# 3

# LUSTER

he first rush, as she plummeted toward the sidewalk, was terrible. But before she could force a scream through her tightened throat, she fell into the green light, which swirled and twisted around her.

Then her fall was slow and strange, and though it seemed to take a long time, it was a time like dreaming. Afterward, she could no more have said how long the fall actually lasted than she could have numbered the stars in the sky.

Her landing was sudden but soft. She lay still for a moment, staring at the sunny sky above her, wondering where it had come from. After another moment she closed her eyes, as if to shut out the strangeness. Where was her grandmother? Where the hunter, the church, the snow-covered city?

Where was *she*?

She took seven deep breaths, trying to calm herself. After a moment she realized she was lying on something soft — moss, from the way it felt beneath her fingers.

*Moss?*

She turned her head to the side. She was indeed lying on a thick cushion of something that, if not moss, was close to it. Ahead of her loomed huge silver-barked trees, unlike any she had ever seen before.

She cried out in fear at the sight. Though she knew she had left her own world far behind, the proof of that journey offered by the strange trees jolted her like an electric shock. Only the fact that her grandmother had told her this would happen — at least, told her she was going to fall into another world — kept the wild panic fluttering in her chest from overwhelming her completely.

How was she to get home?

The thought surprised her. The truth was, home itself would not have mattered much, were it not for her grandmother. She had lived alone with Grandmother Morris since her parents, Ian and Martha Hunter, had abandoned her. She had been three at the time, and in the years that followed, she had suffered her way through a series of humiliations in school, picked on for everything from her deep red hair to the fact that she had no parents — as if she could do anything about either situation!

Many were the nights when, after crying herself to sleep, she had dreamed of leaving her own world behind and disappearing into the one she found in books, particularly the collections of fairy tales — *The Blue Fairy Book, The Red Fairy Book,* and others — that she had dug out of her grandmother's attic.

She looked around. Was that the kind of world she had entered now?

Remembering the tales, she wondered if she would find an old woman here in the woods. If so, would she be a cruel witch, or a magical helper? The question made her remember her grandmother's request: "Find the Old One. Tell her, 'The Wanderer is weary.'"

Well, if that's what her grandmother wanted, then the Old One, whoever she was, must not be too bad. Now if she only had some idea of how to go about looking for her!

After a moment, she realized she was hot. Standing, she shucked her winter coat. Still hot, she peeled off the blue sweater Grandmother Morris had knit for her the year before.

"That's better," she said, more to hear her own voice than anything else.

It *was* better, she realized. Not only because she was down to her preferred jeans and T-shirt, but because the air itself was better, far purer and cleaner than she was used to breathing. After several deep breaths she found herself almost giddy with the sweetness of it.

"I'm *here!*" she shouted.

Immediately she regretted the action. She had hoped perhaps her grandmother had friends here who were looking for her. But it suddenly occurred to her that someone else, someone not so friendly, might be seeking her as well.

With a sudden shiver, she wondered if the Hunter would be able to cross to this world. Was he seeking her even now? Biting her lip, she turned in a slow circle. Save for a soft breeze rippling through the leaves of the trees, she saw no sign of movement.

She repeated the circle, seeking a path, a sign, *anything* that might show her the way she should go next.

Nothing.

Fear began to rise in her again — fear not simply of being lost, but of everything that had happened this night. Or was it this *day?* Though it had been dark when she had leaped from the tower, it was now full light.

Part of her wanted to believe that the whole thing was a dream; that she would soon wake, snug in her bed, in her familiar, if somewhat nasty, world. Part of her quaked with astonishment at what she knew in her heart was real.

That astonishment increased as she began to look more closely at the world into which she had fallen.

At her feet grew something that was clearly a flower. Yet when she bent to examine it, the swollen purple blossoms, covered with a fine silvery fuzz, were so unlike anything she had ever seen that they sent a shiver along her spine.

Draping her coat and sweater over her arm, she walked around the edge of the clearing, searching for a path.

The silvery bark of the trees had a blue undertone that gave her the same kind of shiver the purple flower had. The deep green leaves hanging from their branches were round, smooth-edged, and nearly the size of her hand — not really strange, yet too different from any she had ever seen before to feel comfortably familiar. Cara ran her fingers over the smooth, peeling bark of a tree. To her surprise, a smell like cinnamon filled the air.

She began to circle the clearing a second time, feeling a growing sense of panic. If she could not find a way to determine which direction to go, she would have to enter the forest aimlessly.

*Or should I just stay here,* she wondered, *and see if anyone comes to get me?*

She shook her head. She knew that staying in one place if you were lost was the standard advice. But it only made sense if you could assume someone would be looking for you. She could hardly count on that in this situation; more likely no one in this world even knew she was here. Under the circumstances, waiting in one place to be found would be nothing more than relying on luck. And if there was one thing Grandmother Morris had taught her, it was that you had to make your own luck if you were going to survive in the world.

Halfway through her second circuit of the clearing she heard a faint, crystalline sound. She paused, held her breath, listened more carefully. Yes, there was no mistaking it: running water.

She smiled. *That* would give her something to head for. If she was going to find a path anyplace in this forest, it would most likely be near a stream. People always needed water.

With that thought, she struck off through the trees.

The soft forest floor smelled richly of leaves turning into soil. The forest itself was thick and deep, and once out of the clearing she saw a great variety of trees, many with gnarled trunks nearly as wide as her bed was long. Fortunately the undergrowth was sparse, so it was easy to wind her way among it. A mossy substance, mostly green, but with patches of brown, orange, and red, grew thickly on many of the trunks. Other mosslike things hung like streamers from the trees' lower limbs. Above them the weaving of branch and leaf was so dense that only an occasional shaft of light pierced the gloom. Something with bright wings fluttered past her.

She had often gone for walks in the woods with her grandmother, but none of the places they had visited had the sense of age that this one did; in no place had the trees seemed so old, so . . . dignified.

20

\*     \*     \*

It was not long before she came to a laughing stream. At once, she felt something begin to ease inside her. Her grandmother had always told her that if she was troubled she should find a place to sit by the water, and this was about the most perfect "sit by the water" spot she had ever seen. The stream, about four feet wide, was so clear she could see every leaf and pebble that lay beneath its surface. Gurgling and chuckling to itself, it rolled between mossy banks, here and there splashing around a polished brown stone that thrust above the surface.

She sat down on the bank. After a moment, she took off her boots and socks and dangled her feet in the water, which was cool, but not too cold for comfort.

*I wish Grandmother Morris was here.*

The thought threw her mind back to those last moments in St. Christopher's. What had happened after she jumped? Had help arrived? Was her grandmother all right? Or had the Hunter managed to hurt her, even —

Cara clamped down on the thought, forcing it from her mind. Her grandmother had to be all right.

Lifting the amulet over her head, she looked at it again. Had the white hair coiled inside really come from a unicorn's mane? Her mind reeled with the thought, and again the strangeness of all that had happened made her feel as if she were adrift on some strange sea, with no shore in sight.

Wiping away the single tear that rolled down her cheek, she looked at the amulet.

"What is going on?" she asked, speaking as if it could answer.

So intent was she on her fears that she didn't notice the slender figure that slipped from the shadows and began to slink toward her. She continued to stare at the amulet until a pale hand darted over her shoulder and tried to snatch it from her fingers. She spun in anger, then screamed at what she saw.

Standing before her, clutching at the amulet, trying to tear it from her hand, was a manlike creature slightly more than three feet tall. He had an enormous head, and eyes that were large even for that. A few strands of brownish hair straggled over a scalp the color of a mushroom. His small nose turned up so sharply that it looked like little more than a pair of holes in the middle of his face.

The creature wore a dark green tunic, belted at the center, and brown boots that reached almost to his knobby knees. His lean arms rippled with muscles.

"Skraxis!" he shrilled. He grabbed at the amulet again, this time managing to tangle his fingers in the chain.

"Let go!" cried Cara desperately. The amulet was her only link to her own world. If the creature managed to steal it, she might never find her way back.

For a moment, the two of them struggled over the

amulet, the pale creature hissing and shrieking, Cara grim and silent.

Finally she yanked so hard that she managed to wrench the chain from the monster's grasp. The sudden release caused her to topple backward. Still clutching the amulet, she smashed against a sharp rock. Pain washed over her like a wave as she fell into the rushing stream.

Shrieking with rage, the creature came splashing after her. Dazed by pain, Cara was unable to fight back as he grabbed her by the neck and began slowly forcing her head below the surface.

The cold water kept her alert, even as blackness began to swim before her eyes. *Give him the amulet!* screamed a voice in her brain. *If you don't, you're going to die!*

But some other part of her, aware that her grandmother had sent her here to keep the amulet from falling into the wrong hands, forced her to cling to the golden chain.

The darkness grew deeper, more solid around her. Suddenly the fire in her lungs drove her to a final burst of energy. Thrashing wildly, she tried to break free.

Her efforts made no difference; the creature continued to hold her down. At last there was no energy left, and she felt herself sinking into oblivion.

# 4

# IN THE CAVE

hen Cara woke, she was in a cave. Almost instantly, as if by reflex, her fingers flew to her throat.

The amulet was gone!

The horror of that discovery distracted her for a moment from the hot patch of pain throbbing in her side. She would be trapped here forever. Even worse, she had let her grandmother down.

She clamped down on the panic. She was alive, and that was the first thing. Grandmother Morris always said if you were alive, you had a chance. Suddenly she remembered her battle with the goblinlike creature in the forest. How in heaven's name had she gotten from there to here?

Where *was* "here," for that matter?

Trying to stay calm, she forced herself to start taking stock of her surroundings. Dim light from a single torch showed her that she was lying on a bed made of moss and leaves. She turned sideways, her movement causing the "mattress" to release a faint odor of flowers. It was pleasant. Unfortunately, moving also caused a wave of dizziness.

She closed her eyes, counted to ten, then opened them again. Slowly. Trying not to cry, she began to look about the cave.

The rocky walls were bare, save for a large decoration made from the boughs of a flowering bush or tree. Below the boughs stood a huge, rough-hewn chair. Its seat was rounded up on the edges, and the depression in the center was filled with moss and leaves, much the same as her bed.

Then her eyes fell upon the occupant of the cave. She gasped, her reaction an equal mixture of surprise and fear.

More than anything, he looked like a bear that had started to become a man but hadn't finished the process. Tall and broad shouldered, he had a shaggy coat of fur that covered most of his body, and a short, broad muzzle that ended in a black nose.

He started toward Cara. She gasped, and if she had had the strength, she would have bolted from her bed. Lacking that, she tried to convince herself that if the creature had wanted to hurt her he would already have done so. But was he her rescuer or simply a jailer?

He bent over to peer into her face, and the unexpected intelligence in his large black eyes made her shiver. Broad nostrils quivering, he put a rough, fur-covered paw against her cheek. In a voice only a half tone from a growl he said, "Garzim?"

"What?"

"Garzim?" he repeated. Then, with a look of frustration, he turned away.

Cara pushed herself to her elbows, trying desperately to think of some way to communicate with the creature. Always eager to help, she had been upset by the look of disappointment on his face when he realized he could not speak to her.

He returned a moment later, carrying the base of a thick branch. When he held it in front of her she saw that it had been hollowed out to hold liquid. The manbear grunted and thrust it toward her.

She hesitated, then took the crude cup and drank from it.

The manbear smiled — a somewhat frightening sight, given the large, sharp teeth he thus displayed — and grunted approval.

Cara smiled, too, partly because she felt she had made positive contact with the creature, partly because what she had expected to be water was actually a tea of some sort. It tasted quite wonderful. Even better, it soon made her feel good enough that she tried to get to her feet.

That movement was a mistake. A wave of dizziness overwhelmed her and with a groan she sank back against the bed.

The creature made a sound of distress and bent over her.

"Don't worry," she mumbled. "I'm all right."

The absurdity of claiming she was all right when she couldn't even stand made her remember her grandmother's frequent claim that she, Cara, would claim she was all right even if she belonged in a hospital. Though she tried to hold it in, the thought of her grandmother caused a tear to trickle down her cheek. *Where is grandmother now?* she wondered.

"Guh-izz glack?" growled her new friend.

Though his voice was rough, and Cara had no idea what the words meant, she could tell they expressed sympathy. Hardly thinking about it, she reached out and put her hand on the creature's thick, furry arm.

"Guh-izz glack," he repeated, more gently this time.

Then — so quickly that she later decided it must have been an effect of the drink the creature had given her — she fell back to sleep.

When the pain in her side woke her again, the cave was even darker than before. The silvery light filtering in at what she now realized was the entrance of the cave made her think it must be night.

How long had she slept? And where was her new

friend? The moment of loneliness that overwhelmed her was quickly replaced by a tremor of fear. With her protector gone, could the goblinlike creature that had attacked her in the woods trace her here and try again?

Her fear doubled when she heard something move at the front of the cave. She prepared to leap from the bed, hoping that her legs would hold her. At the same time she tried to stay calm, telling herself it was probably only her host, returning from whatever he had been doing.

Then fear and hope and all attempts at calm were washed away in a tide of wonder, as a creature of such exquisite loveliness that the very sight of him brought tears to her eyes stepped into the moonlight.

In shape, he was much like a horse, though somewhat smaller and more finely built. His hooves were cloven, like a goat's, rather than solid like those of a horse. Mane and flowing tail seemed spun of silver cloud and moonlight. From between his enormous dark eyes thrust a spiraled horn, three feet long at the least, that glowed as if lit from within.

Except for the trembling that had overtaken her, Cara sat without moving as the unicorn began to walk to her. The sound of his hooves against the stony floor of the cave was like distant silver bells.

She wanted to cry out to him, tell him how beautiful he was, but worried that if she spoke he would turn and go. Not from fear; his grace and power were such that she could not imagine him being afraid of her — or of anything, for that matter. It was simply that the moment was so fragile she feared anything might shatter it.

She held out her hands.

The unicorn continued to walk toward her. When he was about five feet away, he lowered his horn and pointed it directly at her chest.

Cara caught her breath. What was he going to do? Unsure whether she had even enough strength to stand, she braced herself to try to run.

Yet, as if enchanted, she could not bring herself to move.

The horn drew closer. Still she did not flinch, not even when it pressed against her shirt. Only when it pierced her flesh and began driving on toward her heart did she cry out.

# 5

# LIGHTFOOT

he moment of pain was brief but intense. When it faded, a tingling spread over Cara's skin, as if she were being shocked by a thousand tiny batteries.

The unicorn stepped back in surprise.

Cara looked down at her chest. The fabric of her shirt was torn where the horn had pierced it. Yet the flesh beneath was unbroken, bloodless, the only sign of what had just happened a tiny, star-shaped scar.

The unicorn laid his horn gently upon her shoulder. Then, to her astonishment, he spoke to her: "I see I am not the first of my kind that you have met. Alas, you have a wound that not even I can heal."

The puzzling message came not in words as Cara knew them, sounds made in the throat and carried on the air. Instead, the silvery creature spoke inside her head, his meaning carried to her in a strange internal combination of images, sounds, feelings — even smells — that she could not have explained, yet that was so perfectly clear she understood even the note of surprise that underlay his thought.

"I'm not going to hurt you," he added. "I just wanted to make it possible to communicate with you. It will be easier for me to heal you if we can speak."

"What do you mean?" she asked, trying to keep her voice from quavering.

"Don't speak out loud! I can't understand you that way. Just form the thought and send it to me. You'll need to stay in contact with me, at least for now."

Though the horn was already resting on her shoulder, she gingerly set her hand on it for good measure. It was as smooth as the inside of an oyster shell, and pleasantly warm.

"Where am I?" she asked.

She sensed him receiving the message. *I'm talking to a unicorn!* she thought, so excited she almost missed his answer.

"You are in the Cave of the Dimblethum," he told her. "In the Forest of the Queen, on the edge of the wild, in the world of Luster."

"Luster?"

"The home of the unicorns."

For a moment, Cara felt as if she could not think at all. Then the questions came in a flood. "What has happened to me? Who are you? Who is the creature that lives in this cave? How can I get home? Do you know my grandmother? Why did you —"

"Wait, wait!" interrupted the unicorn. "I can't possibly answer all those at once. Let's start with some of the easier ones. My name is Lightfoot. And yours?"

"Cara."

"What has brought you here, Cara? Very few humans can cross the borders of Luster these days." He paused, then looked at her oddly and repeated, "Very few." This time the underlying tone of his message was not surprise, but concern.

She started to tell her story, but found herself lapsing into speech without realizing it. She started again. It was surprisingly hard to only *think* what she wanted to tell him, and not say it out loud.

"You'll get better at it," he said reassuringly. "Try again."

Concentrating, she managed to get through the whole story without slipping into speech more than three or four times. The unicorn looked startled, and somewhat worried, when she mentioned her grandmother's request that she "Find the Old One."

"What's the matter?" she asked.

"Nothing," he replied. "Go on with your story."

She looked at him suspiciously, but continued the tale. When she was done he said, "This is more serious than I realized when the Dimblethum came to fetch me."

"The Dimblethum?"

"Your host and rescuer. You're resting in his bed

right now. He's a gruff beast, and generally a loner, so he is somewhat disturbed at having you here — though to tell you the truth I think he rather likes you. It's good for him, if you ask me. Shake him up a bit."

"Where is he now?"

"Gathering some herbs to help you regain your strength. I can heal any serious wounds you might have suffered when you were attacked, but recovery involves more than just healing. Crossing from your world to Luster probably took its toll on you as well. You'll need to rest for a few days. As to the healing — do you have specific wounds I can tend to?"

In the excitement of meeting the unicorn, she had nearly forgotten the pain in her side. But his question reminded her of the wound, and at once she felt it stab through her.

"Here," she said, pointing.

She realized that she should have thought it rather than said it, but the pointing got the message across. Lightfoot stepped back. Returning his horn to her shoulder, he thought, "Show me."

She pulled up her shirt. The raw wound underneath was so ugly it made her gasp to see it. The pain suddenly increased, as if her being aware of the injury made it somehow worse.

Lightfoot turned his head to get a better look at the problem. Whatever he thought of it, the information did not reach Cara, because she was no longer in contact with him.

After a moment he turned his head back and placed his horn on the wound. She cried out at the flash of pain that accompanied the healing. Then the flesh drew together and all pain vanished.

"You fixed it!" she cried in delight.

He nodded, but turned away from her. He took three steps. Then, to her horror, his legs buckled and he crumpled to the floor of the cave.

"Are you all right?" she cried. Realizing he could neither understand nor answer her, she threw aside the covers and stood. Instantly she fell back to the bed. Closing her eyes, she took a deep breath then slid to the floor. She made her way to the unicorn on her hands and knees. Placing one hand on his silky flank, she repeated desperately, "Are you all right?"

She had barely formed the question before he was reassuring her. "Sorry! I should have warned you. A healing takes a great deal out of me — and this healing was more complicated than I expected."

"Why is that?" she asked, feeling worried.

He hesitated, then said, "You have an old wound, very deep. It is a wound of the spirit, not the flesh, and not something that can be quickly cured, even by the power of my horn."

She flinched and drew her hand back from him. A lump of unexpected pain lodged itself in her throat.

The unicorn waited a moment, then leaned against

her. "I do not know the source of the wound," he said gently. "I cannot read your mind — I only understand what you send me."

"I want to rest now," she responded, her voice sharper than she intended. She started to crawl back toward the bed, then thought better of it. Moving closer to Lightfoot, she lay her head on his side and sighed. The loss of her parents was something she did not talk about. Never. Not with anyone.

With a skill born of long practice, she pushed her secret sorrows to the back of her mind and slept.

She was woken by something pulling her hair.

Before she could force her eyes open she heard Lightfoot whicker. A small voice chattered an indignant reply.

Now she did manage to open her eyes.

Crouching near her was a creature just over a foot high. It looked like a cross between a monkey and a squirrel. It had thick fur that grew in two shades of gray, dark on its head and back, lighter on its face, limbs, and stomach. Its bushy tail flicked back and forth as it stared at her from enormous eyes that seemed much too large for its face. Those eyes — dark, with bright blue pupils — were lively and intelligent.

Cara was accustomed to small animals being timid around humans, so she was startled when the gray creature skittered up to her face. Extending a three-fingered hand, it touched her cheek, then rubbed it with its thumb.

"Don't be frightened," Lightfoot told her. "He's harmless. Annoying, but harmless."

"What . . . who is he?" she thought.

"The Squijum."

Cara reached toward the little creature. When her hand made contact with him, he blinked but did not run. His fur was soft and warm.

"*The* Squijum?" she thought to Lightfoot. "Does that mean he's the only one?"

"As far as I know."

"If he's the only one, where did he come from?"

"I don't have the slightest idea," replied the unicorn. "And I'm sure I don't care," he added pointedly.

The Squijum turned his head and chittered at Lightfoot. Even without her connection to Lightfoot, his indignation would have been clear to Cara. *With* the connection, she understood him to be saying something along the lines of, "Mean hornhead not love good Squijum phooey bad hotcha!"

Lightfoot snorted in response.

Suddenly a shadow stretched over them. With a screech the Squijum scrambled over Cara's side and cowered behind her.

Cara turned to look over her shoulder. For a moment her heart leaped in horror. Almost as quickly, she felt a surge of relief. The creature standing at the entrance of the cave was the one she had seen the first time she woke here — the Dimblethum. She wondered if he, too, was the only one of his kind.

He appeared to be smiling, though it wasn't easy to tell, given his bearlike face. Holding up a big, furry paw, he said, "The Dimblethum has something that belongs to you."

# 6

# THE QUEEN'S AMULETS

"The amulet!" cried Cara. "Where did you find it?"

The Dimblethum looked at Lightfoot, who made some noises in his throat. With a shock, Cara realized that he was repeating her words, translating them for the Dimblethum. But it made sense; just because her connection to Lightfoot let her understand the Dimblethum, there was no reason to expect that *he* would be able to understand *her*.

When Lightfoot was done translating, the Dimblethum made a sound deep in his throat that she took to be a chuckle. "Old Dimblethum has his ways," he said. Crossing to where she sat beside Lightfoot, he dropped the amulet into her lap.

She picked it up with her free hand, then cried out in sorrow when she realized that the golden chain had been broken.

"Peace," said Lightfoot. "Chains can be mended. It is enough that we have it back."

Blushing at the rebuke, Cara turned to the Dimblethum and said, "Thank you." Lightfoot translated for her. The manbear nodded and made a growl of acceptance.

"How did you get it back from the delver?" the unicorn asked, echoing Cara's earlier question. He spoke aloud for the Dimblethum's sake, at the same time sending the message to Cara. From the picture that formed in her mind, she understood that by "delver" he meant the creature that had attacked her in the woods.

The Dimblethum chuckled again. "Friends of the Dimblethum followed delver through the forest. Friends of the Dimblethum kept watch, kept track, kept hot on trail. Friends of the Dimblethum showed the way. Easy to follow delver. Easy to crunch delver, bring back amulet."

Now the creature scowled and held out his big hand in a gesture that Cara understood to mean that he wanted her to hand him the amulet. Broken chain dangling over his furry fingers, he held it up and said, "What is not easy is what to do next. This cannot stay here."

"Why not?" asked Lightfoot.

"Look carefully. This is one of the five."

39

"Hotcha!" cried the Squijum, running up the Dimblethum's side as if he were climbing a tree. "Let's see, let's see!"

The Dimblethum plucked the Squijum from his side and dropped him to the floor.

"Want to see!" he sputtered. But he stayed where he had landed — at least until the Dimblethum held the amulet before Lightfoot. Then he scurried underneath the larger creature and looked up eagerly.

After a moment the unicorn sighed. "You're right, it *is* one of the five."

"What are you talking about?" asked Cara.

Lightfoot closed his eyes. "Many centuries ago the Queen ordered the creation of five amulets to be used as rewards for those who had given great service to Luster. The wisdom of this decision is still much argued, for the special property of these amulets was that under the right circumstances they would let the bearer pass between Earth and Luster without going through one of the main gates. This is a great power. Like most great powers, it carries the possibility for great mischief. How did you come by this amulet, anyway?"

"My grandmother gave it to me."

"Who is your grandmother?" asked the unicorn curiously.

"Her name is Ivy Morris."

"That sounds familiar," he said after a moment. "I suppose I should have paid more attention in history."

Cara was trying to take in the idea that her grandmother had done something important in the history of this world when the Dimblethum growled, "The amulet must go to the Queen."

"Wait a minute," Cara objected. "My grandmother told me to find the 'Old One.' *That's* where I want to go. And the amulet stays with me!"

At once she wondered if she would make the others angry. But Lightfoot actually laughed — a beautiful, bell-like sound.

"What's so funny?" she demanded.

"One of the Queen's many names is the 'Old One.' So the Dimblethum is suggesting the same thing your grandmother wanted." He sighed, then added, "Unfortunately, I think the Dimblethum is right."

"Of course the Dimblethum is right!" growled that creature. "If this amulet falls into the wrong hands — "

He broke off, shaking his head at the thought.

"I can help; I can guide!" chittered the Squijum.

Lightfoot's response to the little creature's claims was a derisive snort.

"Small and fast!" the squijum chittered, scampering around the Dimblethum's feet. "Small and fast, can look and find! Want to go! Hotcha!"

"If I say no, I suppose you'll follow us anyway," said Lightfoot.

"Yes! Yes! Glorious yes!" he cried, hugging his tail.

"How about you?" Lightfoot asked, turning to the Dimblethum. "If we go to the Queen, will you accompany us?"

The creature made a series of whuffles and growls that translated to: "The Dimblethum will come part of the way with you. But despite your friendship with him, you know he has little love for your kind, invaders that you are. He will not enter the court of the Queen."

"Invaders?" Cara thought to Lightfoot.

"I will explain later," he replied.

Once it was decided that they were to carry the amulet to the Queen, the conference quickly ended. It was clear that the Dimblethum was not the sort to sit around and chat; decision made, he was ready to leave. And since there was nothing to pack, no relatives to notify, no mail to cancel, there was not much for it but to get up and go. However, therein lay the problem: Both Cara and Lightfoot were still too weak to travel.

"Tomorrow morning, at first light," promised the unicorn. "I'll be ready then."

The Dimblethum made an unhappy noise deep in his throat. "The longer we stay here, the more apt the delvers are to come for us. They will be mad that the Dimblethum took the amulet back. The Dimblethum is more than a match for three or four of them. If they send more, the Dimblethum and his friends could be in trouble."

"We'll be in as much trouble if we try to travel too soon," replied Lightfoot. "Both the child and I will slow things down, and make us easy targets. By morning I will be at full strength, and can even carry her if necessary."

The Dimblethum grumbled but admitted the sense in this. Scooping Cara into his great arms, he deposited her in the bed once more. He roamed restlessly about the cave for a while and finally went back out into the night.

Once he was gone, Lightfoot knelt beside Cara's bed. She placed her hand on his shoulder.

"I have so many questions!" she thought to him.

"My mother says I have an answer for everything," he replied, sounding amused. "Of course, she also claims most of them are neither right nor wise. But I'll do what I can."

"Where is your mother?" asked Cara. She had a thousand other questions, all of them more pressing. But her sudden sense that the unicorn was perhaps not as old as she had first thought, combined with her own interest in missing mothers, pushed the other questions aside.

"She is at Summerhaven," said Lightfoot. "With the Queen."

Cara detected a note of uneasiness beneath his light tone. Remembering his earlier comment about it being unfortunate that the Dimblethum was right, she said, "You don't really want to go there, do you?"

"I don't want to talk about it," he replied sharply. "When you said you had questions, I didn't realize they were all going to be about me!"

Cara lifted her hand from his shoulder, a little

surprised that he could be so testy. After a moment she tried again. "Why did the Dimblethum call you invaders?"

Lightfoot sighed. "My friend does not like it that we unicorns came here from Earth. Actually, I don't think he minds *us* so much as the fact that in opening gates between Earth and Luster we made it possible for *others* to enter here as well. He holds the unicorns responsible for everyone who has come here as a result — including the delvers." He paused, then said, "Also, I think something happened between the Dimblethum and the Queen. Unfortunately, I've never been able to get that story."

"Is the Queen a unicorn or a human?" asked Cara.

Lightfoot snorted at the idea that the Queen might be a human. "Her name is Arabella Skydancer," he said, "and she is the oldest and the wisest of our kind. Unfortunately, she is thinning now. Sometimes you can see right through her."

"Thinning?"

An uncomfortable silence fell between them. After a moment Lightfoot muttered, "I have said more than I should."

Cara clenched her jaw. She hated that kind of half secret.

"How far away is the Queen?" she asked, looking for a question that Lightfoot *would* answer.

"Many days. How many depends partly on how fast you can travel — that, and how much trouble we have along the way."

"Are you expecting trouble?"

"It depends on what the delvers are up to."

"Tell me about the delvers."

"Nasty creatures," replied Lightfoot. She could feel his flesh shiver beneath her fingers. "They live underground, and they are the sworn enemies of the unicorns."

His message didn't come precisely in words, of course; part of it was an *image* of a delver.

"Why are they your enemies?" asked Cara.

"Many reasons," replied Lightfoot. He paused, then added, "Our path will take us to Grimwold's Cavern. Perhaps he will tell you more about them."

"Grimwold?"

"He is the Keeper of the Unicorn Chronicles, and he knows more stories than anyone in the world. However, right now I am only interested in one story, and that is the one in which we are caught. In that story, the only clever thing for either of us to do is get some rest so we will be ready to travel in the morning."

Cara began to protest. Her mind was spinning with a thousand more questions. But she had already pushed herself further than she should, and her body was insisting that she sleep. No amount of curiosity was able to overcome that need.

Lying back, she quickly fell into a deep slumber, waking only when the Dimblethum returned with leaves and berries. She watched as he brewed some tea, which he brought to her in one of his wooden cups. Remembering the last drink he had served her, she took an eager sip.

"Gack!" she cried. "This is terrible!"

Making a face, she tried to hand the cup back to him.

He growled, which made her flinch, even though by now she understood that the sound was more likely to be the Dimblethum's version of speech than an actual danger sign.

Resting his horn on her shoulder, Lightfoot said, "Drink it. It will help you regain your strength — which you're going to need."

Cara grimaced but took the cup back from the Dimblethum and downed the entire brew. When she was finished she rubbed her hand over her mouth and said bitterly, "That's worse than the stuff Grandmother Morris gives me when I'm sick."

The thought of her grandmother sent a wave of worry washing through her. Again — as she would often in the days to come — she wondered if the old woman had escaped the man who had been chasing them.

"Go back to sleep," Lightfoot told her. "We travel at first light, and you need all the rest you can get."

She closed her eyes but did not sleep. Now that the edge of her exhaustion had been dulled, the questions and fears that filled her mind came to the fore again. She was impossibly far from home, from her grandmother, from everything she had ever known and loved, and she had no idea whether she would ever see any of them again. A tear trickled from the corner of her eye.

She lay still in the darkness, looking into the darkness inside, fighting back the memory of her earliest loss, the most painful one of all. The hurt was still strong, after all these years. After a time it merged in her mind with her last afternoon on Earth and the terrifying pursuit in the church. She slipped into a fever dream as her imagination kept struggling and failing to form the face of the man who had chased them. She cried out into the darkness, certain that if she could only see that face, it would solve a great riddle for her.

# 7

# JOURNEY

The Forest of the Queen, Cara decided, must go on forever. They had been traveling since first light, and nothing seemed to have changed. The trees still stretched as far as she could see in every direction — not that she could see very far.

It didn't bother her, really. She loved being in the woods, and now that she had Lightfoot, the Dimblethum, and the Squijum for company, she felt neither as lonely nor as frightened as she had the day before. Her mood was helped by the forest itself, which was deeply beautiful, filled with great trees, mossy boulders, and babbling brooks. Brightly colored birds flew overhead, and butterflies floated in the few shafts of sunlight that managed to pierce the forest canopy.

Oddly, her worst moments came when she saw the most beautiful sights. Before she could block the thought, she would think, *I wish Gramma could see this!* — which would immediately make her aware of how far from home she was and of her concern for her grandmother.

At those times she would wrap her hand around the amulet, and holding it tight, think, *I'll come back to you, Grandmother! I won't leave you!* She meant it; she knew too well what it was like to be abandoned.

Though the Dimblethum appeared to be lumbering along, he moved with a speed and silence that — given his size — was astonishing to Cara. As for the Squijum, he kept scampering ahead, disappearing from sight, then racing up from behind them. He was forever skittering up the trunk of one tree and zipping back down another, and twice Cara saw him make a long leap from one branch to another. She caught her breath at the sight. Though it was no more than she had seen squirrels do at home, watching a creature she had actually spoken to do it made the stunt seem vastly more daring.

Cara had started out walking, but after an hour she found herself stumbling and dizzy. The second time she tripped over a root, Lightfoot knelt and told her to climb on his back. She was thrilled at the thought of riding a unicorn but a little worried as well. It felt not properly respectful — a little like blowing bubblegum in church.

"It would certainly astonish Moonheart to hear you say that," Lightfoot responded, when she expressed her concern.

"Who is Moonheart?"

Lightfoot snorted. "My uncle. He's also one of the crankier unicorns you are apt to meet. I don't think he can imagine anyone feeling a need to show *me* respect."

This talk of uncles and respect prompted Cara to ask something else she had been wondering: "How old *are* you, anyway?"

"Old by your terms, quite young by ours."

"What does that mean?"

"Specifically? It means that even though I am slightly over a hundred years old, Moonheart and the others treat me as if I were what you would call 'a teenager.' "

"How do you know about things like teenagers?" she asked in surprise.

"Oh, we watch your world fairly carefully. Look out — low branch coming up."

Cara ducked as they passed under the branch. Her long red hair spilled forward so that it draped across Lightfoot's shoulder, looking like wine on white silk.

Since she was not speaking aloud, it was perfectly easy to carry on the conversation while she was bent low to his neck. "How do you watch our world?" she asked. "And *why*?"

"You make us nervous," he replied. "The unicorn hunters — who drove us from Earth to begin with — have not forgotten us. They are forever trying to find a way to come here. That is one reason the amulets are so dangerous."

"There are still people on Earth who hunt unicorns?" she asked in surprise. "I thought everyone believed you were imaginary." She blushed, wondering if she had insulted him.

"That's what we would like them to think," he replied. "But there are some who know the truth, some friends, some enemies."

She felt a sense of embarrassment at coming from a species that had hunted unicorns, and wished that she could separate herself from the brutality of the idea. She decided to change the subject.

"What did you mean when you said that you were not the first of your kind that I had met?" she asked.

"Don't you remember?" he asked in surprise.

"Maybe I do," she said slowly. "Was it when I was very little?"

"I don't know. I simply know that I could tell that I was not the first unicorn to heal you."

"I knew it!" she cried. "I always thought I had been visited by a unicorn when I was little. But after a while people convinced me that I must have been imagining it."

"It's just as well," he replied. "As I said, we prefer people to believe we don't exist."

She had more questions, but just then their path led them by a narrow waterfall that wavered down the face of a cliff towering at least a thousand feet above them. At the base of the fall was a pool, from which ran a stream that crossed their path.

"Hold tight," said Lightfoot. Before Cara had a chance to ask why, he started to run, then leaped nimbly over the stream. The Dimblethum splashed through, grumbling to himself as he went. The Squijum crossed by climbing a tree and leaping from its branches to those of a tree on the other side.

A clearing bordered the pool on this side of the stream, and they decided to stop for a rest. Lightfoot nibbled pale green flowers from a vine that grew at the edge of the trees. The Dimblethum pointed to some berries and with a nod indicated that Cara should eat them. She was more than happy to oblige and even happier when they exploded in her mouth with a burst of flavor sweeter and tangier than any she had experienced at home.

The Dimblethum started to pick berries from a spot close by her side. Looking up at his towering presence, Cara wondered if he was standing so close to be sociable, or if he was there to protect her. Either way, she was glad of his presence. She wished very much that she could talk to him.

Having eaten her fill, she found herself thirsty. She looked at the stream, wondering if it was safe to drink

52

from it. Unable to ask the Dimblethum, she went to Lightfoot and placed her hand on his shoulder.

"I'm thirsty."

"Wait until I clear the water."

"What do you mean?"

"It's one of our tricks," he replied, and this time she felt a bit of a chuckle beneath the answer. Walking lightly across the grass, he knelt at the edge of the pool and lowered his horn so that the tip was immersed in the water.

Cara hurried over to stand beside him.

The surface of the pond seemed to tremble as rays of silver extended from Lightfoot's horn across the water — though whether they were a reflection of the horn, or something stranger, Cara could not say for sure.

In the center of the pond a large fish broke the surface, leaped twisting and golden into the air, then returned to the water with a loud *smack!*

A moment later Lightfoot stood and shook his head, spattering silver water in all directions.

Cara put her hand on his shoulder.

"Safe to drink," he thought to her. "Actually, it was all right before I did that, though I couldn't have been certain until I tried it. Anyway, it will taste better now."

"Thank you," she replied.

Kneeling, she cupped her hands in the water, which was crystal clear, and lifted some to her lips. It was like drinking diamonds. She drank more, dipping her hands greedily into the stream. When she was full, more than full, she rinsed her face and turned to Lightfoot to ask him what he had done to the water.

Before she could speak, the Squijum began to shriek.

Lightfoot spun, reared on his hind legs, trumpeted in anger. The Dimblethum began to roar. Cara slipped her hand into her pocket and clutched the amulet.

# 8

# DELVERS

band of delvers — at least a dozen of them — stood in the shadows at the edge of the clearing. Each was holding a spear topped by a wicked-looking metal point.

Cara held her breath. Even if her friends managed to stand against these numbers — which seemed unlikely — she could not imagine them coming through the battle unscathed. She began to tremble. Though she had only known them for a day, the idea of any of them being hurt was more than she could bear. She tried to force her mind to erase the terrible images it was creating, images of Lightfoot being speared by a delver, falling, bleeding. . . .

*Stop it!* she told herself. *You have to be ready to help.*

The thought astonished her. How could *she* help in the fight that seemed to be brewing? Yet she realized that she had no choice. If battle came, she would join in.

The two groups stood staring at each other for a long moment. Then, to Cara's astonishment, three of the delvers carefully placed their spears on the ground. Holding their empty hands before them, they took ten steps into the clearing.

Cara edged closer to Lightfoot and laid her hand on his flank.

"What's happening?"

"I don't know. Just listen. I can't talk to you now, I have to pay attention to the enemy."

She made no response but kept her hand in place.

One of the delvers spoke. His voice was harsh, and the words Cara heard held no meaning at all. But through Lightfoot she understood the delver to be asking if they could talk rather than fight.

Lightfoot dipped his horn in response to the delver's request. The Dimblethum growled suspiciously. The Squijum seemed to have disappeared altogether.

Cara wondered how the unicorn would communicate with the delvers. Would he have to pierce their hearts, as he had her own? To her surprise, he was able to approximate their language with sounds made deep in his throat.

"What business do the Children of the Earth have

with Lightfoot, son of Dancing Heart, son of Arabella Skydancer?"

She blinked in surprise. Was Lightfoot the Queen's grandson?

"My name is Nedzik," replied the delver spokesman, his huge eyes shifting from side to side as if he was expecting trouble at any moment. "I come to you on business that is shameful, but necessary."

The other delvers muttered nervously.

"Go on," said Lightfoot.

"Though there is no love lost between unicorn and delver, we live in the same world — "

"Through treachery," growled the Dimblethum.

Lightfoot shot him a warning glance. The Dimblethum fell silent, though Cara could see it was an effort for him. Lightfoot turned back to the delver. "Go on," he said again.

Nedzik hesitated. He looked as if he was considering dropping the matter or simply fighting instead. The others shifted uneasily. Finally he spoke again.

"Though we live in the same world, many of my people hate the unicorns so violently that they would do anything to strike at them. They would do this even if such a blow might bring great damage, even destruction, to all of Luster." He paused, looked behind him to the others, then continued. "That is the way things stand now. That is why we have come to speak to you, though doing so means we are betraying our king."

He was blinking rapidly, and Cara realized that the sunlight hurt his enormous eyes.

"What does the Delverking plan?" asked Lightfoot. Though it was not in his words, Cara could sense the confusion and fear that the delver's message had created in him.

Nedzik took a step back and the other two weaponless delvers gathered around him. After a moment of whispering, he stepped forward again.

"The king wishes to open a door to the world of men so that they can enter Luster and hunt the unicorns."

The shock that ran through Lightfoot caused Cara to momentarily lift her hand from his flank. When she put it back, the delver was still speaking.

" . . . a thought long in his mind. But until now, he did not have a way to implement it. That changed when Gamzil came upon the human child that stands next to you and tore from her the amulet she was wearing."

The Dimblethum growled at the memory, causing the delver spokesman to flinch.

"Gamzil is a fool and did not recognize the amulet for what it is. He tried to steal it only because it is a pretty bauble. Not long after he came crying back to our caves without it, a man came to us, a human, who had just crossed here from Earth."

Cara caught her breath. The delver was almost certainly speaking of the man who had chased her and her grandmother into St. Christopher's. How had he made it through? Did he have an amulet of his own — or had he somehow managed to jump through the opening she had created? A wave of guilt washed through her, and she was glad that Lightfoot could not read her thoughts unless she sent them to him.

"This man began to ask questions," continued Nedzik, "and it was not long before King Gnurflax, who is smarter than he is wise, may the rocks not crush my feet, realized what he was seeking. When he also realized that Gamzil had had this very amulet in his hands and then lost it, his rage was mighty indeed." Nedzik shook his enormous head. "Alas, poor Gamzil. Even a fool does not deserve such a fate. Anyway, the king has sent out many groups in search of the child and the amulet. It was only luck that let us find you first."

The Dimblethum's growl grew deeper. The delvers looked profoundly embarrassed.

"What the king plans to do with the amulet has not been made widely known," continued the delver. "Those among us who do know his intentions are disturbed but for the most part willing to go along. My cousins and I think this is madness. We believe that flinging open the doors will mean death and destruction for all of us.

"Make no mistake: What we do now is treason. Should the king discover us, should word of this reach his ears, it will mean our lives. But so, we believe, will the success of his plan. He seeks the

59

child and the amulet. You must flee, flee with all speed, flee with one eye before you and one eye watching behind. If you let the amulet fall into the hands of my people, the madness of our king will bring doom to us all."

He began to back away from them.

"Wait!" said Lightfoot.

Nedzik took another step back, then paused. "We must go. Every moment we talk with you rather than fight you we risk our lives."

"You have our gratitude," said Lightfoot, bowing his head. He hesitated, then said, "Will you travel with us? Should we meet others of your kind the battle may go against us. If you truly believe your king's plan will cause such disaster, help us avert it."

"That we cannot do," said Nedzik, and Cara could sense a note of regret in his words. "We have done more than we should as it is." He paused, then added, "We can do this much more. We will point the chase in another direction. That should give you some time. Use it wisely."

With that, the creatures faded into the forest so swiftly and completely it was as if they had never been there at all.

The Squijum came racing down a tree. "Nasty phooey strange hotcha no-good trustem?" he chattered, his lush gray tail twitching violently.

Lightfoot shook himself, a shudder that ran from his shoulders through his flank, and muttered, "This is enough to make me wish my uncle were here."

"What do you think we should do?" growled the Dimblethum.

"Head for Grimwold's Cavern as fast as we can. It's the closest safe haven. Besides, we may be able to get a message to the Queen from there."

"How?" asked Cara.

"Talk later!" cried the Squijum. "Now now shake butts move feet hotcha get going!"

"The Squijum is right," said Lightfoot. "The sooner we're away from this place the better. And we have at least a seven-day journey ahead of us."

"Not necessarily," said the Dimblethum. "There is a shorter way. . . ."

Lightfoot snorted. "Shorter, certainly — unless *she* catches us. In that case, we will never get there at all."

"*She?*" asked Cara nervously.

"Firethroat, Firethroat!" squeaked the Squijum. He began to run in circles around Lightfoot's hooves, crying, "Run run hide hide cover butts not safe hotcha!"

Lightfoot sighed. "Of Luster's seven dragons, Firethroat is the oldest and wisest. She is also the one least to be trifled with. She guards her territory well, does not take trespass lightly, and has no use for fools — a fact my uncle says would make it particularly dangerous for *me* to come in contact with her."

"The choice is simple," said the Dimblethum, backing up to a tree and rubbing his shoulders against it. "The Dimblethum and his friends take the long way and spend seven or eight days trying to avoid the delvers. Or they take the short route and spend a day and a half hoping Firethroat is not angered by them walking the edge of her territory." He pushed against the tree harder, sighed, then added, "The Dimblethum does not think the delvers will expect anyone to go that way. Even if they do, they will not follow unless King Gnurflax is more desperate than the Dimblethum thinks. So the Dimblethum says take the short route. If Firethroat is in a bad mood and eats the Dimblethum and his friends, at least the amulet is saved from the delvers."

For that there was no answer. So it was decided that they would take the dragonpath to Grimwold's Cavern.

"It's just as well, in a way," Lightfoot said to Cara later on. "It's a much prettier route, and you will see some amazing things. Still and all . . ."

He left the sentence unfinished. She could tell he was contemplating the fate of a fool in the claws of a dragon.

# 9

# THE HUNTED

They set off through the forest and did not stop when darkness fell. Lightfoot, putting all his energy into finding the way — and avoiding detection — was distracted and unwilling to talk.

Cara began to stumble again. After a bit the Dimblethum picked her up and carried her in his arms. She fell asleep nestled against his warm and furry breast. When she woke, she gestured to him that she wanted to walk. He hesitated, then set her gently on her feet. She wished she could speak to him; she wanted to thank him for the ride.

By the nearly full moon that shone through the drooping trees she saw that they had entered a swamp. Ahead of her, the Squijum was riding on

Lightfoot's back as the unicorn picked his way along a trail that led between large stretches of brackish water.

Strange dark things fluttered through the night air above them. Occasionally one would swoop close to Cara, and the whir of its rapidly beating wings would give her a start. The first time this happened she cried out in fear, but after that she kept her silence — partly because the Dimblethum had laid a heavy paw on her shoulder and scowled at her, indicating that such outbursts were a bad idea.

So eager was she to please, to prove she was fit for this adventure, that when something snakelike slithered across their path she stopped short but managed to hold in her cry of fear. The serpent stared at her for a moment. Suddenly, without warning, it reared up and hissed at her, spreading a vivid red hood that actually glowed in the darkness. Then she did scream, and jump backward as well.

She bumped into the Dimblethum, who seemed as startled as she was, for he, too, let out a sound of surprise. Then, leaning over her, he roared at the serpent. The sound hurt Cara's ears. The serpent hissed again, more softly. The Dimblethum made a menacing growl deep in his throat. Cara's heart pounded, and her skin grew cold as she stared at the serpent, wondering whether it would strike at her. The Dimblethum continued his low growl until the serpent finally dropped to its belly Slithering forward, it slipped silently into the murky water.

64

Cara didn't object when the Dimblethum picked her up and carried her again.

In this way, passing through swamp and field and forest, along the edges of low cliffs, beside swiftly running crystal streams, they arrived in two days at the edge of Firethroat's territory.

They had stopped to sleep twice, at which times Cara had been fed nuts and berries and a kind of root the Squijum dug up.

"What is it?" she had asked the first time he came scampering up with one of the dark brown roots in his paws and handed it to her.

"We call it *tarka*," replied Lightfoot, resting his horn on her shoulder. "Twist it and see what happens."

When she did as he directed, the root's nubbly husk popped open, revealing a crisp, white interior.

"Try it," said the unicorn.

To her surprise, it tasted like sweet almonds. "Good!" she said, smiling at the Squijum.

"Yah, yah hotcha like it," he replied, dashing off into the darkness. He returned a few minutes later with another of the roots. Stopping three or four feet in front of her, he chittered something she could not understand, then tossed her the root. She caught it before it landed in her lap, prompting an enthusiastic burst of chatter from the Squijum.

Acting on impulse, she picked up a nut and tossed it to him. Leaping into the air, the little creature caught the nut a foot and a half above the ground.

Then he bounded over to her, dropped the nut in her lap, and ran about twenty feet away.

"You like to play catch!" she cried in delight, tossing him the nut again.

The Squijum caught it handily, and Cara spent another fifteen minutes tossing him various objects she found on the forest floor. He caught almost all of them, missing only if her throws were absurdly wide of the mark. The leaps, twists, and turns he made in accomplishing these catches were so wild that she found herself laughing out loud, the first time she had done so in longer than she could remember.

Lightfoot and the Dimblethum took turns watching at night. Feeling safe in their care, Cara slept soundly. Yet she found herself tormented by strange dreams in which she was hunted by some faceless horror.

The second night she was woken from one of these dreams by the Dimblethum, who placed a huge paw gently over her mouth to keep her from crying out. After a moment, when he was sure she was awake and calm, he uncovered her mouth.

Soon after, Lightfoot came to her. His horn looked as if it had been carved from the bright and shining moon. Placing it across her shoulder, he said, "We're being trailed."

Fighting down her fear, she replied, "How do you know?"

66

"The Squijum was out hunting and spotted a camp. We need to move ahead as fast as possible while its owner is still resting."

Cara furrowed her brow. "Just one of them? I thought the delvers would be hunting us in packs."

"It's not a delver," replied Lightfoot. "It's the man."

Fully awake now, she rose quickly, silently, and followed Lightfoot out of their camp. The Dimblethum lagged behind. When she turned to look back, she saw him moving about the spot, trying to erase all signs that they had been there.

The Squijum was nowhere to be seen.

Digging her hand in her pocket to make sure the amulet was in its place, she trudged on through the darkness.

So obsessed were they with the danger behind that they did not remember Nedzik's warning to flee with one eye watching before them.

Thus it was that they did not see the delver camp until they had nearly stumbled into it.

Lightfoot stopped so abruptly that Cara bumped into him. Only the effort she had spent training herself not to cry out when they were traveling through the swamp kept her from betraying their presence with a shout.

Moving cautiously up beside Lightfoot, she froze when she saw not far ahead a low fire, little more than a bed of glowing coals. It was surrounded by dark forms that she took to be sleeping delvers. The reason she assumed they were delvers was that the two figures keeping watch by the fire most definitely were.

More than ever, she was glad of the ability to communicate with Lightfoot without speaking. "What do we do now?" she asked.

"I believe a quiet retreat is in order," he replied silently, beginning to back away.

Cara had long ago noticed the unicorn's ability to move through the forest without making a single sound. She, alas, possessed no such skill. Despite her best efforts, she stepped on a dry twig that broke beneath her foot. It was a tiny sound, yet in the silence of the forest it exploded against her horrified ears like a firecracker.

Lightfoot froze where he stood. She did the same until the delver guards leaped to their feet and, with a bloodcurdling scream, started after them.

"On my back!" ordered Lightfoot.

She obeyed without hesitation. No sooner had she scrambled onto his shoulders than he was off like a rocket, hurtling into the darkness. Hunched low over his shoulders, Cara wrapped her hands in his silky mane and prayed that she would be able to hold on. Branches whipped against her as they careened wildly through the forest. Dark shapes rose before them, then vanished to the side as Lightfoot veered around them.

So tightly were Cara and Lightfoot connected that for a moment she felt as if she *were* the unicorn, as if it were her legs doing the running, her aching lungs and hammering heart fueling the flight from the delvers.

They plunged through a misty hollow, up a steep bank, in and out of patches of moonlight, until suddenly Lightfoot stopped, flanks heaving, and stood silent, listening.

In the distance they could hear delvers crying out in anger and frustration.

"We've lost them," he said triumphantly.

It was only then that Cara realized how terrified she had been. Trying to stop the trembling that suddenly overtook her, she said, "You must be able to see in the dark. I had no idea where we were going."

"Half the time, neither did I," confessed the unicorn.

Cara caught her breath in surprise, then started to laugh.

Their moment of triumph was short-lived. From the dark and the distance they heard a terrible roar, followed by angry battle cries. The sounds were confusing, jumbled together, and muted by distance. But when silence fell, there was no question what they meant.

"They've got the Dimblethum," whispered Cara in horror.

# 10

# THE TINKER

ara and Lightfoot stood about a hundred feet from the delver camp. They had debated fiercely about who should go back to study the situation. When Lightfoot claimed he could move more silently, Cara pointed out that he was also more likely to be seen because of his white coat and luminous horn.

"Actually, I can dim the horn," he told her. "It would be a dangerous thing if I couldn't."

"That doesn't change the fact that it's a lot easier to see that white coat of yours than it would be to spot me. I mean look at me — I practically blend into the forest!"

Indeed, her jeans and T-shirt were so stained and

mud spattered that they looked like the camouflage clothes the boys in her class sometimes wore.

"I can't let you go down there alone," said Lightfoot firmly. "If they heard you, how would you get away?"

In the end they decided they would go together, but Cara would make the closest approach to the camp, with Lightfoot hiding nearby. She agreed solemnly not to get more than fifty feet away from him.

They also decided that it would be foolish to take the amulet with them.

"You know, not all my relatives would approach this the same way," said Lightfoot, resting his horn on Cara's shoulder as she carefully hid the amulet and its broken chain in a hollow tree. "I can think of some that would insist we abandon the Dimblethum and head for Grimwold's Cavern as fast as possible."

She thought about that for a minute. "It might be the sensible thing to do," she said. "After all, the most important thing is to keep the amulet from falling into the wrong hands."

"That's true," said Lightfoot.

Cara paused, her hand still in the tree trunk. "But leaving the Dimblethum doesn't feel right," she continued.

"That's true as well."

She could feel confusion beginning to creep over her. "So the question is, should we risk the mission, and the safety of *all* the unicorns, in order to rescue one friend?"

"Some of my relatives would say there is no question. We have a clear duty to keep the amulet away from the enemy. This is not just *our* journey. The safety of the unicorns, and possibly all of Luster, depends on defending the amulet against those who would abuse it."

Cara slowly drew her hand from the tree. She began moving her arm back and forth, as if she were trying to decide whether to reach in and take back the amulet. The choice seemed to be crushing against her brain. "Are you trying to tell me we shouldn't go back for the Dimblethum?" she asked.

"I'm just pointing out the questions involved. I should probably also point out that most of my relatives don't think much of the Dimblethum." He paused, then added, "Of course, most of them don't think much of me, either."

Though she longed for Lightfoot to make the decision, Cara sensed that he was going to defer to her in this matter — perhaps because he was confused himself. But she was torn, too. Her mind was telling her that for the good of all they should flee with the amulet, taking it as far from this place as possible. Her heart was screaming that they could not leave their friend.

In the end, her heart made the choice. Asking herself what her grandmother would do, she found herself thinking instead about her parents. The painful memory of the way they had abandoned her made it impossible for her to do the same to anyone else.

"We're going to get him," she declared.

"That's a very immature decision," said Lightfoot.

The criticism stung like a slap. "Why do you say that?" she asked sharply.

"Because it is what I would choose," he replied, sounding amused. "And my uncle has assured me many times that I am very immature."

"If your uncle wants to handle this, let him come out here and wander around in the woods with the delvers," said Cara. "In the meantime, we have to go see what they're doing with the Dimblethum."

Creeping through the darkness, away from Lightfoot and toward the delvers, Cara could easily have wished they had decided to press on in their journey. Each movement was an agony of indecision as she tried not to make a betraying sound. Each dew-wet leaf that brushed her face, each twig that prodded her side, seemed to her racing imagination the touch of an enemy.

Finally she drew close enough to get a clear view of the delver camp through the undergrowth. By the flickering light of the low fire she saw that the Dimblethum had been bound to a tall pole. He sagged against his ropes, as if weary and beaten. Even in the low light she could see at least two hideous wounds.

The delvers stood in a circle around him, prodding him with their spears. They were speaking to him, but without Lightfoot at her side, she heard only rasping, guttural sounds. The Dimblethum spoke not at all; whether he was refusing to answer or had actually lost consciousness she could not tell in the dim light.

Each time one of the delvers poked at the manbear she wanted to scream at them to leave him alone. Finally she could stand to watch no more. Moving quietly, she returned to Lightfoot's side.

"What can we do?" she asked after describing the hideous scene.

He shook his head mournfully. "I do not know."

They trailed the delvers for the better part of the next day. It was a horrible, frustrating time, partly because they were moving backward, away from Grimwold's Cavern, but even more because in that time they were not able to do anything to help the Dimblethum.

To add to their worries, they had no idea what had happened to the man who was hunting Cara. She couldn't help but wonder if he was stalking them even as they were following the delvers.

To top things off, the Squijum — who would normally have reappeared by this time — seemed to have vanished altogether.

"You don't suppose anything happened to him, do you?" asked Cara once when they were taking a break.

"Hard to tell with that one," replied Lightfoot.

"Something *could* have happened to him. Or he may simply have lost track of us — though he is a very good hunter. He may even have lost interest; his attention span is not all that great. But there is nothing we can do about him now. We need to focus on the Dimblethum. I'd suggest you rest while you can. There's no telling when they'll start moving again."

Though she couldn't stop worrying, Cara did try to relax. They were only taking a break because the delvers had stopped for the same purpose. There were an even dozen of the little monsters, about half the group that had first captured the Dimblethum. According to the snatches of conversation they had been able to catch, the others had remained to continue looking for "the girl with the amulet," as they referred to her.

Cara thought it was rather amusing that while they were out looking for her she was trailing them. It was the only amusing aspect of the situation. Her heart ached for the poor Dimblethum. She had caught glimpses of him stumbling along, his paws bound behind him, delvers prodding him with their spears should he falter or slow. Oddly, the delvers seemed not to worry about anyone coming after them. She decided that they were so used to being the hunters that it never occurred to them that things might go the other way.

The delver party got ready to start out again. It was a noisy process, which made it easy for Cara and

Lightfoot to keep track of them without getting too close. Cara had noticed that while the delvers occasionally moved through unmarked forest, they more often followed faint but definite paths. What surprised her was that twice these paths crossed wider paths defined by pairs of shallow ruts.

"Is this some kind of road?" she asked Lightfoot the first time they crossed one.

"Yes. It was made by some of the humans."

"There are other humans in Luster?" she asked excitedly.

"Not many."

She wanted to know more, but he was focused on the problem of the delvers and the Dimblethum and didn't want to be bothered talking about such things. She did notice that though the delvers crossed these roads, they did not follow them.

She and Lightfoot were crossing one of the roads themselves, some minutes behind the delvers, when they heard a horrible clatter to their right.

"There you are!" cried a friendly voice. "I've been waiting for you!"

They turned. To their astonishment an oddly dressed man was trotting toward them. He was drawing a cart behind him, which he pulled by means of two wooden poles. Hanging from the roof of the cart were all manner of things, including a number of pots and pans, all of them clanging and clattering like a cooking set being rolled down a stairway.

Cara was terrified that the racket would draw the

delvers, but Lightfoot told her that it was more likely they would stay away, since they did not care much for humans, and only humans would make such a racket.

Still, she would have insisted that they move on, so that they not lose sight of the Dimblethum, had she not seen what was sitting on top of the man's wagon.

"The Squijum!" she cried.

"Oh, yes," said the man, slowing to a walk. "It was he who brought me to you."

"Good Squijum! Happy good hotcha-gotcha!" cried the little creature, leaping from the wagon to an overhanging tree. He began swinging through the branches, which let him reach Cara and Lightfoot considerably ahead of the man. He leaped down to her shoulder.

Cara stroked his fur as she stared at the approaching man.

Bald and bearded, with a roundish nose, he wore high leather boots, loose trousers, and a remarkable coat that seemed to be made almost entirely of patches of various bright fabrics. The coat had an astonishing number of pockets. Gold chains drooped in graceful arcs from every one of them.

"Thank goodness I found you," he said, clattering to a stop. Dropping the wooden poles of his wagon, he wiped his high bald head with a handkerchief he fished from his trousers.

The cart was like a tiny house on wheels, about

four feet wide and eight feet long. It had a pitched roof, and high blue walls. Painted on its side in large, old-fashioned letters, were the words:

THOMAS THE TINKER
I Mend What I Can

"Actually, you're right on schedule," he said, pulling one of the chains to reveal a large pocket watch. He stared at the watch for a moment, then frowned. "Or maybe you're not." He pulled an even larger watch from another pocket and stared at it. "Oh, well, never mind," he said, shoving both watches back into pockets other than the ones from which they had come. "You're here, and so am I, and that's what matters. Shall we take a stab at rescuing your friend?"

# 11

# THE CART

Three hours later, Cara crouched in the narrow aisle that ran down the center of the Tinker's wagon. The Squijum sat next to her, nearly bursting with the effort of keeping still. With Thomas hauling the cart, they were heading for the delvers' camp.

Cara was surprised at how smoothly the cart traveled. She had expected to be bounced and jolted for the entire journey.

The inside of the cart had also surprised her. Rather than the hopelessly cluttered jumble she had anticipated it was so tidy as to be almost stark. Whatever Thomas carried here was packed behind rows and rows of small doors, tiny ones at the top of the cart, larger ones at the bottom.

Despite the need to remain silent, she had tried to open a few of the little doors. When they had proved to be locked, she had tried the others. Every one of them (dozens in all, counting the smallest) was locked.

It had been very frustrating.

In her hand she held the knife Thomas had given her. "When the time comes, I want you to jump out of the wagon," he had told her. "Cut the Dimblethum free and guide him back inside. Then close the door — quickly and *tightly!* — and I'll get you out of there."

The whole thing had been set up so fast it had left her head spinning. But that was the first thing she had noticed about the Tinker: He was fast. It didn't make any difference what he was doing — walking, talking, thinking, or planning — he did it rapidly. Lightfoot had seemed alternately amused and disgusted by the man, but since they had no other way of saving the Dimblethum, he had had little choice but to accept the assistance.

Cara wished she were able to talk to the Squijum. She wanted to know more details about how he had found the Tinker.

Suddenly the cart stopped. Moving silently, she pressed her eye to the secret hole Thomas had showed her in the back wall. It took a moment for her to make out the scene. It was fully dark now, and they were in the delvers' camp, which was once again lit by a low fire. The creatures, none of them any higher than Thomas's waist, had gathered around the Tinker. Several were shifting their spears in a menacing fashion.

Thomas spoke to them rapidly in their own language. His hands flying, he pointed first to their spears, then to the cart.

For a terrifying moment, Cara wondered if he had betrayed them and was sending the delvers to kill her.

She beat down her suspicions and tried to spot the Dimblethum. But the limited view offered by the peephole made it impossible to see him. She hoped she would be able to find him fast enough when the time came!

As she watched, one of the delvers reluctantly handed Thomas his spear. The Tinker took something from his pouch and made a series of swift strokes over the spearhead. Then he tested it against his thumb, and with a smile handed it back to the delver, who did the same thing. His hideous face broke into a wide grin and he nodded to the others.

*Wonderful, Thomas,* thought Cara. *Sharpen their weapons for them. That's going to do us a lot of good!*

But he only sharpened two more of the weapons. When he took the third he examined it and made a series of clucking noises that indicated big trouble. Turning to the owner he said something to him, then reached into one of his pockets and drew out a watch.

Cara braced herself. That was the sign.

But when Thomas opened the watch, nothing happened. He shook it in disgust, closed it, put it back in his pocket. Then he dug out another one.

He motioned to the delvers and they gathered closer.

Thomas opened the watch and, even though she had been expecting it, Cara cried out at the flash of blinding white light that filled the clearing. Her cry, however, was nothing compared to the screams of the delvers, who clamped their hands over their enormous eyes and fell to the ground screaming in pain.

Cara shot out of the cart. After the flash of light, the clearing seemed extraordinarily dark, and it took her a second to spot the Dimblethum. As the night before, he was tied to a pole. Racing to his side, she slashed the rough cords that held him.

The look of gratitude on his face made the risk and the effort all worthwhile. He stumbled forward and she feared that he would not be able to walk. If that happened she didn't know what she would do, for she surely could not carry him.

He did not fall, but he did need to lean on her shoulder. Staggering under his weight, she guided him back to the cart. Chaos surrounded them as the still-blinded delvers, most of them not yet back on their feet, groped their way about the clearing, screaming and cursing. She could not understand any of the words except Thomas's name, which they screamed over and over in tones that made her blood run cold.

One delver nearly stumbled into them, but the Squijum leaped at him from behind, causing him to spin and fall to his knees. Hurrying past him, Cara led the Dimblethum into the cart, turning him sideways so that his broad shoulders could fit into the narrow aisle that ran down the center.

The Squijum leaped in behind her. Slamming the door shut, she fastened the bolt and prayed.

Thomas was as good as his word. With her eye pressed to the peephole, Cara could see the trees flashing by as he pulled them through the forest to the place where they were supposed to rendezvous with Lightfoot. This time she decided that there must be something magical about the cart, for no one could pull it over the root-ribbed forest floor so swiftly and easily without magic.

Lightfoot was waiting impatiently in a clearing just off the side of the little road, about two miles from the delver camp. He had wanted to come on the mission, but the others had persuaded him that there had to be at least one of them left should things come to disaster, and he was the logical one to stay behind.

"From what you've told me, we'll need you to heal the Dimblethum when we get him back," Thomas had said. He had paused, then added (not without a note of jealousy), "I wish I could do *that* kind of mending. Anyway, no sense in risking you at this stage of the game."

Lightfoot had fussed and fumed but agreed to stay behind, muttering that there were times when he found it utterly annoying that he did not have hands. However, once they pulled the Dimblethum out of the cart, he was in his glory. Making the others step aside, he used his horn to heal the numerous wounds that split the manbear's pelt.

Cara noticed with some surprise that the horn glowed brighter as it was doing the healing. What did not surprise her was that as soon as Lightfoot was done, his knees buckled and he fell to the ground.

"We need to get farther away from here," said Thomas nervously. "Let's get them into the wagon."

"They'll never fit!" said Cara.

"Oh, ye of little faith," laughed Thomas. "Watch this."

Though she watched, Cara was never really sure just what it was that the Tinker did to the cart. He began pulling out rods and folding down slats. Humming to himself as he worked, he reminded her of nothing so much as a kid playing with one of those toys that, with the right motions, can be turned into something altogether different. And indeed, when Thomas was done, the blue cart was twice the size it had been.

"How did you do that?" she asked in astonishment

as the Squijum raced around the cart, chattering with excitement.

"This is a very special wagon," said Thomas with a chuckle.

How special became even clearer when he offered to let Cara pull it, after they had loaded the Dimblethum and Lightfoot inside.

"You're joking!" she said, looking at the cart, which was now the size of a large camper trailer.

"Give it a try," he replied gleefully.

Stationing herself between the poles, she grabbed them firmly and tried to take a step forward.

The cart rolled easily behind her.

"Very special indeed," he said, giving the cart an approving pat.

The only problem with having the cart so large was it would not pass easily through the forest. They were forced to follow the road instead, though Thomas said that was just as well, since the delvers would tend to avoid it.

"They won't be able to see well enough to follow us for another few hours, anyway," he continued. "Then they'll probably have a long fight about whether they *should* follow us, or report back to the king, or just run away and hide for a month or two. So the odds are we won't need to worry about them for a while."

"There's someone else hunting for us," said Cara nervously. "Another human."

"I know," said Thomas with a nod. "The Squijum and I met him on the road. Unfortunately, I was a little confused at the time. I'm afraid I completely bollixed the directions I gave him. In fact, now that I think of it, I probably sent him the wrong way altogether. I expect he's a long way away from us now." He gave her a wink. "Silly of me," he said, "but it's done now. Oh, well — I was pretty sure he was no friend of the Queen's."

Cara smiled. Much as she had come to love Light-foot, the Dimblethum, and the Squijum, they were all very different from her. Thomas's presence made her realize that she had missed human company more than she would have thought possible.

"How did *you* get here?" she asked him now as he strolled along beside her.

"Fell in by accident," he said. "Pretty silly of me, now that I think about it. But then, I've done a lot of silly things in my time."

"How long ago did it happen?"

"Oh, it's hard to say." He stopped and did some calculations on his fingers. "About a hundred and fifty years ago, give or take five years on either side."

"Right," she sneered. "And I'll be ninety-two on my next birthday."

He chuckled, which he seemed to do fairly often. "Such a cynic for one so young. I have drunk from the Queen's Pool — a reward for a little something I did when I first got here. Won't make me live forever, which is a pretty frightening idea, anyway

86

now that I think of it. But it does stretch things out a bit."

She looked at him, wondering if he was teasing her. The thing was, here in Luster such an outlandish statement made almost perfect sense.

"Ah, here we go," he said before she could ask another question. "This looks to me like a good place to bed down for the night. And just in time, too," he added, holding out his hand at the same time that Cara felt the first drops of rain begin to spatter against her forearms.

At Thomas's direction, she positioned the cart about ten feet off the road. Rushing about with his usual speed, he quickly blocked up the wheels, folded out a side compartment complete with a bed, unrolled a canopy from the back, and started a small fire in its shelter.

"There we go," he said, settling on the steps that he had flipped out from under the back of the cart. "Cozy as a house and twice as easy to pick up and move."

Cara went in the back of the cart to check on Lightfoot and the Dimblethum, but both of them were sleeping soundly. The Squijum, which had scurried in behind her, snuck onto the Dimblethum's stomach. Covering his eyes with his tail, he sighed softly and fell asleep.

"Now I know this cart is magical," muttered Cara, climbing back down to sit beside the Tinker.

# 12

# DRAGONPATH TO GRIMWOLD

The next morning Lightfoot and the Dimble-thum were still a little shaky. However, they both pronounced themselves fit to travel.

"Mind if I come along?" asked the Tinker, as he started to fold up his cart. To Cara's astonishment, he continued folding until it was about the size of a man's wallet.

"Convenient sort of a thing, isn't it?" he said with a smile, slipping the cart into his pocket. "Only real problem I have with it is when I want to get at my tools. Then I have to unfold the silly thing all over again."

The Dimblethum came to her while she was standing with Lightfoot, and said, "For what you did, the

Dimblethum thanks you. Now the Dimblethum and you are even, each rescuing the other."

Cara was startled. "I didn't come get you so we would be even," she said, somewhat sharply. "I did it because . . . oh, never mind."

Lightfoot translated her words for the Dimblethum, who looked truly puzzled, and a little hurt. But later he gave Cara a flower, one of the fuzzy purple ones. She tucked it over her ear and wore it for the rest of the day.

Most of this day was given over to retrieving the amulet. They had to retrace their journey of the day before, and it was late afternoon when they finally reached the area where Cara had hidden it. For a little while they were not able to find the specific tree. Cara was beginning to panic when the Squijum located it, working by scent.

"See, see!" he cried triumphantly. "*Can* look and find!" Emerging from the hollow tree with the amulet and its broken chain, he crooned to himself, "Hotcha good finder guy!"

That accomplished, they needed to plan what to do next.

"If we press on, we can reach the edge of Dragon Territory tonight," said Thomas. "That will give us an extra bit of safety if the delvers are still patrolling the area; it is unlikely they will enter Firethroat's domain."

"Which makes them smarter than us," muttered Lightfoot.

\*     \*     \*

Late in the evening they stopped to rest. The Dimblethum built a small fire while Thomas unfolded his cart. Later, after they had eaten, he asked Cara if she would let him examine the amulet.

"Well, now I see what the fuss is all about," he said, as he turned it over and over in his hands. "It's not every day that one of the Queen's Five turns up out in the open. Would you like me to fix this silly chain?" he asked.

"That would be nice," said Cara.

"I like fixing things," he said as he worked. "The world is always breaking, here and there, this way and that. Fix a bit of it, and I feel like I'm helping."

Reaching into his jacket, he pulled out a ridiculously tiny tool.

"Funny thing about chains," he said. "They're everywhere, once you know how to look for them. I like chains."

When Cara laughed at this, he shook his chest, causing the hundreds of golden links that hung there to sparkle in the firelight.

"There's lots of kinds of chains," he continued. "You can't see most of them, the ones that bind folks together. But people build them, link by link. Sometimes the links are weak, snap like this one did. That's another funny thing, now that I think of it. Sometimes when you mend a chain, the place where you fix it is strongest of all."

As he spoke, he held up the chain, which was whole again. Passing the amulet to Cara, he said, "Never was a chain that couldn't be broken. Sometimes it's even a good idea."

Putting away his tools, he crawled under the wagon and slept.

Despite her worries about her grandmother, Cara found herself beginning to fall deeply in love with the world into which she had fallen.

"It's so lovely here," she marveled as they stood on top of a high hill, gazing over a spread of green territory dotted with small lakes, friendly rivers, and patches of forest.

"Earth used to be like this," replied Lightfoot. "Not all green, of course; it always had its mountains and deserts. Luster does, too, for that matter. But Earth was once clean and bright and beautiful."

"How do you know about that?" she asked.

"It's in our stories. It's where we came from, after all. Grimwold can tell you more."

"Who is this Grimwold, anyway?"

"A friend of the unicorns," said Lightfoot. "He came here long ago and stayed, as friends sometimes do. More than that I had best not say. He is very possessive and does not like others to tell his stories."

"Is he human?"

"Close enough. Scratch right there, please."

She obliged, scratching his shoulder where she had been resting her hand. She was about to ask him about Summerhaven when he whispered, "Look!"

To their left stood a range of snowcapped mountains. Cara had been eyeing it nervously as they traveled and had been relieved when her companions had assured her that they were not going to have to cross it. Now she looked at it again, wondering what Lightfoot wanted her to see.

Suddenly she caught her breath. Far away, soaring above the highest of the peaks, was the form of a dragon. It was tiny to the eye, but given its distance from them, she could tell it must be enormous.

"Firethroat?" she asked without opening her mouth.

"None other," replied the unicorn.

Even the Squijum was quiet as they watched the great creature swoop and soar above the mountains. Suddenly she turned and sailed in their direction. Cara felt her heart leap in a strange combination of wonder and fear as the dragon opened her mouth and shot forth a column of flame nearly as long as she was herself.

"She's beautiful!" thought Cara, even as she wondered if they were about to die. Then, to Lightfoot: "Should we run?"

"No! If she hasn't seen us — which is unlikely — it will only attract her. If she has, it will anger her, make her think we are up to no good. Our best choice is to stand still and hope she is in a quiet mood."

The dragon continued to spiral and weave through the air. As she drew closer, Cara could see that she was red, a deep red, like blood and fire. Just when Cara thought that she couldn't hold still for another moment, the dragon banked to the left, flapped her wings, and — moving faster than Cara would have thought possible — returned to the mountain. A moment later she had vanished.

"Yowee hotcha yipes!" squeaked the Squijum, vaulting onto Lightfoot's back. "Big eater make me supper gone gone good yipe now!"

Cara laughed in spite of herself. "Since she didn't attack, do you think she approves of us?"

"I wouldn't go so far as to say that," replied Lightfoot. "Just that she doesn't disapprove. Madame Firethroat does not dislike unicorns. It is uninvited company she disapproves of. I suspect she found our little group odd enough that she would rather watch us than eat us. Likely she guesses that we're heading for Grimwold's Cavern. As long as we don't do anything to annoy her, I think she'll let us alone."

"What would annoy her?" asked Cara nervously.

"Hunting on her territory, mostly," said Thomas. "She guards it jealously and considers anything that lives here to be hers. That, and anything that might hurt the land. She has no use for delvers, of course, with all their digging and changing things."

Lightfoot translated the comment for the Dimblethum, who replied, "No one has much use for delvers, except delvers. The Dimblethum and his friends should move on. They may have passed inspection, but Lady Firethroat has been known to change her mind. They should not press her tolerance."

They picked their way down the hillside, which was rocky but easy to walk on. Lower down, the waving grass was as high as Cara's waist, and Lightfoot invited her to ride on his back. The grassland was rife with flowers that grew on spikes so tall she could pluck them simply by stretching out her hand. She started weaving them into Lightfoot's mane until he shook his head and told her to stop.

Sometimes the Squijum rode on the Dimblethum's shoulders, sometimes with Cara. Sometimes he simply scampered off through the grass. Once he disappeared for a long, silent time. Cara started to worry, but finally he reappeared, smiling to himself.

"Don't do that again!" said Lightfoot harshly.

"Hungry small quiet! Not good not eat! Feed good!" protested the Squijum. But his voice was quiet, and he sounded abashed, even ashamed.

"Nothing that happens here is too small for Firethroat to notice," replied Lightfoot. "*Nothing*. Take a meal and you may make a meal, if you know what I mean."

The Squijum sulked and did not talk for several hours, while Cara scanned the sky nervously, wondering if Firethroat would now return for them. She continued to scan the sky as it grew dark, and myriads of twinkling stars began to appear above her. Their strange patterns and unusual brightness made her feel farther from home than ever.

They slept that night in the shelter of a low cliff. When the sun woke them they continued their journey. After the first hour, they veered to the right.

"We're leaving Firethroat's territory," said Lightfoot, and Cara felt both relief and regret to be turning away from the mighty dragon.

The region they traveled through now was one of high hills and rocky valleys. Late in the day they picked their way down the side of a hill to a valley through which ran a particularly lively stream. Halfway along the valley they started up the side of the hill again. After a moment, Cara realized that they were following a path. It led to a wooden door, set in the side of the hill.

"Grimwold's Cavern," said Lightfoot.

The Dimblethum stepped forward and banged on the door.

"Are you sure it's safe?" asked Cara nervously.

"Of course it's safe," said Lightfoot. "It's Grimwold's job to be here when we want to talk to him."

"His job?"

"I told you, he's the Keeper of the Chronicles. That's how he earns the right to be here. Anyone who wants to stay in Luster — "

His words were interrupted by the door swinging open. "All right, all right," said a gruff voice. "I hear you! What is it you want?"

Cara took one look at the strange little man standing before her and cried out in astonishment, "It's you!"

# 13

# GRIMWOLD

"Who did you think it would be?" replied the little man sharply. "My cousin Droopwillow? He doesn't live here. Never did." He paused, then added, "Don't think he lives anywhere now, for that matter."

"But I've seen you before," Cara stammered, too surprised to notice that he was speaking to her in English. She stared at him to be sure that it was true. Yes, it had to be. The dark brown skin; the huge eyes, just this side of being so big they were grotesque; the thick, bushy brows that sprouted over them like silver waterfalls; the rounded pug nose — they all added up to the face she had seen every day on her grandmother's dresser.

INTO THE LAND OF THE UNICORNS

Of course, there it had been surrounded by an ornate wooden frame. The image had not been a photograph like all the others on the dresser, but a painting, one her grandmother had done herself.

Whenever Cara had asked about the painting, Grandmother Morris had laughed and said, "Oh, *him*! an old friend from a long time ago — another life, almost. I painted that back when I was about fourteen."

Cara blinked at the memory. If her grandmother's words were true, then the little man standing in front of her had been a little *old* man for at least fifty years.

Lowering his extravagant eyebrows, Grimwold stared at her and said, "What do you mean, you've seen me before?"

"I . . . I think my grandmother must have met you. She has a picture of you on her dresser."

Grimwold smiled. "The ladies always did fancy me. What did you say your name was?"

"Cara. And how can you understand me without Lightfoot telling you what I'm saying?"

"It's my job. I take it you're Lightfoot," he added, turning to the unicorn. "Son of Dancing Heart, if I remember correctly, which I'm certain I do. Still breaking your mother's heart?"

Lightfoot blew air through his nostrils in a sign of anger. "We come seeking shelter and information. We also need to contact the Queen, if at all possible."

"Certainly, delighted, wonderful," grumbled the dwarf. "As if I don't have enough sorting and filing

98

and figuring without you starting a new story on me. Well, come in, come in; you're outside now, and we're not going to get anywhere with you standing on the doorstep. I suppose the other three have to come in as well. I don't have their stories, you know, or at least not much of them. Not in the job, not in the job. Enough to do without keeping track of the likes of them."

The Squijum chittered angrily, but Cara had taken her hand from Lightfoot's shoulder, so she couldn't make out his words.

The door was wide enough for Cara and Lightfoot to enter side by side. The Squijum scampered in with them, racing around Lightfoot's cloven hooves. The Dimblethum lumbered through behind them. Thomas came last. Grimwold stood by the door until they were all inside. Then he slammed it shut and lowered a huge wooden crossbar to secure it.

They had entered a long tunnel. It was lit by softly glowing lanterns. To Cara's surprise, the walls were of wood rather than stone — a rich, dark wood that reminded her of the paneling in the old library where she and her grandmother had spent the afternoon that had ended with them being chased into St. Christopher's. How long ago had that been? She had lost count of the days.

Again she felt a stab of worry about her grandmother.

Mounted between the lanterns were beautiful paintings in intricately carved frames. Most of the images were of breathtaking landscapes populated by unicorns. Sometimes the unicorns were galloping, sometimes rearing and pawing the air, sometimes simply gazing out over their world. The remaining pictures were portraits, mostly of unicorns. Cara was amazed at how their faces varied, so that each displayed a distinct personality.

A handful of the portraits were of humans, or near-humans, since one was of a mermaid and another of a centaur. Cara wanted to stop to study the paintings, but Grimwold was hurrying them down the stone-paved hall. She was scurrying along, trying to keep up, when suddenly she did stop, so abruptly that the Dimblethum bumped into her.

"What is it?" asked Lightfoot, coming back and resting his horn on her shoulder.

Cara pointed to a small portrait of a beautiful red-haired girl in her early teens. "That's my grandmother!" she said, accidentally speaking aloud.

"It is?" asked Grimwold, sounding nearly as surprised as Cara. "Why didn't you tell me so in the first place? How is dear Ivy?"

"I don't know," said Cara desperately. "She was in terrible trouble when I left her."

Grimwold didn't look surprised. "I knew there was a tale in all this," he said. "Well, come along. We had best get on to the Story Room. I'm going to have to make notes. From the sound of it, I'm going to be part of this one, at least in a small way. Earth and sky, but I hate it when that happens."

100

Cara could have sworn she heard the Dimblethum chuckle. She glanced at him. His mouth was set in a straight line. Even so, he could not hide the twinkle in his eyes. She wished she knew what he was thinking!

The wood-paneled hall opened into a high cavern where the light came not from lanterns but from a single stone basin as wide as Cara was tall. Multi-colored flames leaped from its center, sending shadows flickering and dancing across the walls. The path wound between stalagmites that thrust upward from the floor and stalactites that hung down like huge stone fangs. A few pairs of stalactites and stalagmites had met, fusing into stone columns. Their smoothly shifting contours made them look as though muscles rippled beneath their slick surfaces.

The cavern was so large the bowl of fire could not clearly light its perimeter. Even so, the shifting flames revealed numerous doors and tunnel openings.

*I wonder if you can get lost in here?* thought Cara as Grimwold led them past the bowl of fire. To her surprise, it was cool — a witchfire that cast light only. She noticed then that it was smokeless as well.

Beyond the stone basin ran a stream about ten feet wide. Reflections of the firelight danced on the surface of the dark water. The stream was easily crossed by means of a number of wide, flat stepping stones. The Squijum bounded over ahead of them, then came leaping back. An angry gesture from the Dimblethum sent him scampering away again. Cara guessed that the manbear wanted no interference while trying to cross the stones.

Another wooden door, another wood-paneled corridor; this time the walls were broken on one side by doors, on the other by wood-framed openings that stretched into the darkness. The passage ended at a large door carved with strange designs. When Cara put her hand on Lightfoot's shoulder, she realized they said, "Story Room." It took her another moment to realize that if she could read them while in contact with Lightfoot, he must be able to read them as well.

"Let's get to work," said Grimwold.

Swinging wide the door, he invited them into what was, without doubt, the most wonderful room Cara had ever seen.

# 14

# THE STORY ROOM

I t was clearly a room made for writing. Books, scrolls, stacks of paper, notebooks, pens, and pots of ink seemed to cover every available surface — of which there were many, since the room held five long, low tables. The dark wooden walls were lined with maps, pictures, and intricately woven tapestries. Unlike the portraits in the first hall, these pictures seemed to illustrate specific events.

The walls (of which there were also many, for the room was full of nooks and crannies) were made of stone and wood. Natural outthrusts of stone had been carved into seats; some were even padded with cushions. Three of the larger indentations in the cavern walls had been transformed into lantern-lit reading nooks featuring shelves carved right into the stone. The shelves held pens, papers, and some little wooden figures.

In one wall a merry fire blazed in a huge fireplace. Unlike the cavern's witchfire, this one cast a lovely warmth. A broad shallow pit carved in front of the hearth provided a spot to sit and gaze into the flames.

It took Cara a moment to realize that the chairs were of many sizes. She suddenly suspected that the rugs scattered about the floor were, in fact, resting places for guests.

To the left of the fireplace a little stream sprang from an opening about five feet above the floor, creating a tiny waterfall. At its base was a pool about three feet in diameter. No stream ran out of the pool, so Cara assumed the water must somehow drain from the bottom.

Next to the little fall stood a rack that held a collection of cups and noggins of many sizes and shapes.

*I want to live here!* thought Cara.

"Find a place and settle in," said Grimwold as he scurried behind one of the tables. Mounting a stool, he spread a piece of curling paper before him, then set a polished rock at each corner to hold it down. Muttering to himself, he began trying to select a pen.

Lightfoot folded his legs and curled up on a deep purple rug. The Dimblethum and Thomas each picked up a wooden chair and moved it closer to the fire. After running about for a moment, the Squijum finally leaped into Thomas's lap; wrapping his tail around himself, he settled down with a sigh. (Three minutes later, however, he was climbing onto shelves and examining things.)

Cara hesitated, then positioned herself beside Lightfoot. Though she had wanted to sit with him all along, she had been afraid he would think she was clinging to him. Then she realized that if she didn't sit with him, she would not be able to understand anything the Dimblethum or the Squijum said.

"All right, what's your story?" asked Grimwold, looking directly at Cara.

"I beg your pardon?"

"Your story, your story," he said impatiently. "That's my job, to collect all the stories that involve the unicorns."

"Not only to collect them," said Lightfoot sharply. "To record them and make them accessible. You'll have the story in good time. Right now, *we* need the story behind what is happening to this child. Cara, show him the amulet."

Rising, Cara pulled the amulet from beneath her T-shirt. Lifting the chain over her head, she carried it to Grimwold. He gasped. "One of the Queen's Five," he muttered as he examined it. After a moment he looked up at her. "Did Ivy give this to you?"

Cara nodded.

*"Why?"*

She took a breath, then told him what had happened the evening she and her grandmother had been pursued into St. Christopher's. Grimwold made notes as she spoke, his pen scratching across the paper. When she was finished, he picked up the amulet and let it dangle from his fingertips. He stared at it with an expression that Cara found strange and terrible. After a moment he looked at Lightfoot and said, "I fear that the Hunters have returned."

"Who are the Hunters?" asked Cara.

Before Grimwold could answer, Lightfoot came to stand beside her. She placed her hand on his shoulder.

"Use the common tongue," the unicorn said to Grimwold. "The others must hear this as well."

To Cara's shock, she felt an undertone of fear in Lightfoot's message, a fear so strong it frightened her as well.

"Certainly," said Grimwold, "though much of it will be things that you already know."

"That is all right," said Lightfoot. "Cara, come sit with me while Grimwold tells of what has been, of the enemy that drove us from Earth so long ago."

They returned to the purple rug. Cara knelt with her hand on Lightfoot's neck and stared at the old man expectantly. The Dimblethum growled and shifted in his seat. The Squijum left off his explorations and returned to Thomas's lap.

Looking directly at Cara, Grimwold said, "This is the story of the hunting of the unicorns, and how it began. At least, it is the short version of that tale, for I could tell it in a way that would take many evenings and let you know the deeds of many heroes, both human and unicorn."

He lowered his voice, speaking more intensely. "Their sacrifices led to the creation of the first door between Earth and Luster, the path the unicorns followed to safety and freedom. This is the story behind that story, the story from which springs all other stories gathered here in the Unicorn Chronicles, all other songs sung on this world. It is a tale woven from greed and loss, lies and truth, bravery and sacrifice, ending and beginning."

As Grimwold continued, Cara felt herself moving into the trance of the story. The power of his telling brought the tale to life inside her, drawing her back to a time long gone....

"Back in the morning of your world [said Grimwold] when things were sweeter rougher stranger cleaner and more savage than they are today, the unicorns came forth. No one knows from whence they came. No one knows why. They just were. Their numbers were few, as if the world could only hold so much of their magic. And magic they were, for in their horns, in their hooves, in their very *being*, they carried the power to transform things.

"At first even the unicorns did not know the extent of their powers. But as time went on they found that they could clear water, heal wounds, quicken growth.

"In that early time the unicorns lived in harmony

with the world, bringing it sweetness and guarding some of the small animals for whom they took a fondness. They gathered much wisdom, which they stored in their heads, as they had no means of writing it down. Of course, in the newness of the world, there was less to know, and among them the unicorns could hold all that they had learned. Because they can communicate so easily, the knowledge was accessible to all.

"Eventually another creature came to power. That was man. And though your species has many virtues, child, there is a strain of savagery running through it that has driven much of the best and most beautiful that your world once offered into extinction, or — as in the case of the unicorns — exile."

The Dimblethum growled softly, as if remembering some old anger. Grimwold nodded toward him, acknowledging his right to complain, then continued his story.

"Man hunted. He hunted for food, for skins to warm himself and his family, even for sport. But he did not hunt the unicorns.

"Now death comes for all things, even unicorns, though they are remarkably long-lived. When the first of their kind died, a great mourning overtook the unicorns. The twelve oldest came to her body and with their horns changed her flesh to soil, her bones to water, her mane and tail to flowers. But they could not change her horn, for it was too powerful. The horn stayed as it was.

"From its perfect beauty flowed inestimable tragedy."

Cara felt Lightfoot shiver.

"A man found the horn and brought it back to his people," continued Grimwold. "But to make himself seem braver and more honorable, he did a dishonorable thing. He told a great lie about the ferocity of the unicorn from which he had taken the horn, claiming that she had attacked him in the wood, and that he had battled it to the death. In that falsehood lay the seeds of the tragedy that followed."

# 15

# A TALE OF BLOOD
# AND SORROW

"The story of the fierce unicorn was repeated often, and the wide-eyed children who heard it had no reason to disbelieve. Yet the power of the horn was such that it began to transform the man who had found it. The lies retreated from his heart and with them the need to feel higher than his fellows. Slowly he learned to use the horn to heal, to help, to protect.

"Eventually he even tried to take back the story of how he had obtained it. But lies have a life of their own and are harder to kill than either men or unicorns.

"People began to come from great distances to be touched by the horn. But since the horn was no longer part of a living being, the magic it held could not be replenished. Over the years its power was slowly drained, until at last it was empty of everything save beauty.

"Now, even before the horn had lost its magic, other men had desired one of their own, longing for the power and prestige that would come to whoever possessed such a miracle. With the horn drained, the dream of owning one became even more intense, for no healer who walked the Earth at that time had the certain power of the horn.

"Even so, only the bravest went seeking unicorns. For while the horn had lost its power, the lie told by its finder had grown in strength. Men now believed the story of fierce and deadly unicorns as if they had experienced it firsthand."

"We can be fierce if need be," said Lightfoot proudly.

"It is something you learned in the terrible years that followed," replied Grimwold. He paused, then turning to Cara said, "It started with a girl about your age. She was the child of a great hunter, a man both ferocious and determined. His wife had died giving birth to the girl, and thereafter he had lived alone in the forest with only his child for company. He called her 'Beloved,' for he had given all his heart to her.

"Beloved fell ill. On the first day of her sickness, the hunter tended her himself. But on the second day she was much worse, so he went to the village and brought the healer back to their forest home.

"But the healer could do nothing. 'Alas that we no longer have a unicorn's horn,' he muttered as he left the hut.

"The father's quick ears heard these words.

"With each passing day, Beloved's condition grew worse. On the third day after the healer's failure, the hunter said to himself. 'I shall find me a unicorn. I care not for its ferocity. I care not for my own life, should Beloved die. I will hunt, and I will find, and I will tear the horn from its head.' "

Cara could feel Lightfoot shudder. Horrible as the story was, she wondered what it would be like to have a father who loved her like that.

"Such was the hunter's love for his daughter," continued Grimwold, "that he never questioned whether his vow was good or evil, wise or foolish. The child alone was in his mind and his heart as he went a-hunting.

"His quest carried him far and wide. But each night he returned to the cottage to care for Beloved and tend her needs. He was a solitary man, and even had he known someone who could come and help with the child, he would not have known how to ask. Alas, each night when he returned to the cottage, the child was worse than when he had left her. The days drew on. She begged him to stay by her side until she died, as she was sure now that she must do.

"But the hunter had become obsessed with the quest for the horn. Wild-eyed, he refused his daughter's pleas and instead strapped her to his back and carried her with him on his hunt. It was not hard, for her illness had wasted her and she weighed but little. Nor did she complain, for she loved her father and longed to be with him."

Cara sighed, thinking what that must have been like. Grimwold glanced at her, but made no comment.

"In the forest," he continued, "the hunter left Beloved in a place he deemed safe, a place his hunter's skills told him was not visited by great cats or other fierce beasts. Then he began circling out, searching for a unicorn, haunted by the fear that he would come back and find his daughter dead from her illness.

"Late that afternoon a breeze caught and carried Beloved's scent to a unicorn named Whiteling, who was wading in a stream some miles away. The smell of her pain and need, of her approaching death, touched his heart. He began seeking the child even as her father was returning from his hunt.

"Whiteling reached the clearing first. He did not enter at once, for unicorns were wary around humans. But something about the child drew him in — her innocence, perhaps, or her pain, or simply the knowledge that he could heal her. Silently, on feet that could cross a field of flowers without crushing a petal, he began to walk toward the girl.

"She lay equally silent, eyes closed, breathing shallow.

"Lowering his horn, Whiteling pointed it at Beloved's breast even as her father drew near the clearing. The hunter's heart filled with terror when he saw the very beast he had been seeking, the beast he had been taught from boyhood was ferocious beyond all others, heading for his daughter. He reached into his quiver, drew forth an arrow, nocked it to his bow."

Cara drew a sharp breath. She could feel Lightfoot grow tense beside her.

"The unicorn bent to heal the child. The father loosed his arrow. It flew straight and true, piercing Whiteling's heart at the very moment that his horn pierced the heart of the ailing girl. He screamed and reared, trumpeting his pain.

"Bellowing with rage, the hunter raced into the clearing. Whiteling turned on him and the two began to fight.

"The battle was brief, but bloody. When it was done, both man and beast lay dead on the forest floor. The only living thing in the clearing was Beloved, who had watched the tragedy through wide and terrified eyes.

"Whiteling had cured her illness. Yet her heart was filled with an icy pain. Here is the reason: When the arrow struck Whiteling, he had snapped up his head so fast that the tip of his horn caught beneath Beloved's breastbone and broke off there. That piece of horn was now lodged in her heart, which was doomed to be forever wounded, forever healing, both in the same instant."

Cara put her hand to her chest, trying to imagine the feeling.

"Though it took seven days, Beloved buried her father in that clearing, digging his grave with the broken horn that she had hacked from Whiteling's head with her father's knife. When she was done, she stood atop her father's grave. Holding the alicorn with both hands, afire with pain, she swore that she and her children, her children's children, and all the generations that followed would be foes of all unicorns, and hunt them and kill them until the last days and the ends of the Earth.

"Only then did she return to the cottage that she had shared with her father. Eventually she found another hunter and married him, and gave birth to seven sons. Each son was trained in the ways of the wood, and the trail, and the hunt; each sought unicorns to slay, which they did by acting out their mother's story and placing a young woman in the woods.

"The hunters believed this lured the unicorns because they wanted to savage the innocent girl. But the real reason was even stranger. In the moment of Whiteling's death, the unicorns had been taken by a kind of madness. He was the first of their kind to be killed, and each unicorn had felt the moment when his horn had been broken. Each had seen, for an instant, through his eyes. And what they had seen was a young girl, lost in pain and fear. These two things, the girl and the broken horn, were fused in their minds, and they sought ever and again to find the missing bit of horn and to bring peace to young maidens — usually to the unicorns' own grief and sorrow.

"The sons of Beloved grew old and died. But Beloved herself did not, for the piece of horn lodged in her heart kept her alive, ever wounded, ever healing. Grandsons she had, and great-grandsons after that. And as is true for many families in your world, they came to be known by what they did; they came to be called the Hunters. Of course, many are known as Hunter who do not come from this clan. And there are many born to the clan who do not know its true past. But from each generation Beloved herself selects a handful to carry on the family quest: to seek and to slay unicorns."

Grimwold paused and shook himself, as if coming out of a trance. Looking directly at Cara, he said, "After a time the unicorns opened the first door to Luster. They fled here to have a world of their own, where they would be safe from the Hunters, and the curse of Beloved. But that is another story and a long one at that. What you need to know now is that for centuries the Hunters sought to enter this world, in order to carry on their quest for revenge. Then something happened, and for a long time we did not hear anything of them. We even dared hope that the line had finally died out or given up.

"We were wrong. I am sure that the man chasing you is one of the clan. His goal is to gain the amulet so he can open a door to Luster to others of his

116

kind. Perhaps the Hunter and the delvers are in league. Even if they are not, should the delvers succeed in opening a door, the Hunters will be ready. The slaughter will begin again."

Cara felt a cold terror in her heart — partly because of what Grimwold had just said, but even more because she finally knew the identity of the man who had chased her grandmother and her into St. Christopher's.

She knew, but she dare not tell.

# 16

# THE SCRYING POOL

ightfoot shifted uneasily beside her. "I do not like that story," he said. "It makes me unhappy."

"I did not tell it to brighten your day," replied Grimwold sharply. "I told it because you have become part of it."

"But how do you know that the man who is chasing us is a Hunter?" asked Cara.

"Who else would seek the amulet? Someone else might have heard of it, I suppose. But when you add the amulet to the tracking, the pursuit of you and your grandmother, it smacks to me of Hunters."

"Do you think he would have hurt my grandmother?" she asked.

Grimwold frowned. "It is hard to say. Though their quarrel is only with the unicorns, they can be ruthless in their pursuit."

Cara groaned. "What should we do now?"

"Let us try to contact the Queen," said Grimwold.

"How do we do that?"

"Through the scrying pool," he said.

Cara wrinkled her brow. "What's that?"

Rather than answering directly, Grimwold said, "Follow me." He rose and led them to a door in the side of the Story Room.

When they stepped through it, Cara caught her breath in wonder and desire. If the Story Room was the best room she had ever seen, the *contents* of this next room were — especially for someone who could think of little better than to live in a library — overwhelming.

It was a room of books, shelves and racks and rows of books. And every one of them looked old and mysterious, as if it held secrets too fascinating to be put in more modern-looking volumes. Scrolls there were as well, and four or five polished wooden stands where thick books lay open with ribbons marking their pages.

"What are all these?" she asked.

"The Unicorn Chronicles," replied Grimwold. "They hold the history of all that has happened since the unicorns first came to Luster."

"But where did they come from?"

Grimwold shrugged. "From me. From the unicorns. The unicorns bring me their stories and I write them down."

"You wrote all of these?" she asked in astonishment.

"I have been here a long time," he replied, as if that explained everything. "And please remember, I do not invent the stories — I simply record what the unicorns tell me. You will be in here, too, before long, because you are part of one of their stories as well. Though should things go wrong with this one . . ." He trailed off, as if the possibility was too horrible to contemplate.

"But where do the things to make them come from?" she asked. "The paper and the ink and the pens and — well, *everything*!" she finished, waving her hands in a gesture that took in not only this room, but the one they had just left, and the hall beyond that, with its paintings and portraits.

"You are not the only human who has come to Luster," said Lightfoot gently.

"More's the pity," growled the Dimblethum.

They had reached an arched door at the far side of the library. Grimwold paused with his hand on the thick metal latch and said, "The unicorns have lived here for a long time now. In the time since they first opened the passage to this world, humans have stumbled, fallen, lied, cheated, bought, magicked, and hoped their way here. Whether or not they are allowed to stay is a complicated matter. But any who do are expected to serve the Queen. My job is to chronicle the days of the unicorns. Others there are who make paper, who bind books, who fashion things of beauty and worth."

"Or fix things," said Thomas cheerfully.

"Where do the other humans live?" Cara asked.

"Here and there," said Grimwold with a shrug. "Usually in clumps and clusters, the way humans tend to, though some are solitary, and live in cottages built far from the beaten path."

"Some just travel," added Thomas.

Grimwold, who clearly did not like to be interrupted, shot him a nasty look. Thomas took out one of his watches and looked at it as if it contained important information.

"The people who find their way here often tend to be loners," continued the dwarf. "So some do not live any place at all but wander the paths of Luster, doing errands when the Queen summons them."

Thomas smiled and nodded.

Grimwold snorted and opened the door he had been holding. The others followed him out of the library into a cave that had been left in its natural form. In its center three tripods supported small cauldrons filled with something that glowed a soft orange. By this dim light, Cara saw irregular stone walls, and a scattering of stalactites and stalagmites. Centered between the tripods was a stone basin much like the one that had held the cold fire in the main cavern. However, rather than fire, this basin held dark, cold-looking water.

"The scrying pool," said Grimwold. Then he ordered Lightfoot to dip his horn in the basin.

The unicorn nodded and stepped forward. When he bent his horn to the water, silver shimmered across the surface of the basin.

"Stand beside me," the dwarf said to Cara, positioning himself at the edge of the basin.

She stood where he indicated.

"Look into the water."

Again, she complied. To her surprise, the surface of the water began to shimmer. Slowly an image began to appear. It was not her reflection, nor a reflection of the cavern, but an entirely different place, green and pleasant looking.

"Summerhaven," said Lightfoot, who was standing behind them. He backed up a step or two. "I'd just as soon you not tell the Queen I'm here," he said to Grimwold.

The Squijum had jumped onto the rim of the basin and was looking into the pool with fascination. "Very much good pretty," he said, reaching out to touch the water.

Cara expected Grimwold to snap at the little creature and shoo him away. But before the dwarf could move, the water roiled and darkened.

"Yikes!" squealed the Squijum, leaping onto Cara's shoulder.

Grimwold cursed in astonishment.

"What is it?" asked Cara. "What's happening?"

"Something has interfered with the connection," he said. He shivered, and the look in his eyes sent a chill down Cara's spine as well. "This has never happened before," he continued. "The pool is a powerful magic. The Queen herself set it up for me. I cannot imagine what could —"

*"Look!"* said Lightfoot.

All eyes turned to the pool. A message had appeared on the surface of the troubled water, written in large, flowing letters, as if from some great pen.

It said: "Surrender the Amulet."

It was signed, *"Beloved."*

# 17

# UPWARD

"You must leave this place at once," said Grimwold.

"Why?" asked Cara, who was still shaking with the shock of the message.

"Because she knows that you are here."

They had returned to Grimwold's writing room. The old dwarf was pacing back and forth in front of the fireplace, chewing his lips.

"This is worse than anything I could have imagined," he said. "Beloved has not been heard from for years. I had even dared hope she might finally have died. Now you arrive with this amulet, a Hunter hot on your trail, and the ancient enemy tracing your path. I do not like this. I do not like it at all."

Cara shifted nervously in her seat, feeling vaguely

guilty, as if the entire situation were somehow her fault. She started to say something, then stopped herself.

"Why not destroy the amulet?" growled the Dimblethum.

"Be my guest," said Grimwold. Gesturing toward the fireplace, he nodded to Cara and said, "Throw it in, if you wish."

"Won't the Queen be angry?" she asked, at the same time wondering what such an action would mean for her own chances of getting home.

Grimwold shrugged. "Probably not. I suggested it merely for the sake of demonstration. If you throw it in, it will not melt. Hammer it, it will not bend. To destroy it would take a magic more powerful than can be found in this cave."

"Things that cannot be broken are generally a bad idea," said Thomas.

Cara shivered. "Where is Beloved now?" she asked. "On Earth — or here in Luster?"

"I do not know," said Grimwold, "though I dearly hope that she is still in your world. Bad enough that she has some agent in this world — probably one of the Hunters, which is even worse — without her being here herself."

"If she knows where we are, knows to send a message here saying she wants the amulet, isn't it likely that she will have someone in place to steal it as soon as we leave here?" asked Lightfoot.

"Absolutely," replied Grimwold. "Which is why

you must leave in secret. I will take you to one of the back tunnels. It will let you out in Firethroat's territory."

"Yikes!" squealed the Squijum.

"She should not bother you," said Grimwold. "I have long since made peace with the Great Lady. In fact, she herself suggested this emergency exit."

"What do we do after we leave?" asked Cara.

"Make for Summerhaven and the Queen with all the speed that you can manage. I had hoped to summon help, an honor guard to take you and the amulet safely to court. Now you will need to travel as swiftly and secretly as you can. *The amulet must not fall into Beloved's hands! If it does...*"

He shook his head, as if the magnitude of the catastrophe was beyond his power to describe.

The trip through the tunnels was longer than Cara had expected, mostly because it had not occurred to her that Grimwold could have such a lengthy passage underground. They traveled first through a corridor lined with wood, then for a long way through natural rock, crossing underground streams, traversing caves so huge she wasn't sure they would find the other side, and narrow places so small the Dimblethum could barely squeeze through them. Finally they left the caverns and entered an earthen tunnel supported by beams.

*Man-made!* Cara thought to herself, then realized

that here on Luster *handmade* was the most she could say and be sure that she had the truth.

The Squijum rode on her shoulder for most of the journey, nervously crooning nonsense syllables in her ear. His fluffy tail curled around her neck felt as friendly and safe as the stuffed animals that lined her bed at home.

*Home.* The thought nearly stopped her in her tracks. She could not think of home without thinking of her grandmother. And she could not think of her grandmother without a pang of fear, wondering what had happened to her in the tower of St. Christopher's — though now that she knew *who* had chased them there, she was even more confused.

Aside from the Squijum's chatter, they traveled in silence. Once or twice Lightfoot made a point of stepping beside her. When she put her hand on his shoulder he thought to her, "I just wanted to see if you were all right."

Eventually they reached a set of five earthen steps. The steps led up to a wooden door. The door slanted toward them. The angle was so sharp that when Cara pressed her forehead to the door, its base was still some five feet ahead of her, level with her knees.

Grimwold said something to the Dimblethum. The creature put a pawlike hand on Cara's shoulder to draw her back. Stepping past her, he pressed his shoulder against the door. It opened into twilight, revealing a sky just starting to blossom with stars.

Cara now saw that the reason for the door's angle was that it was set in the side of a hill. Once outside, she saw that the door's exterior had been disguised with grass and wildflowers and rocks that she guessed must somehow have been glued in place. (Or, she realized, held there by some sort of magic.)

Grimwold pointed ahead of them and began to speak to Lightfoot — giving the unicorn directions, Cara assumed.

The dwarf turned to her. "It was a great pleasure to meet you, Miss Cara," he said with such obvious sincerity that she suddenly felt somehow more at home here. "Not all stories are good, not all endings are happy. May your story, on which may ride the fate of us all, be both good and happy. Give my regards to the Queen, and to your grandmother, if you are lucky enough to see them."

"I will," replied Cara, somewhat confused by the combination of gloom and hope in the dwarf's words.

Grimwold turned and stepped into the hillside. When he closed the door, it was almost as if he had never been there.

The Dimblethum made some growling noises. Cara put her hand on Lightfoot's shoulder, too late to understand the meaning of the growls, but in time to catch the unicorn's response, which was basically, "As fast as possible." Turning his attention to Cara, he added, "Would you like to ride?"

She scrambled onto his back, twining her fingers

in the spun silk of his mane, pressing her knees to his sides. No need to urge this steed to speed, or for a bridle to guide him. She merely held on as he sped through the grassland, straight into the domain of the dragon.

The Squijum and the Dimblethum traveled beside them, the Dimblethum usually on his hind legs, but occasionally dropping to all fours. Thomas ambled along behind, seeming not to hurry, yet never falling very far back.

They were nearing the foothills. A full moon had risen, painting the entire landscape with silver light. Suddenly the Squijum screeched and leaped onto the Dimblethum's back. "Look see look look look!" he cried, pointing moonward.

Cara looked up and gasped. Dark against the darkness of the night, Firethroat was flying. She crossed the moon once, and then again, her great and terrifying shape stark against the silver orb. On the second pass Cara realized that the dragon was getting closer. For a moment she tried to convince herself it was mere coincidence, but too soon it became obvious that Firethroat was heading straight for them.

"Run!" she cried to Lightfoot, forgetting that her spoken words carried no meaning for him. It didn't make any difference; the thought was so strong in her that she didn't need to try to send it to him. It flowed from her in a wash of panic so powerful that he reared back and pawed at the air.

Cara slid from his back, landing with a thump on the soft grass. Part of her remembered Lightfoot's warning that to run would only anger the dragon. But with that great, bat-winged form swooping toward them from the darkness, such advice was hard to heed. Scrambling to her feet, she shot off through the grass. Something grabbed her neck. She screamed before she realized it was the Squijum, who had leaped onto her shoulders and was gibbering with a fear that matched her own.

To her astonishment, Lightfoot held his ground. He stood in the moonlight, wind streaming through his mane, staring up at the dragon as if daring her to take him.

Cara caught her breath as Firethroat swooped low above the unicorn. The creature was enormous, her head the size of a car, the span of her wings wider than a house. Lightfoot, even the Dimblethum, suddenly seemed tiny in comparison.

Raising her head, the dragon shot a column of fire into the sky. Then she flapped those enormous wings a single time and swooped over Cara. Closing her right claw around the girl, the dragon turned and headed upward.

Cara screamed and kicked as she was lifted from the ground. But the talon that had closed around her waist was like a band of iron: smooth, hard, unbreakable. Her stomach lurched as the world fell away below her. Her legs dangled uselessly, and with nothing supporting her she was terrified that she would fall. At the same time, irrationally she was struggling to escape the dragon's grip, even though success would have sent her tumbling to the ground, increasingly far below. The Squijum, which still clung to her neck, was screeching in terror.

The dragon wheeled, and, almost as an afterthought, veered toward the ground again and snatched up Lightfoot with her other claw. Then into the air she rose. As Cara watched the land fall away below them she spotted Thomas and the Dimblethum, the latter roaring and stretching his fists toward the sky. Slowly they dwindled, until they were nothing but specks.

The dragon flew on.

# 18

# IN FIRETHROAT'S CAVE

irethroat flew higher and higher, until Cara felt that all of Luster was spread below them, a world of forests and plains, broad swamps and great rivers. In the distance, sparkling in the moonlight, a vast body of water stretched on farther than she could see, some huge lake, or inland sea, perhaps even an ocean.

Cara looked to her right, where Lightfoot dangled from the dragon's other claw, which held him around the middle. She wanted to speak to him, but it was impossible without direct contact.

To her surprise she was quite warm. She soon realized that the warmth emanated from the dragon's belly.

The Squijum, muttering in terror, had burrowed

between her body and Firethroat's claw. Cara worried that he might tickle the dragon into dropping them. But once he stopped squirming she realized it was almost comforting to have the little fellow snuggled against her.

They were above the mountains now, rising higher with the beating of Firethroat's great wings. The land below them, marked with cliffs and crags, grew wilder and rockier the higher they flew.

Was Firethroat planning to eat them? Perhaps she was simply going to drop them from some great height. Why was she angry with them? Simply for invading her territory? Or had they committed some other crime? She remembered Lightfoot saying that Firethroat had no patience with fools. She also remembered Grandmother Morris asking if anyone could be sure that he was not a fool.

The dragon banked to the right, and Cara felt dizzy as the world tipped beneath her. Then they swooped toward the side of a mountain. For a moment her heart leaped with new fear as she thought the dragon was going to dash them against the cliffs. At the last moment Firethroat flapped her wings just enough to lift them above the edge of the cliff onto a broad shelf of rock that fronted an enormous cave. After depositing them on the flat surface, the dragon settled in herself. She had no need to fear her prey would run away; the only possible routes were over the cliff or past herself.

On wobbly legs Cara stumbled to Lightfoot and

placed a hand on his shoulder. *Are you all right?* she thought.

*Better than I'm likely to be in a few moments,* he replied.

Suddenly the Squijum bolted from her shoulder and attempted to race past Firethroat. The dragon put out one enormous claw to block the little creature's path. Squeaking with distress, the Squijum scrambled over the claw and disappeared on the other side.

Firethroat made a dangerous noise deep in her throat. Cara wondered if the dragon would now cook her and Lightfoot out of mere annoyance. Instead, Firethroat simply looked at them, which was almost as frightening. Indeed, after a few moments in the dragon's gaze Cara felt as if she *had* been cooked.

The dragon did not move. After a time Cara forced herself to look back. She realized, with some surprise, that Firethroat was quite beautiful — if *astonishingly* large. The eyes that stared at her were nearly the size of her bedroom windows. Tendrils of smoke curled from flared nostrils so big that you could easily have roasted a turkey in either of them.

Reddish scales that had the appearance of burnished metal covered her massive head. Her long neck disappeared into the darkness of the cave, though the end of her tail looped forward again so that its pointed tip lay only a few feet from Cara. Finally Firethroat said, "So. You are the one for whom I have suffered so much humiliation."

134

Though Cara had her hand on Lightfoot's shoulder, she didn't need the connection to understand the dragon. The beast spoke in perfect English!

Cara was so surprised that she ignored the dragon's strange statement and asked, "How do you know my language?"

"Each species has its gifts," replied Firethroat. "The unicorns are healers. You humans have your hands and your inventive brains, always thinking of new things to make. We dragons have — among other things — the gift of tongues."

This time Cara understood that the dragon was whispering, and realized that if she spoke with her full voice it would probably blow them off the mountainside.

Cara paused. The next question felt dangerous, as if once asked, it would open the door to a problem that could overwhelm them all. And yet there was no way back, no choice but to ask it. Realizing that the very presence of the dragon seemed to demand that she speak formally, she asked, "How have I brought humiliation upon you?"

Firethroat made that terrifying noise in her throat again. The smoke curling from her nose became thicker, darker.

"I am very old," she whispered. "It has been many hundreds of years since anyone dared trifle with me. Yet two days ago a man came to this cave while I was out flying. Few men there are in Luster and even fewer that would dare come here. This man dared

135

to come, and much more. He went to the store of my treasures, which no man on Luster has ever done. Worse still, he disturbed that store, rummaging through it for the greatest prize of the lot, which he stole from me, to my shame and humiliation, and to your great sorrow."

"What was it that he stole?" asked Cara nervously.

Firethroat snorted twice. Little gouts of flame licked around the edges of her enormous nostrils.

"One does not become as old as I am without being wily as well. Before I came to Luster, many a man wished to kill me for the sake of impressing some fair lady whose span of days would be no more to me than the mayfly is to you. Most of these men were easily defeated. Yet I knew the day would come when some man would catch me while I was contemplating the poetry of the sky and the messages written in the clouds and not thinking about men and their treachery. I knew that in that moment I would die.

"So I wove a great enchantment. It took the help of many, for many were the magic makers, witches and wizards and sorcerers of all sorts, who were in my debt. Together we took my heart from my body and placed it in a golden casket. So long as my heart was in that casket it was safe, and I could not be harmed.

"The man who came to my cave yesterday did what no man has ever dared to do, or even thought of doing. He stole my heart, and told me he would not return it until I did his bidding."

The dragon closed her eyes for a moment, and Cara felt a flash of pain and embarrassment so overwhelming that she almost wished she could fling herself from the cliff.

"He who holds the casket holds my heart. He who holds my heart, holds me, and can command me as he wishes. This was the price of the magic, the geas that is laid on me. I have no quarrel with you or your companions. But the man who holds my heart asked for you, and I had no choice but to obey."

"Who is it that holds your heart?" asked Cara, sickeningly sure that she knew the answer already.

Firethroat did not speak. From behind the dragon a clear strong voice said, "I do."

Footsteps echoed across the floor of the cave as the man stepped from the darkness, stood beside the dragon's head. He was tall, with red hair. His eyes were dark, his face hard and lean. In his hands he held a large casket made of gold. Placing it on the ground, he put one foot on top of it, triumphant, confident.

Firethroat groaned.

Cara's heart was beating like a captured bird, and something thick seemed to have lodged itself in her throat.

The man turned to her and spoke. She did not

need to hear his voice to know he was the man who had pursued her into St. Christopher's — to know he was that man, and so much more.

"Hello, Cara," he said.

She closed her eyes and swallowed. Then she whispered, "Hello . . . Daddy."

# 19

# FAMILY MATTERS

ightfoot cried out and flinched away from her as if he had been burned. In the instant before he moved, she could sense the feeling of betrayal that washed through him. Firethroat closed her eyes, like someone pulling the shade over a window. It was a gesture of understanding, of resignation, of defeat.

As for Cara, her heart was running wild with so many emotions that she simply could not move. She stared at the man she had longed for for so long, a deep and indefinable ache stretching through her body. At last she saw the face for the voice in the tower, the secret face that had haunted her dreams since she entered Luster.

Trying to keep her voice from breaking, she whispered, "Where have you been all this time, Daddy?"

"I have been doing the family's business. *Your* business, Cara Diana. I have been guarding our world against the intrusion of murdering beasts like the one that stands beside you. Even more, I have been seeking a way to enter *this* world, so that the hunt can end at last, and we can rest."

"Is that why you left me?" she asked. It was hard to force the words past the pain in her throat.

He shook his head sadly. "I never left you, sweetheart."

She blinked in astonishment, her heart leaping. Of all the things he might have said, this is the one she would most have longed to hear. But she did not know what to make of it, whether to trust it.

"What do you mean?" she asked at last.

"I didn't leave you. Your grandmother stole you from me."

A wave of coldness, filled with terror and sorrow, washed over her. "What do you mean?" she asked again weakly.

He sighed. "Do you remember that once when you were little you became very sick?"

She nodded. "And a unicorn came and healed me. I stopped believing that for a long time. But now I know it's true."

"Your grandmother summoned that unicorn," said her father. "She was always a friend of unicorns, and they would do as she asked. But in saving you, she had created a problem." He sighed. "That problem was me. I swear I do not know why I fell in love with your mother, Cara, don't know if Grandmother Beloved set me on that path to get to your grandmother. I did know, though I never understood why, that it broke Ivy Morris's heart when her daughter married a man named Hunter." He sighed again. "At the time I didn't know the secret of our family. But after the unicorn had come, Beloved called me, and I was initiated. You have to believe me, Cara. I did not abandon you. Your grandmother took you from me because she was afraid I would use you to get at the unicorns."

"And would you have?" she asked.

Her father hesitated. "Yes," he said at last.

Cara felt as if her heart was being torn in half. How could her grandmother have done such a thing to her? Yet how could she not? She had been to Luster, been a friend of unicorns. Knowing what her son-in-law's family would do if they could enter this world, she would have been forced to take action.

Cara wondered whose pain had been greater — her own or her grandmother's?

Or maybe even her father's?

She wondered if there was anyone in the world that she could trust.

She wondered if the hurt would ever go away again.

"Is Grandmother Morris all right?" she asked. "Did you hurt her in the tower?"

The question caused her father's face to twist with

pain. "What kind of a man do you think I am?" he cried.

"I don't know!" she screamed. "I don't know anything anymore!"

A horrible silence filled the cave.

Ian Hunter knelt, careful to keep one knee on the casket, and looked directly at her. Spreading his arms to welcome her in, he whispered, "I have missed you so, my Cara, my dear one." His eyes were large and dark with sorrow. "You don't know yet what it means to be part of our family, Cara, don't know the burden we carry, protecting Earth from his kind. Since you fell through here ahead of me I have been terrified that one of them would kill you before I could save you."

"Lightfoot has been kind to me," she said, confused.

"They are cunning," her father replied with a sneer. "They knew I was coming and wanted you on their side. But you were born to help bring an end to them. Give me the amulet, sweetheart. Once I have it, we can go home."

"And then what?" she asked, her voice, her body, trembling.

"Then the final hunt will begin. After a time the unicorns will be gone and our family's task will be ended. Beloved will be able to rest at last and so will I. Then you and I can be together again. You don't know how I've longed for that day, Cara, how much I regret the lost time. But Grandmother Beloved called, and I had no choice but to answer. And you — you had disappeared. I wanted to hunt for you, but first I had to be trained for our great mission. Yet I always knew that one day I would find you again."

Cara closed her eyes, imagining it.

"What about Mommy?" she asked.

She had meant to say, "my mother," but it had been eight years since she had last seen the woman she called by that name, and when she thought of her, thought of the night she had disappeared, it was the word "Mommy" that forced its way through her throat.

"Mommy is waiting for you," said her father.

Cara heard the dragon shift behind her, but it was a momentary noise, and then the great beast was quiet once more.

Her father held out his hand. "Bring me the amulet, Cara Diana."

Still she stood without moving, as if frozen by hearing once more the name he had called her when she was but a toddler, the name he called her when he threw her in the air, and played peekaboo, and tucked her in at night.

"Bring me the amulet," he said again, his voice strong.

Slowly she stepped forward. Raising her hands to her neck, she lifted the mended chain that held the amulet.

Lightfoot whickered, and even though she was not

connected to him, she could hear in that sound fear, and sorrow, and his sense of betrayal.

Tears in her eyes, she took another step forward, studying her father's face, uncertain if she would be able to do what she had to do.

"I'm waiting, Cara," he said, voice gentle, eyes hard.

Cara ran toward him, raising her arms as if to embrace him. But just before she reached him she stopped and threw the amulet. It soared above his head.

"What . . . ?" he cried, then he turned to scramble for it.

But the Squijum was faster; it had already caught the amulet and was racing into the darkness. Ian Hunter lunged for the little creature, then suddenly twisted back, a look of fear on his face.

He was too late. Cara had seized the golden casket that held Firethroat's heart and was backing away from him, toward the unicorn and the dragon.

"Cara!" he screamed. "What are you doing?"

She said nothing.

"Cara, give that back to me. You don't know what kind of catastrophe you could create. *Give it back to me!*"

"I'm sorry, Daddy," she said softly. "I can't do that."

"Cara, I'm your father. I demand that you give it to me."

She laughed, but it was a painful sound, a laugh that held eight years of sorrow and loss.

144

He spoke again, more calmly. "Cara, you are a Hunter, one of the clan. You were born to this. It is the final chapter of our story, the chance to end the hunt forever. Your blood binds you — my blood, the blood of Beloved that runs in our veins. It's family, Cara Diana, Cara Diana *Hunter*. Family. You belong to us, to Beloved."

"Family isn't blood," she said bitterly, continuing to back away. "Family is who loves you, who takes care of you."

"I wanted to take care of you!" he cried, his words pouring out in a howl of pain. "You were stolen from me!"

The sorrow in his voice pierced her, and she wanted to run to him. But she saw that even as he mourned her loss, he was judging the distance between them, preparing to leap.

She took another step back, then turned and ran.

She wanted to call on Firethroat for help, but feared that if she unleashed the dragon's wrath, the beast would destroy her father. She didn't want to destroy him, merely wanted him sent back to Earth, far from her and the unicorns. She hadn't thought further ahead than keeping the amulet out of his grasp.

His leap brought him within inches of her. She ran faster, heading for the front of the cave, uncertain where she would go after that.

"Come back here!" he roared, scrambling to his feet, sprinting after her.

145

Firethroat, freed from Ian Hunter's hold on her heart, was stirring.

"Don't hurt him!" cried Cara, and, because she held the dragon's heart, Firethroat was bound by her command.

Her father tackled her. They fell together, near the edge of the cliff. He would have wrenched the casket from her then, but Lightfoot trumpeted and began to pelt the man with his hooves. Hunter drew back. Then, as if invincible to the pain, he lunged forward again. Stretching his arms, he tried to tear the golden casket from his daughter's hands. Lightfoot struck his hands away just before they closed on the casket.

Cara scrambled to her feet. Her father, intent on the casket, grabbed her legs. She fell again, closer to the edge. They began to wrestle. Lightfoot bugled a warning, but it went unheeded. They rolled over once and then were gone over the edge of the cliff.

It was different from the leap from the tower of St. Christopher's. Then, she had leaped into light, with a glimmer of hope that she might come to something better. Now, she only fell, through the night in the mountains, toward not a street but a heap of snow-covered rock so far below it made the distance from tower to street seem like a baby step. She fell with no hope, only primal terror ripping through her.

Her father was near but no longer holding her. She could barely see him, falling, falling, just a few feet away. Some small part of her brain registered with interest that they were falling at the same speed, though he was so much heavier.

She had heard the old story that when someone is drowning their whole life flashes before them. But drowning would be a slow death compared to this. Their speed was breathtaking. The cliffside flashed by. She couldn't breathe, couldn't think, as she saw oblivion racing toward her and then — *Snatch!* Firethroat plucked her from the air and soared upward again.

Her father was still falling.

Cara was still clutching the casket that held Firethroat's heart. Without thinking, she commanded the dragon to do her will.

"Save him!" she screamed.

# 20

# THREE DROPS
# OF BLOOD

ara sat, trembling, at the edge of the cliff, holding the golden casket against her chest. The Squijum crouched on her shoulder, crooning nonsense into her ear. Lightfoot stood behind her. She wondered what he was thinking.

Ahead of them dawn was creeping over the mountains. Suddenly, Firethroat burst into the light, appearing as if from nowhere. Her claws were empty.

Cara and her friends scrambled back from the cliff edge as the dragon returned to her cave.

"It is done," she murmured, folding her wings.

"What did you do with him?" asked Cara nervously.

The dragon regarded her with one enormous eye.

"I returned him to Earth," she said at last. "Not an easy thing to do, I assure you. But flying between worlds is another gift that dragons possess."

"Where?" Cara asked. "Where did you leave him?"

"Someplace empty," said the dragon with maddening vagueness. "I cannot go where there are people, of course. I left him safe, dry, and alive. What he does next is up to him. I care only that he does not return to Luster."

"Thank you," said Cara. "I know it was not easy for you." Stepping forward, she placed the casket on the cave floor, not far from the dragon. "Here," she whispered, pushing it forward. "Your heart is your own again."

She watched a great claw reach forward and draw the golden casket away.

Then the last of her strength left her, and the pain and the loss came flooding in. Turning from the dragon, from her friends, Cara bolted into the darkness at the back of the cave. When she stumbled and fell, she made no move to get up, simply lay on the floor, sobbing her grief and pain, until a welcome darkness blanketed her mind.

When she woke, it was dark again. The only light came from a sprinkling of stars behind her, and — to her right — a faint glow from the dragon's fiery nostrils.

Whimpering, she curled into a ball, trying to blot the memory of the previous night from her mind.

149

After a while she realized that someone was standing over her. Opening her eyes, she saw the glow of Lightfoot's horn. A look of gentle concern filled his eyes. He knelt beside her and she wound her arms around his neck, burying her face in the clean perfection of his mane.

"Do you hate me?" she thought.

"Why?" he asked, seeming startled by the question.

"Because I am a Hunter."

"You are Cara," he replied, "and you are not chained by blood. You are a friend of unicorns."

Though she tried to hold it in, another sob tore out of her. Clinging to Lightfoot, she wept until her lungs were sore, her face a soggy mess, whispering, "Daddy, Daddy, Daddy."

"I have no way to heal a wound such as this," said Lightfoot sadly, when she was done.

She said nothing, only tightened her grip on him, holding him as if she were tottering on the edge of an abyss far deeper and more terrifying than the one from which Firethroat had saved her.

"Are you all right?" he asked after a while.

She shook her head. "How can I be all right? I missed him so much for so long. And then..."

"Family ties are strange," he replied. "I have thought about them often, but never — "

He was interrupted by the Squijum. The little creature had been sitting in front of them, holding the amulet. Suddenly he darted forward and placed the golden bauble on Cara's knees. As Lightfoot stepped

150

back, the Squijum chittered something, then scrambled up Cara's arm to her shoulder and kissed her on the cheek. As if startled by his own boldness, he scampered back down and raced to the mouth of the cave, where he sat on his haunches, chattering incomprehensibly.

"I wish I could understand you," she said, half-amused, half-irritated.

"An interesting thought, young human," said Firethroat, interrupting the Squijum's chatter. "And perhaps the solution to a vexing problem."

"What problem?" asked Cara.

The dragon sighed, sending a wave of warmth in Cara's direction. "I owe you a great boon for what you have done."

"A boon?"

"It is something like a reward," explained Lightfoot. "Dragons do not like to be in anyone's debt, and you have done this lady a great service. It would be wise to accept whatever she offers with as much grace as you can manage."

"But you already saved my father," whispered Cara.

"It was commanded of me," said Firethroat. "But my heart was freely returned, and the boon must be freely given."

Cara paused, feeling the world was moving too fast for her. After a moment she said, "I would be most grateful to accept your boon, Lady Firethroat."

The dragon made a sound of approval. "Come with me," she said. "I would prefer to do this in private."

151

Cara followed Firethroat deep into the cave, then into a separate chamber. Here the darkness was complete, save for the dim light that came from the dragon's nostrils. Suddenly, Firethroat opened her mouth and shot forth a brief gout of flame.

Cara gasped in wonder, for at once the chamber came to life with a thousand colors, as piles of gold and jewels reflected back the burst of flame. For a moment Cara thought the purpose of the flame had been to show her what was in the room. She wondered if this was to be Firethroat's boon, some piece of fabulous treasure.

She was wrong, on both counts. Firethroat had used her flame to light a torch mounted in the wall. Now its low, flickering light danced on the gems, some as big as Cara's fist, that littered the floor.

The dragon cast her eye over a pile, then reached into it and pulled forth a jeweled chalice. "This should do," she said, passing it to Cara.

"Thank you."

The dragon chuckled. "That is not the boon."

Cara blinked.

"You didn't *want* it to be the boon, did you?" asked Firethroat.

She shook her head, hoping she wasn't getting herself into more trouble.

Firethroat stared at her. "You held my heart in your hands and returned it to me, when you could have made me your slave."

Cara shivered. The thought had never occurred to her. She found it repulsive.

"I want you to understand the granting of this boon," said the dragon. "This is only the third time in more thousands of years than I care to remember that I have done this for a human. Come here — step close."

Hesitant, nervous, Cara did as the dragon asked. As she watched, Firethroat ran the first talon of her right front foot up and down the scales of her neck.

"Here!" she said at last. Grasping one of the scales, she wrenched it from her neck. Blood welled from the wound, steaming hot.

"Catch it!" she ordered.

Cara held the chalice beneath Firethroat's neck. Three large drops of blood fell, steaming and smoking, into the chalice.

"Now drink them."

"What?" cried Cara.

"Drink them. *Quickly,* while they are still hot and the magic is strong."

Cara stared into the steaming chalice. Lightfoot's words about accepting the boon with grace sounded in her head. Closing her eyes, she lifted the chalice to her lips. Then she threw back her head and drank.

Fire scalded her throat, raced along her veins. The chalice fell from her hands. She closed her eyes, stiffened, nearly fell, straightened, stood firm.

"Are you all right?" asked Firethroat, not in Cara's

153

language, but in the ancient tongue of the dragons, a language of fire that came from deep in the belly.

And Cara *understood*.

"*This* is my boon," said Firethroat, "the best I have to offer. It is the gift of tongues, of knowledge of the languages of all creatures. Now there are none in Luster to whom you cannot speak, none to whom you must be a stranger."

"It is a great gift, and I am deeply honored," said Cara.

"Small return for the return of my heart," said Firethroat.

With a flick of her wing, she extinguished the torch. Then she led the way from the chamber.

# 21

# THINGS BROKEN, THINGS MENDED

nce again Cara dangled from Firethroat's foot. But this time there was no fear, only wonder, as — safely wrapped in the dragon's claw — she looked out on the world spread wide below them.

Firethroat had agreed to return Cara, Lightfoot, and the Squijum to the place from which she had first snatched them, with the hope that they might be able to rejoin Thomas and the Dimblethum and continue their journey.

"I would take you all the way to Summerhaven," the dragon had said, "but even I cannot fly that far carrying both a unicorn and a human."

They had discussed the matter for a while, Cara joying in her ability to talk to her friends with ease and freedom. Finally they had decided that their wisest course would be to return to Grimwold's Cavern and try once more to contact the Queen.

"After all," said Lightfoot, "with the Hunter gone, Beloved's connection to this world may be severed."

He paused for a moment when he noticed the tremor of grief that twisted Cara's face at the memory he had stirred up.

"He would have destroyed us all, you know," he said softly.

She nodded. "I know. Even so . . ."

"Even so," agreed Lightfoot.

As they retraced their flight of the night before, Cara tried to pick out some of the landmarks Lightfoot had told her they would pass on the last leg of their journey to Summerhaven: the River Mallow, Chiron's Tor, Spirit Lake. Each, he said, had a story attached. And each story, of course, was stored in Grimwold's Cavern.

She longed to know them all.

It was because she was looking so hard for the landmarks that she was the first to spot the surprise awaiting them. "Look!" she cried to Lightfoot, pointing into the distance.

He stared for a moment, uncomprehending, then threw back his head and bugled his delight.

"Oh yeah much good hotcha!" burbled the Squijum, who was clinging to her neck.

*     *     *

The Dimblethum and Thomas were waiting for them when they landed.

"You're back, you're back!" roared the manbear, waving his arms in delight. Then he stood still, embarrassed at his own outburst.

"We are!" cried Cara, throwing her arms around him, at least, as far as they would reach.

He looked at her, astonished that she could speak to him. "How did...?" He paused, then looked at the dragon and nodded. "The Dimblethum sees that you have a story to tell," he said.

"Well, I'm the one she'll have to tell it to," said Grimwold, stepping up beside them.

Cara was not surprised to see him there. But her attention was focused beyond him. There, standing in a rough circle, were at least a dozen unicorns, dazzling in the sunlight, dazzling in their beauty and perfection.

*You should not be hunted,* she thought to herself.

The largest of the unicorns stepped forward.

"It's my uncle," whispered Lightfoot. He did not sound happy.

"I bring you greetings from Queen Arabella Skydancer," said the unicorn. "She commends you on your courage and thanks you for your efforts on behalf of Luster. I am commanded to escort you and your friends to the court at Summerhaven, where you will be presented to the Queen."

"Wonderful," muttered Lightfoot bitterly. "I've

spent the last three years trying to get out of doing just that. Some reward!"

A week later, after a journey filled with marvels and wonders, Cara entered the court at Summerhaven. It was a place of green splendor, grown, not built, and at its center was a unicorn so old and so beautiful that words could not describe her. She was small and slender, as luminous as a rainbow, as fragile as a promise. You could see through her, as if you were seeing tomorrow.

To Cara's sorrow, neither Lightfoot nor the Dimblethum was with her when she entered the court. Both had come to her late in the night before they reached Summerhaven and bid her farewell.

"The Dimblethum is not really welcome there," said the manbear, putting his huge paw against her cheek, where it lay as delicately as a butterfly.

"And I am not ready to return there," said Lightfoot. "But I will see you again, I promise."

She wondered if it was true as she watched them slip into the night. She wiped a tear from her cheek.

"Chains," said the Tinker, coming up behind her. "They bind us, whether we want them to or not. But a heart without chains would have nothing to hold it, might simply blow away."

Then he held her in his arms while she wept and wept, for her father, for her grandmother, and even for the ever-wounded, ever-healing Beloved, chained to her rage for longer than anyone could imagine.

Together, Thomas, Cara, and the Squijum went to stand before the Queen. When Arabella Skydancer laid her horn across Cara's shoulder in blessing, the girl whispered, "Are you the Old One?"

"I am," said the Queen.

"Then I have a message for you. I have carried it from another world, through danger and heartbreak across this world to you. I am to tell you that the Wanderer is weary."

"Then it is time to bring her home," said the Queen. "Would you like to be the one to fetch her?"

"I would," whispered Cara. "Very much."

"Then so it shall be."


And so it was.

But that, of course, is another story altogether.

It is recorded, like all such stories, in the Unicorn Chronicles.

# Song of the Wanderer

*Dedicated to all the readers who have waited,*
*patiently and impatiently, for this second volume,*
*with my deepest apologies for taking so long.*

# CHAPTER ONE

# A MEETING
# WITH THE QUEEN

The Queen will see you now, human child."
Cara scrambled to her feet. She had been sitting beneath a large quilpum tree, enjoying the spicy smell of its bark while she watched the unicorns graze in the blue-green meadow ahead of her. The afternoon was warm, and she had been drifting at the edge of sleep. Now she was totally alert.

Laughing Stream, the unicorn who had spoken to her, watched with an amused expression as the girl began brushing leaves and twigs from her pant legs.

*I wish I had some better clothes,* Cara thought anxiously. *I'm hardly dressed to visit a queen!*

Indeed, she had been wearing the same jeans and T-shirt since she had first entered Luster a few weeks ago, and they were filthy. She put a hand to her long red hair and sighed. It was even worse than her clothes.

"Ready?" asked Laughing Stream.

Cara nodded. "Ready."

"Then follow me."

Though Laughing Stream was trying to be serious — this was important business, after all — the unicorn was not able to hide the hint of amusement in her voice. Cara would have been offended, except it hadn't taken her long after meeting Laughing Stream to realize that the unicorn found almost *everything* amusing. Her name had been well given.

Besides, the girl had no energy to spare on being offended. Her thoughts were all on what would happen when she saw the Queen. It was a conversation she had been eagerly awaiting since she'd arrived at Summerhaven three days earlier.

She had already seen the Queen a few times, but always in a very formal way. Today, at last, they were going to discuss how Cara would return to Earth to fetch Ivy Morris, the woman the unicorns knew as "The Wanderer," but whom Cara thought of only as Gramma.

The last time Cara had seen her grandmother, she was ringing the bell in the tower of St. Christopher's church to help open the gateway to Luster — the gateway through which Cara had fled with the amulet she now wore around her neck. From that moment, Cara had ached to know if her grandmother was safe, if she had survived that horrible night.

So intent was Cara on her thoughts that she paid no attention to where she was walking and soon stumbled over a root. She managed to keep from crashing to the ground, but just barely. Laughing Stream snorted, then tried to hide her amusement. Unicorns rarely stumbled.

They came to a circle of trees that reminded her of weeping willows, save that their trunks and leaves both had a distinct bluish tone. Their long, slender branches swept the ground, creating a kind of lacy wall. Laughing Stream led the way through an arched opening in that wall.

In the center of the trees shimmered a pool of crystal-clear water. A scattering of leaves, silver-blue and shaped like the blades of spears, floated on its surface. Standing at the edge of the pool was Arabella Skydancer, the Queen of the unicorns, sometimes known as "the Old One." She was small, her shoulders no higher than Cara's. Her mane was like the foam on the crest of the long ninth wave, her spiral horn like a lance of pearl. She held herself with a sense of ancient dignity that Cara found almost overpowering.

The Queen nodded to Cara and stared at her for a long moment. Finally, in a voice like soft summer wind, she said, "It is time for us to talk."

Cara lowered her head and made a kind of curtsy. Only a few days earlier she would have had to be touching the Queen in order to understand her. But now that the dragon Firethroat had given her the gift of tongues, she could speak with ease to any of the intelligent creatures of Luster.

The Queen laughed. A kind laugh, sweet and gentle. "No need to be so formal with me, child. Come, sit beside me. We will speak of what needs to be done . . . and of things you need to know."

Folding her slender legs, the Queen settled to a bed of young ferns. She was very old, but her age showed only in the way she was beginning to fade. Sometimes you could see right through her, as if she were already part ghost. Yet now, lying on the ferns, she looked as much like a young foal as an ancient queen. Except for her eyes. They were so deep and so old that looking into them made it hard to imagine anything had ever been young.

Cara settled beside her.

"Have you recovered from your adventures?" asked the Queen.

Cara thought before she answered. Her journey through Luster had been harrowing. But here at Summerhaven, safe and well fed, her body had quickly regained its full strength. As for her heart . . . well, that was a different matter. It was only days ago that she had discovered that the man who had chased her and Grandmother Morris into St. Christopher's had been her own father. She still stung from the knowledge that he was a Hunter, one of the ancient clan sworn to stalk and kill the unicorns. Even worse, through her father she herself was descended directly from the strange woman known as Beloved, the greatest enemy the unicorns had ever known.

She didn't know how to discuss these things with the Queen. They were painful and embarrassing. And frightening. Given her family history on her father's side, it sometimes surprised her that the Queen and the other unicorns would talk to her at all.

Yet her grandmother had been a great friend of the unicorns — such a good friend, according to her father, that she had stolen Cara away, kidnapped her, rather than let her fall into the hands of the Hunters.

But if that was so, why had her grandmother never spoken of it? Why hadn't she prepared her for all this? Cara loved her grandmother and longed to see her safe. But she also had some hard questions to ask her.

"I'm not sure I'll ever recover," whispered Cara.

"Each wound has its own time for healing," replied the Queen. "The wounds of the heart are much deeper than those of the flesh."

Cara nodded gravely.

"Now, let me speak to you of Luster," said the Queen. "If you are going to journey across our world in order to fetch the Wanderer, there are things you should understand."

Cara looked at her in surprise. "I thought I would use the amulet to return home." As she spoke her hand crept to her throat, and the chain that held the amulet her grandmother had given her — the amulet that had opened the way for her leap into Luster.

"Certainly the amulet will carry you between Luster and Earth," said the Queen softly. "But unless you make the crossing from the right place, you could still end up very far from your grandmother."

Cara felt suddenly weary. "Does that mean I have to go all the way back to where I was when I first got here?"

"Alas, if only it were that simple. But ours is an oddly patchwork world, Cara. We touch old Earth in a hodgepodge of places, connections that change with the passing of the seasons. That's why the first stage of your journey will be to the home of the Geomancer."

"The Geomancer?"

"She's a kind of . . . oh, an earth-magician. Her magic is that of soil and stone, of water and rock. She will be able to work out the best place for you to cross back to your own world."

"Is it far to where she lives?" asked Cara nervously. This was turning out to be more complicated than she had expected.

"Only two or three days. And you won't be traveling alone. We will choose a small glory of unicorns to travel with you. Only three, alas. I thought long and hard about this, whether it would be better to send a large group and seek safety in numbers, or a small group and hope for safety in stealth. I finally decided that a small glory would be wisest. After all, the delvers are already aware of you, and a large group would be more apt to attract their attention."

Cara shuddered at the mention of the delvers. The vicious, goblin-like creatures were sworn enemies of the unicorns. Her fear of them was intensified by the fact that one had attacked her shortly after she'd first arrived in Luster.

"I've asked Moonheart to lead the group," continued the Queen.

"That's nice," said Cara, despite the fact that the idea made her a little nervous. Moonheart was one of the Queen's nephews, and though he had been kind enough in the few days since she had met him, she found him distant and aloof. She suspected this might be partly because the very first unicorn she had met in Luster — and the one to whom she had really given her heart — was his own nephew, Lightfoot. For some reason Cara had not been able to discover, Moonheart considered the young unicorn a disgrace to the family.

Whatever the reason, Lightfoot and his big, lumbering friend the Dimblethum had quietly slipped away from their group just before they'd arrived at Summerhaven. Cara missed them both desperately. They had been her first friends in Luster; had helped her, taught her, and guided her on her journey to find the Queen.

Well, at least Thomas the Tinker and the Squijum were still with her. She would see them later, after her audience with the Queen.

Suddenly Cara realized that she had let her attention wander — an old problem that had gotten her in plenty of trouble in school.

"I know Moonheart may seem a little . . . formal," the Queen was saying. "But he is experienced in the ways of the forest and the mountain, and as brave as any unicorn you can find in all of Luster."

"It will be an honor to travel with him," said Cara quickly, feeling she had been terribly ungrateful to question the Queen's choice. *You're getting spoiled!* she told herself. *Not long ago, the idea of even seeing a unicorn would have been enough to make you think that your greatest dream had come true. Now you're getting choosy about which ones you want to travel with!*

"You will need him, and the others," said the Queen. "Luster is beautiful, but it is not without its dangers. Remember, our world is not developed in the ways that your world is. You will not find wide roads and solid bridges to cross this wild country. And along the way you may find strange and ancient creatures, beings that you thought no more than myths or legends."

Cara grinned. "You mean, like unicorns?"

The Queen laughed — a sound that made Cara think of distant wind chimes. "Like unicorns. But not only unicorns, child. We were the ones who opened the way, with the help of an old magician named Bellenmore. But once the gates were opened, others came through as well. As you know, we have dragons here. Dragons, and other creatures, too — some of them kindly, others more . . . unpredictable."

"Tell me more about the gates," said Cara.

The Queen paused for a moment, as if the subject was painful. "Seven gates link Luster to Earth," she said at last. "Stepping through any of them will carry you from one world to the other. I have kept them open in the hope that the day might come when we could finally return to Earth, or at least visit our old home more freely. Alas, I fear it was a fool's hope."

172

When Cara started to object the Queen shook her head. "Oh, yes, child. Even a queen can be a fool — perhaps more a fool than most. Many in my court feel it is time to close the gates, and not merely for safety's sake. They want to bring full end to our old connection. My heart speaks against this. But the truth is the choice may be beyond me anyway."

"Why?"

The Queen looked away, almost as if she were gazing into another world. "The ancient magic that formed the gates seems to be fading. It is possible they will vanish of their own accord sometime in the near future." She shook her head. "That will be a loss for both worlds. Anyway, for now — and for as long as the gates are open — each entrance to Luster is closely guarded at all times. And their location on Earth is a very deep secret, as it must be to keep the Hunters from passing through."

Cara felt herself blush at the mention of the Hunters from whom she was descended.

The Queen, as if sensing her discomfort, said softly, "I care much less about your roots than about how you have chosen to grow, child. You have well demonstrated both your loyalty and your courage. I am satisfied."

Cara felt a hot lump of sorrow in her chest when she thought of the moment in Firethroat's cave when she had been forced to choose between her father and the unicorns. *But he had been going to open a new gate, so he could lead the Hunters into Luster where they would kill —*

She cut off the thought. She had made her choice: She stood with the unicorns.

Yet the memory of her meeting with her father raised another question, almost as painful: *Where was her mother?*

According to her father, she was waiting to see Cara again. The thought pierced her with longing. But was it true?

Again she had let her attention wander. With a start, she realized the Queen was speaking.

"Tonight we will have a ceremony at which you will pledge yourself to the quest. Tomorrow, your journey will begin."

Arabella Skydancer paused, and Cara could sense a deep sorrow in her. "May that journey be successful. An old wound separates your grandmother and myself, and I would like to heal it. Bring the Wanderer back to me, Cara. Bring her back, because I dare not finish fading until you do."

"Finish?" asked Cara nervously.

"I am old," said the Queen, and the sudden weariness in her voice seemed to crush Cara's bones. "Older than I should be. I yearn to leave this life behind and move on to what is next. But I have promises to keep, and wounds to heal, and I cannot go until I do. So bring your grandmother back, child, for her sake . . . and for mine, so I can rest at last."

Cara felt a coldness in her heart. "Are you saying that if I bring my grandmother back —"

She couldn't bring herself to finish the sentence. The thought was too horrible. But she didn't really need to ask the question. Arabella Skydancer had made her meaning clear: She was waiting for the Wanderer to return so that she could die.

# CHAPTER TWO

# "Do You Accept This Task?"

Night fell. The moon, waning since the night Cara had confronted her father in Firethroat's cave, was a mere sliver now. The greatest light came from a huge star that the unicorns called "The Magician's Eye."

When the star reached its highest point, the unicorns gathered, arranging themselves in a half circle so that all of them were facing a large black stone. The stone, which had a perfectly flat top, was about three feet high, three feet wide, and five feet long.

When the gathering was complete Arabella Skydancer appeared, climbing silently onto the stone platform by way of its sloping rear side. She stationed herself at its center. Her milky white coat seemed to glow in the moonlight. She gazed out on the gathering, then called Cara to come and stand before her.

The girl stepped forward. Surrounded by the glory of unicorns, she felt unexpected tears well up. To be in this place, with these enchanted creatures, was a dream come true. But now she had to leave. Never mind that the leaving was to fetch her grandmother, something she desperately wanted to do. It still hurt.

She brushed a strand of her red hair away from her face, then reminded herself not to fidget and dropped her hand back to her side.

Arabella Skydancer, the Queen, the Old One, stared down at the girl for a long moment. Finally she said, "Cara Diana Hunter, do you accept this task of your own free will?"

"I accept this task of my own free will," replied Cara, using the ancient words of ceremony that the Queen had taught her that afternoon. "I will give it all my heart, all my strength, all my energy."

"So be it," said the Queen. Raising her head, she said, "I call Moonheart to come forward and join us."

A large unicorn stepped into the circle and came to stand beside Cara. He was so tall that he and the Queen were eye to eye, even though she was standing on the black rock. His horn was a pearly wonder: Extending a full three feet from his forehead, it glowed as if with some inner light — though Cara knew that he could quickly quench that glow if he needed to move unseen through the night.

The Queen spoke softly. "Moonheart, I ask you to accompany this child as she goes to seek the Wanderer. Do you accept this task of your own free will?"

Moonheart lowered his horn until its tip touched the stone between the Queen's cloven hooves. "Ivy Morris was a friend of mine," he said solemnly, "and our fates are tangled together like the strands of a callum vine. I accept this task with joy. I will give it all my heart, all my strength, all my energy."

Cara looked at Moonheart in astonishment. How was his fate woven with that of her grandmother?

"There will be danger," warned the Queen.

"I understand that."

"You may even be required to return to Earth."

A shudder rippled along Moonheart's silken flanks. But all he said was, "I will do what I must."

"Then guard the child," said the Queen. "Guide her

as well. Have you spoken to those we selected to travel with you?"

"I have," replied Moonheart. Turning toward the assembled unicorns, he made a series of low whickers, which Cara understood to be a call.

Two unicorns stepped from the group. One, a male, was the biggest unicorn Cara had yet seen. Coming from the other side of the group was a female who, though much smaller than the male, had such a look of ferocity that Cara found her almost terrifying.

"Greetings, Finder," said the Queen, addressing the big unicorn.

"Greetings, My Queen," he replied softly, in a voice that reminded Cara of a cello.

"And Belle," said the Queen, turning to the female. "Though I shall miss having you as part of my guard, it pleases me that you will be part of this journey."

Belle nodded, but said nothing until the Queen repeated the ceremonial words. Then she made her pledge and affirmed that she accepted the task of her own free will, just as each of the others had.

When the swearing in was finished, the Queen stepped down from the rock. Coming to each of them, she placed her horn across their shoulders in sign of blessing. "I shall eagerly await your return. May your journey be successful, for each of you is dear to my heart — as is the Wanderer you go to seek."

She returned to the stone platform. "Travel safe, travel well," she called, her voice stronger than Cara would have thought possible from such a seemingly frail creature. "May those who have gone before be always with you."

From behind them, in response, came the voices of the assembled glory. "Travel safe, travel well. May those who have gone before be always with you."

The Queen turned and left the circle.

The other unicorns waited until she was out of sight, then began to drift away as well. Several came over to bid a special farewell to one or the other of the unicorns going on the journey. But finally it was just Cara standing with the three who were to accompany her. She was longing to ask Moonheart about his connection with her grandmother, but before she could get up the courage, he said, "We leave at first light. I suggest you all get a good night's rest."

Then he, too, turned and left the clearing.

Cara felt uneasy as she watched him disappear into

the forest. Though it would be a great honor to travel with him, she found herself longing for Lightfoot. The younger unicorn was not only much friendlier, he actually seemed to like her — a feeling she did not sense from Moonheart.

She wondered if one reason she and Lightfoot got along so well was because they were both young.

*Well, "young" isn't exactly the right word,* thought Cara with a smile. Her friend was more than a century old, after all. But, according to what he had told her, that was approximately what being a teenager was to a human.

What she had not been able to get Lightfoot to tell her was why he had refused to return to the court at Summerhaven. No one here had been willing to speak of it, either — though in the few days Cara had been here, it had become clear to her that the unicorns at court were as unhappy with Lightfoot as Lightfoot was with them.

Her wandering thoughts were called back to the present by Finder, who said shyly, "I'm glad we'll be going with you."

"For all the use you'll be," muttered Belle.

"Fighting isn't the only way to be of help," said Finder gently.

Belle snorted, then turned to go.

"Wait!" said Cara.

Belle turned back.

"Thank you for agreeing to come."

"Moonheart asked," replied Belle sharply. "Of course I agreed."

"Belle is very fierce," said Finder, sounding a little nervous.

"Have to be fierce if you're on delver patrol," snapped Belle, her voice dripping with scorn. "Only way to survive."

"You can always hide," replied Finder. Then, quickly, he turned away. Cara had a feeling that if he were human he would have been blushing.

"I will see you in the morning," said Belle brusquely. Then she turned once more and left the clearing.

"Don't mind her," said Finder after Belle was gone. "She doesn't like to talk much."

"I guess not," said Cara, who could not help but wonder if her own family history had anything to do with Belle's attitude.

"I, too, will see you in the morning," said Finder gently. He nuzzled the top of her head once, then turned and disappeared into the darkness.

182

◆　　◆　　◆

Cara remained in the center of the clearing for some time. Though it seemed that the unicorns had all gone, she knew they would not leave her entirely alone; one or two were always somewhere nearby to guard her. She understood this was to protect her from delvers, but sometimes she suspected, sadly, that this was also to protect *themselves* from *her*. Despite all she had done, she was not sure the unicorns entirely trusted her. Given her family background, she could understand that. But it still hurt, especially considering what she had given up to be here among them.

Her thoughts were interrupted by the snapping of a twig. Turning quickly, she saw a man step from the darkness beneath one of the trees. The brief instant of panic faded when she realized it was Thomas the Tinker. As always, her friend was dressed in an outlandish coat, the original material of which had nearly vanished beneath a myriad of brightly colored patches. The coat had almost as many pockets as patches, and gold watch chains hung in graceful arcs from every one of them. A stray shaft of moonlight piercing through the forest canopy reflected off the chains, and also off the shiny scalp of Thomas's balding head.

"I didn't know you were here," she said as he crossed to join her.

"Wouldn't have missed a ceremony like that," he said, speaking as rapidly as usual. "I understand you're leaving first thing tomorrow?"

"That's the plan. Moonheart isn't the type to wait around once something has been decided on."

"Unicorns are like that." Thomas took one of his watches from a pocket, opened it, glanced at it, shook it, closed it, then placed it in a different pocket. He returned his attention to Cara. "I'd be glad to travel with you for at least part of the way, if you like."

Cara's delighted response was interrupted by a triumphant cry of "Hotcha gotcha!" as a furry ball of energy came flying out of a tree to land on her shoulder.

She jumped in surprise, then sighed as she realized it was only the Squijum. The creature raced down Cara's side and began to scamper in circles around her feet. "Want to come!" he chattered. "Want to come along!"

Cara knelt to bring herself close to him. Just over a foot high, he looked like some odd cross of squirrel and monkey. His thick fur grew in two shades of gray — light on his face, limbs, and stomach, storm-cloud dark on his head and back.

184

"It could be dangerous," she said earnestly.

The Squijum's enormous eyes grew even bigger, the bright blue pupils flashing. "No scared! No scared!" His bushy tail thrashed back and forth. "Good fight! Good run! Hotch hittem bad things! Bite bite bite! Want to come!"

"I doubt you could stop him if you tried," said Thomas, who was rummaging in one of his numerous pockets. After a moment he produced a hard biscuit, which he tossed to the Squijum.

The creature caught the tidbit with one three-fingered hand and scampered back up the tree, where he began munching on it. "No stop!" he confirmed between bites. "No stop Squijum!"

"Suit yourself," said Cara, secretly glad to have him along. Though she sometimes pretended that he annoyed her, she found his unreserved affection comforting.

The Squijum followed her to her resting place after she told Thomas good night. Buildings were not allowed in Summerhaven. Even so, she had a private spot to call her own — an open circle, about eight feet in diameter, surrounded by a wall of shrubs that grew so thickly it was impossible to see through them. In one spot the shrubs overlapped for about four feet; an opening about a yard wide between the overlap formed a kind of hallway through which Cara could enter. She wasn't sure, but she had a feeling that some human friend of the unicorns had caused the bushes to grow this way. Or maybe the unicorns themselves had done it, using their magic to create a comfortable resting place for their guests.

Within the circle she had a bed of moss and leaves, which she covered with a finely woven cloth Thomas had given her. Most nights the air was so sweet and warm that Cara was perfectly comfortable sleeping outside. It had rained only once since her arrival at Summerhaven; on that night she had slept in Thomas's wagon.

The Squijum entered the circle with her. Once inside, he went bounding around the green walls, now disappearing among the leaves, now bouncing out again to cry, "Hotcha gotcha!"

Cara settled herself on her bed, then stared into the star-spattered sky. She wondered — as she did several times a day — where her grandmother was, what she was doing.

Though the other questions — whether her grandmother was a captive of the Hunters, or whether she was even alive — were too awful to consider, they sometimes managed to creep in at the edges of her mind. Usually she was able to push them away.

Usually, but not always.

She stared at the stars above her, so many more than she ever saw in the light-choked sky of the cities where she had grown up. The *many* cities. She wondered now if all the moving she and her grandmother had done had been because they were fleeing the Hunters.

Or had it simply been because her grandmother was a Wanderer and could not stay in one place?

A falling star caught her attention. She began trying to pick out the patterns of the stars. Though different from the ones she knew at home, they were gradually becoming familiar to her.

She located the constellation Thomas had taught her to call "The Ravager." As she studied it, other questions came crowding in on her. The Queen had said it would take two or three days' travel to reach the Geomancer. But how long beyond that would it take to reach her grandmother? Would the journey really be as danger-ous as the Queen seemed to think? And, the biggest question of all: Would her grandmother even be there when she finally made it home?

*Of course she'll be there,* she told herself angrily, trying to ignore the fearful voice inside that kept insisting the Hunters would have come and taken her grandmother by now. *It wasn't Gramma they were after,* she reasoned, trying to make the fear subside. *It was the amulet. That was why my father followed me through the opening into Luster. Besides, he was alone. There was no one else there to bother Gramma.*

Though she kept repeating this idea, she could never entirely convince herself it was true.

Another frightening possibility occurred to her: What if Gramma Morris had already gone somewhere else to live, in order to throw the Hunters off the trail?

She tried to push the idea away, telling herself it was stupid. But her mind would not let go of it. She knew her grandmother would do whatever was necessary to shield the unicorns. The thought of making the long journey home, only to discover her grandmother was gone, had fled somewhere else, tormented her — partly because her heart was already tender on this matter, still unhealed from the loss of her parents. Which led her wandering thoughts back to the horrible question her father had planted in her mind, the question that had nagged at her ever since: Had her grandmother really stolen her from her parents in order to keep her away from Beloved?

And if she had, was that so bad? But why hadn't she said anything?

The questions blurred together. The Squijum, who had crept onto her bed and nestled in beside her, had fallen asleep. He was making a sound somewhere between a purr and a snore. The night air whispered around them, rich with scents of earth mold and moonflower.

She was still gazing at the Ravager when her eyes grew too heavy to keep open, and she fell asleep.

Her first dream was simple and sweet.

It was the second dream that made her wake up screaming.

CHAPTER THREE

# THE JOURNEY
# BEGINS

The dream had started simply enough. Cara was in the rented house she had shared with her grandmother for the last year or so, sitting in her own room. Feeling lonely, she went to look for her grandmother. But Ivy Morris wasn't there — not in the kitchen, nor the little living room, nor her own snug bedroom.

Finally, to ease her loneliness, Cara turned to their old black-and-white television, which her grandmother had insisted stay off most of the time.

To her surprise, it was already on.

And the picture was in color.

When Cara realized what was on the screen, she tried to turn away. To her horror, she couldn't; her eyes were locked on the image it presented.

This was how Cara saw for the first time the face of Beloved, the ancient enemy of the unicorns and her own many-times great-grandmother. Beloved, who as a child had watched her own father — a man who had been led by a lie to believe unicorns were evil — fight to the death with Whiteling, the unicorn who had come to cure her when she was horribly ill. Beloved, who still carried in her heart the tip of Whiteling's horn, which had broken off when her father attacked the unicorn and had forever after been both constantly wounding and constantly healing her. Beloved, who blamed Whiteling for her father's death (and her own never-ending pain) and, as a result, had vowed to destroy all unicorns.

The woman was shockingly beautiful, her face neither young nor old. Though her hair had turned pure white, it was still as thick and glossy as a unicorn's mane. Her eyes were gray, the deep gray of thunderclouds, save for their center, where they glowed a fiery red.

"You belong to me," the image whispered.

"I don't!" Cara cried. "I *don't!*"

"You're mine, Cara Diana Hunter, and always will be!" The scarlet pupils of Beloved's eyes were blazing now, so large and bright they almost obliterated the gray surrounding them. Her voice dropped to a whisper, low and seductive. "There is no point in fighting me, child. Blood calls to blood. And you *are* of my blood, my many-times great-granddaughter. So come to me. *Come to me!*"

"No!" cried Cara. She screamed — a real scream, so loud that she woke herself. She sat up, staring into the darkness, then gasped in new horror as she realized she hadn't been dreaming after all. Even though she was now awake, she could still sense Beloved in her mind.

"Get out!" cried Cara. "Get out!" Frantically, she shook her head from side to side, as if she could somehow fling Beloved away. "Get out, get out, *get out!*"

Beloved didn't go. "Accept your destiny, child of my children's children," she crooned in Cara's mind. "Accept who you are. No need to wander in vain. Come home — home to *me.*"

Trembling with horror, Cara beat at her head, trying to drive out the intruding presence.

"Come to me," whispered Beloved one last time, her voice desperate, longing.

And then, suddenly, she was gone.

Cara lay panting on the grass, scarcely aware of the Squijum crouched at her side, muttering nervously, "Hotcha Wowie bad dream! No good, much yell yowie yowie yowie."

Seconds later, Thomas and Moonheart came running into her clearing, both kneeling beside her to ask what had happened, if she was all right.

She flung her arms around Thomas's neck and clung to him, weeping.

Later, after she had grown calmer, Cara told them what she had experienced. At the first mention of Beloved's name, she could see a hint of fear in Moonheart's eyes, a flicker of distrust that added sorrow to her own fear.

The unicorn turned to Thomas. "What do you make of this, Tinker?"

"It could be just a dream."

"It wasn't!" said Cara indignantly.

The Tinker nodded. "I'll take your word on that. But if it wasn't a dream, then I'm troubled by the question of how Beloved was able to make a connection with you. Something like that can't come out of nowhere. There has to be some contact point, some key."

"Are you carrying anything Beloved might have a connection with?" asked Moonheart sharply.

"I don't think so," said Cara. "Unless . . . could it be the amulet?"

Moonheart snorted a dismissal. "If she could reach you through the amulet, she'd be on her way here already. No, there had to be some other way she made the contact."

"What?" asked Cara, more nervous than ever at this idea. "What could it be?"

"I don't have the slightest idea," said Moonheart, "which is part of what bothers me." Then he made her tell the whole story over again.

When she was done, Moonheart shook his head in dismay. "I can't find the connection." He turned to Thomas. "Will you stay here until morning?"

The Tinker nodded. "Of course."

"Send for me at once if there is any more trouble," said Moonheart. Then he turned and left the clearing.

Thomas stationed himself against the green wall of the hedge. The Squijum curled beside Cara. "We'll be right here if you need us," Thomas assured her.

Even so, after a time the two of them slept.

Cara, however, stayed awake until morning, sometimes closing her eyes but mostly staring up into the clear, star-spattered sky.

Moonheart seemed more cheerful when he returned at sunrise. "Come with me," he told Cara after she had eaten a breakfast of berries. "Finder and Belle will be waiting for us."

"I'll catch up with you later," said Thomas. "I have a bit of business to do before I go. Don't worry," he added reassuringly when he saw the look on Cara's face. "I'll rejoin you. I promise."

With the Squijum bouncing along beside them, they walked for a mile or so through the forest, crossing a stream, then climbing a rocky crest. On the other side of the crest stood Finder and Belle. They nodded and whickered as Cara and Moonheart strode up to them.

"Are you ready to go?" asked Moonheart.

"Certainly," said Belle, while Finder simply nodded.

Cara was always amazed at how quickly a journey could begin here in Luster. At home there would have been a great deal of packing and fussing before such a major expedition could get under way.

*Or would there?* she wondered as a dim memory of a swift and sudden move made at midnight nudged its way into her mind. With a stab of longing she remembered a little house she had once loved: a house with a climbing tree in the backyard and a good friend next door, a house abandoned in the middle of the night, never to be seen again.

She had cried about that for a time, and then forced it from her mind.

But though she had forgotten it, she now realized she had never really let anyplace feel like home again. Home was someplace you could lose, someplace she did lose every year or so. Letting herself feel at home meant nothing more than setting herself up for another round of grief when it came time to leave.

She had liked the places they had lived; some of them, at least. She had had happy moments in most of them.

But after the little house with the tree, none of them had ever been home again.

One thing that made it easy to set out quickly this time was that the unicorns carried nothing, and expected Cara to travel pretty much the same way. Since it was high summer and the land was laced by clear streams and rich with good things to eat, this was all right with her.

"What about Thomas?" she asked as they set out. "Should we wait for him?"

"He'll find us," said Moonheart. From the tone of his voice, Cara got the feeling that the very fact of Thomas accompanying them was an annoyance Moonheart didn't want to think about.

Cara had spent enough time with the Tinker to know that Moonheart was probably right about Thomas finding them. The man had a knack for showing up in unexpected places. So she set aside her misgivings and made no objection to their setting out.

It was a curiously quiet beginning to their journey.

*Well, what did you expect?* she thought, chiding herself. *Fanfares? A cheering crowd? These are unicorns; they do things differently. Besides, last night's ceremony was our formal farewell.*

They traveled in silence for a time — not only the silence that comes from not speaking, but the silence of unicorns on the move. The only sound at all was the rustle of leaves beneath Cara's feet as she walked, and an occasional squawk from the Squijum. But the little creature seemed to understand that the unicorns wanted to move without sound for the time being, and so made an effort to restrain his chatter.

As Cara moved into the rhythm of the day, she noticed again how differently time seemed to pass in the wild. In the cities where she had lived it was frantic, divided into little chunks. Here, it seemed to roll on more smoothly.

When the sun was straight overhead, they stopped in a shady glade to rest for a bit. Moonheart used his horn to freshen the water in a small pool, and Cara drank deeply, reveling in its clear, cool flavor. Finder pointed her toward a clump of berry bushes, a kind she had learned to call "sunberries." The bright yellow fruits were small, with a bittersweet taste she had grown quite fond of.

As she was gathering the berries, Finder came to stand at her side. "I've heard many stories about your grandmother," he said in his soft way. "I think she and I have a lot in common."

Cara looked at him in surprise.

"We both like to explore," said Finder, by way of explanation.

Cara had been wondering why someone who seemed so timid had been chosen for the expedition. "Do you explore a lot?" she asked.

"Oh, yes. Often I am the first unicorn to see a place. The unfinished" — Finder broke off, and a heavy silence hung between them for a second until he concluded — "the new places, places where no one has ever been before — they don't bother me the way they do some of us."

He stretched his neck forward and delicately nipped several sunberries from a thorny stem, his muzzle and beard startlingly white against the blue-green leaves. Then he nodded to her and turned to walk away. He whisked his tail as he went. It brushed her arm, feeling like silk at it slid across her skin.

When Cara rejoined the glory, Belle said quietly, "Someone is following us."

"Any idea who it is?" asked Moonheart.

"Not even *what,*" said Belle. "Though I doubt delvers could travel that quietly."

Cara looked for the Squijum, thinking perhaps he

199

could go back to check for them, but the little creature was nowhere to be seen. "Perhaps it's Thomas," she said hopefully.

"Possible," said Belle. "But not likely. He usually makes considerably more racket."

"Keep watch as we travel," ordered Moonheart.

Belle nodded but said nothing.

Their first night they stopped beside a small pond, where Finder showed Cara several things to eat, including a lumpy pod called *skug*, which grew on the roots of one of the water plants. Though the pod looked dreadful, once she had peeled it and washed it in the clear water of the pond, the blue interior proved to be crisp and sweet. She ate a half dozen or so of the pods and felt quite pleasantly full.

She grew nervous as darkness approached, reluctant to sleep for fear Beloved might try to contact her again. But finally the previous night's lack of rest, combined with the exhaustion of the day's journey, proved too much for her, and she nodded off.

The night passed with no repeat of her "dream" of Beloved, and Cara woke feeling both refreshed and enormously relieved.

♦    ♦    ♦

Two days' journeying brought the travelers to the edge of a river that the unicorns called "Diamond Drop." It ran deep and swift, and Cara wondered aloud how they would cross it.

"About an hour upstream we'll come to an easy ford," said Finder, who was standing next to her. And indeed, when they had followed the river for three or four miles, they came to a place where it grew broad and shallow.

Cara thought about undressing before she started across, then decided against it. Even though she couldn't think of any reason *not* to be naked in front of the unicorns, the idea made her uncomfortable. So she took off just her shoes, then waded in. *After all,* she told herself, *it won't take my clothes long to dry. And besides, they could use a good washing.*

The water was crystal clear and, for the most part, no more than a foot or two deep. Cara noticed red fish, as long as her arm, swimming placidly about her feet as she splashed her way across.

When she had nearly reached the far bank, she found a quiet pool, deeper than the water surrounding it. She took advantage of the spot to swim around and clean her clothes a bit.

◆　◆　◆

The day was warm, the sun bright, and it was not long before her clothing dried again. She felt better, and she certainly smelled better. But her long red hair was getting more and more tangled, and she began to think she might never get the knots out of it.

From the river they headed north. After a mile or so of thick forest, they came to a meadow where the waving grass stood nearly as high as Cara's shoulder.

"Would you like to ride?" asked Finder.

"That would be nice," said Cara gratefully. She tried to climb onto his back, but he was so big she had to twine her hands in his mane to pull herself up. He didn't flinch.

She was delighted to be astride a unicorn again. Yet, to her surprise, it made her a little sad, as well. She realized she was missing Lightfoot.

As they started across the meadow, the Squijum gave a squeal of delight and went bounding into the grass, where he disappeared from sight. Cara heard him now and then, shouting, "Hotcha wowie! Bad bug. Wanna eat you!"

Finally his voice faded away altogether.

The meadow was thick with flowers of all shapes and colors, including a purple blossom that grew on a thick stalk and attracted clouds of insects. Their humming filled the air — as did the scent of the blossoms, which was a little like cinnamon. Cara found herself growing drowsy and had to fight to keep herself from falling forward on Finder's back.

Thomas was on the far side of the meadow, leaning against his multicolored cart and whistling casually. The Squijum sat placidly on his shoulder, munching on a biscuit.

"How did you get here?" cried Cara in delight.

The Tinker shrugged. "There are many paths to most places."

"So you weren't the one following us?"

The Tinker looked surprised. "I came from a completely different direction."

"I told you he wasn't the one," said Belle quietly.

"Let's move on," said Moonheart. "We have a lot of ground to cover today."

Thomas picked up the handles of his wagon and fell into place beside the unicorns. The pots, pans, and

SONG OF THE WANDERER

tools hanging from the roof clattered noisily as he walked.

"Will you quiet that dratted thing down?" snapped Belle after they had gone about a quarter of a mile.

Thomas frowned, then shrugged and turned to the cart. "Shhh!" he hissed.

The pots rattled once, as if annoyed, then fell silent. After that the cart rolled along without a sound, no matter how rugged the terrain they were crossing.

As they traveled, Thomas hummed a melody that was oddly familiar to Cara. Yet she could not figure out where she had heard it before.

The sun was dipping low in the sky when they came to a rocky set of foothills. At the top of the first hill Cara spotted a house. It had a spiky look, caused by at least a dozen turrets and other things — structures she could not identify — sprouting from its roof.

It was startling to see a house here in Luster; in fact, it was the first building she had seen since she'd arrived. "Who lives there?" she asked.

"M'Gama," said a gravelly female voice. The words seemed to come from less than an arm's length away.

Cara turned, but could see no one. "Who said that?" she asked nervously.

"I did," snapped the voice. "And unless you have a good reason for being here, you had best leave now, before *she* turns you all into some very decorative rocks."

# CHAPTER FOUR

# THE GEOMANCER

Cara put a nervous hand on Finder's shoulder. "Show yourself!" snapped Moonheart. Belle moved into a fighting stance.

At the same time — and somewhat to Cara's surprise — Finder said with a chuckle, "No need for such dramatics. Listen, whoever you are. We come to the Geomancer on the Queen's business."

"Can you prove that?" asked the voice suspiciously.

Moonheart nudged Cara. "Show her the amulet."

Fumbling at the neck of her T-shirt, Cara drew forth the amulet that had carried her into Luster. Its crystal lid caught a ray of the setting sun. Coiled beneath the lid was a luminous strand of white hair.

"That's one of the Queen's Five!" said the voice in surprise.

"Now do you believe us?" asked Finder serenely.

"I suppose I must." As the voice spoke these words, Cara saw some of the rocks beside her begin to shift and change. Within moments she was staring down at a *very* small woman.

"Oh, that *is* clever," said Thomas appreciatively.

The newly revealed dwarf had a high brow and deep-set eyes. She wore a tunic of brown cloth. Her skin was also dusky brown. In one hand she clutched a short spear. Her head reached barely to Cara's waist.

"Follow me," said the dwarf, once she was totally visible. "I will take you to M'Gama." Without another word, she started up the hill, her stubby legs moving so fast that Cara and Thomas were hard put to keep up with her.

The three unicorns, of course, climbed the hill with no problem at all. The Squijum kept racing forward to weave in and out between the woman's feet, until she uttered a burst of angry words and jabbed at him with her spear. He squawked in alarm and scurried back to clamber onto Cara's shoulder. Cara hadn't been able to make out the dwarf's exact words, but she thought she had heard "snack" somewhere among them.

207

◆   ◆   ◆

Cara was panting when they reached the top of the hill. But though she had to stand with her hand pressed against her side, she was delighted with the house they had come to. From below she had assumed it was built of wood. Now she could see that it was made — all four stories of it — from earth and stone. In fact, from the way the sides merged into the rocky terrain behind it, from up close the dwelling seemed almost to have grown directly out of the hilltop.

Each level of the house was somewhat smaller than the one below, making it look like a stony wedding cake, though not nearly so regular. The main entrance was formed by two tall stones, about four feet apart, with a third placed flat across their tops. The door, also made of stone, stood open.

The dwarf led the way into the house, which was cool and dark inside. Stepping in, Cara felt as if she had entered the hill itself.

Most of the first room was taken up by a stone table on which were scattered bits of earth and rock of all sorts — everything from clots of mud to sparkling gems the size of acorns. A variety of branches stood in a tall, slender pot at one side of the table, some freshly cut, others long dry.

"M'Gama!" cried the dwarf. "We have visitors!"

"Bring them up," replied a voice from somewhere above them.

The dwarf sighed. "Follow me," she said. Then she darted through a door at the back of the room.

Cara wondered how the unicorns felt about being inside — about climbing stairs. But they crossed the room with no comment, their hooves tinkling like silver chimes on the stone floor.

As they passed through the next door Cara saw a room that looked like a kitchen to her left. She didn't have time to study it because the dwarf was urging them up the stairs. These were made of stone as well, the steps being very wide and broad. It took a moment for Cara to realize that they were carved directly into the side of the hill.

The first flight of stairs brought them back into the open, onto a kind of terrace. Remembering how each level of the house was smaller than the one below it, Cara realized they must be standing on the roof of the room they had first entered. The terrace was about ten feet wide, with a stone wall at its edge that reached just to her knees. The Squijum immediately leaped onto the wall and began racing back and forth along it.

Beyond the wall Cara could see the valley they had just traversed. The land rolled on, beautiful and wild, most of it covered with forest. She felt a pang of love for Luster's unspoiled beauty, and ached again at the thought of leaving it.

A gentle nudge from Finder brought her back to the moment, and she realized the unicorns had started up the next level of stairs. Though made of stone like the first level, these were on the outside of the house. They led to another terrace, from which the view was even better.

"Pretty!" said the Squijum happily.

They continued climbing.

"Stairs," Cara heard Belle mutter. "What a stupid idea!"

The final set of steps ended on top of the house. The roof was wide and flat. Open to the valley on one side, it merged directly into the hill on the other. From it sprouted several poles and narrow towers with a variety of whirling arrangements that made Cara think of tiny windmills.

In the center of the roof stood a remarkable-looking woman. Dressed in a flowing robe dyed in deep shades of red, purple, and green, she stood well over six feet tall. The way her hair was piled above her head added several inches to that already considerable height. Her smooth, gleaming skin was nearly jet-black. She had high cheekbones, full lips, and a broad nose. She was astonishingly beautiful — which was somewhat surprising to Cara, who had vaguely been expecting some wizened crone.

"Welcome to my home," said the woman. Her voice was rich and deep. "I am M'Gama, the Geomancer." She gestured toward the dwarf who had escorted them up the stairs. "And this is Flensa. She guards me well."

Cara noticed that while M'Gama's left hand was covered with rings — four or five to each finger — her right hand was bare.

"Guards you from what?" asked Belle.

"From intrusion. From disturbance. From things that would distract me from my study and my work." She closed her eyes for a moment and added, "And from delvers, of course."

"Yike!" yelped the Squijum, leaping onto Cara's leg

211

and climbing to her shoulder. "Delvers bad. Much not good hotcha phooey!"

"Precisely," said M'Gama, smiling ever so slightly.

"But why would the delvers want to bother you?" asked Cara.

"Because they are earth-creatures. I do not mean," she clarified quickly, "Earth as in the world from which you and I — and the unicorns, for that matter — originally came. I mean creatures of the soil and stone that make up the world. As my magic is earth-magic, there are many things I have that the delvers would like to possess. Tools. Spells. Knowledge. Things I would rather they not take from me. Now, what is it that brings you to my home?"

"We require a reading," said Moonheart.

"Oh, really?" M'Gama raised an elegant eyebrow. "And what would that be for?"

"The child is to return to Earth, to fetch her grandmother, Ivy Morris."

The Geomancer's eyes widened when she heard the name. "So, the Wanderer is going to return to us at last."

She didn't sound entirely pleased at the idea, which

surprised Cara. Everyone else she had met in Luster had been delighted at the thought of the Wanderer returning.

"It is the Queen's wish," said Moonheart sharply.

M'Gama bowed her head. "Then it is my bidding." Extending her right hand, the one bare of jewelry, she said to Cara, "Come, young one. Let us begin the work."

Cara, not entirely sure she wanted to go off with this woman, glanced at Moonheart. At his nod of approval, she stepped forward and took the Geomancer's hand. Together they walked to a door at the back of the roof, which led into the hill itself. Inside was another set of stairs, not so wide as the ones by which Cara had ascended. They started down.

At about the time the light began to fade behind them, the darkness ahead was lessened by a series of clear glass bowls that sat in niches in the wall. Each bowl was filled with a glowing liquid.

As they passed the first bowl, M'Gama dipped a forefinger into the liquid, then painted a line of it across her forehead, where it continued to glow. At the next bowl, she did the same to Cara. The liquid was cool and tingled a bit on her skin.

After another few minutes Cara said, a little nervously, "I don't remember this many steps going up."

M'Gama uttered a low, silky laugh. "Of course you don't. We've gone far below the first level of the house."

"Why?"

"My magic and my study are rooted in the earth. Therefore, I must go into the earth to practice them."

*Very deep into the earth,* thought Cara as they continued to wind their way down. She tried to count the steps but lost track after the first hundred.

They came at last to a room — a cave, really — crammed with globes, maps, star charts, astrolabes, bubbling retorts, candles with multicolored flames, and pots exuding strange smells. A fire pit carved into the center of the stone floor held a pile of glowing red embers. In the farthest corner stood an intricately carved stone cabinet. Behind its crystal doors Cara could see shelves stacked high with sticks, stones, and clods of moist earth. In front of each item was a card covered with tiny, precise writing. Though the writing was in a language she did not know, Cara had a sense that the cards were labels.

"Pieces of reality," said M'Gama when she noted the

questioning look in Cara's eyes. "These bits of earth are the touchstones of my craft, and the source of my knowledge." She crossed to the fire pit and, in a single, graceful motion, lowered herself so that she was sitting cross-legged on the floor. Patting the stone next to her, she said, "Come and sit beside me. I must learn many things from you before I can do the work that will tell us from where you should depart."

Cara did as the woman asked, imitating her posture. When she was settled, M'Gama extended her right hand and said, "Let me see the amulet."

Cara hesitated a moment, unwilling to let the amulet out of her grasp. But since the Queen had sent her to M'Gama, she decided it must be all right. Slowly, she drew the chain over her head and passed it to the Geomancer.

Rather than look at it, as Cara had expected, M'Gama closed her fingers over the amulet, clenching it so that the chain flowed down from either side of her fist. She closed her eyes and began swaying slowly from side to side. After a moment she crooned a soft, wordless song that reminded Cara of the tune Thomas had been humming earlier that day. Green light began to flow between her fingers — the same green that had shone when the amulet had opened the door to Luster.

Finally M'Gama opened her eyes. "These amulets contain great magic," she murmured, her voice husky. She uncurled her fingers, and the glow vanished. "They hold the power to pierce the walls between worlds, to open a hole from what *is* to what *might be.* Now, tell me where you need to go."

Cara described her home. As she spoke, M'Gama asked many questions. After a while she nodded, then went to one of the globes and began to study it. "You can return to the others now," she muttered, without even glancing up at Cara. "This will take some time."

"Is it all right if I stay?"

"Suit yourself. But please do not speak from this point on."

Sitting in silence, Cara marveled at the cat-like grace with which M'Gama moved around the cave. On a table near the back wall the Geomancer placed several items that she pulled from the cabinet: a smooth, red stone; two long, green feathers; a small bottle of water; and a dried twig. She then took a double handful of dried leaves from a niche in the wall and tossed them onto the embers in the fire pit. Cara gasped as a burst of flame rose from the pit, stretching nearly to the ceiling. But within three or four seconds the fire died down, to be replaced by thick, blue smoke.

As the smoke curled up from the fire pit, it coalesced into a perfect globe that began to turn slowly on its axis. M'Gama sat before the globe, hands on her knees, staring at it as if all the knowledge of the world were somehow concealed beneath its surface.

After a time she began to chant.

A sweet, musky odor filled the cave.

Points of light appeared on the surface of the smoky globe. They began to move, slowly at first, then faster and faster. Soon they looked like lines instead of points. More and more appeared, zipping madly over the globe until it seemed to be made of light instead of smoke.

M'Gama's voice rose higher and higher. "A la manna hayim!" she chanted swaying back and forth. "A la manna hayim!"

Her body began to tremble; suddenly she uttered a shrill cry, then collapsed onto the stone floor.

The globe vanished. The embers were quenched. Even the glowing lines on their foreheads went black, leaving Cara in a darkness so complete it was as if the world itself had disappeared.

# CHAPTER FIVE

# "I AM WANDERING, WANDERING . . ."

M'Gama?"

Cara whispered the name, half afraid that someone — or some*thing* — other than M'Gama might answer from the darkness.

When there was no answer at all, she tried again, more loudly. *"M'Gama?"*

Still no answer.

She started to stand, thought better of it, and began to crawl across the floor. The stone was smooth and cool beneath her hands. The air smelled the way it does after a lightning strike.

Hoping she was heading in the right direction, she searched ahead of her with her hands so she would not accidentally come down too hard on M'Gama's body. She continued to whisper the Geomancer's name, wishing M'Gama would respond — if only with a groan — so she would know she wasn't feeling through the dark for a dead woman.

Finally her fingers brushed flesh instead of stone. The moment of shock gave way to relief when she realized the flesh was warm and had flinched slightly at her touch. Scooting forward, Cara rose to her knees and drew the woman's head into her lap. "M'Gama," she whispered urgently. "M'Gama, are you all right?"

The Geomancer shuddered, then took a deep breath. She seemed startled to find Cara holding her, and began to struggle to rise. After a moment she dropped her head back and murmured, "I'll be fine. I just need some time. That was . . . harder than usual."

She fell silent again, though whether she was asleep, unconscious, or merely too tired to speak, Cara wasn't certain. Only the sound of M'Gama's breathing kept the girl from total panic. She felt as alone as she had ever felt, swallowed by the blackness around her.

She closed her eyes to see if it made any difference in the quality of the darkness.

It didn't; the world was equally black either way.

Deprived of sight, her other senses seemed to grow sharper. Somewhere in the distance she heard the slow drip of water. The musky smell of the herbs M'Gama had thrown on the fire lingered around her. She could feel the weave of M'Gama's garment, the threads bold and clear beneath her fingertips.

As time went on, Cara's mind began to wander, tracing back over all that had happened to her since she'd first fallen into Luster. Again she found herself missing Lightfoot and the Dimblethum. She thought with fondness of the Dimblethum's strange face, like that of some bear that had begun to turn into a man, then stopped halfway through the process. Despite his gruffness and his growls he was gentle in his strength.

She never had found out how he and Lightfoot had become friends. She wished Lightfoot was with her now. They had already shared so much danger together it felt strange to be setting out on this adventure without him.

Thinking of the dangers she had shared with Lightfoot inevitably led her to a more disturbing memory . . . that of her father.

She didn't want to miss him, didn't want to love him anymore. But she couldn't stop herself from wondering where he was, if he was all right. Firethroat had said only that she had taken him to a place that was safe, but empty. Was he even now wandering through some wilderness? Wandering like her, only without friends?

She forced the thoughts away. Her father was an enemy of the unicorns, and she could not afford to feel pity or love for him.

In the darkness her mind drifted to her grandmother. She tried to envision her face — something she did almost daily anyway, for fear that if she did not the image might fade from memory. Sometimes, at first, the memory was fuzzy. That always scared Cara. But she found that by focusing on the details, by first recalling the long braid, then the high forehead, the soft skin with its lines like crumpled paper, the gray eyes, the wide mouth, that the picture would sharpen until she saw her grandmother clearly and distinctly once more.

As she did that now, as she began tracing the lines of her grandmother's face in her mind's eye, she thought she heard the old woman singing — a high, thin sound that seemed made up of equal parts of courage and despair.

"Gramma?" she whispered.

The singing continued: "Oh, where's the thread that binds me, the voice that calls me back?" The voice was distant and quavering, but distinct.

"Gramma?" whispered Cara again. "Gramma, where are you?"

"Cara? Cara, is that you? Oh, come and get me, my child. Come and get me. I am wandering, wandering and so far from home."

"Gramma, where are you?"

Her own words, uttered in a desperate cry, came echoing back to her, eerie in the darkness.

But the echoes were all she heard. Her grandmother's voice was gone. Cara strained to hear it again, listening until she thought the black silence would drive her mad. Finally, trembling, she lapsed back into thought. Was she losing her mind? If not, where had the words come from? More importantly: What did they mean?

So absorbed was she in these questions that when someone touched her on the arm she started violently, nearly dropping M'Gama's head to the stone floor.

"*Shhhhh!*" hissed the intruder.

With relief, Cara realized it was Flensa. She could sense the woman next to her, so tiny that though Cara was kneeling and Flensa was standing, the dwarf's mouth was right next to her ear. "This has happened before," whispered Flensa. "Though not often. We must wait."

She sounded angry, as if she blamed Cara for M'Gama's condition. Cara tried to ask a question, but Flensa shushed her again. "Wait," she whispered. "Wait."

After what seemed like hours, M'Gama groaned and stirred again. "Flensa?"

"Here, My Lady."

"Help me to my feet."

"Best to wait a bit, My Lady."

"Then bring me something to drink," said M'Gama, sounding half annoyed, half amused.

Flensa moved away so silently that Cara only knew she was gone by the sudden absence of her body's heat. She wondered how the little woman could see in the dark.

The dwarf returned a few minutes later, something Cara could tell not by her footsteps but by the faintest sound of water sloshing.

"Drink, My Lady," whispered Flensa.

M'Gama moaned, but drank. "Better," she whispered. Reaching behind her, she closed her hand on Cara's arm. "Is that you, child?"

"Yes."

"Are you all right? I am truly sorry if I frightened you."

"I'm all right," said Cara, speaking the truth, though just barely. "But I have to tell you about what happened while you were asleep."

Quickly she spilled out the story of hearing her grandmother's voice, of her strange and desperate words.

"What does it mean?" Cara asked when she was finished. "What does it mean?"

M'Gama was silent for a time. When at last she spoke, her words were of little comfort. "There is a deep strangeness in this. I cannot make sense of it. Was the voice true? I cannot say — though it is certainly possible. A great deal of magic was loose in this cave a little while ago. On the other hand, when one is alone in the dark, the mind can conjure up all sorts of things that have the feel, the seeming, of reality, and yet are not real."

"But what should I do about it?" asked Cara urgently.

"Exactly what you are doing," said M'Gama. "Are you not doing as your grandmother has asked? Are you not in search of her even now?"

"Yes," said Cara. "But I felt as if . . . I don't know . . . as if there was something more my grandmother needed — wanted . . ." Her voice trailed off. "Only I don't know what."

"Then until you do, I think the best thing is to continue the journey you have begun. But keep yourself open, child — always ready to receive what may come. There may be more for you to learn, information that may arrive in unexpected ways."

"I'll try," said Cara, though the idea made her nervous, given the vision of Beloved that she had experienced the night before they'd begun their journey. "How soon can we go back to the others?"

M'Gama laughed. "Give me another few minutes. Flensa, bring some light, please."

The little woman left without a sound. A moment later she returned, carrying one of the bowls of liquid light that had lined the steps leading down to the cave.

The light was low and greenish, but steady, not like the flickering of candles. Shining up into Flensa's face, which was grotesque enough in the daylight, it made the dwarf seem truly eerie. The light was not strong enough to reach the corners of the cave, which remained in shadow.

"Help me to my feet," whispered M'Gama. With Cara's support she was standing by the time Flensa reached them. "All right," she said, taking a deep breath and drawing herself to her full height. "Let us return to the upper world."

Flensa led the way. Though M'Gama had to lean on Cara's shoulder when they started, she seemed to grow stronger by the moment. By the time they had climbed the first twenty or so steps, she released her grip and walked on her own.

Cara stayed close to her, just in case. After another twenty steps she asked softly, "What did you see, M'Gama?"

"When we're out of the caves and with the others I'll tell you. I only want to say it once."

Cara didn't like the sound of that.

◆　◆　◆

By the time they reached the top of the stone stairs, the backs of Cara's legs were aching and she was breathing hard. She saw that it was full dark out — a disappointment, since she had been looking forward to the daylight.

"Oh, well," she muttered as they stepped through the door. "Probably would have hurt my eyes anyway."

"Yowie!" cried the Squijum when he saw them. "Good come back hotcha miss much girl gone too long!" Then he scrambled onto Cara's shoulder and began to tug at her tangled hair.

"Stop it!" she said crossly, too tired and nervous to appreciate his greeting.

"Be nice!" ordered the Squijum, giving her a little smack with his paw. But he settled down, clinging to her shoulder for a full thirty seconds before he darted away again.

"Well?" asked Moonheart. "Were you successful?"

"The work was more difficult than I expected," said M'Gama slowly. "However, I found your answer. Not that you will like it."

"That's encouraging," said Thomas dryly.

227

"There is nothing here to be taken lightly," snapped M'Gama. "As I walked the lines of the world to look for your answer, I could feel someone trying to find me, trying to discover what I was doing."

"Do you know who it was?" asked Finder nervously.

"Yes. It was the one you call 'Beloved.'"

A coldness rippled across Cara's shoulders. "*Did* she find you?" she asked in horror.

M'Gama shook her head. "I have tricks of my own. But eluding her was . . . unpleasant. As was the answer to your question."

"What do you mean?" asked Finder.

"I have found the place where Cara must make the transfer back to Earth."

"And . . . ?" prompted Moonheart.

M'Gama glanced nervously at the skies. "Let us go below. Some things are best not spoken of in the open."

# CHAPTER SIX

# PATH TO THE SEVENTH DRAGON

Without another word, M'Gama led them down the broad stone stairs that started on the outside of her home and then, two levels down, shifted inside. The night air was cool, the sky thick with stars. Cara walked beside Finder, her hand on the big unicorn's warm, silky shoulder.

At the main floor they turned and headed into the hill. To Cara's surprise they entered a large chamber — half room, half cave — that could easily have held a dozen unicorns without feeling crowded. It was lit by the same glowing bowls that had lined the stairs Cara and M'Gama had descended to reach the deeper part of the dwelling. Their light filled the center of the chamber but did not reach all the way to the back.

A waterfall ran down the right wall, reminding Cara of how thirsty she was.

"Food and drink for all," said M'Gama, as if she had read the girl's mind. Flensa quickly began bringing bowls from the kitchen that Cara had noticed earlier. The bowls were made of stone. The ones she gave the unicorns were large — so big, the dwarf could barely get her arms around them — and filled with dried flowers.

After watching the dwarf carry in the first bowl, Cara went to help her.

"Where did all this come from?" she asked when they were alone in the kitchen.

"Here and there," said Flensa. "I prepared it while you and my lady were in the earth." She paused, and her face looked troubled. "I also went out to search for any sign of the ones that Belle says are following you. I had to cut short my search when I sensed my lady was in trouble."

Cara looked at the dwarf curiously. "How did you do that?"

Flensa shrugged. "M'Gama and I have a . . . connection."

Cara hoisted one of the bowls, and staggered under the weight. She glanced at the dwarf in surprise, wondering how the tiny woman could carry them so easily.

They arrayed the bowls along a table, which was also made of stone and built at a comfortable height for the unicorns to eat from while standing. Once these bowls were all in, Flensa gestured for Cara to stay in the main hall. She scurried back to the kitchen and returned a moment later with a cart bearing a large black kettle, from which she dished up three helpings of a simmering vegetable stew. The stew seemed to be made mostly of roots; Cara recognized one of the ingredients as *tarka,* something the Dimblethum had taught her to eat.

The Squijum, who had been climbing the stalagmites at the back of the room, came scurrying back. "Food, food! Hotcha wowie much good!" he said, looking for his own bowl. When he realized there wasn't one, Flensa laughed — the first time Cara had heard her make such a sound. Then she produced a final bowl from beneath the cart, a bowl filled with nuts, berries, and uncooked *tarka.*

"Yum!" cried the Squijum, diving at it so ferociously

Cara was afraid he would send the entire contents scattering across the table.

Flensa disappeared back into the kitchen.

"Isn't she going to eat?" asked Cara.

"She prefers to do so alone," replied M'Gama.

They dined in silence for a while. Cara, anxious to hear what M'Gama had learned, had a hard time settling down to eat. But the stew was surprisingly good, and (even more surprising) somehow soothing. *It tastes like home,* Cara decided at last.

Finally M'Gama pushed aside her bowl. "Now we must talk." Raising her voice, she cried, "Flensa! Bring the maps."

A moment later the dwarf scurried in, clutching an armful of scrolls, each almost as long as she was tall. She placed them in front of M'Gama, who sorted through them until she found the one she wanted. After clearing a space on the table, she unrolled the scroll, setting small stones at the corners to hold it in place.

"Look," she commanded.

The company gathered around her, some on the far side of the table, some right next to her. Cara studied the map for a moment, then asked, "Why are there so many blank spaces?"

"Unicorns are neither mapmakers nor land claimers," said Thomas.

"Those are human traits," added Moonheart, with a faint touch of disdain.

M'Gama snorted. "Human traits that are occasionally useful even to unicorns. But Luster is a young world, and has not been deeply explored."

Finder, who had come to stand behind Cara, was poking his big head over her shoulder. "I have been to some of those empty places," he said shyly.

She glanced at him in surprise.

"Why do you think Moonheart asked me to come?" he murmured.

Cara put her hand on his neck, comforted, as always, by his gentle strength.

"Look," said M'Gama, calling Cara's attention back to the map. The place names were written in an ornate script that she could not read, but M'Gama whispered them aloud as she traced the path they must follow with her fingertip.

"You'll start here, at my home," said the Geomancer

softly. "Travel west for five days, until you come to the River Silver, which flows down from the north."

"Grimwold's territory is somewhere around there, isn't it?" asked Moonheart.

"It is," replied M'Gama. "At least, the outer edges of it. If I can contact him, I'll let him know that you are heading in his direction."

The thought pleased Cara. Grimwold was the Keeper of the Unicorn Chronicles, and though he was a bit cantankerous, she had grown fond of him on her first visit to his caves — partly because he had known her grandmother from the time she was as young as Cara herself was now.

"Once you reach the Silver, you must move carefully, for you will be skirting delver territory. Follow the river north, until you come to a forest. You will pass through wooded areas along the way, of course, but you will know this forest when you see it, for it rises abruptly from a stretch of flat grassland and stretches like a wall for as far as you can see in either direction. This stage of the journey will take you several days."

"Can you be more precise?" asked Thomas.

"Not really. The river winds and twists and sometimes shifts in its course. If the water is high, you may find yourself making lengthy detours. Even so, it is the only good way through this territory. It will take at least ten days."

"It seems like such a long way," said Cara. "And not anywhere near where I entered Luster."

"That's because the world has shifted since you first came here," said M'Gama. "It will shift again, before too long. Autumn is approaching, and the days are growing shorter. On the day when the light and the dark are in balance, this spot will cease to be of use to you."

Cara felt a twist of fear. "How much time do we have?" she asked urgently.

M'Gama closed her eyes, as if consulting some internal calendar. "The shift will occur as the sun sets on the thirty-first day of your journey."

"Does that give us enough time to get there?"

"It depends on what happens along the way. It also depends on what happens once you cross over to Earth. If the Wanderer is waiting and you can turn around and come right back, that is one thing. But remember, the connection works both ways. Once the shift occurs, the place I am sending you will no longer take you to your old home. And if you have already gone through, using the amulet to return from Earth will not bring you back to that spot."

"Where will it bring me back to?" asked Cara nervously.

"I do not know. Therefore, I suggest you try your hardest to return before the shift occurs. Now, let me finish giving you the directions." Again she drew their attention to the map. "Once you reach the forest you must be extremely cautious. There is an enchantment on the woods that makes it hard to pass through them. If you go the wrong way, you may find yourself wandering in circles without ever finding the way out." She dropped her voice to a whisper. "Ever," she repeated darkly.

"Then how do we get through them?" asked Cara.

"There is a true path, which will guide you safely as long as you stick to it. The entrance is marked by a pair of black stones, each twice as tall as a unicorn, that stand about an armspan apart. You will find them a half day's journey to the east of where the river enters the forest. Take that path all the way through the forest."

"Wait a minute," said Thomas nervously. "Doesn't that path lead to . . ."

M'Gama finished the sentence for him. "It will take you to the Northern Waste that is home to the seventh dragon."

"Yike!" cried the Squijum. He jumped onto Finder's shoulder, causing the big unicorn to flinch.

"Who is the seventh dragon?" asked Cara.

"Ebillan!" whispered Thomas. The dismay in his voice frightened Cara, who had come to count on the Tinker as being sure and steady no matter how bad the situation.

M'Gama turned to Cara. "Seven dragons came from old Earth to Luster. Their names, in the order of their arrival, are Firethroat, Redrage, Fah-Leing, Master Bloodtongue, Graumag, Bronzeclaw, and Ebillan. Of these seven, Ebillan is the smallest but also the most unpredictable, which makes him one of the most dangerous. He is heartsore and angry, and bears little love for humans — dangerous traits in a dragon. Even so, it is to his home that you must travel."

"By 'home,' I hope you mean simply the territory that Ebillan controls," said Thomas.

M'Gama shook her head. "No, I mean his home. At the back of Ebillan's cave is a smaller cave. Its walls are made of crystal, and he allows none to enter it."

"Then how am I going to get in?" asked Cara.

"That is not a question I can answer. I can only tell you that if you stand in that cave to use the amulet, it should take you directly to your old home."

*"Should?"* echoed Cara nervously. She would have preferred a nice, definite *will.*

"That is what my geomancing told me. Can I make a guarantee? Of course not. Very little is certain in this life. Sometimes you simply have to do, and hope."

# CHAPTER SEVEN

# THE BATHING POOL

Cara felt safe in M'Gama's house. Even so, she slept fitfully that night. In her dreams she stood in her grandmother's bedroom and wept, though she could not tell who — or what — it was that she wept for.

She was roused from her troubled sleep by the morning sun peeking over the edge of the second-floor terrace. Her first movements brought a sputter of protest from the Squijum, who was curled at her side with his tail tucked over his eyes.

When Cara stumbled down the stone steps to the main floor, she found the Geomancer standing at the table in the entry room. The table was no longer covered by bits of earth and stone, but held instead an array of clothing.

"You should be better outfitted before you continue your journey," said M'Gama. "Unicorns tend not to think about these things. Also, you should let me help you with your hair."

Cara put her hand to her head. Her thick red hair, usually so neatly groomed at home, was not only tangled but becoming matted. "You're not going to cut it off, are you?" she asked nervously.

M'Gama laughed. "It might be a good idea. But for now we'll simply get it in shape for traveling. Flensa will help you first. I'll join you in a while."

As if summoned by the very mention of her name, the dwarf appeared at Cara's side. "Follow me," she growled. Turning, she led Cara back to the hall where they had dined the night before. She stopped to pick up one of the glowing bowls and motioned for Cara to do the same. This done, they headed toward the back of the chamber, the area that had remained in darkness the night before. Cara could see now that the cave tapered to a narrow opening that seemed to tunnel straight into the hill. The stalactites hanging from the ceiling and the stalagmites thrusting up from the floor looked like giant teeth, giving the tunnel itself the appearance of a long, dark throat waiting to swallow her.

"Where are we going?" Cara asked, fighting to keep the tremor out of her voice.

"You'll see," grunted Flensa.

Though Cara found picking her way among the rocky formations into the dark tunnel somewhat nerve-racking, the traveling was smooth once they entered it. The tunnel sloped downward for a good distance, bringing them at last to a cave lit by several more glowing bowls. The air was cool and moist, making Cara think of the cellar under the little house with the climbing tree back on Earth.

In the center of the cave was a stony pool. Steam drifted across its still surface, much as it does above a pond on a crisp autumn morning. The sound of slowly dripping water echoed around them, bouncing eerily off the cave walls.

"You can bathe here," said Flensa.

Cara waited for the dwarf to leave, but after a moment it became clear that she had no intention of going. Cara hesitated, then, telling herself not to be silly, undressed. Bracing herself for a shock of coldness, she stepped gingerly into the water. "It's warm!" she cried in delight.

Flensa waited until Cara's voice had finished bouncing off the walls before she replied, "What did you expect?"

Cara had never dreamed a hot bath could feel so good. She swam across the pool. It was about ten feet wide and so deep her feet could not touch bottom in the middle. She clung to the far side for a moment, then swam back to the ledge where she had first stepped into the pool. The echoes of her splashing were a little eerie, and yet at the same time somehow comforting.

"This is wonderful," she sighed, leaning against a place where the stone was polished to a smooth sheen. "I wish — what are you *doing?*"

"These herbs are good for your skin," said Flensa as she dumped a double handful of dried leaves into the pool. "Stir them around."

Cara did as she was instructed. At first, the addition to the water made her skin tingle in an unpleasant way. But after a minute or two, the sensation vanished and a spicy odor filled the warm, moist air.

After a while M'Gama came to join them. She helped Cara wash her hair, then massaged a dark blue concoction into it. The earthy smell of the stuff was intense, yet somehow soothing. M'Gama sang as she worked. When the song was finished, she said, "Now rinse it out."

Cara had to duck her head under the warm water of the pool several times before all the stuff was gone. Once it was, M'Gama patted the stone next to her and said, "Now come sit with me."

Cara took the towel Flensa handed her, wondering as she did where it had come from. It was coarse, obviously handwoven, but surprisingly soft. After drying herself, she wrapped the towel around her and went to sit beside M'Gama.

The Geomancer showed her a comb made from dark wood, its ornate handle carved like a dragon. "A friend made this for me," she said as she began to untangle Cara's hair.

It took nearly two hours, some strange-smelling lotions, and (Cara suspected) a bit of magic to get all the knots out. After the first ten minutes, Cara began to grow restless. "We have to hurry!" she said at last. "I have to get moving."

"Yes, you do," replied M'Gama serenely. "But the journey ahead of you calls for endurance as much as speed, and you will do better — last longer — if you set off rested and well prepared. Haste at the start often costs much more time at the end. Turn your head to the right, please."

Cara took a breath and tried to settle herself. Despite her eagerness to begin the journey, she managed to relax a bit, and to listen.

As M'Gama manipulated the comb, she spoke of her work as Geomancer and how she had come to learn the rhythms of the world and the shape of the stones. She told of the lines of power that run beneath the surface of all worlds, and the secrets that can be read in a pebble, a leaf, a twig, or a clod of soil. As Cara listened she felt the world opening up to her, expanding, as if she could see it in a new way. Sometimes rather than speaking aloud, M'Gama would whisper. Three times she sang — secret songs, which could only be uttered *inside* the world, in a cave, as they were now.

When she was done with the combing, she plaited Cara's hair into two thick braids. "This will help keep it from tangling again. Now come. The others are waiting."

Cara put on her clothes, which felt grubby against her clean skin, and followed Flensa and M'Gama out of the cave.

◆　◆　◆

"Oh, well done!" said Thomas, who was lounging near the front door. "Your hair looks very good that way."

"Thank you," said Cara, blushing a little. Then, quickly, she added, "M'Gama did it."

"Come, child," said M'Gama, who was standing at the table once more. "We are not finished yet. Let us see if any of these will fit you."

"Where did this all come from?" asked Cara as she examined the variety of clothing spread out on the table.

The Geomancer turned her palms upward. "People sometimes come to me for information. When they do, they offer me something in return, usually something they have made. I take whatever they offer. You never know when something will come in handy."

"How many humans are there in Luster, anyway?" asked Cara, picking up a pair of leather trousers. She held them to her waist, then sighed and put them back since they were at least a foot too long for her.

M'Gama paused. "Not very many. I suspect if you gathered us all together you might have enough to make a medium-sized town. Of course, I speak only of this continent. What is over the sea, I cannot say. Here, try this on."

By the time they were done, Cara was outfitted in a loose linen shirt covered by a dark green tunic woven from some fabric she did not recognize; a pair of close-fitting brown trousers that were far easier to move in than her jeans had been; and a pair of high boots made of supple, earth-colored leather. Better yet, M'Gama gave her a pack in which she was able to carry two additional sets of clothing.

"Best take this cloak, too," said the Geomancer, rolling another piece of fabric and tucking it into the pack. "You'll be traveling north, and summer is coming to its end. Evenings may be cool."

To finish the outfit, she strapped a short sword to Cara's side. "May you never have to use it," whispered the Geomancer. "But may it perform its job well if you do."

Cara drew the sword and stared at it, feeling a strange mixture of excitement and fear. Somehow having an adult give her a such a weapon made the dangers of the path ahead seem even more real.

"I wish I could have some lessons," she muttered.

"With luck, you won't need it for anything more

than slicing a path through the underbrush," said M'Gama. "Let us rejoin the others."

Feeling more prepared to face her task than she had at any point since her meeting with the Queen, Cara followed M'Gama to where the unicorns were waiting.

"What a transformation!" said Belle appreciatively. "You look much more suited for a fight."

"Much more suited to travel and explore," corrected Finder, earning himself a scowl from Belle.

Moonheart stepped forward. "On behalf of the Queen, I thank you for your help, M'Gama. I will report to her when we return."

"Assuming we do return," said Finder, in a voice solemn enough that Cara knew he wasn't joking.

Moonheart was clearly eager to be moving, a feeling that matched Cara's perfectly, so the good-byes were quick. Yet despite her eagerness to be on the road, when Cara turned to leave she suddenly realized how good it had been to be inside a house, even one as odd as M'Gama's, even if for only a day. Breaking from the group, she ran back to the Geomancer and threw her arms about her waist. "Thank you," she whispered. "For everything."

"You are welcome, child," whispered M'Gama,

stroking the top of her head. "For your sake, if not for the sake of the Wanderer, I wish you success on your journey." She hesitated for a moment, then slipped her hand into her pocket. "I want you to take this," she said, holding out a ring made of green stone that had been polished until it was smooth as glass.

"I can't —"

"Take it!" said M'Gama fiercely. "And may you travel in safety."

"Thank you," said Cara softly. She turned to Flensa, who was standing slightly behind M'Gama. Her ugly little face was set in a deep scowl, and she was clutching her spear as if ready to use it. "My thanks to you, too," Cara said softly.

Flensa nodded but said nothing. Cara rejoined the unicorns, and they started west, away from M'Gama's home, and toward the River Silver.

They had not been traveling for more than an hour when Belle suddenly broke away from the group and trotted back the way they had come.

"Where's she going?" asked Cara.

"Hard to say," replied Finder, who was walking beside her. "Belle is not one to talk. Mostly she just *does*. But she'll be back."

And indeed, in less than ten minutes she returned and said softly, "Someone is following us again."

Moonheart looked concerned. "Do you have any idea who it is?"

Belle shook her head, causing her mane to flow like foamy water over her graceful neck. "The signs are very subtle. Whoever it is knows how to be careful."

"We'll have to do the same," said Moonheart.

And with that they started moving again, faster than before.

"I don't like this," said Cara nervously.

"Fear not, fair lady," said Thomas. He took out one of his watches, wound it, then returned it to a different pocket. "We travel with the best the Queen has to offer." He took out another watch and began to fiddle with it, trying to look casual. Even so, he had sounded slightly nervous himself.

The path they followed was so faint that Cara could scarcely detect it. The unicorns claimed that the signs were clear. Even so, Cara noticed that Moonheart let Finder take the lead for most of this stage of the journey.

When they camped the first night, Cara searched

until she found a smooth stick, thick as her thumb and about a foot long. Then she carved a notch at one end.

"What's that?" asked Thomas, who had been watching her.

"My calendar," she replied. She ran her thumb over the notch. "We have thirty days left."

She tucked the stick into her pack.

Late in the afternoon of the third day Cara noticed a bell-like sound somewhere ahead of them. "Do you hear that?" she asked Thomas.

The Tinker set down the handles of his cart and furrowed his brow, seeming to concentrate fiercely. Suddenly a broad smile creased his face. "I do!"

"Well, what is it?"

"Either a very strange bird, or Armando."

"Wonderful," muttered Moonheart. "Armando. Exactly what we need!" With a snort of disgust, he trotted to the front of the group.

"Who's Armando?" asked Cara after Moonheart was gone.

Thomas raised one eyebrow. "Patience, my child. Anticipation is half the fun in a surprise!"

Cara made a little growl, but said nothing more. They were walking through a sun-dappled stretch of forest, still following the faint path Finder had said was the best route to the River Silver. The air was clean and sweet. The first hints of autumn were tinting the leaves with blue and silver. The occasional song of a bird — a real bird, not the strange sound she had heard earlier — drifted through the forest. When it did, Thomas would name the bird for her and tell her what Earth bird it was most like, or what made it unique to Luster.

Despite her urgent desire to reach her grandmother, she was enjoying the journey — partly because they were making good time, which eased her nervousness. But now she found that in addition to the nagging fear that was always present at the back of her mind, she was subject to a gnawing curiosity — a curiosity that continued to grow as they traveled since the sounds ahead were becoming louder and more interesting. Cara heard bursts of music, occasional laughter, shouts of delight, and — once — a cry of pain.

At last they topped a small rise and, looking down into the clearing before them, Cara saw the source of the mysterious sounds.

# CHAPTER EIGHT

# THE QUEEN'S PLAYERS

Standing in the center of the clearing was a short, chubby man dressed in outlandish clothing. "Welcome, friends!" he cried. "The Queen's Players salute you!"

Then he tumbled forward and stood on his head.

At the far side of the clearing were three gaily colored wagons, much like Thomas's. Clustered between the wagons and the man standing on his head were nearly two dozen oddly assorted people.

Cara, startled by the size of the group, thought, *That's more humans than I've seen since I entered Luster!*

The people were dressed in bright, fanciful clothing, ornamented with bows, ribbons, and plumes. Some of the men wore tight-fitting outfits, checkered with a pat-

252

tern of large black and yellow diamonds. Others wore flared pants and white silk shirts. One of the women was dressed to look like a cat.

One of the men in black tights came running toward the headstander, did two handsprings, then vaulted over the chubby man's skyward-pointing feet.

"Well done!" cried Thomas, applauding. "Oh, *well* done!" At the same time, the Squijum scurried over to the upside-down man, leaped onto his belly, and began digging into his pockets.

"Wait, wait, *wait!*" giggled the man, tumbling back to the ground, where he lay shaking with laughter.

"Hotcha gotcha!" cried the Squijum, pulling a morsel of something from the man's pocket. "Hotcha gotcha, Armando!"

"Stand up, old friend," said Thomas. "I have someone I want you to meet."

The little man scrambled to his feet, brushed himself off, and did his best to look dignified — not easy with the grin that kept twitching at the corners of his mouth and the merry look that sparkled in his eyes. His efforts were not aided by the Squijum, who was sitting on his neck and tickling his ear with one paw.

"All right, Thomas," said the man. "Introduce your companion. The arrival of another two-legs in Luster is always interesting news."

At a gesture from Thomas, Cara stepped forward. In a formal voice, the Tinker said, "Cara Diana Hunter, allow me to present you to Armando de la Quintano, head of the Queen's Players."

The little man looked momentarily startled when he heard her name. But he quickly got his face under control. "Delighted to meet you!" he cried, sweeping forward in a bow that tumbled the Squijum onto the ground before him. Ignoring the creature's indignant squawks, Armando asked, "And what brings you on this rather remote path?"

Moonheart came to stand beside Cara. "We travel on a mission from the Queen," he said.

"What a coincidence!" cried Armando. "So do we!"

"Ours is considerably more urgent," replied Moonheart sourly. "Which means we have little time for foolery."

"More's the pity, for we are little more than fools. Even so, if we are going in the same direction, perhaps we can travel together for a bit." Reaching above him,

254

Armando plucked a purple flower from the seemingly empty air. With a bow, he handed it to Cara.

Blushing slightly, she tucked it behind her ear.

"We are heading for the River Silver," said Moonheart.

"Good gracious!" cried Armando. "So are we!"

This news was so exciting that three of the people behind him stood on their heads, and five others turned somersaults.

"Pack up!" bellowed Armando. "Moonheart and his friends are in a hurry, and we cannot delay them."

Moonheart's handsome face twisted into a scowl. Finder moved close to him and spoke gently, words that Cara could not hear. Moonheart nodded and seemed to relax a little. Belle stood aloof from the Players. Finder, on the other hand, plunged in among them as soon as he left Moonheart's side. From the sounds of their greetings to the big gentle unicorn he was both well known and well loved.

Soon enough they were traveling again, though nowhere near as silently as usual. That was all right with Cara. She didn't mind the extra noise as long as the Players didn't slow them down.

She found herself walking between two of the black-clad men. After a few minutes they glanced at each other over her head, nodded, then shouted, "Hup!" Before she could say a word of protest, they had hoisted her onto their shoulders, where they carried her for the next fifteen minutes.

The Players sang as they traveled, sometimes the whole company belting out a marching song that made Cara's feet want to move at a faster pace, other times a single voice offering a song. Some of these solos were so sad that Cara's eyes brimmed with tears, making Luster go blurry around her. Others were so funny that she found herself laughing out loud.

The sound of her own laugh startled her at first. When she tried to figure out why, she realized it was because she had not laughed since that heartbreaking meeting with her father in Firethroat's cave. She felt a little guilty about the laugh — wondered if it was all right for her to do so when she still carried such sorrow. But the bumptious humor of the songs was proof against such reasoning, and forced her to laugh again and again, whether she wanted to or not.

By the time they stopped to make camp Cara had

had a chance to meet several members of the troupe. They were the oddest assortment she had ever come across: people who had come to Luster from all corners of Earth, and from a variety of times. Yet for all their differences, they had a number of things in common — including a deep love of what they did and an obvious joy in the world around them.

From one of them, a petite woman named Li Yun, Cara learned more of how the Players operated.

"The Queen herself has charged us to wander Luster, fooling, tumbling, and singing for both humans and unicorns," the woman told her. "We put on plays and shows of all sorts, everything from dramas, where we act out important stories from the Unicorn Chronicles, to evenings that consist of nothing but singing, juggling, and general foolery."

"What do *you* do?" asked Cara.

Li Yun smiled. "I am an acrobat," she said — then did a series of flips to prove it.

Later, Cara walked beside an older man name Jacques, who had sunken eyes and a deeply seamed face. Despite his melancholy look, he told her a nonstop stream of jokes that sometimes had her doubled over with laughter. He always seemed surprised when she laughed, and never displayed the least hint of a smile himself. The more solemn he remained, the funnier his jokes seemed.

The second night, the Players put on a show for Cara and the unicorns. Cara sat enthralled as they juggled flaming torches, hurled themselves about the clearing like living cannonballs, and clowned with such hilarious abandon that even Moonheart could be heard to laugh on occasion — usually nothing but a low nicker, though once he startled everyone with a loud bray of amusement.

One of the wagons had a side that folded down to make a theater for puppetry. They used this for a comic story about a bandit and a unicorn, and again later for a strange and unexpectedly moving piece about a rock and a river arguing over whether it was better to roam the world or stay in one place.

To close the show, the old man called Jacques stood alone in front of a fading campfire and sang a haunting song that pierced Cara's heart. She recognized the melody at once; she had recently heard bits of it from

M'Gama and Thomas. But it was the words of the chorus that made her shiver.

> *My heart seeks the hearth,*
> *My feet seek the road.*
> *A soul so divided*
> *Is a terrible load.*

She had heard them before — not here in Luster, but back on Earth, and always late at night. They had been sung by her grandmother when she'd thought Cara was sleeping. Now Cara was a Wanderer, too — wandering in search of her grandmother. *And what else?* she asked herself.

*Answers,* she decided. *I want answers.*

And deeper in her heart, in a place so sore she was not willing to look at it, a voice whispered, *I want to know who loves me.*

She felt a tear trickling down her cheek and lifted her hand to wipe it away.

To her astonishment, the ring M'Gama had given her was glowing. Forgetting her sorrow, she stared at it. But even as she watched, the glow faded, and the ring went dark again.

◆　◆　◆

Shortly after noon of the next day they reached the River Silver, a broad strip of water that did indeed look like a band of silver in the bright sunshine. Cara stared at it in wonder, realizing she had never seen a river this clear back on Earth.

Here the Players and the unicorns had to part company. Before they made their final farewells, Cara sought out Jacques and said, "Would you sing that song for me again — the one you sang last night."

He shook his head. "I don't think so. The 'Song of the Wanderer' is for —"

"Is that the name of the song?" interrupted Cara eagerly.

Jacques looked surprised. "Of course. Didn't I mention that when I sang it? No, maybe I didn't. Everyone in the troupe knows it so well, it didn't even occur to me to say what it was. Anyway, it's not a song I sing very often. Reminds me too much of the one I learned it from. I don't know why I sang it for you. Maybe because you're on a journey yourself it seemed appropriate somehow."

"Who taught it to you?" asked Cara.

The lines that etched Jacques' face seemed to grow

even deeper. "I learned it from the Wanderer herself. Her name was Ivy Morris."

Moving close, looking into his dark eyes, Cara whispered, "Ivy Morris is my grandmother."

Jacques stared at Cara in astonishment. Then, narrowing his eyes, he said softly, "Yes. Yes, I can see it! Wait here a moment. I'll be right back."

He hurried to Armando and whispered in his ear. The ringmaster's usually merry face darkened to a scowl. Jacques whispered again, his face urgent. Finally Armando's shoulders slumped, and he spread his hands in a gesture of defeat. Then he stepped forward and embraced Jacques tightly.

When Jacques finally disentangled himself from Armando, he went to Moonheart. At the old clown's first words, the unicorn shook his head from side to side. Jacques continued to speak, the urgency of his words showing in his face. Soon Finder joined them; after a minute or so, the big unicorn began to speak himself, addressing his words to Moonheart.

Finally Moonheart nodded his agreement. But he didn't look happy.

Jacques, on the other hand, was ecstatic. With an

unusual smile creasing his lined face, he hurried to Cara and said happily, "I'm coming with you!"

"Why? I mean . . . I'm sorry, I don't mean to —" She felt herself blush at the rudeness of her question.

Jacques lifted a hand to silence her. Then he knelt, took both her hands in his, and looked directly into her eyes. "I'm coming because I want to help you on your journey."

"But why?" asked Cara again.

His gaze grew more intense. "I have many reasons. But one among them should be enough."

"What is it?" she asked, starting to feel nervous.

Though the old man was still smiling, Cara could see tears welling up in his eyes. Squeezing her hands, he said softly, "I want to come along because I'm your grandfather."

# CHAPTER NINE

# FIGHT IN THE FOREST

Cara blinked and stepped backward, too startled to reply at first. When she did catch her breath, she said, "What are you talking about?"

Jacques rose to his feet, a hurt look in his eyes. "I thought you'd be pleased."

Cara didn't know what to say. A thousand questions were tumbling through her head, each clamoring to be answered. Was it possible this was true? If not, why would Jacques tell such a story? But if it was, why had her grandmother never mentioned this man? Cara realized, with shock and a little sadness, how little she really knew of her grandmother's past life.

Jacques was still looking at her. In her confusion, she blurted, "But I've never even heard of you!"

The sorrow in his eyes made her wish she could take back the words. After a moment, he said softly, "The wedding of the Wanderer to Jacques the Tumbler is recorded in the Chronicles." He paused again, then added, "Do you know about the Unicorn Chronicles?"

Cara nodded. "I've been to Grimwold's cavern. But I thought he only kept track of stories."

"Our wedding *was* a story," replied Jacques, somewhat ruefully. "A day of celebration and catastrophe. However, even if that were not true, it would have been recorded in Grimwold's cave, for he keeps lists of marriages, births, and deaths for all the humans in Luster."

"No wonder he's so busy!"

"Oh, there aren't that many of us. It's the adventures of the unicorns that really keep him busy. Anyway, you'll find our marriage listed there. Now, it is possible that after Ivy returned to Earth —" Jacques broke off, a pained expression twisting his features, and turned away from her for a moment. "I suppose it is possible you are not my blood granddaughter," he whispered. When he turned back to her his face was calmer. "That makes no difference to me. You are the grandchild of Ivy Morris. I was once the husband of Ivy Morris. As far as I am concerned, that makes you my grandchild."

Suddenly Cara realized that the unicorns had not told the Players the true nature of their quest. "Do you know what we're doing?" she asked softly. "Where we're going?"

Jacques shook his head.

"I am returning to Earth . . . in order to fetch my grandmother back to Luster."

A stricken look crossed Jacques' face. "Are you sure the Wanderer *wants* to return?"

"The last thing Gramma Morris said to me before I jumped into Luster was, 'Find the Old One. Tell her'" — Cara faltered for a moment, just as her grandmother had, then went on — "'Tell her, "The Wanderer is weary."'"

Jacques nodded. "Then she is ready to come back." In his voice Cara heard such an odd mixture of relief and sorrow, hope and pain, longing and anger, that she could make no sense of it.

"Why did Gramma go back to Earth to begin with?" she asked urgently. "I wouldn't have if I were her. I wouldn't now, if I didn't have to get her. I love it here."

"As did she," replied Jacques. "But what you love and what you feel you must do are sometimes different things. More than that, I cannot say. It is your grandmother's story. I will not tell it for her."

Cara rolled her eyes, but Jacques caught her hand and said urgently, "I know that is frustrating to hear. But this is a matter of honor and trust. It is not my story to tell."

Cara held herself stiff for a moment, then relaxed. "All right," she said. "I understand."

Which was almost true.

When the other Players learned Jacques was leaving them, there was a great deal of hugging and crying that had to be accomplished before they would let him depart.

Finder stood next to Cara while this was going on. "Look at Moonheart," the big unicorn whispered.

Cara glanced over at their leader. His nostrils were flared, his eyes hard, his mouth set in a grimace of annoyance.

"He doesn't like sentimental good-byes," said Finder.

When the farewells were finally over, the two groups headed their separate ways. As they walked north along the riverbank, Cara listened to the singing of the Players grow dim behind them; even after the last voices had faded, she could hear the slight *boom* of their drum.

Finally even that was gone.

She looked around her and smiled. What an odd group they made! Three unicorns, three humans, and a Squijum. Even in her wildest daydreams back on Earth she had never imagined that someday she would be trekking across another world, a world of unicorns, in such company. But maybe this was the life of a Wanderer — or at least the granddaughter of a Wanderer.

Her thoughts were interrupted by the Squijum, who came bouncing up from behind, scrambled onto her shoulder, and began chattering in her ear.

She walked beside Jacques off and on during the day, drawn to him, but distrustful as well. It was as if her heart was at war with itself: part of it wanting to accept him at once as her grandfather; another part holding back, fearful, thinking only that here was one more person who could abandon her, betray her.

For his part, he looked sad each time she stepped away from him — or, more precisely, sadder than usual, since his normal look was one of melancholy. That changed whenever she returned to his side. Then his eyes would brighten, and a smile would struggle, briefly, across his well-creased face.

They did not talk much, though late in the day she began to tell him some of the adventures that had befallen her since she'd crossed into Luster. He listened solemnly, and once put his arm around her shoulder and drew her to him, as if wishing he had some way to ease her memories.

Their path took them upward for most of the day. By the time they emerged from the woods into a high, rocky area, Cara's legs were aching. The afternoon sun was dropping lower in the sky to their left when the travelers began to follow a track that led along the edge of a drop so deep it made Cara uneasy to look at the river below.

Evening was falling fast as the path dipped into forest once again. It was much darker under the trees than it had been in the open, and the travelers had gone only a little way into the woods when they decided they should stop for the night.

Cara was glancing around for a good resting place when she heard something rustling in the darkness. She reached for Finder. A twig snapped somewhere off to her right.

"What was —"

Her words were cut off by a hideous screech as a band of delvers burst from the underbrush. They were only about three feet tall, but there were well over a dozen of them, all clutching short spears. In the dim light their enormous eyes seemed almost to glow in their oversized heads.

Immediately the three unicorns positioned themselves around the humans. At the same time, Cara put her hand to the blade M'Gama had given her. Her heart pounded with fear. She had been attacked by a delver only moments after she'd first arrived in Luster and she remembered too clearly the feeling of the little monster's wiry hands around her throat.

The delvers rushed forward. Cara's fear turned to stark terror when they began chanting, *"Get her! Get her! Get her!"*

The unicorns reared and kicked, their cloven hooves slashing through the air like silvery knives.

The first blow was struck by Moonheart, who caught one of the delvers on the shoulder. With a shriek, the murderous creature dropped his spear and staggered back.

The other delvers fell away for a second, then rushed forward again. Shrieking louder than ever, they jabbed viciously at the unicorns' bellies with their spears.

Belle spun and kicked backward, sending two of the screaming monsters into the brush.

Cara watched, trembling with terror, rage, and frustration. The Squijum, clinging to her neck, cried encouragement to the unicorns: "Gittem, gittem, gittem! Hittem, unicorns! Hittem *hard!*"

Beside her, Thomas was fumbling with one of his many watches, muttering angrily to himself about not being better prepared. Jacques had drawn a knife from his tunic. He kept trying to position himself to protect Cara, but that was almost impossible since the delvers were attacking from all sides.

Cara drew her sword. The hilt was cold in her hand. She held it before her, ready to slash, wishing desperately that she knew more about using it.

Suddenly the manikins set up a weird cry, a piercing ululation that was one of the most horrifying sounds she had ever heard. She dropped her blade and clapped her hands to her ears, trying to shut out the delvers' screeching, which seemed to slice into her like a living knife. She could see the unicorns shaking their heads violently, as if trying to drive the cries from their ears.

A half dozen of the delvers stopped chanting. While the rest continued their weird cries, these six tightened their grips on their spears and started forward. Belle trumpeted in rage. Dashing toward them, she struck one down with her hooves.

The others fell back. But the horrible chanting continued and Cara could see that it was making it hard for the unicorns to focus on the battle.

"Aha!" cried Thomas in sudden triumph. "*This* should do the trick." Fingers working frantically, he wound one of his many watches, then held it up and flipped open the lid.

As if sound itself had vanished from the world, a complete and utter silence fell over the battle. The delvers looked so baffled — their huge eyes goggling in shock as their mouths moved, but produced no sound — that Cara couldn't help but laugh.

To her astonishment, no sound came from her own mouth, either.

Thomas winked at her. The unicorns took advantage of the delvers' surprise to rush at them. The silence of the fighting that followed — the absolute lack of cries of anger or shrieks of pain, of trumpets, whinnies, or shouts, of even the sound of feet and hooves — was eerie. Cara couldn't even hear the Squijum, though he was still on her shoulder, shaking his paws at the enemy and clearly shouting all sorts of scathing insults.

For a time it looked as if the unicorns would win. Their flying feet and snapping mouths — more vicious in battle than Cara would have thought possible — kept the enemy at bay. But they were hampered by fighting in the woodland, where the obstructing trees gave an advantage to their small foes.

Then Finder stumbled — tripped over a delver, actually — and fell to the ground. This was all the delvers needed. In an instant they were swarming over the big unicorn like ants on a sweet. And in the silence created by Thomas's spell, neither Belle nor Moonheart could hear his desperate whinnies, nor Cara's cry of rage and horror.

Snatching up her blade from where she had dropped it when the delver chant had begun, Cara raced forward to help Finder. Before she could reach him, more delvers burst through the opening created by

Finder's fall and began leaping to attack Belle and Moonheart.

Cara lashed out with her blade. Despite her lack of training, her first swing struck home. The feel of the blade as it entered delver flesh, the spurt of green blood, made her stomach turn. But her rage at these creatures who attacked her and her friends overwhelmed the fear and disgust.

With a ferocious cry she pulled her blade free. Two other delvers took the place of the one she had struck down. She swung at them, clutching the blade as hard as she could.

At the same time, more delvers poured toward them.

Thomas clapped his watch closed, dropping it to dangle at his side. Sound flooded the scene of the battle, sudden as an unexpected thunderclap. But now the noise was all wild and chaotic. The delver chant was done, the little monsters too absorbed in the fight to continue their evil chorus.

Thomas pulled another watch from his pocket, swung it around his head, and lashed at the delvers with it. Wherever it struck, Cara could hear the hiss of burning flesh. Jacques shouted wildly from behind her.

273

Before she could turn, he came handspringing past her, into the midst of the delvers. He landed on his feet and began slashing about him with a short blade while the delvers stabbed at him with their spears.

All this Cara saw in a flash. Then her attention was all on her own fight, for the delvers were after her as well. She continued to slash out with the blade M'Gama had given her, wishing as she did that she knew something, *anything*, about how to use it properly. Even so, she was able to keep the monsters at bay, and severely wound more than one of them.

It was not enough. Soon a delver grabbed her from behind, pulling her arms back with a fierce yank. Her shoulders bursting with pain, she cried out and dropped her blade. That didn't stop her from also kicking out, and the delver in front of her fell with a surprised cry.

With a snarl, her captor tightened his grip on her arms. He swung her around.

Cara cried out in astonishment.

# CHAPTER TEN

# NEW ARRIVALS

Racing out of the forest, exploding into the battle, came Lightfoot. Not far behind the unicorn, slower but plowing ahead like a living tank, was the shaggy, bear-like form of the Dimblethum.

The unexpected attack from a new flank started the delvers shrieking and wailing. The Dimblethum, roaring with rage, flung the little creatures about like rag dolls. Lightfoot snatched one from Belle's back with his teeth and sent it crashing into a tree. Then he spun about and with a powerful kick from his hind legs sent another sprawling into a bush.

In the moment of surprise, Cara wrenched herself free from the delver who held her. Flinging herself to the ground, she snatched up her sword and rolled over just in time to stab upward at a delver who was about to grab her. She pierced his shoulder. He staggered back with a screech of pain.

She was on her feet at once, ready to slash about her. But the battle was over, ended as quickly as it had begun. Clearly overpowered, the delvers chose to retreat, vanishing into the darkness so quickly it was as if the ground itself had swallowed them.

For a moment, no one spoke. The first to move was Cara. Racing to Lightfoot, she flung her arms about his neck. Though Firethroat's gift of tongues made it possible for Cara to speak to anyone in Luster, with Lightfoot she preferred to speak mind to mind.

"I've missed you so much!" she thought. "Thank you for coming!"

Before he could reply, Belle spoke aloud. "I *told* you someone has been following us!"

Moonheart nodded. "So you did. Would you care to explain why that was, nephew?" His voice was stern, disapproving.

"You might thank him first!" said Cara sharply. "He did just save our lives."

Moonheart looked startled, then angry. But finally

he said, somewhat grudgingly, "The child has a point. Our thanks. Now, answer my question."

"I was following you because I was concerned about Cara."

"You want me to believe that *you* have a sense of responsibility?" asked Moonheart scornfully. "You, who have defied your family and refused your place at court?"

"Believe what you want," said Lightfoot, tossing his head so that his mane rippled like a wave.

"And what of *him?*" asked Belle, pointing her horn toward the Dimblethum. "What's he doing here?"

The hulking creature, who seemed to be equal parts bear and man, stood a few feet behind Lightfoot. He clenched his shaggy fists and wrinkled his short muzzle when Belle asked her question, but said nothing.

"We travel together," said Lightfoot simply.

Belle made a sound of disgust.

Now the Dimblethum did speak. "The Dimblethum, too, cares for the child," he growled. But the words were in his own guttural language, and Cara could see that Belle and Moonheart did not understand them.

"Might I suggest we save our arguments for later?" said Finder gently. "It might be wiser to tend our wounds first. Once that's done, we can tear each other up again if we wish."

Lightfoot actually laughed, and the Dimblethum gave a rumbling chuckle. Moonheart scowled, but said softly, "You are correct, Finder. Let's take stock."

It was bad, but not as bad as they might have feared. Thomas and Jacques each had three or four stab wounds, the Dimblethum one deep cut on his side. The wounds were mostly low because the delvers were so short.

"Probably have to amputate," said Jacques, looking at his legs gloomily. "Both of them," he added, though the wound on his left leg was little more than a scratch.

Actually, of the humans it was Thomas who was most severely wounded, his right shoulder cut so deeply that his arm hung useless at his side.

Cara, consumed with worry about her friends, was surprised to find she had a serious wound of her own — a ragged bite mark on her left hand. She had been so involved in the fight she hadn't even noticed it when it had happened.

278

The Squijum had escaped injury altogether.

The unicorns had taken the worst of it. Cara found it heartbreaking to see the way their crimson and silver blood stained their silken hides. It was mixed with delver gore, which was a muddy green color and smelled of the earth. Finder was badly hurt, though he insisted his wounds were nothing and that he would help with the healing. To Cara's surprise, Moonheart had fared even worse. His flanks were scored with a dozen deep cuts, and bite marks peppered his neck.

"The delvers knew him for the leader, and so attacked him the most viciously," explained Thomas in a whisper as Cara bound his shoulder with a strip of cloth she had cut from her own shirt.

The four of them — Cara, Thomas, Jacques, and the Dimblethum — were sitting under a tree, watching the unicorns examine one another. Though clearly pained by the wounds on his legs, Jacques had been far more concerned about Cara's well-being than his own. Now, finally convinced that she was all right, he was massaging his thigh while he waited for one of the unicorns to heal him. His forehead was beaded with sweat, and Cara could tell he was trying not to cry out.

As she watched the unicorns, she realized that while

she still did not feel comfortable with Moonheart, there was little doubt she owed him her life. Though when it came right down to it, she probably owed her life to each of them. In fact, remembering the cry the delvers had set up when they first attacked, she was certain that must be so.

"Thomas," she said softly. "Did you hear what the delvers were shouting when they attacked?"

"Delvers," growled the Dimblethum in disgust. "Dimblethum crush delvers."

Thomas smiled, then winced as if even that small act was painful. Leaning his head back against the tree, he said softly, "They were crying, 'Get her!'"

Cara's stomach tightened. "Were they talking about me?"

The answer came from Jacques, who said gloomily, "It's possible they were after Belle. She's known to be one of the Queen's fiercest warriors, and the delvers probably have little love for her. But . . . I'd say it's more likely it was indeed you they wanted."

Cara shuddered. "Why?"

"I can see two possibilities, neither good. The first is that they know you are carrying one of the Queen's amulets and they want it. The second, which I like even less, is that they have found out who you really are and have some reason to want *you*. Perhaps they are even in contact with Beloved, though I'm not certain how that could be."

"Jacques is right," said Finder, who had limped over to join their conversation. "We're going to have to be more careful than ever how we travel."

Belle's sharp ears overheard them. "They never should have gotten the jump on us to begin with," she said from where she stood. "I should have been paying closer attention. But my thoughts were distracted by trying to figure out who was following us, not who might be waiting ahead."

"No point in blaming Lightfoot for what's happened," said Finder gently.

"Oh, go ahead," said Lightfoot, glancing at Belle. "You might as well blame me. I'm used to it."

Belle snorted in disgust. Ignoring her glare, Lightfoot turned to Thomas. "Moonheart asked me to tend your wounds. I'll take care of that bite on your hand, too, Cara. But Thomas first, because he's lost the most blood. Finder will take care of the Dimblethum. And Belle will see to Jacques."

Cara knew that in doing all this healing, the unicorns were at the same time weakening themselves and would need to rest for a while to recover.

"Are you going to fix each other, too?" she asked Lightfoot when he came to tend her hand.

"We'll take care of the worst of the damage," he told her as he knelt beside her and pressed his horn to the place where the delver had bitten her.

She started to answer, but her words were choked by the flash of pain that accompanied the healing. She caught her breath, then bit her lip to keep from crying out. In a moment it was over. She looked at her hand. Though the open wound had closed smoothly, the flesh was still red and angry looking.

"An incomplete cure," murmured Lightfoot. "Delver bites are nasty, and I am at less than full strength. Thomas's wounds were even worse than they looked, and took a lot of energy to fix."

Cara noticed that his legs were trembling. A moment later he sank to the ground beside her.

She had learned the first time Lightfoot had healed one of her wounds — a wound also caused by a delver attack — that the process was extremely draining for the unicorns. She guessed that was why they were going to heal only the worst of each other's wounds. It was probably a kind of balancing act, determining which would slow them down the least: the wounds themselves, or the period of rest required after a major healing.

Putting her hand on Lightfoot's neck, she thought, "I am so glad you've come back. I missed you."

"And I missed you," he replied, his thoughts muzzy with exhaustion.

An instant later he was asleep.

They stayed at the site of the battle for the next two days, keeping watch for the return of the delvers and letting the unicorns regain their strength. Cara fretted at the delay. Rubbing her thumb across the notches on her calendar stick, she counted the days over and over, as if by counting them enough she could somehow change the math of the sky and add to the time they had left before the first day of autumn.

She did take advantage of the delay to spend some time with the Dimblethum, whom she felt she had slighted the day before by rushing straight to Lightfoot.

"I am so glad you are with us," she said to him. "I missed you very much."

"And I missed you, little Wanderer," he replied in his deep, rumbling voice.

The name startled her, and she didn't say much after that. The Dimblethum wasn't one for talking anyway. But it felt good, and safe, to sit beside him. Later, he disappeared for several hours. When she asked Lightfoot about it, he said, "I think he's off looking for delvers to crunch."

Toward the end of the second afternoon, Jacques invited her to take a walk with him. It felt good to be up and moving, even if they weren't really going anywhere. They found a stream about a hundred yards from their resting place. Following it, they came to a large pool.

"Don't go too far," warned Jacques when she waded in to wash. "You'll drown yourself for certain."

She laughed and rolled her eyes, which caused his face to grow even gloomier than usual.

Later they led the unicorns to the pool, and Cara helped them clean away the blood and gore that had covered them after the battle.

"Do you know one of the biggest differences between unicorns and humans?" asked Finder, standing knee-deep in the cold water.

"What?" asked Cara, trying to keep her stomach from turning as she used a handful of *tarka* leaves to scour the filth from his coat.

"Hands," said the big unicorn. "I can never be sure if I'm glad we don't have them, or not. They're plenty useful — certainly it would be easier for us to clean up now if we had them. On the other hoof, they lead you into all sorts of mischief."

Cara held her hands in front of her, spread her fingers, wiggled them. Though she sometimes wished she had been born a unicorn instead of a human, she wasn't sure she would be willing to give up her hands for the privilege.

She returned to her task. "There," she said at last. "Perfectly clean!"

Finder climbed out of the pond and shook his head. His mane spattered water in all directions, like a spray of diamonds.

That night Cara carved the seventh notch in her calendar. "Twenty-four days left," she murmured.

The next morning they began to travel again. Moonheart was still limping a little, but his wounds were healing faster than Cara would have expected.

*I wonder if their healing powers work naturally on their own wounds?* she thought as she watched him walk. She studied the scar on Finder's shoulder and, by the end of the day, was surprised to see that it had grown significantly lighter.

The Dimblethum dropped behind several times. Lightfoot told her it was because he was covering their trail and devising various methods to confuse the delvers.

Continuing upstream along the river, they emerged at midday from the woods to an open plain. Though the land was flat and open here, it was often marshy, and trying to find a solid path sometimes slowed their progress so much that Cara would grow nearly frantic with worry.

On the far side of the plain rose some low, rolling hills, which they reached toward dusk of the second day. By this time the unicorns seemed to have completely recovered from their wounds. It was just as well, for their path led directly into the hills, where it was not always easy to follow the river. It had sliced deep into the land, and the banks were often steep and high.

To make things more difficult, it began to rain — a

slow, steady drizzle that persisted all through the night and the next day as well.

On the morning of the fourth day after they had resumed their journey, the soggy, grumpy travelers were walking along a rocky wall when they were startled by a rumbling sound.

Looking to her right, Cara gasped. One of the boulders was rising into the air, revealing a dark hole.

From the darkness came a voice, both cranky and familiar.

"Well," it snapped. "It's about time you got here!"

# CHAPTER ELEVEN

# UNDERGROUND JOURNEY

A small man stepped out of the darkness. His skin was a beautiful deep brown. His eyes, so large they looked almost comic in his serious face, were topped by bushy sprouts of silvery hair. He wore a coarsely woven robe in which shades of red, brown, and orange mixed to make it look rather like a distant view of a forest floor in autumn.

"Grimwold!" cried Cara in delight. "What are you doing here?"

"Well, you were coming to see me, weren't you?" asked the little man, sounding impatient.

"I wasn't sure. I hoped we might, but —"

He cut her off with a wave of his hand. "The Queen sent a message."

"You mean other unicorns have gotten here ahead of us?" asked Cara in surprise.

"Did I say that?" asked Grimwold, rolling his eyes.

"Then how —" She broke off as she remembered the scrying pool with which they had once tried to contact the Queen.

"Arabella has many ways to communicate with me," said Grimwold. "Anyway, she'd heard from M'Gama that you were coming this way and asked me to meet you." He narrowed his eyes. "She didn't mention that there would be so many of you."

"We had unexpected company," said Moonheart sourly.

Grimwold sighed heavily, as if accepting some tragic turn of fate. "Well, I suppose you'll *all* be wanting to come in. Nothing to do about it, I guess. It's not like anyone would really care if it was an imposition, or if I already had more work than I could handle, or anything like that. Come on, come on! We can't stand here all night!"

With that, he disappeared back into the darkness. Thomas began folding up his cart, something Cara always enjoyed watching. It was astonishing to see the huge thing disappear into itself — though she could never figure out exactly how it happened. The Tinker had reduced the cart to something he could easily tuck under one arm when Moonheart motioned for Cara to lead the way.

As she stepped into the dark opening, the Squijum leaped onto her shoulder to ride with her. "Wowza, wowza!" he chattered. "Cranky, cranky old guy!"

"Shhh!" she cautioned. Not because his words weren't true. She just didn't want him to make the situation worse.

As soon as they entered the hillside, she saw a glimmer of light to her right. The passageway turned, then turned again. Rounding the second corner, Cara found herself in a small chamber lined with dark, reddish wood. From the wall hung a lantern, casting a cheery glow. Beneath it stood Grimwold, his hands resting on what looked like the captain's wheel of an old-fashioned ship. On the floor beside him was a backpack.

"You'd better go on a bit," he said gruffly. "Won't be room in here for everyone."

Cara nodded and did as he asked, moving along the stony corridor that stretched to his left. She could hear the others enter behind her, the unicorns muttering in annoyance because the turns were so tight it was hard for them to maneuver.

Finally she heard Lightfoot say, "That's it. I'm the last."

Grimwold grunted. "Are you sure? I was beginning to think the Queen had sent an entire army." He paused, then said, more softly, and clearly surprised, "By Bellenmore's Belt, it's Lightfoot. What are *you* doing here?" He chuckled. "I notice you waited till last to come in. Staying as far from your uncle as you can?"

"I thought you didn't like idle chatter," said Lightfoot sharply.

"Information gathering is never idle."

"Why not just close the door before someone else tries to get in?" snapped Lightfoot.

"What do you think I'm doing?" said Grimwold, sounding equally testy.

Cara heard a *creak*. Looking back past the others, she was able — just barely — to see Grimwold turning the wooden wheel. Next came a rumbling noise, and then a heavy *thud* as the boulder that masked the entry into the hill fell back in place.

A moment later Grimwold joined her at the front of

the procession. He was carrying the lantern that had hung in the small chamber.

"I knew we would be passing near the edge of your territory," said Cara. "But I didn't realize we were so close to it already."

"You're not."

"I don't understand. If we're not near your home, then why are we —"

"This tunnel leads to my home. But it would take us at least a day's journey to get there. Anyway, that's not where we're going."

"I still don't understand," said Cara, beginning to feel frustrated.

"You want to get to the Northern Forest, right?"

"Yes."

"Well, it will take you forever the way you were going. I have a better route."

"All underground?" asked Cara nervously.

"I like being underground. Besides, we'll travel more quickly this way. Making the same trip overland, with all those hills and valleys and forests and other nonsense — not to mention the way that foolish river twists and turns — would take at least twice as long."

Cara felt a surge of relief. Anything that would get them to Ebillan's cave faster was welcome to her.

"You'll probably be safer this way, too," added Grimwold, somewhat as an afterthought.

"That would be nice," said Jacques, who was walking behind them. "I'd just as soon avoid danger as much as possible."

"Sensible," said Grimwold. "Hardly what I would have expected from one of you Players."

Moonheart snorted in amusement.

It was a wondrous journey. They traveled along corridors lined with wood, and others made of stone. Some of the stone passages appeared to have been made by hand; others were obviously natural, sometimes widening so that the entire company could walk side by side. At other times a passage would narrow so sharply that even going single file they could barely squeeze through it. Once they had to stop because the Dimblethum got stuck and howled pitifully until they could free him — which was only possible because Jacques was still behind him, and so could push, while Thomas pulled him from in front.

Moonheart and Belle stood watching this, both looking exasperated.

Shortly after they had freed the Dimblethum, the passage opened into an enormous cave, so big that the light from Grimwold's lantern couldn't penetrate its depths. Ahead of them was a reddish glow. Cara heard a low rumbling sound. As they drew closer to the glow, she could see that it came from a wide gap in the cavern floor.

"How are we going to get over that?" she asked nervously.

Without saying a word, Grimwold pointed to the right, where a narrow stretch of rock spanned the chasm.

"I thought you said this was safer than traveling aboveground," grumbled Jacques.

"I said safer, not risk-free. Besides, if you don't fall off, it's no problem at all."

"I'd rather take my chances in a good, clean fight," muttered Belle.

The rumble grew louder as they walked. From the red glow ahead of them, Cara expected to find the chasm filled with bubbling lava. She was astonished when they reached it to see that the noise was actually made by an enormous cataract — a thundering torrent of water that gushed from a sheer wall about a quarter of a mile to the right, then tumbled fifty or sixty feet to form a river that raged and rolled beneath them and on to their left for as far as she could see.

What made it even more remarkable was that the water exploding from the wall glowed a brilliant red. The spray and mist it threw up were crimson as well, and the river that roared beneath them might as well have been made of blood.

Cara stared at the water in awe. "What makes it glow?" she asked, shouting to be heard above the roar of the water.

Grimwold shrugged. "Could be minerals it picks up as it travels underground. Could be some kind of tiny plant or animal."

"Could be magic," added Thomas.

"Possible," agreed Grimwold, "though if it is, I don't see the point of it."

"Do all wonders need to have a purpose?" responded Thomas.

Grimwold snorted in response, then said, "Follow me." He stepped onto the stone bridge, which was about three feet wide, with an irregular surface. Fortunately it was far enough from the falls that the spray didn't reach it, so the surface was not made slick by water. Unfortunately, the drop to the river below was well over a hundred feet.

"Well, at least it will be a quick death if I fall," said Jacques as he stepped onto the bridge.

Cara followed him, and after a few steps made the mistake of looking down at the glowing torrent. She felt herself sway and had to close her eyes for a moment. After that she forced herself to focus on her feet and not the abyss below.

The Squijum, however, scampered around fear-lessly — shooting ahead, zipping back and forth across the bridge, even climbing over the edge and clinging to the side. Cara tried to ignore him until he got under-neath her feet and nearly tripped her. "Squijum!" she snapped. "Get up here on my shoulder before you kill me. And don't move until we get to the other side!"

"Hotcha stinky cranky girl," he muttered sullenly. But he did as she told him.

They stopped at the top of the bridge's arc to admire the waterfall. Turning to her left, Cara could now see that the river flowed in a straight line for another mile or two, then disappeared out of sight — though whether it plunged over another falls, or the cavern ended and the river simply began flowing through a tunnel again, she could not tell.

Once across the bridge it took another hour to reach the far side of the cavern. Cara had no idea how Grimwold kept on track, for there was no path that she could see, and the space was so large that even the echoes of their footsteps seemed distant. But that he did keep on track there was no doubt, for when they finally came to the far side, they were directly in front of a small tunnel, no more than five feet high and three feet wide. It was tiny compared to the vastness of the cavern wall, and if you missed it you could have spent hours, maybe days, trying to find it — and that was assuming it was the only one and you didn't go wandering off in the wrong tunnel altogether.

"How did you bring us directly to this spot?" asked Cara.

"Practice," grunted Grimwold as he entered the tunnel.

Another hour or so of traveling brought the group to a comfortably sized cave that was dimly lit by glowing, pale blue fungus that grew on rocks surrounding a pool of water.

"We'll stop here for the night," said Grimwold.

"How do you know it's night?" asked Jacques.

The old dwarf snorted. "I listen to my body. Do you have to have the light to tell you everything?"

Jacques shrugged. "If I listened to *my* body, it would be time to rest all day long."

Thomas pulled out one of his watches, opened the top, shook it once, then said, "It's night all right."

Grimwold snorted. Setting down his pack, he opened it and removed a large knife. He began slicing chunks of the blue fungus away from the rock — chunks that he distributed to the others.

"You want me to eat this?" asked Cara in dismay.

"You can wear it if you'd rather. I suspect, however, it will do you more good inside than out."

She took a tiny bite. This was Luster, after all. Maybe it would turn out to be unexpectedly delicious.

It didn't.

"Yuk! Ptooie!" sputtered the Squijum, who had tried a bit at the same time. "Nasty, nasty, nasty!"

*My sentiments exactly!* thought Cara as the Squijum spat the fungus onto the rock where he was crouching.

To her surprise, the others seemed to think it tasted just fine. She wondered if it was one of those weird foods that only grown-ups seem to like. Sheer hunger forced her to take two more bites. Then she gave up.

Now that they had stopped moving, she could feel the coolness of the caves. She took the cloak M'Gama had given her from her pack and wrapped it around her shoulders. She also took out her calendar stick and carved another notch.

Eleven days gone. Would they make it on time, or not?

Despite her worries over the time, despite her hunger and the hard stone floor, exhaustion worked its magic, and she was soon fast asleep.

They spent most of the next day traveling in single file through narrow tunnels, which made it difficult to speak to the person ahead of you — especially if the person ahead of you was a unicorn. And the few times they came out into the caverns, the vast spaces seemed somehow inappropriate for talking, as if the huge underground rooms had a sacred quality.

When they did enter the more open areas, Cara made it a point to take turns walking beside each of her companions. She spent the most time beside Lightfoot and the Dimblethum, of course. But she wanted all of them to know they were important to her, that she cared for them.

It hurt her heart that Moonheart and Belle were so obvious about avoiding the two newest members of their band, always positioning themselves as far from Lightfoot and the Dimblethum as they could and refusing to speak to them unless necessary.

She wished they could all be more friendly with each other.

Dinner was better that night, for they came to a cave with an underground stream and the Dimblethum was able to catch some fish for them. Pale and blind, with enormous, sightless eyes, they were ugly to look at but extremely tasty.

*At least, tasty for raw fish,* thought Cara, finding herself actually thankful that her grandmother had insisted she try all kinds of food over the years, up to and including sushi.

When they had finished eating, Grimwold called them together and said, "Tomorrow I will be sending you back to the world above. So tonight I want to share a story with you."

Cara was surprised to hear a whicker of satisfaction from Belle, who then added, "It would have been quite a thing to travel three days with the Keeper of the Chronicles and not be given a story."

"I give you this one at the request of the Queen."

"What story is it?" asked Cara, excited but also a little nervous.

Grimwold looked directly at her.

"It is the tale of how your grandmother first came to Luster. When you're ready, I'll begin."

CHAPTER TWELVE

# IVY'S STORY

Cara glanced around the cave, which was lit only by Grimwold's lantern. Despite the lack of comfort, despite the chill, despite her exhaustion, she felt an odd sense of happiness. These . . .

She faltered in her thoughts. What to call this group? Not "people" — that word wasn't big enough to properly include the unicorns, the Dimblethum, and the Squijum. And "creatures" seemed too — well, animalistic, or something. Maybe "beings" was the right word.

No. Not beings.

*Friends.*

She felt surrounded by friends. The journey was long and hard, but traveling together had forged them into a kind of family of the road that was filling a need in her heart.

Moonheart, Belle, and Finder had settled themselves in a group to Grimwold's right. Thomas had opened his wagon, which looked particularly strange here inside the cavern, and he and Jacques were sitting on the tailgate. The Dimblethum lounged nearby, growling gently as he picked at the last bits of the fish, while the Squijum was splashing cheerfully in and out of the water. And Lightfoot — her dear Lightfoot — had taken his place beside her. Wrapped snugly in her cloak, she leaned against him to listen.

While the travelers had been trying to make themselves comfortable, Grimwold had opened his pack and taken out a large, leather-bound book, into which several brightly colored ribbons had been inserted as page markers. He waited until everyone was quiet, then said, "When Queen Arabella contacted me through the scrying pool and asked me to help Cara on her journey to the Northern Forest, she also requested that I tell Cara this story." He looked directly at her. "I was well prepared to do so. I had started digging into the Chronicles after the last time I saw you, looking up some stories I had recorded many tens of years ago — stories about your grandmother."

He settled the book in his lap and placed his lantern

on a boulder next to him. Looking at Cara again, he asked, in unusually gentle tones, "How much do you know of your grandmother's past?"

Cara glanced at Jacques, feeling a little embarrassed. "Not much," she said at last.

Grimwold nodded. "Then I'll start at the beginning." He opened the book to a page marked by a scarlet ribbon. "This is Ivy's story — the first part of it, at least. She told it to me herself many years ago. She was a young woman then, and these are her own words, exactly as she spoke them."

*I remember almost nothing of my early years. According to Mr. Preston, the director of the orphanage where I lived, I had been found wandering in the hills outside of the town. It was a small town in England, near the border with Wales.*

*When they brought me to the orphanage, I appeared to be seven or eight years old. Though I could speak clearly and well, I did not know my name or where I had come from.*

*Eventually Mr. Preston named me Ivy. He said he chose this name because sometimes I would sit and stare out the window for hours on end, gazing at the forest and the mountains that rose behind it, as if I were rooted to the spot. But other times I would wander off, going much farther than I should, so that people were frantic to find me. "Ivy has roots, and yet it rambles wherever it can," he said. "Just like you."*

*Except I didn't have roots, not really; how could I, when I had no memory of family or home?*

*The first images I can bring to mind are of my room in the orphanage. The room was small, and I shared it with three other girls. They often teased me because of my strange ways, and sometimes I would cry because of this. But just as often they were friendly, and I have more good feelings about them than bad. And while I longed for a family, the orphanage was not really a bad place. I was cared for, fed and sheltered, and had friends to play with.*

*One day Mr. Preston called me into his office and said, "Ivy, I have someone here I would like you to meet."*

*Sitting in the small sofa was a short, cozy-looking woman who looked like she would be nice to hug. Next to her sat a tall man, lean and hard looking. He had reddish-brown hair, dark eyes, and a hawk-like nose. He smiled. It was a warm smile, friendly and inviting. For some reason, I found it terrifying.*

*"This is Mr. and Mrs. Martin Hunter," said Mr. Preston. "They're interested in adopting you."*

*I took a step back.*

*Mr. Preston laughed. "Don't be silly, Ivy. You want a home, don't you?"*

*I wanted a home more deeply than he could imagine. The very word created a longing so intense, it was almost painful. But not with these people. I didn't know why. I only knew they terrified me.*

*I shook my head.*

*Mr. Preston laughed again, but it was a shorter, harsher sound than the first time. "Don't be silly, Ivy. You know that we can't keep you on here if someone is willing to take you in. You should be pleased. Mr. and Mrs. Hunter have been watching for a long time, and out of all our orphans they've chosen you."*

*I shook my head again, mute with a horror that I could not explain.*

*"Oh, she'll come around soon enough," said Mrs. Hunter with a laugh. The sound was warm and gentle, as cozy as she looked, and I felt myself thawing toward her. But it did nothing to lessen my dread of her husband.*

*Mr. Preston dismissed me. While I was out of the room, the deed was done. Later that afternoon Mr. Preston called me back to his room, scolded me for my behavior earlier in the day, and told me that next week I was to go live with the Hunters.*

*"And you'd best be grateful for this, Miss Ivy," he said sharply. "Be grateful and act proper. I don't want you showing up on our doorstep again because you're not willing to be civil to these pleasant folk who are willing to take you in. I've been glad to have you here, strange poppet that you are. But our goal is to find you a home, and now that you have one, you'd best take advantage of it."*

*That night, I resolved to run away.*

*Two nights later, I did. Rising after dark, I tip-*

toed from my room without waking the other girls. In the kitchen I took a loaf of bread, some fruit, and some cheese — not enough, I now realize, to feed me for more than two or three days. But I was less worried about how I would eat than whether anyone would catch me.

I slipped out through a window that I knew had a broken latch, planning to head for an abandoned cottage I had discovered during one of my "rambles." I thought I'd stay there, at least for the next day or so until the Hunters went away.

I had not traveled far from the orphanage when I heard footsteps behind me. I froze in terror, but only for a moment. Moving quietly, with a stealth I had not known that I possessed, I slipped into the bushes at the side of the road.

It was not long after that I saw a man come riding by. Though he was a tall man, he was leaning low over his horse's neck. He glanced from side to side, and in the moonlight I could see his face.

It was Martin Hunter.

The night was cool, but the chill I felt when I saw him came from something deeper, a terror that I could not explain.

308

*He rode on, but it was a long time before I dared to move again.*

*It was nearly dawn before I made it to the cottage. Though it was cold, and the floor itself was made of earth, my exhaustion was such that I slept for hours.*

*For two days I was left in peace. I wandered the forest and felt both a happiness and a terrible longing that I could not understand. Then, late in the afternoon of the second day, I heard footsteps through the trees.*

*Fearing it was Mr. Hunter coming to get me, I fled, going deeper into the woods, toward the mountains.*

*I moved silently at first, until I was a good distance from the hut. Then I ran as fast as I could, ran until my side felt as if it had been sliced open and my lungs burned as if I were breathing fire. Just when I thought I was safe, I heard someone behind me again. I stumbled forward, nearly blind with exhaustion — and stepped into emptiness. I remember the terror of falling. Then, for a time, there was nothing.*

*When I came to my senses it was dark, and I was in tremendous pain. My leg, especially, hurt; when I tried to move it I quickly realized I had broken it. I wanted to scream but didn't dare for fear Martin Hunter might still be looking for me; though I didn't know why he was chasing me, I was certain I didn't want to be caught.*

*The night seemed endless. I drifted in and out of an agony-filled daze, trembling so violently from pain and shock that I feared I would crack my teeth. It wasn't until morning that I saw I had fallen over a cliff. The bushes had saved my life — perhaps saved it twice: first by cushioning my fall, then by hiding me from the man who was after me, though whether he realized I had gone over the cliff, whether he had found a way down to look for me, I had no way of knowing.*

*Every moment hurt. I vomited from the pain. Yet I couldn't stay where I was. It took several hours, and I blacked out several times during the process, but I managed to drag myself out of the bushes.*

*I was in a narrow valley, bordered on both sides by cliffs some thirty or forty feet high. I could hear a stream gurgling through the center of the valley, so I pulled myself in that direction, both because I was so parched I could hardly swallow and because I figured if I had any chance of getting help, of being found, it would be near the water.*

*But, truthfully, I did not expect anyone to find me. I expected to die there.*

*I had thought about death many times, wondered what it was like, what it would mean. Yet somehow I had never quite believed it would happen to me.*

*Now I did.*

*By the time I dragged myself to the stream, my leg felt as if someone had hammered nails straight through the bone and now was trying to pull them out again. I plunged my face into the icy water and drank, then rolled over and blacked out again.*

*When I woke, the sky — what I could see of it, for much was blocked by the cliffs — was a deeper black than I had ever experienced. The stars, in turn, were more brilliant than I had imagined possible. I gazed up in awe, so startled I nearly forgot my pain in that first moment.*

311

*It reminded me soon enough that it was there.*

*I grabbed a low branch of a nearby shrub and clenched it in my hands, trying to keep from crying out. I wanted to be found, but not by anything that might have been prowling through that darkness.*

*My silence did me no good. I was found, anyway, and a good thing for me that I was.*

Grimwold paused and looked up. The listeners were silent, even the Squijum, who had curled himself up on Cara's lap. She stroked his gray fur, wondering why her grandmother had never told her these things.

Glancing around at the others, she was startled to see that Moonheart looked troubled, as if he was deeply bothered by the story.

"Shall I go on?" asked Grimwold.

"Of course," Cara would have said, save that the question was clearly directed to Moonheart.

The others glanced in his direction.

After a moment he nodded and said, "Continue."

*What was that all about?* wondered Cara. But she didn't have time to ponder it, for the story had begun again.

312

*He came so quietly* [read Grimwold] *that I had no idea he was approaching. When I first saw him, so white in the starlight, his shape blurred by my teary eyes, I thought perhaps it was the moon. But as he came closer, I realized I was being approached by a unicorn — which made me think I had died, or gone mad. So I was only a little terrified when, once he was close enough, he bent his head and pierced my chest with the tip of his horn, driving it toward my heart.*

*For a moment I felt as if my skin had turned to light, as if my blood had become electricity. Then the strange tingling passed; with it went much of my other pain as well.*

*"Alas, poor maiden in the woods," said the unicorn. "I am sorry to frighten you. But I needed to do that so we could communicate."*

*To my astonishment, he spoke not in words but in pure meaning — meaning that came from images, sounds, memories, even smells that formed directly inside my head. "Where did you come from?" I asked eagerly. "How did you find me?"*

*"Don't speak aloud! I can't understand if you*

313

*do. Just form the thought and send it to me. You'll have to stay in contact with me to do it."*

*I didn't want to lose contact with him, not now, not ever. Gripping his foreleg with my hand, I thought again, "Where did you come from?"*

*"Earth, originally. Now, from another world."*

*I found the strangeness of these words nearly as frightening as any of the other things that had happened to me.*

*"How did you get here?" I asked. "Are you lost? Are you scared?"*

*"I came through a gate. I came because you needed me."*

*This was so startling I broke my contact with him for a moment, dropping my grip on his foreleg as if it had burned me. He nickered softly, and I placed my hand on his leg once more. It was smoother, silkier, than anything I had ever felt.*

*"How did you know I needed you?" I asked.*

*He paused, and when he finally answered, I could sense a deep pain in his words. "We unicorns have long had a connection to young maidens in the woods."*

*"There are more of you?" I asked eagerly, for I*

314

*had heard the legend that there is never more than one unicorn on Earth at a time — not that I had believed there were any at all until I saw this one.*

*"Not here," he said, sounding as lost and lonely as I felt. "Not here." Before I could ask another question, he said, "I can heal you if you would like."*

*"Please!"*

*He had me stretch out flat on the ground, and then examined me. Finally he said, "I am going to ask you to do something difficult."*

*"What?"*

*He gestured with his horn toward a nearby shrub. "Wedge your foot in those branches, then pull yourself back until the leg is straight again. It will hurt like fire. But the leg is badly broken, and I can heal it better if the two parts of the bone are more in line. Do you think you can do that?"*

*"Of course," I said, trying to sound braver than I felt.*

*And I did, though the searing pain made me scream.*

*The flash of agony when he healed me was even worse. But that was over in an instant. I sat up.*

315

*To my astonishment the leg was solid and whole once more. The pain, though not completely gone, had faded to a shadow of what it had been.*

*"Now I must rest," the unicorn said. He started to kneel, but his legs buckled before he could get all the way down, and he collapsed beside me. I pressed myself against him, trying to keep him warm. But in truth it was his presence that kept me warm through the night.*

*In the morning I was able to walk, which felt better than I would have imagined.*

*"We must get away from here," said my unicorn. He led me along the ravine, then into another, then up an isolated mountain to a craggy area where he showed me a hidden cave. Once we were inside, I could tell he felt calmer, more relaxed.*

*"Now we must talk," he said.*

*"About what?" I asked.*

*Before he could answer, a man leaped out of the darkness. I recognized him at once. It was Martin Hunter.*

*"This is for Beloved!" he screamed.*

*Then he plunged his sword into the unicorn's side.*

# CHAPTER THIRTEEN

# THE JEWEL

G rimwold paused in his story, rubbed the back of his hand over his brow, then glanced at Moonheart, almost as if seeking permission to continue.

But it was Cara who urged him on. "What happened next?" she asked eagerly. She was fascinated by this secret history of her grandmother. Yet at the same time, the intrusion of another Hunter into the story left her once more horrified by the chain of family that tied her to the vengeful Beloved. She would have given her life to protect the unicorns, and she couldn't help feeling vaguely guilty whenever she thought of her father's side of the family.

"Give me a moment," said Grimwold. He went to

the stream from which they had taken the fish, dipped in his hand, took a drink of water.

Then he returned to his place and, by the light of his lantern, began once again reading Ivy's words:

*The unicorn reared back. Silver and scarlet blood pumped down his silken coat as he pawed the air with his hooves, trumpeting in pain and fury.*

*The man slashed out with the sword again. As he did, I flung myself at him, grabbing his arm. Startled, he turned toward me, raising his hand to strike me. But the unicorn struck first, his hooves thudding against the man's head.*

*Our attacker cried out, then crumpled to the cave floor.*

*My unicorn stood for a moment, blood pulsing from his side. Then he, too, collapsed.*

*I threw myself down beside him, put my hand on his neck. I was sobbing, but forced myself to stop. "Are you all right?" I thought, realizing it was a stupid question even as I asked it. "What can I do for you?"*

"Get help," he thought, and the message as it came to me was red and swirling with pain. "Get help."

"How?"

"Back of the cave . . . another cave . . . find gate."

"A gate?" I asked, feeling confused. Why would there be a gate in a cave?

"Gate to . . . Luster. Find . . . other unicorns. Tell them . . . Moonheart needs help."

Cara gasped. "Moonheart?"

"I never knew about this!" said Lightfoot, sounding equally surprised — and slightly amused.

"There is a great deal you don't know, nephew," said Moonheart severely. "Continue with your story, Grimwold."

The old dwarf nodded and began to read again.

At first, I was not willing to leave my unicorn, my Moonheart. But I could do him no good where I was. So I made my way to the back of the cave. I traveled a little distance in darkness, through a

319

narrow passage. Then I saw a light ahead of me. Turning a corner, I entered another cave, larger than the first. I stopped short, gazing in awe at the most amazing thing I had ever seen.

The gate — it had to be the gate — floated in the center of the cave, its base a foot or so above the floor. It was a perfect circle, twelve feet high at least, with a surface that shimmered like water and glowed with the tender green of springtime. I was delighted — and terrified. I walked up to it nervously, then pressed my hand against the surface. I felt a pleasant tingling. I pressed harder, and my hand went through. At once the tingling flowed along my arm.

I cried out and pulled my hand back. Then I walked around to the other side of the circle. It looked exactly the same as the front. Standing at the edge of the circle so I could see both sides — it was no thicker than a penny — I thrust my hand forward again.

To my astonishment, though my hand went in, it didn't come out on the other side!

I pulled my hand out, gasping with fear, and was relieved to find it still attached to my arm.

*What was on the other side of the circle? Not the other side here in the cave — I had seen that. What happened if you went through the gate, as I was supposed to do?*

*I wanted to run away. But Moonheart was counting on me.*

*I began counting myself, intending to step through the circle at three, at five, at ten, but hesitating each time. "I'll do it when I get to twelve," I promised myself, starting again with one.*

*And I did. When I reached twelve, I plunged through the circle — and into the world that would claim half my heart for all my life.*

*Though I had crossed from a cave, I stepped out onto a mountainside. Though I had crossed from morning, I stepped out into twilight.*

*In a circle of trees a little way below me stood a glory of unicorns — though I didn't know, then, that "glory" was the proper term for a group of these wonderful creatures. I stumbled toward them, awed by their beauty, terrified that they might run. I needed them, needed them desperately, to come help Moonheart.*

*To my relief, they remained standing, watching*

*me. After a moment I gained control of myself. Slowly, holding one hand before me, I approached them as you would a skittish animal. I didn't know, then, how foolish that made me seem; didn't know that I was the skittish animal.*

*They held still, let me come to them. I placed my hand on the neck of the one closest to me.*

*"Moonheart needs help," I thought desperately.*

*"He wants us to come to the other side?" he replied. I could sense the horror in his response, feel it in my stomach as if it were my own.*

*"Yes. A man attacked him. He's been stabbed. He's bleeding. I'm afraid he might . . . might die."*

*The unicorn's anger, surging into me through our connection, almost knocked me over. I staggered away, losing my contact with him. He spoke to the other three unicorns, and they raced up the hill. Leaping into the glowing circle, they disappeared from sight.*

*And that was how I first came to Luster.*

Grimwold closed the book.

"That's it?" demanded Cara.

"That's the story the Queen asked me to tell you," he replied with some asperity. "The tale of how your grandmother came to be here. I assume she had her reasons for wanting you to know it."

"But what happened next?"

"I survived," said Moonheart dryly.

"What were you doing on Earth to begin with?" asked Lightfoot.

Moonheart closed his eyes. "I was having a Wander Year. A year, mind you," he said emphatically, opening his eyes and looking directly at Lightfoot, "not an eternity. I wanted to see the Seven Gates, both to satisfy my curiosity and because I knew I would someday be charged with the care and guardianship of them. That was a responsibility I took seriously."

The Squijum, distracted by something, bounded off Cara's lap and scurried into the darkness.

Moonheart snorted and continued his story. "The glory that was guarding the fourth gate welcomed me — until I told them that I could sense something wrong on the other side, could sense a maiden in the woods who needed help.

"'That's no business of ours,' said the leader —

Silkmane was her name — 'we stay in Luster, where we belong.'

"I knew she was right. But all through the night, Ivy's feeling of need, of terror, of pain, continued growing in me. Finally I went to Traveler, who was standing the late watch, and said, 'I am too restless to sleep. I'll take your place for a while.' He was only too happy to agree, and went contentedly off to stand drowsing with the others.

"I waited, biding my time, until I felt certain none were alert. Then I bolted through the gate."

"*You* went against orders?" snorted Lightfoot in astonishment.

Cara, her hand on Lightfoot's flank, thought, *Hush! He'll never finish the story if you embarrass him!*

Moonheart looked uncomfortable, but ignored the question. "It didn't take me long to find her. But there was a mystery then, and it remains now: Why was I able to sense Ivy's need when none of the others could? Why was I able to sense that need all the way from the other side of a gate? What made that need so compelling that I was willing to abandon common sense, to flout the rules, in order to respond? That is not the way of things as we know them. That is not *my* way."

He turned his head so that he was speaking directly to Lightfoot. "And yet, I have never regretted what I did. After all, it brought Ivy Morris to live among us. And when my Wander Year was over, I did the right thing and went back to court."

His voice held a hint of accusation, aimed directly at Lightfoot, and something sharp and angry seemed to float in the air between them.

Cara, uncomfortable, said, "I still want to know what happened next."

"The others found and healed me," said Moonheart.

"And what of the Hunter?" asked Cara, knowing that she must be in some way related to him, as she was to all the Hunters. With a shudder she realized he might even have been her grandfather on her father's side.

"He woke as the others were healing me. When he saw so many of us together, he tried to flee. But we couldn't let him go, now that he had found the gate — couldn't let him take that information back to the others."

"You didn't . . . kill him, did you?" asked Cara.

"He would have killed me," said Moonheart coldly.

325

"But no, we didn't kill him. We brought him back here and put him in the hands of a person who deals with such things for us. She put him to sleep, rather like the princess in your 'Sleeping Beauty' story."

"And he's still sleeping?" asked Cara in astonishment.

"Do you have a better idea for dealing with him?" snorted Belle.

"No. I just . . . no."

"Actually, there are times I almost wish to wake him," said Moonheart, "for there are questions I would still like answered. Our feeling is that the reason he wanted to take Ivy from the orphanage was to use her as a lure for a unicorn, in the way that Hunters have always placed young maidens in the woods. Yet the Guardian of Memory was thousands of miles from that place, so there was no unicorn for him to catch until I arrived. Why set a trap where there is no unicorn? Hunters are not fools about these things. It was almost as if he knew I would be coming. But though Beloved and her Hunters have many skills, reading the future has never been one of them. So how could he have known? And why was it Ivy, in particular, who he wanted — wanted so much that he tried to track her down when she fled? He could have taken some other girl from the orphanage if all he wanted was a maiden to lure a unicorn."

Moonheart shook his head, causing his mane to ripple over his neck. In the glow of Grimwold's lantern it looked like liquid light. "I have pondered these questions many times but have not been able to make sense of them. And yet, I do not regret what happened, for it brought Ivy to my side, and that was a great joy. She traveled with me for the rest of my Wander Year, and we had many adventures together. When the year was over she was offered a home at court with the Queen. She turned it down, which was a bit of a scandal. But it was as if there was something in her that could not bear to be at rest. She was always looking, seeking. Sometimes I wondered if because I was a Wanderer myself when we first met that she had been somehow infected by my own restlessness. But I think it was more than that. Alas, whatever it was that made her a Wanderer was one mystery she kept to herself."

"Indeed," said Grimwold, and Cara had the sense that he was deeply annoyed at not knowing the whole story.

"There's nothing wrong with wandering," said Finder quietly.

"No, there's not," agreed Moonheart, "not if that's what you're born to do. But with Ivy there was always a sense that she was not merely wandering, but that she was looking for something — something she could not even name."

"Or perhaps that some secret sorrow kept her in motion," said Jacques, who had been silent to this point. "I sometimes felt that she feared if she stayed in one place too long, some old pain or loss that she could not speak of, perhaps couldn't even really remember, would rise up and devour her."

"There are things even a unicorn can't heal," said Moonheart sadly.

*I wonder if Gramma's wandering had anything to do with losing her parents?* thought Cara.

"Eventually your grandmother became a messenger for the Queen," said Grimwold. "Which is not a bad job for someone who is a wanderer by nature. She was one of the few to travel regularly back and forth between the two worlds. She has more adventures recorded in the Chronicles than I can count."

"She was using the amulet all that time?" asked Cara, putting her hand to her neck.

328

Grimwold shook his head. "No, the amulet was given to her at the end, when she decided to return to Earth for good. She had done the Queen a great service then, and no one wanted her to go. But she insisted. The amulet was so she could return to Luster when she wanted. It has a particular quality in that regard. While I know it dropped you in the wilderness when you first arrived, its magic was tuned in such a way as to bring the Wanderer back to the Queen, wherever she might be."

"Yet she didn't come back," whispered Jacques, his face still and solemn, its lines deep with age and loss. "I don't know why."

"She used to sing about her wandering," said Grimwold. Then, to Cara's surprise, he began to sing "Song of the Wanderer" himself. After a moment, Jacques joined him, their voices blending in an unexpectedly lovely harmony.

It was a long song, filled with a need so deep it was like the sound of a heart being torn in two.

*Across the gently rolling hills,*
*Beyond high mountain peaks,*

## SONG OF THE WANDERER

*Along the shores of distant seas,*
*There's something my heart seeks.*

*But there's no peace in wandering,*
*The road's not made for rest.*
*And footsore fools will never know*
*What home might suit them best.*

*But, oh, the things that I have seen,*
*The secret paths I've trod,*
*The hidden corners of the world*
*Known to none but me and God.*

*Yes, the world was meant for knowing,*
*And feet were meant to roam.*
*But one who's always going*
*Will never find a home.*

*Oh, where's the thread that binds me,*
*The voice that calls me back?*
*Where's the love that finds me —*
*And what's the root I lack?*

And between each verse the now familiar chorus:

*My heart seeks the hearth,*
*My feet seek the road.*
*A soul so divided*
*Is a terrible load.*

*My heart longs to rest,*
*My feet yearn to roam.*
*Shall I wander the world*
*Or stay safe at home?*

"That was her final gift to us," said Jacques when they were done. "That —" He broke off. Pointing to Cara's finger, he cried, "What does *that* mean?"

Cara glanced down. M'Gama's ring was glowing, as it had the first night she'd heard Jacques sing the song.

"I don't know," she whispered. She held up her hand. The green light of the ring, almost dazzling in its intensity, began to fade even as they all stared at it.

"Where did you get that?" asked Grimwold gruffly.

"M'Gama gave it to me," said Cara, still staring at her hand even though the ring had lost its light.

"She always was one for a touch of mystery," muttered Grimwold. "As for gifts — a song and a ring are all fine, but odds are good you are going to need yet another gift before this is over, if the message I got from the Queen is correct. She said you were heading for Ebillan's territory?"

The Dimblethum growled at the mention of the name.

"Yes, well, that's very impressive," said Grimwold, nodding at the manbear. "But it will take more than growls to convince that dragon to let you pass in peace."

"Do you have any suggestions?" asked Cara.

"He is fierce and unpredictable," said Grimwold. "The best way to reach him is through his greed."

"Alas," said Finder, "we have nothing to bargain with."

Grimwold smiled. Reaching into his robe, he drew forth a scarlet gem the size of a duck egg. "This may be of use," he said, sounding just a trifle smug.

He extended it to Cara.

"Are you sure you want to give this up?" she asked, awestruck by the size and beauty of the jewel.

"What am I going to do with it?" he asked scornfully. "Eat it? I don't want to throw it away on a fool's errand. But if you can make good use of it — if it will help you bring back the Wanderer — then take it."

Hesitantly, Cara accepted the jewel from his hand. It looked like fire and felt like ice. Staring into it, she felt herself being lost in its crimson depths, wandering among its facets, almost as if she had entered another world. Forests of red, rivers of red, towering mountains and deep caverns, all blazing red, rolled out before her.

As she walked along the scarlet paths, one tree in particular seemed to call her. Unaware now of Grimwold, of her friends, of anything save the jewel, Cara let her mind drift forward.

The tree had a big hollow at its base.

Cara stooped to peer into it.

Inside sat a woman dressed in a white robe — the only white Cara had seen in this red world. The woman had her hands clasped before her and her head bowed so that her long red hair covered her face.

Suddenly she snapped her head back, flinging her hair behind her. Cara gasped at the beautiful face revealed by this gesture. The wide-set blue eyes, the high cheekbones, the full lips were all achingly familiar to her, familiar for a simple reason: They belonged to her mother.

# CHAPTER FOURTEEN

# THE WILDLANDS

For a moment Cara couldn't move, couldn't speak, was afraid, indeed, that her heart would stop beating. Finally she whispered, "Mommy?"

Her mother, whom she had not seen since she was three, stared at her for a long time without answering.

"Don't you know me?" asked Cara, her voice quavering.

Suddenly her mother's eyes grew wide with astonishment. "*Cara?* Cara, is that you?"

"Yes! Yes, it's me, Mom. What are you doing here?"

Her mother looked around. Then, her voice troubled, she said softly, "I don't know. I don't know at all! Where am I, Cara? *Where am I?*"

"How did you get here?" Cara asked urgently. She stepped forward, reaching toward her mother. But the moment she touched her, the vision was over. It ended not with a flash of light, nor a roar of thunder. Her mother's image simply vanished, and Cara found herself once more in Grimwold's cave, staring at the scarlet jewel that lay in her trembling hand.

She took a deep, gasping breath. When she looked up, the others could see tears trembling in her eyes.

"What just happened?" she whispered.

"What do you mean?" asked Jacques. He was bending over her, his leathery face wrinkled with concern.

"What just happened?" repeated Cara, a note of wildness creeping into her voice.

Moonheart stepped forward. "You were staring into the jewel — studying it as if you were reading something hard to understand. Just as I was starting to wonder if something was wrong you cried out and shook your head."

"I was here all that time?" she asked, still trying to catch her breath.

"Where else would you have been?" asked Grimwold, his voice unusually gentle.

Closing her fingers over the jewel — holding it as tightly as if it were her own heart, trying to escape — she told them what had happened.

Jacques was the first to speak, the first to break the silence that followed her story. "What does it mean?" he asked. His voice was ragged, almost desperate, and Cara suddenly realized that if he was indeed her grandfather, then her mother would be his daughter — a daughter he had never seen.

Grimwold shook his head. "I have no idea." He sounded disturbed, even frightened.

Cara loosened her grip on the jewel. Feeling foolish, yet knowing she had to ask, she pointed at it and said, "Is it possible. . . could my mother be *inside* this thing?"

"I hesitate to say anything is *impossible*," said Grimwold. "But I doubt that is the case. More likely the jewel offered a focal point for you to connect to your mother — possibly because it is connected to whatever magic holds her."

"But there are other possibilities, too," said Thomas.

Cara turned to him. "Like what?"

He took a watch from one of his pockets, consulted it, and returned it to a different pocket, jingling his chains as he did. "One is that you simply imagined the whole scene, saw it because you want your mother so much."

Cara started to object, but he raised his hand.

"Another is that the jewel itself carries an enchantment, one that makes you see things that are unsettled in your life. It could be a positive enchantment, forcing you to face issues you haven't dealt with. It could be a negative one, meant to torment you and lead you into false action."

"Why would someone cast a spell like that?" asked Cara, appalled at the thought and resisting the idea that she had not actually seen her mother.

Thomas shrugged. "The ways of magic users are strange and mysterious. But it doesn't even have to have been a purposeful spell. It might be some natural property of the jewel, or some side effect of it having been kept in a place where magic was in use. But there is one more possibility to consider: What if the message is false?"

"What do you mean?"

"Remember back in Summerhaven, when you dreamed of Beloved? I suspect that dream came because Beloved was trying to reach you — though I'm not sure *why* she was able to do it then."

"What are you talking about?" demanded Grimwold.

Quickly, Cara told him the details of the horrible experience she had had the night before they left Summerhaven.

"The Tinker is right," said Grimwold. "This may well come from Beloved. If it does, she was probably using the jewel as a focus point to reach you. But if so, what was the focus point the first time? And why hasn't she tried again until now? That's something I'd dearly like to know."

"But why would Beloved send me a vision of my mother?" asked Cara desperately.

"It could be designed to throw you off balance, or turn you from your path," said Thomas gently.

Cara felt as if she would choke on the confusion and despair swirling in her breast. "How can I know for sure?"

"There *is* no way to know right now," said Grimwold. "That is why such messages are usually of so little use, and may even be dangerous. They can lead you into journeys you were not meant to take, turn you toward paths you were not meant to follow. For now, simply hold the vision in your heart. Later, you may learn something that will help you understand it — and understand what to do about it."

She opened her fingers. The jewel lay in her palm, flashing scarlet and crimson in the torchlight.

"Should I look in it again?" she asked fearfully.

338

"Not now," said Grimwold, closing her fingers back over it.

"You had better keep it," she said, thrusting it back toward Grimwold. "I could never give it to Ebillan, not after what just happened. You'll have to give me something else to use."

"Do you think I keep things like this just lying about?" demanded Grimwold indignantly. "Bits of treasure to cough up on demand?"

Cara blushed as she realized that Grimwold had freely given her something worth a fortune to help her on her quest, and that now she was demanding he take it back and give her something different. "I'm sorry," she murmured. "But I don't know what to do with it."

"Do whatever you want," said Grimwold gruffly. "I've given what help I can. I need some rest now. I'd suggest that you lot do the same. Tomorrow I'll lead you to the best place to reenter the world above."

When everyone had settled for the night, Grimwold extinguished his lantern.

The blackness of the cave was utter, and complete.

Even so, and though she knew she should rest, Cara could not get to sleep. Despite her exhaustion, the story of her grandmother's entrance into Luster, and even more the strange episode with the crimson jewel, continued to circle in her mind.

She could not decide which was more complete: the darkness of the cave, or the darkness inside her.

The next day Grimwold led them through a series of tunnels, then up a long slope that brought them out onto the side of a low mountain.

"This is as close as I can take you to your destination," he said. "The River Silver is that way. I wish you well on the rest of your journey."

He turned away, and Cara thought that was all he was going to say. But after a moment he turned back, turned to face her specifically. "When you find the Wanderer, give her my greetings. Tell her . . . tell her she owes me a story." He turned once more, and vanished into the darkness. A moment later a boulder slid silently into place, blocking the entrance.

"Come," said Moonheart. "We'd best get moving."

♦　♦　♦

It was Finder who took the lead now, picking his way skillfully down the mountainside so that even the humans could travel without too much slipping and sliding. They heard strange cries as they walked, and more than once the sound of something slithering away from them. Cara realized with a start that there were probably hundreds — maybe thousands — of kinds of animals here that she was totally unaware of. If the ones she had seen so far were any indication, they would be like the ones she knew on Earth, and yet some-how . . . different.

They reached the Silver before noon. The river was considerably smaller here, closer to its source. They followed it north for the rest of the day. Late in the afternoon, they came to a flat stretch of grassland. On the far side of the grassland, rising like a wall, just as M'Gama had described it, was the Northern Forest.

It was nightfall by the time they reached the edge of the forest, and they made their camp at the corner formed by the river and the forest.

Cara took out her calendar stick and carved the day's notch. Thirteen days. Grimwold's shortcut had brought them here ahead of schedule.

Her heart felt lighter than it had in days.

♦   ♦   ♦

The next morning they traveled east along the forest's edge. About noon they came to the black stones that M'Gama had described. They were unmistakable — smooth, about three feet in diameter, and towering to ten feet in height. They stood about five feet apart, and Cara shivered as they walked between them.

But the path was there, just as M'Gama had promised, true and straight.

As darkness began to fall, they found a resting place at the base of an enormous tree. Its bark, remarkably smooth for such a big tree, was silvery-blue. The trunk was so big that Cara, Jacques, and Thomas together could not reach their arms around it. Its massive roots rippled the ground for yards in all directions, creating long, low mounds, sometimes heaving right out of the soil so that their tops looked like long, silver snakes stretching out from the tree. Cara made a pile of leaves between two of these roots, and in this way created a cozy bed for herself.

The next day the territory they entered was wilder still. Cresting one hill, Cara noticed an area off to her right that seemed oddly out of focus. At first she thought it was due to a light mist that hung over the area. But as she kept staring at it, that didn't seem right. When she drew Finder's attention to it, he said, "No one has explored that area yet."

"But why does it look that way?" she persisted.

"Because no one has explored it yet," he repeated.

"What does exploring a place have to do with how it looks?"

"I'd rather not talk about it," answered Finder. His discomfort only increased Cara's curiosity. But when she tried another question he made it clear that he wouldn't say any more on the topic.

The going was more treacherous now — the hills steeper, the forest thicker and denser. Once, the path led them into a swamp, where they nearly lost the Dimblethum when he stumbled into murky water that began to suck him down as if trying to swallow him. His roars of distress were deafening, and for the first time Cara saw fear in the great creature's eyes. Jacques and Thomas struggled desperately to pull him out, but it was only when Cara and the Squijum found some vines that they were able to use as ropes that they managed to get him free of the clinging muck. His shaggy coat was thick with slime, and though he longed to wash it off, he was afraid to enter the water again. It was not until late the next day, when they found a clear stream, that he managed to get clean.

Three nights later they made camp beside another stream. As usual, Thomas and Jacques placed themselves on either side of her, each about four feet away. She knew they did this so that she would feel safe, and she appreciated it. The Squijum curled up at her feet, then on her chest, then beside her head, then disappeared for a while, then came back to lie beside her again. She was vaguely aware of his restlessness as she drifted on the edge of sleep, but not bothered by it since he was that way most of the time. The unicorns, who needed less sleep than the others, stood to one side, talking softly among themselves.

All around them were the sounds of the night — the breeze that moved softly through the leaves above them, the shrill chirp and singing of the insects, the flick of wings from creatures that flew only in the dark. In the distance something howled mournfully at the moon. Cara rolled over, and the leaves rustled beneath her. To her right a shelf of fungus attached to the trunk of a large tree glowed pale blue.

The night wore on. The sounds began to fade. Yet Cara could not sleep. Finally she sat up. Rummaging in her pack, she found the jewel Grimwold had given her. Moving as silently as possible, she got to her feet. She stood for a moment, uncertain what to do.

*I need more light,* she thought.

But M'Gama had warned them against leaving the path.

*I won't go far,* she promised herself. *Certainly not out of sight of the camp.*

Looking around, she found a spot only a few yards away, where the trees were not blocking the moonlight. She crossed to it, trying to move as quietly as if she were a unicorn herself. Once in the light, she held up the jewel and stared into it, waiting to see her mother again.

# CHAPTER FIFTEEN

# MOANS IN THE DARKNESS

Nothing happened.

Cara stared harder, holding her breath, willing the magic to work once more.

Nothing.

Angry and frustrated, she resisted an urge to fling the jewel into the darkness. Forcing herself to breathe deeply, she gazed up at the black velvet sky. The stars were flung across it in wild abandon, jewels themselves, winking with distant fire. She sought out the few constellations she had learned so far: the Queen, the Guardian, the Snake, the Ravager.

Her eyes lingered on the Ravager, and as they did she found herself drifting into a waking dream once more. She felt a moment of fear when it began. Then,

346

thinking she might see her mother again after all, she released herself to it.

She was in a cave lit by torches. The torches indicated a path, and she followed it, drifting as if her feet did not touch the floor. Down she went, deeper and deeper into the cave, into the dream. She came at last to a great wooden door. She touched it with her fingertips, and it swung silently open.

On the far side, where she had hoped to find her mother, she saw instead Beloved.

The woman gestured to her. Unable to resist, caught as if in a spell, Cara took a step toward her.

"Welcome, daughter of my daughters," whispered Beloved. Her eyes were warm, her tone soft and caressing. "Come closer."

Telling herself she shouldn't, longing to hold still, Cara took another step forward.

"Closer," whispered Beloved.

Cara was trembling now. But she took another step.

Beloved reached out to embrace her.

"Where is my mother?" asked Cara. "Do you know?"

"Of course I do. Give me the amulet, and she is yours."

Cara longed to obey. She felt her hand going to her neck. With a ferocious effort, she stopped herself. *No!* she thought. *No, I won't!*

"Give it," whispered Beloved eagerly.

Feeling as if her heart were splitting, Cara lifted the amulet from her shirt. She gazed down at it. Her fingers shook as she touched it once again. With a sudden cry, she turned and ran, out of the cave, and out of the dream.

Awake, Cara found herself standing in the moonlight once more, in the night of Luster, just outside the circle of her friends. But the terror had seized her, and without thinking she ran into the forest, slipping and stumbling as she did, running as if she could leave her life, the tangled web of her family, far behind.

She charged on until the air burned in her lungs, and her side throbbed with pain. When her legs could no longer hold her, she tripped over a root and fell crashing to the ground.

She lay there for a time, gasping and sobbing. Finally she rolled over and looked up.

Now she was seized by a new terror. *What have I done?* she thought, furious with herself for letting her fear drive her away from her friends.

Suddenly, M'Gama's warning about not leaving the path echoed in her ears.

"How could I have been so stupid?" she cried.

Immediately she regretted speaking aloud, and wondered if there was anyone nearby to hear.

She pushed herself to her feet, looking desperately for some sign of the way that she had come. But the forest was deep here, and neither starlight nor moonlight could penetrate the leaves. The darkness was complete.

She was lost in the wildlands of Luster.

She stumbled forward, her hands outstretched as if she were blind, until she came to a tree. She wrapped her arms around it, clung to it as if to a life raft that would support her in the sea of darkness that surrounded her.

She had scarcely caught her breath when a new terror shook her. For out of the deep and surrounding darkness came a low, shuddering moan.

Cara tightened her grip on the tree. As the first jolt of fear subsided, she began groping above her, search-

349

ing for branches she could use to pull herself up, away from the ground.

She heard the moan once more. It was still frightening. But it didn't sound angry, and — more importantly — it didn't sound any closer than it had before. So whatever it was, it wasn't coming after her, as she had feared.

She tried to slow her breath, to make herself as still and silent as possible.

A light breeze stirred around her, rustling the leaves with its coolness. She began to edge around the tree, hoping to put it between herself and the source of the moans. After a step or two, she turned around, realizing it would be better to have her back to the tree and be facing out so she could detect any approaching danger — though what good that would do in the forest darkness she wasn't sure.

When Cara reached the far side of the tree, she slid to the ground and curled herself into a small, miserable ball. Her flight into darkness, being lost, the strange moans in the night, and, most of all, the vision of Beloved — it was all more than she could take.

As she huddled there, trying not to cry, she heard

the moan once more. It was low and sorrowful — sounding, in fact, much like she felt. It roused a kind of pity in her, and she began to wonder if she should go in search of the sound to see if she could offer some help.

*Don't be stupid!* she told herself. *Stay right here until sunrise. If the moaning is still going on when it gets light, then you can go look.*

But her heart wouldn't listen to her mind, and as the next moan came shuddering out of the night, she found herself forgetting her own problems and wondering what would cause anyone to make such a mournful sound.

For a long time after that she heard nothing. The sudden silence frightened her almost as much as the moaning had.

*What if whoever it was has died?* she fretted. She lay in an agony of indecision, unwilling to venture into the darkness, knowing she couldn't see to find anyone anyway, and yet still feeling she ought to do something.

After what seemed like hours, she heard another moan. She was almost relieved. Pulling herself to her feet, she started toward the sound. She moved slowly, both because she could not see, and because she wanted to remain silent in case whoever was making the sound was dangerous after all.

She stumbled twice within the first few steps she took and realized that getting to her feet had been a bad idea. She dropped back to her hands and knees. Putting her right hand ahead of her, she swung it from side to side, then lowered it gently to the ground, trying not to snap any twigs or rustle any leaves as she did. Then she moved her right knee forward as well.

She repeated the process with her left hand and knee.

Her progress was excruciatingly slow. But then, she was in no particular hurry, her concern about whoever was moaning being nearly balanced by her fear.

Wings fluttered overhead, and she wondered what kind of animals flew at night in this forest. In the distance she heard a howl — like a wolf's, but lower and deeper.

Realizing again how little she knew of Luster and its wildlife, she shuddered. But she also continued her forward motion.

Suddenly, as if announced by the howl, the moon appeared. Though its silver-blue light was mostly blocked by the forest above, her eyes were now so dark-accustomed that even these shreds of light allowed her to move much more easily.

Another moan told her she was off course. She adjusted to the left and continued forward.

A few feet more brought her to a large boulder — so big that as she worked her way along it, she thought at first it was a cliff. But soon enough she felt it curve, and could see by the faint dapple of moonlight that it was only a stone after all.

Now she moved more cautiously than ever. Even so, when she put her hand down onto a thick stack of feathers, she shrieked and scurried backward.

At the same time, a harsh voice cried, "Gaaahhh! Don't kill me!"

Cara pressed herself against the rock, trying not to betray her position by so much as a breath.

After a moment of silence, the voice cried, "Well, if you *are* going to kill me, stop fooling around and let's get it over with, gadfound you."

"I don't want to kill you," said Cara softly. She felt braver now, thinking that anything so afraid of getting killed was unlikely to be out to hurt *her*.

"Then what are you doing here?" asked the voice suspiciously.

"I heard you moaning and came to see what was wrong."

"I was *not* moaning!"

This remark startled Cara so much that she said, "If it wasn't you, then who was it?"

"I don't know. But Medafil does not moan." The voice hesitated a second, then added, "Besides, wouldn't you moan if you were trapped, and had probably broken a wing, and you figured the delvers were going to come and kill you at any moment?"

"Yes," said Cara. "I would. Definitely."

"Well, there you go," said Medafil. "It wasn't me. But it would have been all right if it had been."

"How are you trapped?" asked Cara.

"Why don't you come around and see?" asked the voice wearily.

"How do I know you won't eat *me* if I do?"

"What would I want to do that for?" replied the voice, sounding shocked beyond belief.

"Because you're hungry?"

"Gaaaah! If I wanted to eat you I would have come

354

around that dadgimbled rock and done it by now. At least, I would have if I could move."

This didn't entirely make sense to Cara, but she pushed herself to her feet anyway. Still somewhat wary, she stepped a few feet away from the rock before she continued around it.

What she saw in the dim moonlight filled her with wonder, terror, and pity.

# CHAPTER SIXTEEN

# MEDAFIL

The creature was magnificent, even in distress. His head was that of an eagle, or would have been if not for the tufted ears that rose from its sides. His wings, too, could have been those of an eagle, except that they were vastly bigger than any eagle's had ever been. But there the resemblance to an eagle ended. From the shoulders down, Medafil's body was that of a great, tawny lion — though twice the size of any normal lion.

"A gryphon!" Cara whispered in awe. "You're a gryphon!"

"Well, what's so surprising about that?" the creature snapped. "You're a girl. Very unusual around here. Even so, you don't see me lying here with my mouth hanging open, gawping at you about it."

"But I've never seen a gryphon before."

"How old are you?"

"Twelve."

"Well, it's been longer than that since I've seen a girl. So who's the more surprised, eh? Now, if you want something really surprising, consider the fact that a gryphon let itself be trapped like this. Gaaaah! It's . . . humiliating."

Looking more carefully, straining to see in the dim light, Cara realized that the gryphon's right front leg was caught by a thick snare. Walking cautiously to him — she wanted to trust him but she also knew that his beak could take off one of her own legs with a single snap — she knelt to examine the snare.

It was made of many strands of wire, woven together to form a cable as thick as her thumb. One end of it was anchored under the boulder, though how that had been done, she couldn't imagine. The other formed a loop around the gryphon's leg that had been pulled so tight it nearly disappeared beneath his fur. That the fur was wet with blood testified to his struggles to break free.

"Who would have done this?" she asked, horrified and outraged all at once.

"Delvers," replied the gryphon, his voice filled with disgust. "Who else?"

"But why?"

Medafil shrugged one of his wings, creating a small breeze. "Why do birds fly? That's the way they are."

"How did they capture you?" asked Cara, trying to work her fingers into the wire loop to see if she could loosen it.

"I'd rather not say," replied the gryphon. He sounded embarrassed. But before Cara could press the point, he added, "Oh, all right, I'll tell you. They cheated. They played on my weak point."

"What's that?" she asked, still working at the wire.

The gryphon clicked his beak in annoyance. "I like shiny things. I collect them. Old family habit. Can't help myself. The delvers have lots of shiny things, of course. Bladratted creatures rooting around in the ground the way that they do are always coming across gold and jewels. So they made this."

"What?" asked Cara.

"This," he said impatiently, moving his front leg. She gasped. Hidden beneath his enormous paw had been a gem-encrusted sphere that would have been worth a fortune back on Earth. "They left it out here for me to find, knowing I wouldn't be able to resist it. And they set that snare to catch me when I went after it."

"I would have thought they'd have been watching to see when you got caught," said Cara, glancing around nervously. "Why haven't they come to get you yet?"

"They're in no hurry. The trap may have been here for weeks already. They probably check it every other night or so."

"Weren't they afraid that someone would steal the . . . the bait?"

"Well, anyone who tried would have been trapped just like me. Besides, who else would there be to take it?"

Given the fact that they were in a deep, nearly unin-habited wilderness, Cara could think of no answer for that question.

Turning back to the snare, she said, "I think I'd bet-ter go look for the others. I don't think I can do this by myself."

"Gaaaahhh! Don't go. If the delvers come while you're gone, they'll kill me. Gadbingled things will probably eat me, too. Very undignified way for a gryphon to die."

Cara didn't want to face the delvers again herself. Even the idea made her shudder. But she couldn't leave the creature here to face them on his own. So she began working at the wire snare again. For a time it seemed that the more she worked, the tighter it got. Once the gryphon hissed in pain and stretched his great beak toward her as if he was about to bite her. When she gasped, he stopped and drew his head back, blinking a bit and looking ashamed. She made no comment.

*I wish I hadn't left my sword behind when I ran off,* she thought as the wire began to shred her fingertips. Her blood was matting in the gryphon's fur, mingling with his own.

*The unicorns can heal the cuts,* she kept telling herself, mostly as a way to try to ignore the throbbing pain.

Finally deciding that she was not going to be able to loosen the snare, she groped around until she found a sharp rock and began to saw at the wire.

"Gaaah!" cried Medafil. "You're cutting me!"

"Well, I've already cut myself!" she snapped, growing impatient with the creature. "Do you have a better idea?"

"Gramding it," he muttered, which she took to mean, "No."

At first she thought the rock would be no more effective than her fingers had been. But finally she felt a strand of the wire snap. Another went, and then another. It took a full ten minutes, but finally she had severed the entire cluster of wires.

As soon as she was done the gryphon surged to his feet, shrieked with triumph, and flapped his wings. Dust and twigs blew all around her.

"Well," said Cara dryly. "I guess your wing isn't broken after all."

"I couldn't tell at first," sniffed Medafil. Tucking his wings against his sides, he sat, much the way a cat does.

Cara had to look up to see his face. His eagle eyes blinked down at her, and the sharp blade of his beak made her nervous.

"What are you doing here, anyway?" he asked.

Cara started to reply, but realized she wasn't sure how much she should say about her mission. She had begun to realize there was more going on in Luster than she had first thought. "I'm looking for someone," she replied evasively.

Medafil scowled at her. "Are you a friend of the Queen or not?"

Cara felt herself relax a bit. The clear implication was that only a friend of the Queen would be welcome here. "Friend," she said happily.

"And who are the 'others' you mentioned earlier?"

"I'm traveling with a band of unicorns."

"Then what are you doing out here on your own? Don't you know the danger of leaving the path in *this* forest?"

"I had a . . . a vision. It frightened me, and I ran away. That was pretty stupid, I suppose. But I wasn't thinking straight. About the time I realized I was lost, I heard you moaning —"

"I wasn't moaning," said Medafil sharply. Then, letting his wings sag, he said, "Oh, all right, I was moaning. A little. And you're not going to forget it, are you? Think you have a hook in me now, don't you?"

"Why are you so suspicious?" asked Cara.

"I'm not! And never mind anyway. Now, do you want me to take you back to these unicorns of yours?"

"That would be wonderful."

"All right. I owe you that much at least. But there's no point in looking for them until morning. And

362

there's not much point in staying here, either. Why don't we go back to my aerie?"

"I don't know," said Cara nervously.

"Why are you so suspicious?" asked Medafil mockingly. "If I wanted to eat you, I could do it right here."

"Maybe you want to share me with your mate," replied Cara quickly, surprised at her own boldness. "Or maybe you've got a nest full of babies who prefer their food live."

Medafil turned away. "I have no mate," he said bitterly.

The hurt in his voice was so sharp that Cara's suspicion was replaced by pity. "I'm sorry," she said, stepping forward to stroke his side. "I didn't mean to —"

"Never mind," he said sharply. "Climb on my back, and let's get out of here. No, wait. Go get that bauble they used to trick me with. No sense in leaving it around here for the delvers. Unless you're secretly working for them."

"Don't be silly!"

"Well, you can't be too careful," said the gryphon.

Cara picked up the jewel-crusted sphere, then climbed onto Medafil's back.

"Ready?" he asked. Without waiting for her to an-

SONG OF THE WANDERER

swer, he began to run, flapping his great wings as he did. She leaned forward to grab his feathered neck.

A moment later they were airborne.

Cara cried out in delight as they rose into the night sky. Medafil circled higher and higher. In the moonlight she could not see the details of the land, only the broad strokes of it — the forest, the mountains, and, in the distance, a glimmering body of water. "What's that?" she called.

"What's what?"

"The water over that way."

Medafil shuddered beneath her. "Gaaah! That's Lake Death. Don't talk about it."

He turned away from the lake, beating his wings harder still. They continued to rise. In the moonlight Cara saw the rocky slope of a mountain. The air was cold and thin, and as they neared the mountain she could see that they had passed above the tree line.

"Home," said Medafil a moment later as he settled onto a rocky ledge. Cara slid from his back onto a surface that was littered with an odd collection of items: clean-picked bones, some tiny, some nearly as long as she was tall; a scattering of shiny baubles, some of which looked quite valuable; and a dozen or so long, tawny feathers that looked very much as if they had come from Medafil himself.

"Sorry," said the gryphon, kicking aside a bone. "Not very tidy. Bachelor quarters, you know. View's good, though."

Following the gesture of his wing, Cara turned to look out on the world below. Vast and unsettled, silvered by moonlight, the beauty of the forest that stretched into the distance was so stark, it made her catch her breath. She stared at it for a time, drinking in the wonder of it, then rubbed her arms. "Cold up here," she said.

"Come inside," said Medafil. "It's warmer."

She followed him into the cave that opened at the back of the ledge. "Don't you have any light?" she complained as she stumbled over more debris.

"Why should I? I can see perfectly well in the dark."

"Well, I can't," she replied testily.

"Well, you don't live here," he snapped back. "But if it means that much to you, I'll see what I can do. Hold still. I'll be right back."

This speech was followed by the sound of him rummaging through the debris on the floor. "Drat!" he muttered. "I know that thing was around here some-where. Ouch! Dingfangled pointy things. No, not that. Grambabbit, where is the spartbongle anyway?"

After several minutes of this, he exclaimed tri-umphantly, "There you are, you splitgiddled thing. Thought you could hide from me, did you? Hah! And hah again! Now shine. Shine!"

Nothing happened.

"Drat!" said the gryphon. "I forgot how to make it work. Here, see if you can do anything with the dim-buggery thing."

He dropped a large sphere into Cara's lap. Smooth and cool to the touch, it was nearly the size of a bowl-ing ball. Fortunately, it weighed scarcely more than a feather.

No sooner had Cara placed her hands on it than the sphere began to glow with a soft light.

"Gaaah!" cried Medafil. "I forgot! It only glows for humans. That's why I never use the spligfitted thing."

"It's beautiful," said Cara in awe. "Like a giant pearl lit from inside."

"Well, you can't have it. So don't even think about trying to steal it."

"For heaven's sake! Why are you so suspicious?"

"It's my job. I'm a treasure guardian. I have to be suspicious."

"Don't you trust anyone?"

"Not hardly. Certainly not humans. No, I take that back. There was a human I trusted once, for a while. Until she broke my heart. A girl like you. Little older, maybe. Hard to tell with you humans. We used to call her the Wanderer."

"She's my grandmother!"

"Gaaah!" cried Medafil angrily. He stood, looking suddenly menacing in the pearly light.

Cara shrank back against the wall.

"She owes me something," said the gryphon, looming over her. "An old debt. I think it's time to collect."

He started toward her.

# CHAPTER SEVENTEEN

# SHELL AND SPHERE

Cara stood and began backing away from the gryphon, holding the sphere between them like a shield. "What is it?" she stammered. "What does my grandmother owe you?"

"A kiss! She promised. She promised, and then she left without giving it. A cheat, a cheat after all. And I trusted her!"

Cara blinked. "Is that all? Well, come here, then. I'll be glad to kiss you."

"You will?" asked Medafil suspiciously.

"Certainly." She nearly added that she had always kissed the neighbor's cat back at home, but decided against it. She wasn't sure Medafil would like the comparison.

He sat in front of her, wings tucked against his sides, eyes closed, tail curled around his front paws. Cara set the sphere gently on the cave floor. Then she placed her hands on the gryphon's neck. Stretching upward, she kissed him firmly on his beak.

Medafil opened his eyes. "Well, that's better!" he said happily.

"But why did my grandmother leave without kissing you?" Cara asked. "She always keeps her promises."

"Gaaah! I don't want to talk about it! Well, if you must know, we were having an argument. She was stubborn, even for a human." He sighed. "She said she was coming back. But she didn't. She didn't come back."

"I'm going to get her," said Cara gently. "That's why we're out here in the wilderness to begin with."

Medafil blinked in surprise. "What are you talking about?"

So she told him her story, beginning with the night she had jumped from the tower of St. Christopher's and landed in Luster. As she spoke, he stretched on the floor beside her. After a few minutes she heard a deep *thrum* and realized that he was purring. The purring stopped when she described the path M'Gama had told them to follow.

"Ebillan!" he cried, sitting up. "Gaaah! You can't go there. You'll never come back!"

"I have to go."

Medafil let out a heavy breath. "Well, I may be able to help you through the forest. But when it comes to Ebillan, you're going to be on your own. Gaaah, what a terrible idea!"

He stood and began pacing back and forth, his tail twitching as he did. Suddenly he stopped. "I just remembered something that you should have. Something I want to give you."

He went to the back of the cave. After several minutes of listening to him mutter and fuss, Cara picked up the sphere and walked to where Medafil was standing. "I can see why you have a hard time finding anything," she said, gazing at the pile he was pawing through. It was an odd mixture of natural and hand-crafted items — large gems, ancient-looking daggers, lumps of gold, pieces of driftwood, candles, a crown, two shields, and dozens of other things jumbled together in a huge heap.

"Need a housekeeper," muttered Medafil. "Ah, there we go!"

Reaching forward, using his claws delicately, almost like fingers, he extracted a large seashell from the pile. "Here," he said proudly, passing it to Cara.

Shifting the sphere so that she could hold it in one hand, she took the shell. Its outside was a pale, creamy color and rough to the touch. Turning it over she could see that its deep purple throat — smooth and shiny as burnished metal — curved into hidden depths. "It's beautiful," she said. "But why —"

"Hold it to your ear," said Medafil eagerly.

Cara smiled indulgently, figuring the gryphon thought the old trick of "hearing the ocean" in a shell was some special magic. Not wanting to hurt his feelings, she put the shell to her ear, ready to feign surprise.

Her pretend surprise quickly turned to complete astonishment. Though it was indeed the familiar "roar of the ocean" that she heard at first, it soon faded, to be replaced by the voice of a young woman. Though Cara had never heard the voice before, it was oddly familiar.

The words it sang were even more familiar:

*My heart seeks the hearth,*
*My feet seek the road.*
*A soul so divided*
*Is a terrible load.*

"Where did you get this?" she asked, taking the shell from her ear. She noticed that M'Gama's ring was glowing again, more brightly than ever.

"The Wanderer gave it to me," replied Medafil. "She was supposed to give me a kiss, but she gave me that instead."

"Is that her voice?"

"Of course!" The gryphon looked at her suspiciously. "Don't you recognize her voice?"

"I never heard her voice when she was young," said Cara. "She was much older by the time I was born."

"That makes sense," said Medafil with a nod. "I keep forgetting how quickly you humans age. Anyway, keep the shell. Keep the ball, too, if you like. I don't have much use for it since I can see in the dark. Sort of."

"Thank you," said Cara sincerely. "I don't think I can take the ball, though. It's too big and too fragile. I'm afraid I would break it the first day."

"Oh, nonsense. It's not fragile at all. Watch!"

Reaching forward, the gryphon knocked the glowing sphere out of her hand. Immediately it went black. She heard it hit the stone floor with a bell-like sound, then start to roll away. She could hear Medafil pounce and slam one huge paw down on the sphere, which let out a clear, high note.

"Pick it up," said Medafil.

Groping forward through the darkness, Cara found the gryphon, found his leg, found the sphere. As soon as she picked the ball up, it began to glow again.

"Put one hand on top, the other on the bottom," said Medafil. "That's right. Now twist your hands in opposite directions."

Again, she did as he directed. The sphere began to grow between her hands.

"Oops," said the gryphon. "Try the other way."

She reversed the direction of the twisting. The sphere began to shrink, reducing to the size of a cantaloupe, then a grapefruit, then a tangerine. When it was no bigger than a cherry, she stopped for fear of making it disappear altogether. She held it up for a moment, marveling at its brightness.

"Put it in your pocket," said Medafil.

She did as he instructed. The minute it left her hand the light was extinguished again.

"I'm glad it goes out," she said, "since it would be dangerous if it stayed on all the time. On the other hand, it would be good to be able to let go of it when I'm trying to do something. Is there a way to keep it glowing without holding it?"

"How should I know?" said Medafil, shrugging his wings. "I can't work the gatbangled thing at all! Look, it's getting light. I'd better take you back to your friends before they get worried. Or even worse, before they decide to start looking for you. If they leave the path, we may never be able to find them."

Cara could see just the faintest glimmer of light in the sky at the front of the cave. When she walked toward it and could look out toward the horizon, she saw that fully half the sun was already above the edge of the world.

"You're right!" she said, suddenly terrified that her impulsive action would leave the others thinking something terrible had happened to her — and lead them into danger when they tried to find her. "Let's go. Now!"

"Actually, I'm not sure I want to," said Medafil, sounding sly and stubborn. "Maybe I want you to stay here with me."

"Oh, don't be silly. I have a job to do!"

Medafil sighed. "You sound just like your grandmother."

Cara smiled. "Take me back, and I'll give you another kiss."

"Gaaah! You gave me one kiss because you had to. I don't want another unless you want to give it to me. Come on, let's go."

She mounted his back, and he raced toward the front of the cave. He sprang forward, leaping out over the ledge. When Cara saw the sudden drop beneath them, hundreds of feet down to deadly, jagged rocks, she couldn't help but cry out. But Medafil had spread his great wings and, without even flapping them, he caught an updraft and roared into the sky.

Cara saw Moonheart and the others before they spotted her. When they did look up—it was Finder who spied Medafil first—there was a sudden uproar in the camp. Watching it, Cara could see they feared

Medafil was on the attack; Belle and Lightfoot were already moving into battle position.

Leaning against the gryphon's neck, Cara called, "Don't go too low yet. Let me shout to them first."

Holding his wings steady, Medafil glided down to about fifty feet above the travelers, then banked sideways in a curve so they could see Cara mounted on his back.

"It's all right!" she shouted, waving to them. "He's a friend!"

She could see them relax. A moment later, Medafil landed.

"Thank goodness!" cried Jacques as Cara scrambled down from the gryphon's back. "When I woke and found you were gone, I was afraid something terrible had happened."

"Well, something *terrifying* did happen," said Cara.

As she spoke, the Squijum scrambled up her side to perch on her shoulder. "Bad girl!" he scolded. "Gone long scare Squijum bad! Much naughty!" And with that he gave her hair a yank.

"Ouch!" said Cara. "Cut that out."

"Yike! Don't yell!" He gave her a little kiss on the

cheek, then leaped off her shoulder and ran to hide behind Thomas.

When everyone had gathered, she introduced Medafil, then quickly filled them in on all that had happened the night before, starting with her vision of Beloved.

"Hmmmm," said Thomas, taking out one of his watches and glancing at it.

"What?" asked Cara.

"I'm not sure. But there's something familiar about how it happened. I'm trying to figure out what the connection is, what makes this vision like the one you had back in Summerhaven. But I can't put my finger on it."

"We thank you for taking care of our friend," said Moonheart formally, making a slight bow to Medafil.

"Gaaah! She is a friend of the Queen, whom I honor. She is the grandchild of the Wanderer, whom I love. Of course I took care of her. What kind of framdatted care are *you* taking, leading her into Ebillan's territory?"

"It is the path we were given," said Moonheart.

"How are you planning to get there?" insisted the gryphon.

"We'll continue as we are going now," said

Moonheart. "Through the forest and to the edge of his territory."

"You'll never make it unless you follow my advice. Well, you probably won't follow my best advice, which is to not go there at all. But at least let me help you."

"How?"

"The forest is enchanted. Unless you go the right way, you'll wind up wandering in endless circles and never find your way out." He reached back to preen one of his wings with his beak, then said modestly, "I happen to know the paths."

"The only path we need is the one we're on right now," said Moonheart. "If we stay on it, we'll be just fine." These last words he delivered with a significant look at Cara.

"I know a shortcut," said Medafil, sounding almost desperate now.

Cara, ever aware of the calendar stick she carried in her pack, caught her breath. "Moonheart, that might make all the difference," she said softly.

"How do we know he's not simply going to lead us into some trap?" said Moonheart.

Cara, uncertain how to answer, finally said, "We just have to trust him."

Moonheart looked uneasy.

"Trust beak-faced wingcat?" squeaked the Squijum, peeking out from behind the Tinker's boots.

Medafil started to lunge at the little creature but managed to hold himself back.

"Why not trust now?" asked the Dimblethum. "Can always crunch later if need to."

Moonheart sighed. "Lead on," he said.

"I think I'll go home instead," said Medafil.

But Cara put her hand on his shoulder. "Please?"

"Gaah! Dradfingled girlthings. Always could talk me out of common sense. All right, follow me."

And with that, he plunged into the forest.

It took three days to reach the far side of the forest. During that time Cara grew deeply fond of the crotchety gryphon — despite his constant warnings of impending doom. And he more than proved his worth when he twice kept them from being lured onto a false path that would have sent them wandering in the untracked wilderness.

At night, after they had made camp and settled in to rest, Cara followed two rituals. The first was to take out her calendar stick and cut a notch for the day just past.

The notches were growing numerous, the days left for them to reach Ebillan's cave before the transit point would shift again fewer and fewer.

Once she had marked the stick, she would return it to her pack and take out the shell Medafil had given her. Whenever she held it to her ear to listen to her grandmother's voice, M'Gama's ring would begin to glow with a gentle green light. One night Jacques saw her with the shell and asked about it. Without saying anything, she handed it to him. He put it to his ear. After a moment his eyes widened, then filled with tears.

He sat listening to it for a long time.

The Dimblethum was enormously useful in keeping them fed as they traveled, for he seemed to know every plant that could be used in any way for food. Yet he grew fidgety as they continued. When Cara asked him why, he growled, "The Dimblethum does not like dragons. Most especially, he does not like Ebillan."

This did nothing to make her feel any more comfortable.

Cara noticed that Lightfoot often walked alongside Belle. She wanted to ask him about it but wasn't able to maneuver him away from the others until late in the second day. They were walking at the back of the group, Cara with her hand resting on Lightfoot's shoulder. They were silent for a while. Finally, gathering her courage, she said, "Do you like Belle?"

"What do you mean?"

"You know! Do you *like* her? Do you want her to be your girlfriend?"

Lightfoot curled his lip. "The warrior queen for a girlfriend? Now there's a scary thought. Besides," he muttered, "it wouldn't make any difference if I did."

"What do you mean?" asked Cara.

But he shook his head and said, "If we're going to talk, let's talk about something sensible!"

They spent most of the third day after she met Medafil — the twentieth day of their journey — climbing. At the end of the day they came out on a low cliff. Stretching before them was the Northern Waste, a vast, bleak-looking stretch of land, rocky and nearly bare of vegetation. Smoke curled up from cracks in the ground. Ahead, and to the right, Cara could see a muddy pool that popped and bubbled.

"A vacation paradise," muttered Jacques.

"Ebillan's territory," said the gryphon. He reared back and flapped his wings as if he wanted to get away from the land. "This is where I leave you bitdingled fools. Unless you decide to do something intelligent and turn around, too."

Cara looked at Medafil in surprise. Somehow she had assumed he would continue to travel with them. But, of course, he had no connection to their quest and had only come this far as a courtesy.

She went to stand in front of him. "Thank you for your help."

"Gaaah! What have I done but help you to your doom? Dingbongled dragon will probably eat you before you go two miles into his territory. Why not turn around and come back with me?"

"I can't. You know I can't."

"Gaaah," said Medafil. But this time it was little more than a sigh, and his wings sagged as he said it. "I knew you were stubborn from the minute I met you." He looked around, then straightened his shoulders and said, "All right. I was just testing you, hoping you would see the wisdom of turning back. If you insist on going forward, then so be it. Let's get going."

382

Thus it was that, on the twentieth day of their journey, the Dimblethum, the Squijum, four unicorns, three humans, and one gryphon climbed down the cliff into the Northern Waste that was the territory of Ebillan, the seventh dragon.

To their left the sun was low in the sky. From it stretched brilliant ribbons of red and orange, their garish light making the desolation appear all the more stark. Then, against one of the ribbons of light, Cara saw something else.

"Look," she whispered. "Ebillan. He's coming!"

# CHAPTER EIGHTEEN

# To Bargain
# with a Dragon

Ebillan's body was sinuous, and his long tail writhed and twisted like a snake even as he flew. He was jet-black, save for his eyes, which were a blazing red, and his nostrils, which glowed like hot coals. As he swooped toward them Cara noticed that he was considerably smaller than Firethroat. Even so, each of his bat-like wings was easily as long as a schoolbus.

Suddenly he threw back his head and shot a gout of flame into the darkening purple sky.

Finder stepped back nervously.

"Just a warning," murmured Thomas, and though the words were reassuring, Cara thought he sounded less like he was offering a fact than trying to convince himself that this was the case. She stepped closer to

Lightfoot, who stood tense and ready. Belle was beside him, one foot pawing the stony soil as if she was about to launch herself forward. Moonheart had stepped to the front of the group, where he stood without flinching.

Cupping the air with his wings, Ebillan dropped gracefully to the ground, landing about twenty feet in front of them.

"Yike!" whispered the Squijum, who clung cowering to Cara's neck. The Dimblethum, standing behind her, put one heavy paw on her shoulder.

She glanced over at Medafil. "Gatbimbled thing," muttered the gryphon.

"How dare you enter my territory?" growled Ebillan. His head wove back and forth as he spoke, and his long tongue flicked out of his mouth, nearly lapping against the travelers.

"We come on a mission from the Queen," said Moonheart.

This seemed to surprise the dragon. He looked at them suspiciously for a moment, then said, "An odd group for the Queen to send on a mission."

"We were fewer when we started," said Moonheart. "Others . . . joined us along the way."

385

"What, precisely, is this mission?" hissed Ebillan. Distrust dripped like venom from his words.

Moonheart nodded toward Cara. "This child seeks the Wanderer, in order to bring her back to Luster."

"What does she have to do with me?" The dragon's tail was writhing faster now, knotting about itself, almost as if it were a separate creature. Suddenly he thrust his head forward. A broad crest sprang up around his neck, snapping out so fast it made Cara jump.

Moonheart stood his ground without flinching. "According to the calculations of the Geomancer, the girl's path lies through your cave," he said quietly.

Ebillan threw back his head and roared in fury, sending another column of fire shooting straight above him. "*Through my cave!* You expect me to let this . . . this *human* enter my home?"

"It is the Queen's wish that the child be given free passage," said Moonheart.

"What the Queen wishes is of little interest to me. She's your queen, not mine." The dragon dropped to a crouch, much like a cat about to spring. His tail writhed more wildly than ever. "This is my territory, and I do *not* welcome trespassers, sent by the Queen or not. Those who set foot here pay with their lives."

The sinuous neck reared back. It was about to shoot forward when Cara stepped up beside Moonheart and cried, "Stop!" The word seemed to come from somewhere deep within her, rising from her belly and scorching her throat.

The dragon blinked at her in astonishment. "You speak our tongue?"

It was only then that Cara realized she had addressed Ebillan in the language of the dragons. Smiling slightly, she said, "I have been given the gift of tongues by the Lady Firethroat, who considers me a friend of dragons. I do not think she would take it kindly were she to find that you had eaten me."

Ebillan settled back on his haunches. His tail still writhed, but a little less rapidly now. "Why didn't you tell me this to begin with?"

"I didn't know you were so lacking in courtesy that I would have to claim my dragon friendship merely to save my life."

"Yike!" muttered the Squijum, tightening his grip on her neck. "Be nice!"

"I have little love for humans," muttered Ebillan, sounding slightly embarrassed.

"I do not seek your love," replied Cara sharply.

"Just as well," said Ebillan, and now sarcasm dripped like flame from his words, "as you have little chance of earning it. But what, then, *do* you want?"

"Only what Moonheart has already stated: the right to pass through your cave in order to return to my grandmother's home. I do not seek this boon without offering you something in return."

"Ah," sighed the dragon, sounding almost happy. "You wish to bargain."

"I *offer* to bargain," replied Cara. Reaching into her pack, she closed her fingers over the enormous jewel that Grimwold had given her. She longed to keep it so she could try to see her mother in its crimson depths again. But it had been given to her for this purpose, for bargaining with the dragon. So she pulled it forth and displayed it on her palm, even though doing so felt like taking out a piece of her own heart.

Medafil, standing behind her, sighed when he saw it. "Pretty!" he whispered. *"Pretty!"*

Ebillan's eyes widened in interest. "Very pretty indeed." He extended a claw to take it.

Cara pulled her hand back. "Do we have a bargain?"

The dragon's nostrils flared. "I wish to examine the offer."

Cara hesitated. Lightfoot, who was standing close behind her, whispered, "You can trust him. You have to trust him."

"Indeed she does," said Ebillan. "Don't forget, girl, that I could easily kill you — all of you — and simply take the jewel if I really wanted to. But that is not the dragon way. Now, let me see it."

She stepped toward him, holding up her hand. With talons that looked like burnished metal, he lifted the jewel delicately from her palm.

"Very pretty," said Ebillan again. Then he dropped it back into her hand. "But I think you can do better."

The surge of relief that Cara felt at not having to give up the jewel was quickly replaced by confusion and a touch of anger. "What's wrong with it?" she asked, trying to keep her distress out of her voice. If the dragon wouldn't take this fabulous jewel, what else could she possibly offer him?

"Nothing is wrong with it," said Ebillan smoothly. "In fact, it is flawless. But I believe you can do better."

Cara thought for a moment, then pulled M'Gama's ring from her finger. Hoping the Geomancer would forgive her, she said, "This was a gift from a friend. It is a piece of great beauty, but even more, it is close to my heart. To me, it has much value."

Ebillan took the ring and studied it. "Interesting, but not good enough." Returning the ring to her hand, he added, "Hold on to it, though. It may be of use to you someday."

"How?" asked Cara eagerly as she returned the ring to her finger.

Ebillan snorted. "I am not an oracle. You will have to discover that for yourself. Now, do you have anything else to bargain with, or are you ready to turn around and go?"

For a moment Cara feared that all was lost. Then she remembered the glowing sphere Medafil had given her. She glanced back at the gryphon. Hoping he would not be angry, she reached into her pocket and pulled it forth.

"This is not only beautiful, it is useful," she said. Her words were rueful, for she had planned to use the bauble herself to light her way through darkness for the rest of her life. Twisting the sphere as Medafil had taught her, she expanded it until it was nearly a foot across and looked like a small moon glowing in her hands.

"Very clever," said Ebillan. He took it from her, easily gripping it between two claws, despite its size. To her surprise, the sphere continued to glow, reflecting off the burnished surface of the dragon's talons. He examined it for a moment, then returned it to her hands. "Charming, but I have little need for such a light since I can provide my own."

"Arrogant dragon," muttered Medafil angrily.

Ebillan rolled an eye in the gryphon's direction but did not bother to respond. Instead, he said again to Cara, "Do you have anything else?"

"No," she replied angrily, "I don't!"

Then, her heart sinking, she realized that she did, indeed, have one more item that the dragon might accept. It was a minor thing compared to the others, but closest of all to her heart, even more precious than the sphere, the ring, the jewel.

Slowly, sorrowfully, she reached into her pack and took out Medafil's second gift to her. She heard a little cry of sorrow from Jacques as she brought forth the shell that held her grandmother's voice. Ebillan, however, snorted contemptuously at the sight.

Cara held in a flash of anger. "Though this is more humble," she said enticingly, "it carries a special beauty and is more dear to me than anything else I have offered."

Looking at her with new interest, the dragon took the shell.

"Hold it to your ear," Cara whispered.

Ebillan did as she directed. After a moment he closed his eyes and nodded. The hint of a smile appeared at the corners of his vast, scaly mouth.

Faintly, very faintly, Cara could hear her grandmother's voice singing the now familiar words of "Song of the Wanderer." M'Gama's ring flickered on her finger. It was all Cara could do to keep herself from reaching forward to snatch the shell from Ebillan, to tell him that he couldn't have it after all. She prayed he would reject it, feeling that giving it up was like giving up her closest link to her grandmother.

Then she retracted the prayer, knowing that giving up the shell might be the only way to regain her grandmother.

The dragon put down the shell and sighed. "It will do," he said softly.

Throat tight, heart aching, Cara nodded and whispered, "Then it is yours."

# CHAPTER NINETEEN

# THE TINKER'S DIVERSION

Ebillan's cave was halfway up a stony mountain. Since the black dragon was much smaller than Firethroat and had no interest in carrying them anyway, they had to walk the entire distance across the bleak and blistering territory, which took them nearly a week.

Finder led the group now, picking a safe way across the treacherous lands of the Northern Waste through some process that only he understood. By the end of the second day, even Belle had expressed a grudging admiration for the skill with which he steered them away from sinkholes and gas vents — a skill that became more obvious when he had started down one path and then abruptly turned back only moments before a gout of vile-smelling flame erupted from the ground, sending rocks the size of Cara's head several dozen feet in the air.

Every evening at sunset Cara made another mark on her counting stick. When they reached the foothills that led to Ebillan's mountain home, only four days remained until the beginning of autumn and the end of the cave's usefulness as her point of passage.

With her goal so close and time so short, Cara found herself nearly frantic with impatience at being forced to trudge along a seemingly endless path. She watched the sky anxiously. The days were growing shorter; even more than her wooden calendar, they assured her that the first day of autumn was nearly upon them. She was terrified of arriving too late, of finding that she would not be able to use the cave as a transit to her grandmother's home after all.

"I can fly you if need be," offered Medafil.

"A noble suggestion, and one we may yet need," said Moonheart. "But we do still have a little time, and I would rather Cara not enter Ebillan's home without all of us to guard her."

"You don't think he'll betray us, do you?" she asked.

"Dragons claim to be bound by their word," said Moonheart. "Even so, I would just as soon not push our luck on that front too hard."

And so they trudged onward.

Though Thomas's cart moved easily over the foot-hills, when they reached the base of the mountain itself two days later he folded it down to its smallest size — no bigger than a man's wallet — and tucked it into one of his pockets.

"Well," he said, squaring his shoulders, "a tinker's trade takes him many places. Even so, this is one spot in Luster I had never planned to visit. Ah, well. Upward, friends!"

And up they went.

It was the next-to-last day of summer.

Ebillan was lolling at the mouth of his cave when the group arrived. They were exhausted by the climb and ravenously hungry as well, since they had found little to eat during the final stage of their journey.

"I wondered if you would make it," said the dragon casually. "Perhaps you are more serious about this trip than I realized."

"If I weren't serious, you wouldn't have that shell right now," snapped Cara, in no mood for the dragon's rudeness.

"And if I weren't kinder than you think, *you* would be nothing more than a bit of well-grilled meat," replied the dragon smoothly. "I'm tempted to simply return your shell and tell you to go back the way you came. I don't need your snippiness here in my home."

The Dimblethum growled. Cara, repenting her rash words and terrified that she might have ruined the bargain, put a cautioning hand on his thick arm.

The uncomfortable silence that hung between Cara and Ebillan was broken, unexpectedly, by Thomas.

"You don't happen to have anything that needs fixing, do you?" asked the Tinker in a cheerful voice. "Something in the treasure pile that's a little bent and worn, perhaps?"

"What are you talking about?" asked the dragon. Though his voice was surly, it was clear that he was intrigued.

"My trade," said Thomas. "I am a traveling tinker. I mend things. It's my job. Knowing dragons — I have met a few in my day; in fact Fah-Leing is rather a friend

396

of mine — it wouldn't surprise me if you might not have need of my services."

The expression on Ebillan's face was unreadable.

"I can fix practically anything," continued the Tinker encouragingly.

The dragon made a noise deep in his throat. "All right," he said at last. "Come inside."

They entered the cave, which was rank with the smell of sulfur.

"Wait here," said the dragon. Then he turned and headed for the back of the cave.

The sound of Ebillan's scales slithering across the stone floor made Cara shiver. She took Medafil's sphere from her pack and twisted it between her hands until it was about half a foot wide. Its pearly light revealed two openings at the back of the cave. Ebillan vanished into the one on the left.

"Big hotmouth bad ptooie!" muttered the Squijum once the dragon was out of sight.

"Shhhh," cautioned Lightfoot. "His ears may be better than you think."

"And you're the perfect size for a quick snack," added Belle, glaring at the Squijum.

While they were talking, Thomas sidled over to Cara. "If I can get him distracted, and I think I can, head for the back of the cave and go on through to your home. It may be your only chance."

"Won't he be furious?"

"Not if I do my work well enough. And time is precious. We can't waste any more of it. Shhh! He's coming back!"

At first, Cara thought Ebillan hadn't brought anything with him. But when he reached them, he opened his mouth. Out fell a gem-studded goblet made of gold and so big Cara would have had to use both hands to hold it. One side was torn by a jagged split, as if the goblet had been pulled apart by some great force.

Thomas bent to pick it up. "Ow!" he cried. Standing, he began passing it from hand to hand. "Still hot," he explained.

"Fix it," said Ebillan.

"Your wish is my command," replied the Tinker so smoothly that Cara couldn't tell if he was being sarcastic or not.

He placed the cup gently on the floor, then began to

unfold his cart. "Convenient sort of thing, isn't it?" he asked, glancing up at Ebillan as he worked.

The dragon nodded, obviously astonished—something Cara would have thought impossible.

Once the cart was at full size, Thomas went inside. Cara could hear the clatter of tools as he rummaged around. "All set," he said happily, reappearing a few minutes later. "Now, Ebillan, if you could warm this up for me again. Just a bit! I only want to soften the metal."

Heating things "just a bit" turned out not to be something that came easily to the dragon. Finally Thomas discovered that, using a pair of tongs, he could soften the metal of the goblet by holding it inside one of Ebillan's nostrils. Soon the musical *clink* of the Tinker's tools was echoing from the stony walls of Ebillan's cave.

"Beautiful piece," said Thomas as he worked. "What happened to it, anyway?"

"I'd rather not say," growled the dragon.

"Probably did it himself," muttered Lightfoot, who was standing next to Cara.

Ebillan hissed angrily. "You forget yourself, unicorn.

My hearing is indeed better than you think. But you are right. I did do it myself. This cup was the cup of my heart. From it I drank the flaming dragonwine that is used in our pledging ceremony. With it I pledged myself to the Lady Nakreema."

"What happened to it?" asked Cara, feeling a tug of sympathy for the dragon in spite of his nastiness.

The flames flickering around Ebillan's nostrils grew brighter. "Long ago, even before the unicorns left Earth, the dragons began to flee to another world. Their reasons were much the same. Earth was becoming hostile to magic, and to magic's children. And they were being hunted, though not so fiercely as the unicorns later were by Beloved and her descendants.

"A magician named Bellenmore—the same one who later helped the unicorns—opened a gate for us. Not all fled. Some of us refused to leave our home, refused to let the humans force us out. Nakreema and I argued about whether to leave. She insisted we had to go. I, being stubborn, insisted on staying. Finally she left without me. I swore a dragon oath that I would see her again, that either I would come for her if things got better, or go to live in that other world myself if things on Earth got worse."

He turned his head away from them. When he spoke again, his voice was soft, like a whisper of flame. "Finally, of course, I did have to leave. But I had waited too long, decided too late, and though dragons can move between worlds, the gate to this new world was closed to us by the very magic that had opened it. Thus when the last seven dragons of Earth—Firethroat, Redrage, Fah-Leing, Master Bloodtongue, Graumag, Bronzeclaw, and myself—finally admitted defeat, and agreed that we had to flee as well, Luster was the only choice left to us."

"A tragic story," murmured Jacques mournfully.

Ebillan swung his head back. "Luster is not my home! That other world, the world where my lost love lives, is not home. *Earth* is home. But Earth, like my love, is lost to me. No dragon can live there now. Too much of the magic has been drained, and we would quickly sicken and die. Even if not, we would be hunted and killed—or, even worse, imprisoned. Do you wonder, human child, that I have little love for your kind?"

He lifted his head and shot forth a gout of flame. It struck the cave's ceiling, then spread across it and down the walls. For one terrifying moment Cara thought it would engulf them all. But Ebillan closed his mouth, and the flame vanished. He dropped his head to the floor. "I tore that cup as a sign of my own broken oath," he whispered sadly. "I did it in a moment of rage and sorrow. Now I repent of my rashness and wish to have it repaired."

Thomas looked up. "I shall do my best," he said. Then, putting his tongue firmly between his teeth, which he did whenever he wanted to concentrate, the Tinker returned his attention to the goblet.

Ebillan settled before him, watching the work with fascination.

Cara stood back, watching as well—watching the dragon watch the Tinker. She was torn about what to do, wanting to take advantage of the opening Thomas had offered, yet terrified that if she did, it would put her friends in jeopardy.

And outside, the sun was sinking toward the horizon, bringing an end to the next to the last day of summer.

Thomas glanced in her direction and seemed startled to see she was still there. He motioned toward the back of the cave with his head, urging her to go.

402

She placed a hand on Lightfoot's shoulder. "Thomas is doing all this so that I can slip away," she told him, speaking mind to mind. "I'm going to go through now."

"Do you think that is wise?" he asked fretfully.

Almost without her thinking about it, Cara moved her fingers to the gold chain that held the amulet around her neck. She glanced around. Ebillan's eyes were still fixed on Thomas and the golden cup. "It's now or never," she thought to Lightfoot.

"Go in safety," he replied. "Come back soon."

Moving silently, as silently as she had on the night when she and her grandmother were pursued into St. Christopher's by the Hunter she later discovered to be her father, Cara slipped toward the back of the cave.

She peered into the opening Ebillan had entered, the one on the left.

In the distance she could see the glitter of gold.

She stepped to the right.

A short passage led to a smaller cave. It was made of crystal, just as M'Gama had said.

Still moving silently, Cara made her way to the cave. Entering it, she felt as if she had stepped into a diamond. The faceted walls caught the light of Medafil's sphere, reflecting it around her until the brilliance was almost painful. Quickly she twisted the sphere down to marble size and tucked it into her pocket.

Now the crystal cave was dark and silent. Feeling slightly guilty yet at the same time wildly excited, she clutched the amulet, then whispered the spell that would return her to Earth.

"Luster, let me go."

The world swirled green around her. She felt as if she were falling, then as if she were being blown across time by the breath of God. How many minutes, hours, days went by, she could not guess.

Then, so suddenly it left her blinking, she was standing in the kitchen of the house she had shared with her grandmother during the last year.

Luster was gone. She was back on Earth at last.

She glanced around. The kitchen was clean and tidy, just as her grandmother always kept it.

That was a good sign, but not proof. Part of her was still terrified that her grandmother might be gone, that this might be someone else's house now. What would she do then?

She slipped the chain back over her neck and tucked the amulet under her shirt.

She thought about calling out, then decided against it. She didn't want to startle Grandmother Morris with her sudden arrival—or possibly alert some new tenant to the fact that there was an intruder.

But what was the best thing to do now? For all that she had thought of this moment, ached for it, worked toward it, she was not sure how to handle it.

Torn between eagerness and dread, Cara moved to the door that led to the living room. Cautiously, silently, she swung it open.

A woman stood by the window, gazing into the night below. At the sound of Cara's entrance, she turned.

Cara cried out in horror.

# CHAPTER TWENTY

# BELOVED

Welcome, wandering child," whispered the woman. She winced and closed her eyes, as if experiencing some horrible pain. After a moment the spasm passed. Opening her eyes again, she said, "I have been waiting for you to return, my many-times great-granddaughter."

Heart pounding, chest tight, throat so dry she could hardly speak, Cara whispered, "Where is my grandmother?"

"She is wandering, of course. Just as you have been doing. Since she isn't here, I thought I would come and wait for you instead."

A terrible emptiness seemed to swallow Cara. To come all this way and find that her grandmother was gone seemed too much to bear. But then, it would have been even worse to find her a prisoner of Beloved. Fighting to speak calmly, she said, "Is my grandmother safe?"

Beloved shrugged. "I expect so. I don't really care. It's you I'm interested in."

"Me?" asked Cara nervously.

"I've come to take you away with me, dearest. Remember, I am your grandmother, too, though many times farther back. It is time for you to join us, child. Time for you to take your place in our family."

Beloved smiled and took a step toward Cara, then winced again. Even in pain her pale skin was smooth, her features unutterably lovely. Her winter-white hair, curling and wispy like a unicorn's mane, hung well below her waist. The gray irises of her eyes were cold and looked like stone, though in their centers the pupils blazed a hot, terrifying red.

Cara backed away. Without intending to, she began to lift her hand to her neck, reaching toward the amulet. The hungry flicker in Beloved's eyes made her stop. Of course! Beloved wanted the amulet. Her father had told her as much, told her that when Beloved had it, she would be able to open her own gate into Luster, and lead the Hunt into the very world where the unicorns had fled to be safe.

Cara's mind began to race. She had to keep the amulet away from Beloved. But how? She thought, briefly, of trying to fling it through the window. Her heart flinched at the thought; in doing so, she would lock herself out of Luster, too.

She might have done it anyway, only Beloved stood between her and the window, and it seemed likely that if she tried the woman would somehow intercept the amulet.

Her second thought was that she should simply slip back into Luster. But she feared that if she did, Beloved might come with her. She was fairly certain that was how her father had gotten into Luster the last time.

That might not be all bad. Maybe once they had Beloved in Luster they could — what? Kill her? Cara couldn't imagine the unicorns doing that, though Beloved had been responsible for the death of so many unicorns. Imprison her? Cure her? Put her to sleep forever, like the Hunter who had attacked Moonheart all those years ago in the cave in England?

BELOVED

Or would she run amok, cause destruction beyond imagining? Cara had no idea how powerful Beloved was, how much magic she controlled. Once in Luster might she be able to summon the Hunters, open a door for them to invade?

"You seem frightened," said Beloved gently. "I'm not going to hurt you, child."

"You'd hurt the unicorns if you could."

Beloved's red eyes blazed, but she kept her voice soft, almost a purr. "There is a great deal that you don't understand," she murmured. Another spasm of pain twisted her face.

"Where is my grandmother?" asked Cara again. "What have you done with her?"

"I told you, she is wandering."

"Where? I want to know *where!*"

Beloved smiled. "Give me the amulet, and I'll tell you."

Cara gasped and felt as if Beloved had somehow managed to reach inside and grab her own heart. Was this what it would come down to? Trade the amulet for her grandmother? The unicorns for the Wanderer?

She knew at once what her grandmother would want, and shook her head. "I can't do that."

Beloved shrugged, as if it was of little matter to her.

Cara stared at the woman, trying to understand her. If only Beloved could know the unicorns the way she did, could see how kind and good they were, maybe she would let go of her quest for vengeance.

"The unicorns are my friends," she said softly. "They're not bad, like you think. They're not —"

"Quiet!" shrieked Beloved. "You miserable brat, who do you think you are to tell me about the unicorns? What do you know, what can you know, in the tiny amount of time you've been alive? Did the unicorns kill *your* father? Did they curse *you* with a pain-laced life that goes on and on, never letting you die?" Her features writhed, and then she gained control of them once more. "The unicorns are nice," she simpered. "The unicorns are kind. You driveling nitwit. What can you possibly know about their evil, their deceit, their vileness?"

Panting, Beloved lunged toward her.

Cara ducked aside. Beloved spun and, with astonishing speed, lunged again. This time she caught Cara by the arm. They tumbled to the floor together.

"I *will* have that amulet!" shrieked Beloved, clawing at Cara's neck.

Cara grabbed the woman's wrists and tried to push them back, but Beloved was strong, terribly strong. Then another spasm of pain struck. Beloved shuddered and cried out, and her grip weakened. Cara wrenched herself away, then rolled over so that her face was to the floor. Tucking her fists against her jaw, her arms tight against her sides, she pressed down, trying to meld herself with the carpet.

Beloved pulled at her arms, and then her hair. "Roll over!" she cried. *"Roll over!"*

Cara pushed herself down even harder, praying for the moment to end, for Beloved to vanish. But like a madwoman, she continued to claw at Cara. Then, suddenly, the attack stopped. For an instant Cara thought Beloved had given up. Then she felt her hands on her ankles. Before Cara could do a thing about it, Beloved had flipped her over.

Cara pulled back her feet, then thrust them forward as hard as she could, catching Beloved in the chest. Eyes widening in astonishment, the white-haired woman staggered back against the wall. Cara scrambled to her feet and headed for the window. She *would* fling the amulet out, even if it meant she could never get back to Luster herself. But she hesitated for just a moment, stopped by a new fear: What if someone else found it, someone who shouldn't go to Luster?

*They wouldn't know how to use it,* she told herself.

The instant's hesitation was all Beloved needed. She hurled herself across the room and grabbed Cara from behind. With her tight embrace pinning Cara's arms to her sides, Beloved began to whisper in the girl's ear. "You mustn't be like this," she crooned. "Grandmother Beloved doesn't like it. Be good, and Grandmother Beloved will be good to you. Be nice, and Grandmother Beloved will be nice to you. I'll teach you secrets you never imagined, Cara. There is so much waiting for you, child. Things you've never dreamed of, things the unicorns would never have told you about." She paused as another wave of pain shuddered through her, and then went on again, her voice low and seductive. "I know deep and secret places in the world, unsuspected beauties, mysteries beyond anything most humans can even guess at. Give yourself to me, Cara. Let your blood answer its call. You are one of my children. You *are* a Hunter, and it's not right, not good, for you to resist me like this. Just relax, dearheart. Relax and let Grandmother Beloved take care of everything for you. No need to think, no need to worry. Relax. Relax."

Her voice was soothing, hypnotic. Against her will, Cara began to sag in the woman's arms. She could feel one of Beloved's hands creeping toward the chain that held the amulet — could feel it, but didn't seem to be able to do anything about it.

"Relax," whispered the voice, which came to her as through a fog. "Relax into the mystery and the beauty that only I can give you. Relax, and when you do, I can take you back to your mother. Relax and —"

"That's enough!" A familiar voice, strong and sharp, cut through the velvet of Beloved's words. The woman's grip faltered, and Cara slithered out of her arms.

"Jacques!" cried Cara. "How did you —" She broke off. Not only was her grandfather standing in the doorway that led to the kitchen, but next to him was Lightfoot.

A new wave of terror washed over her. "Lightfoot, what are you doing here? Go. *Go!*"

Her words were drowned in Beloved's shriek of rage. "To me, my children!"

From the hallway, where they had been waiting in silence, rushed seven men. They were dressed in black and armed with glistening swords.

Cara cried out in fear and confusion when she saw that the man at the front of the group was her father.

Lightfoot reared back and trumpeted a challenge, the tip of his horn grazing the ceiling.

The men raced toward him. His hooves flashed forward, raining silver blows among them. The attackers dropped back, but not before one managed to slash open Lightfoot's side with his sword. Crimson and silver blood spurted from the wound.

Jacques hurtled forward in a series of handsprings, which ended with his feet smashing into the chin of one of the Hunters. The man let out a startled cry, then crumpled to the floor.

"One down!" crowed Jacques, looking happier than Cara had ever seen him.

Two others turned toward him. He began to leap and spin like some demented dervish, his agility astonishing for someone his age. One of the men rushed forward. Jacques ducked underneath his arm, came up be-hind him as he rushed past, and gave him a solid kick in the back of the head that sent him sprawling.

"Fools rush in," Jacques murmured in satisfaction.

Now half the men had turned their attention toward the old tumbler. The others, swords raised and ready, stood facing Lightfoot.

Though Cara had started forward when she saw Lightfoot wounded, Beloved had again grabbed her from behind. Now, despite her desperate struggles, the woman held her fast.

Bugling in fury, Lightfoot lunged toward them, plowing past the men, knocking two of them down, ig-noring the second and third wounds that scored his sides. Cara struggled to break free.

The room was a madhouse of sound and fury, the battle made awkward by the close quarters. The men bumped into furniture, scrambled over it, leaped over it, stumbled and fell over it. One screamed in pain, then fell writhing to the floor when Light-foot's flashing hooves struck his arm and snapped the bone.

"Enough!" cried Beloved in a voice so powerful it

sliced through the chaos and turmoil, so commanding that all eyes turned toward her.

All eyes save Cara's.

For Beloved held her from behind. The woman had one arm around Cara's neck. Her other hand, which clutched a silver dagger, was poised above Cara's heart.

# CHAPTER TWENTY-ONE

# BETRAYAL

The battle stopped. Jacques and Lightfoot stood without moving. Three of the men lay moaning on the floor. One of the men still standing raised his sword as if to plunge it into Lightfoot's side.

"Not now, Marcus," snapped Beloved. "Better to do it later, with ceremony and ritual. You'll waste too much magic this way. Kenneth, bring the binding."

A tall man with reddish-gold hair stepped toward Lightfoot. From his hand dangled a golden bridle.

When the unicorn shied away, Beloved said sharply, "Careful, beast!"

The woman's voice was ragged with pain, and Cara could feel the shudder that rippled through her. She tried to take advantage of the moment to squirm free of Beloved's grasp. It did no good. Beloved tightened

417

her grip and brought the tip of her silver dagger to rest directly against Cara's chest.

Lightfoot, watching, shook his head. "Be still, Cara," he whispered.

She slumped back and watched helplessly as the golden bridle was placed over his head. To her horror, the moment it was on him she could see him relax, falling calm and docile under the bridle's spell. She felt as if all hope had been ripped from her heart.

"Good," murmured Beloved. "Now he is ours, to do with as we will." Then, as if she had barely noticed Jacques until now, she said, "Ian, bind the old man. Tightly!"

Ian. Ian Hunter. Cara's father.

Her father, who hadn't even acknowledged her presence.

*That's all right,* she thought fiercely. *He's not my father anymore. I don't want him!*

Even so, it hurt that it was her father who pushed Jacques into a chair, her father who pulled the old man's hands behind his back and bound them with black cord, her father who bound his feet as well, tying them to the legs of the chair so that he couldn't even hobble away.

Bitterness rose within her, so strong she could taste it. How could he do these things?

"Good," said Beloved. She lowered the knife and stepped away from Cara. "Now, Great-granddaughter, let us try talking again. There are things you need to know, things you do not understand. Sit down. I want to take a look at our captive."

Cara did as the woman directed — partly because one of the Hunters came to stand beside her to make sure she didn't try to escape.

Beloved walked around Lightfoot, studying him carefully. He stood, docile and unflinching, even when she poked at his wounds. His flanks were drenched in his own blood, silver and scarlet, and the sight was like acid in Cara's eyes. She longed to heal him but could not; longed to save him but didn't know how.

When Beloved was done, her face glowed with triumph. "This is better than I could have hoped for! Do you know what we have here, my children? A unicorn of the royal family. Not merely of royal blood, but next in line for the throne. We have captured Prince Lightfoot himself."

Cara blinked in astonishment. She had known

Lightfoot was the Queen's grandson. But next in line for the throne? How could this be?

Following hard on that question came another, one she had lost track of in the chaos of the fight: *How had Jacques and Lightfoot crossed to Earth?*

She realized it was possible she might never find out because she might never speak to either of them again . . . might never again see them alive.

She blinked back tears, telling herself to keep strong.

Beloved returned to Cara. Reaching down, she hooked a slender finger under the chain that held the amulet. Tugging at it, she pulled the amulet from under Cara's shirt. It rested in her palm, golden and sparkling, the luminous white hair from a unicorn's mane curled beneath its crystal lid.

"Soon," she murmured. "Soon."

Then she dropped the chain.

"Aren't you going to take it?" asked Cara in surprise.

"I will if I have to. But it will do less damage to the magic if you give it to me freely."

Cara snorted.

"Don't be rude, child. I *could* simply take it if I wanted to. Or I could bargain with you — the amulet for the life of one of your friends over there."

Cara felt her head swim. Would she trade the amulet for Jacques or Lightfoot? Of course! Except . . . except if she did, how many more unicorns would die as a result?

"That would be better. But it would be better still," continued Beloved, "if you simply *gave* it to me because you finally understood that what I am doing is right, and that you have been tricked and used by the unicorns."

Her face writhed, and she gasped for breath. The moment passed, and she composed her features again.

"You have been deceived, Cara — fooled into thinking these creatures are kind and compassionate. This is not true. They are brutal and vicious."

Jacques leaned forward. "That's a lie, a total — "

His words were cut off by a backhanded blow from Marcus.

Beloved sighed. "It is hard to reason with you with all this distraction, Great-grandchild." She glanced up at the man standing beside Cara's chair. "Anders, you and Marcus take the old man into the next room. I don't want to hear from him again."

"Jacques!" cried Cara as the two men picked up the chair to which her grandfather was bound and carried him into the kitchen.

The door slammed shut.

"Why are you doing these things?" asked Cara. "Why won't you leave us in peace?"

Beloved looked down at Cara. In the woman's stony eyes there was, at last, some look of humanity — traces of pity, of anger, of sorrow.

"Listen to me carefully, child. I am older than you can imagine, so do not think you can speak to me of things you scarcely understand. I have lived an eternity etched by pain, staggered through centuries with a fire gnawing at my heart. After the unicorns fled from Earth, I was lost. Where could I turn my anger, how seek my revenge? I tried for a time equal to the lives of many mortals to find a way into Luster so I could lead my children there to finish what we had begun, but I was blocked at every turn. Finally weariness overcame me, and I let my efforts lapse. I couldn't die, but I had nothing to live for. I wept and I brooded, haunted by the image of the unicorn that had pierced my heart, then killed my father. And my heart throbbed in constant agony from the piece of horn that lances and heals it with every breath I take."

She fell silent for a moment, staring out the window. Almost against her will, Cara said, "And then?"

Beloved smiled, a cold and terrifying sight. "And then you happened."

Cara fought to keep her voice from trembling. "What do you mean?"

"I was only vaguely aware of your father; he was but one of thousands of my descendants scattered around the world. I kept an eye on all of them, of course, but in my weariness I had ceased to choose new ones to train in the Hunt. What was the point? My enemies had fled, and I could not get at them. All gone." She paused and smiled. "Well, all save one. There is almost always one unicorn here on Earth. The Guardian of Memory, they call him. Sometimes" — here she paused again and closed her eyes in ecstasy — "ah, sometimes my Hunters would find that one and slay him! Then, for a moment, my heart would be at peace. But another would come. Always, sooner or later, another would come. What I wanted, *craved*, was a path into Luster itself. Only then could the Hunt be properly concluded. Only then could I finish my job and rest. Only then would the wound in my heart finally heal for good and all.

"We sought the gates, but could not find them. However, there was one other possibility. I knew there was a key, an amulet here on Earth with which I could open a new gate to Luster. I knew, too, that it belonged to Ivy Morris. But we could not locate it. She would not stay put, and her wandering defeated my efforts to find her. Until Ian, dear Ian, married your mother. I did not realize, at first, that one of my children had connected to the family of the Wanderer. It was only when you were sick, and your grandmother summoned a unicorn to heal you, that I understood what luck had come my way.

"But the very night that I made contact with your father, that I came to tell him his true heritage, your grandmother disappeared, taking you with her. Oh, the Wanderer was a clever one. She knew I was after her. After you. After the amulet."

Cara groaned. So it was true. Her grandmother *had* stolen her from her parents.

Or had she? Could she trust what Beloved was telling her? Was it possible she was lying, even now?

"Your father was wild in his grief over losing you. But it also proved to him that what I had told him about the unicorns and their evil was true."

"But the unicorn cured me!" protested Cara.

"Because the Wanderer summoned him," repeated Beloved, speaking very slowly, as if she felt Cara had failed to understand something utterly simple. "The unicorns have their human allies, friends who have traded their duty and obligation for a bit of glamour and magic. Of course he cured you! They wanted to use you — use you to get at *me*."

Cara blinked. That couldn't be true, could it? Yet she knew how the unicorns hated and feared Beloved.

She shook her head, trying to drive away the poison Beloved was pouring into her ears. If the unicorns wanted to use her to get at Beloved, they would have been able to do it long before this.

"Where is my mother?" she asked. "What have you done with her?"

"Your mother is somewhere safe," said Beloved. Then, coaxingly, she added, "I can take you to her, you know."

Cara felt her heart leap. She glanced at her father. His face remained still, unreadable.

"Oh, it's going to be so lovely," continued Beloved. "You can be with your parents again, just like you've always wanted, Cara. You'll be home at last, and your heart will be able to rest." She clutched her own heart, her ever-wounded, ever-healing heart. "As will mine. For just as you will gain your heart's desire, so will I when I fling wide the gate and send my children to Luster. For am I not the Ravager? Is it not written in my stars — the very stars through which I have twice made contact with you — that I shall be the one to bring the murdering beasts to justice?"

Cara gasped. "The Ravager! The constellation! That was how you were able to get to me!"

Beloved went on as if she had not heard. "Oh, how the blood will flow when the Ravager finally enters Luster! And once the Hunt is done, once the unicorns are *all* gone, the fire in my heart will be gone, too. Then, finally, I will be free!"

Her eyes were wild now, glazed with the passion of the Hunt as she imagined it. "All I need is the amulet. Give it to me, Cara. Give it to me and you can join me, join your father and find your mother. We'll be together, all of us."

Lightfoot stood, impassive, held by the magic of the golden bridle.

Cara turned away.

"Look at me!" screeched Beloved. She reached out, grabbed Cara by the chin, forced her to stare directly into those blazing eyes. "It is time, child; time to give me the amulet. Give it, or I will take it. Give it freely and join us, or have it ripped away and be cast away yourself, away from the Hunters, away from your family, away from your own blood. Choose, Cara. Choose now. For I *will* have that amulet, what ever way you decide. I'll have it, with you or without you. The unicorns are going to die anyway. Are you going to join me, or not? Do you want — "

"Stop!" cried Cara, clamping her hands over her ears. "Stop!"

"No!" shrieked Beloved. "The time for stopping is past. Choose! Choose now! My blood runs in your veins, Cara. You are part of an ancient story. It is time for you to take your place and play your role. I was a child when it began. You are the child born to help me end it."

Cara wrenched herself away. Beloved lunged at her, clutched the amulet.

"Let me go!" cried Cara. "I choose the unicorns. *I choose the unicorns!*"

Beloved hissed in fury, wound her fist in the amulet's

chain, pulled at it, choking Cara as she tried to wrench it from her neck.

"That's enough," said a deep voice.

A pair of hands grabbed Beloved from behind.

Cara looked up in astonishment. Then she closed her eyes and whispered, "Thank you . . . Daddy."

Her father stood there, holding Beloved by the arms. Kenneth, the only other Hunter who had remained standing in the room, was crumpled on the floor. Lightfoot, no longer restrained by the golden bridle, stood guarding the door to the room where the other two men had taken Jacques.

Beloved, wild with fury, struggled in Ian Hunter's arms. "Traitor!" she shrieked as he pried her fingers from the amulet's chain. "Betrayer!"

"Perhaps," he said grimly. "But was I not betrayed myself when I lost my daughter to the struggle between you and the Wanderer? I lost her again in Firethroat's cave because of your teachings and my own stubborn blindness. I would have lost her a third time tonight. But her courage has opened my eyes."

The muscles in his lean arms rippled as he forced Beloved around so that she was facing him, moving his hands so that they gripped her wrists. Her fingers arched like claws, straining for his eyes. But he held her tight, and she could not reach him.

"It is enough, Grandmother Beloved," he said between clenched teeth. "Let it go. Let it go!"

She spat in his face. He drew back, startled. In his moment of surprise, Beloved broke free of his grip and raked her fingers down his cheek, leaving four streaks of blood.

"I'll let nothing go, you spineless pup!" she shrieked. Then, suddenly, she collapsed, falling limp into his arms. "All these years," she moaned. "All these years! Oh, Ian, Ian, how could you betray me like this?"

Tenderly, Ian Hunter lowered the ancient woman to the floor, where she curled in a miserable heap, weeping. Stepping past her, he reached toward his daughter. Cara stretched her hands toward him, tears streaming down her own face as she did.

Before they could embrace, Beloved was on her feet again. "Betrayer!" she cried.

Then she plunged the silver dagger into his back.

# CHAPTER TWENTY-TWO

# UPSTAIRS

C ara stood frozen with horror, her hands still outstretched to where her father had been standing.
Then something deep within, a rage and a strength she
had not known she possessed, took over. She launched
herself at Beloved. Knocking the knife from the
woman's hand, she carried Beloved backward with her
momentum. Together, they tumbled to the floor.

Again, Beloved clutched at the amulet. But before
she could take it from Cara, Lightfoot entered the fray.
Snatching the woman's robe in his teeth, he hauled her
from Cara.

With a cry of rage, Beloved ripped away. She threw
herself across the floor, toward the silver dagger. Cara
was there first. Kicking the blade, she sent it skittering
toward the hallway.

The door to the kitchen burst open. Anders and Marcus, the Hunters who had hauled Jacques away, came running in.

Lightfoot turned to face them. Anders, sword in hand, slashed at Lightfoot, but the unicorn was too fast for him and danced nimbly away despite his wounds.

Marcus raced to Beloved, knelt beside her, and whispered urgently to her.

She was on her feet in an instant. "To me!" she cried in triumph. "Come to me, my children!"

Even as she spoke, she hurried to one of the fallen Hunters and stood astride his body.

At her call, Anders backed away from Lightfoot. The unicorn, who had been rearing defiantly, dropped to all fours. He watched the men cautiously. Marcus and Anders each grabbed one of the other men who had been rendered helpless during the first fight — one unconscious, the other unable to walk — and dragged them to Beloved's side.

Cara, with no one to stop her, had also raced to a fallen Hunter. Her father. She knelt beside him, tears streaming down her face. His hand closed over hers, weak but warm, and she felt a surge of relief. He was still alive!

But what was Beloved up to?

When the Hunters were gathered close around her — the last of them had dragged himself to her side — she lifted her hands.

"This round is yours, grandchild," she said, her eyes narrow and filled with hate. "But the battle is not over. In fact, it's just beginning, as you will soon see, my stubborn one."

She spread her arms, encircling the Hunters with her black cloak, which seemed to billow and expand as she lifted her arms. As the cloak swirled around her, she uttered some words in a deep, guttural voice.

With a flash, the group vanished.

"I don't like this," said Lightfoot. "What is she up to?"

"Never mind that now!" cried Cara urgently. "My father is hurt. You are, too, I know. But I think he's dying. Can you heal him?"

Lightfoot hurried to her side.

"The cut is deep and bitter," he said after probing the wound with his horn. "Not only blade but poison is at work here. Even so, I think it can be healed. Though why I should heal a Hunter . . ."

"He saved us!"

"Oh, I know," said Lightfoot wearily. "Another renegade. I'll probably end up liking him. Well, let me do my work. You had best go check on your grandfather."

With a throb of guilt, Cara realized she had almost forgotten Jacques. Had the Hunters hurt him? *Killed him?* Longing to stay to make sure her father was properly healed, yet trusting Lightfoot and knowing there was nothing more she could do here, she hurried to the next room.

A cold dread seized her. Jacques, still tied to the chair, sagged in his bonds. His head was slumped onto his chest. Hurrying to his side, she was relieved to find he was still breathing. She saw no blood, no stab wounds. But when she knelt beside him to try to wake him, she noticed an egg-sized lump on the side of his head.

"Poor Grampa," she whispered softly. She set to work untying his bonds. When she had him free, she lowered him gently to the floor. She looked around for something to cushion his head but saw nothing that would work. "I'll be back," she whispered. Then she returned to the living room.

Lightfoot was lying on his side, his eyes closed. He lifted his head when he heard her enter. "It's done," he told her quietly. "Your father will live." Then he dropped his head back to the floor, closed his eyes, and slept.

Ian Hunter still lay facedown on the floor. Cara knelt beside him. His color was good, his breathing regular.

She turned her attention to Lightfoot. The slash that had opened his side was longer than her arm but not deep, and the bleeding had stopped. She thought briefly about trying to sew it shut, then decided it would be better to wait for one of the other unicorns to heal it. She returned to the kitchen and got a pan and a towel. She filled the pan with water and soaked the towel. Then she returned to the living room and washed the blood from Lightfoot's side.

That done, she stood and looked around, feeling oddly lonely at being the only one in the house still awake. Lonely and restless. She felt as if there was still more to do. But what? Her grandmother was gone; where, she didn't know. They couldn't return to Luster until the others had recovered. With a sudden surge of dread she wondered if, when they did return, it would be to Ebillan's cave, or somewhere else altogether. Did time pass the same way here on Earth that it did in Luster? Had the world shifted yet? If so, where would the amulet take them?

She felt a restless need to move *now*. To do something. Anything. Finally she remembered that she had been going to get something to cushion Jacques' head. She could do that for her father, too. Eager to do anything that felt useful, she headed for the stairway. The shabby blue carpet that covered the steps seemed immediately familiar despite the time that had passed since she last saw it.

At the top of the stairs, she turned left. When she entered her old bedroom, the sight of it, so comfortable and cozy, so far from the life she had been living, made her stagger. She leaned against the wall, staring at it in wonder. How far away the girl who had once lived here — the girl she had once been — now seemed.

She went to her bed and ran her hand over the bedspread, smiling at its flowers. She had wanted unicorns, cute and cartoony, and had been angry when her grandmother had forbidden the idea. Now that she had seen real unicorns, she understood.

435

She picked up the single pillow, then frowned. She needed another one, for Jacques. After a moment's hesitation, she headed for her grandmother's room.

Slipping through the door, she turned on the light, then cried out in astonishment.

On the bed lay her grandmother.

Ivy Morris.

The Wanderer.

Calling her grandmother's name, Cara hurried to her side.

The old woman lay perfectly still. She was fully clothed, her hands crossed on her chest, her eyes closed.

*She can't be dead!* thought Cara. *She* can't *be!*

Tenderly, fearfully, Cara reached out to touch the body.

It was warm!

She remembered Beloved telling her that her grandmother was wandering, and not here. Had she lied? Or had she, in her own strange way, been telling the truth?

Her grandmother was here, but not here.

Was her spirit indeed wandering somewhere else?

If so, where? And how could she be called home? Cara felt herself overwhelmed by a sense of mystery.

"What has she done to you, Gramma?" she whispered, kneeling beside the Wanderer's bed. "What kind of spell has she put you under?"

The Wanderer did not answer.

"Wake up!" cried Cara, shaking her grandmother's shoulders. "WAKE UP! I NEED YOU!"

Ivy Morris lay still and unmoving.

Despair washed over Cara like a wave of blackness. Dropping her head to the bed, she sobbed with a hurt she had not known she could feel anymore.

She remained kneeling beside the bed long after her tears had stopped, whispering to her grandmother, cajoling her, begging her to wake.

The Wanderer made no response.

At last, overwhelmed by loneliness, Cara decided to check on the others again. Clutching the pillow she had taken from her own room, she went downstairs, where she tucked it under her father's head. Then she took a throw pillow from one of the chairs — smaller and less comfortable than those from the beds, but still better than the floor — and carried it to the kitchen, where she tucked it under Jacques' head.

The older man stirred as she moved him. "Cara?" he asked in a hoarse whisper.

"Yes, it's me."

"I'm sorry," he murmured with a tone of gloom deeper than any she had ever heard from him, so deep it was almost painful to listen to. "So sorry."

"For what? You saved me. If you and Lightfoot hadn't arrived when you did, Beloved would have taken me away with her." Then she remembered something she had wondered about earlier. "How did you do that, anyway? Come through to Earth?"

But he had drifted into unconsciousness again and could not answer her.

She stroked his brow for a moment, then left the kitchen and climbed the stairs once again, so weary that she had to drag herself up them. They had come all this way to find her grandmother, and, though found, she was still as lost to them as ever.

Returning to her own room, so familiar yet now so strange, Cara took the chair from her desk and carried it to her grandmother's room. She placed it beside the bed and sat down to keep watch.

She remembered how her grandmother used to do

the same for her when she was ill — how she would sit beside the bed and sing to her. Reaching out, Cara put her hand on her grandmother's forehead and began to sing herself. She did the old songs first, the comforting lullabies that had meant so much to her when she was little: "Toora Loora Lura" and "All the Pretty Little Horses" and "Angels Watching Over Me."

She ran through all the ones she could remember, sang them twice, and then a third time, pleased at how many of the words she still knew, oddly sorrowful at how many she had forgotten.

Then, almost without thinking about it, she began another song.

The "Song of the Wanderer."

Her voice high and clear, she sang:

> *Across the gently rolling hills*
> *Beyond high mountain peaks,*
> *Along the shores of distant seas*
> *There's something my heart seeks.*
>
> *But there's no peace in wandering,*
> *The road's not made for rest.*

*And footsore fools will never know*
*What home might suit them best.*


The song seemed to speak to her of her own life now, and her voice began to waver on the second verse as longing and sorrow choked her. Tears swam in her eyes, blurring her vision. So she didn't see her grandmother's lips begin to move.

She did, however, feel M'Gama's ring begin to burn on her finger.

Looking down, she saw that it was glowing again, more intensely than ever before. The green grew brighter, brighter still, until it almost hurt her eyes.

Then it pulled her in.

# THE RAINBOW PRISON

Cara felt as if she were falling — felt, indeed, much as she had the moment after she had leaped from the tower of St. Christopher's. Around her was nothing but green, green that swirled and shifted: the light green of spring grass; the deep green of pine needles; the greens of seawater, of apples in early summer, of sunbeams filtering through the forest.

Beyond the green, or from somewhere within it, she could hear a voice, long loved, long lost, dearly familiar — the voice of her grandmother.

> *My heart longs to rest,*
> *My feet yearn to roam.*
> *Shall I wander the world*
> *Or stay safe at home?*

Then, as had happened in M'Gama's underground workroom, Cara heard the plaintive, heartbreaking cry: "Cara, is that you? Oh, come and get me, my child. Come and get me. I am wandering, wandering and so far from home."

"Where are you, Gramma? *Where are you?*"

"Here." The voice drifted to her from out of the swirling green. "Here, in the rainbow prison."

Cara had gone underground with M'Gama, and even deeper underground when they'd traveled with Grimwold. Now she felt as if she were descending yet again, into someplace stranger than she had yet experienced.

The green still swirled around her, misty and insubstantial. Then she noticed a strand of it that looked more solid. Thick as a rope, it twisted and coiled away from her, into the green distance. Looking to see where it went in the other direction, Cara was startled to discover that it ended at her own hand, at M'Gama's ring. She wondered, for an instant, whether it was flowing out of the ring, or coming from somewhere else and flowing into it.

Suddenly she realized the strand was beginning to

fray, green drifting into green. When she grabbed for it with her free hand, her fingers closed over it as if it were made of fog.

"Cara!" called her grandmother's pleading voice. "*Cara!*"

She sounded more distant than ever.

The ring was growing dim. Remembering the other times it had glowed unexpectedly, Cara began to sing.

Instantly the ring glowed more brightly, and the strand of green grew thicker again.

"Sing, Gramma!" Cara called excitedly after she had finished the first verse. "Sing it with me!"

Trying to send her own voice into the swirling green emptiness, pulling the words not from her mind but her heart, she continued:

> *But there's no peace in wandering,*
> *The road's not made for rest.*
> *And footsore fools will never know*
> *What home might suit them best.*

Her heart lifted when she heard her grandmother's voice join her on the chorus:

*My heart seeks the hearth,*
*My feet seek the road.*
*A soul so divided*
*Is a terrible load.*

*My heart longs to rest,*
*My feet yearn to roam.*
*Shall I wander the world*
*Or stay safe at home?*

On they sang, and on, until they reached the final verse:

*Oh where's the thread that binds me,*
*The voice that calls me back?*
*Where's the love that finds me —*
*And what's the root I lack?*

Now the green rope was strong and sturdy, and Cara pulled her way along it. As she did, her grandmother began the song again. Suddenly Cara realized she was no longer pulling herself along the rope. Instead, the rope was pulling her. Faster and faster she moved until the green around her blurred into a solid-seeming wall. And then she was there, beside her grandmother — her true grandmother, not merely the body she lived in.

"I found you!" she cried, surprised to discover that she was weeping. "I've found you at last." She flung herself toward her grandmother, which was the first time she realized that she, too, had left her body behind. She felt a flicker of fear, but it was lost in her joy at finding her grandmother. And though neither of them was wrapped in flesh, the embrace they shared was real and solid.

"Cara," whispered the old woman after a time. "My Cara. I knew you would come for me."

"But where are we?" asked Cara, not raising her head to look.

"I don't know."

It was not merely the words that Cara found terrifying, it was the tone of hopelessness in her grandmother's voice. "How did you get here?" Cara asked, pulling away a little now.

Ivy Morris looked uneasy. "An old enemy sent me," she said at last.

"Was it Beloved?"

Cara's grandmother looked surprised, and somewhat frightened. "I think you have a lot to tell me, granddaughter."

"That's true for you, too," replied Cara sharply. Then, though she had vowed not to, had promised herself she would hold her questions until this was all over, the words forced themselves out in an angry burst. "Did you really steal me from my parents?"

Ivy Morris flinched back, looking almost terrified. Then her face relaxed. "I should have realized that some of our past would come to light when I sent you to Luster. Yes, dearheart, I did just that."

"But *why?*"

"I suspect you already know the answer."

"All right, I do. What I don't know is why you didn't *tell* me about it. Why did you lie to me all those years, let me think they had abandoned me?"

Her grandmother sighed. "I couldn't bring myself to tell you they were dead — though it might have been kinder if I had."

"But they *weren't* dead!" exploded Cara. "That would still have been a lie. *Why didn't you just tell me the truth?*"

Ivy Morris looked directly at her granddaughter. Her own eyes deep with sorrow, she whispered, "Because the truth was too heavy a burden to place on you."

Cara started to protest, but her grandmother raised her hands to stop her. "I don't mean it would have been too painful for you to hear — though I think it would have been more painful than you might believe, especially when you were little. No, I mean that *holding* the truth is too painful."

Cara drew back from her grandmother, and in so doing noticed, for the first time, the world around them, which she had ignored in the rush and excitement of their reunion.

It had more solid detail than she had expected.

They stood at the edge of a forest, but a forest greener than any she had ever seen, a forest where not only the leaves but the trunks and branches of the trees were green — as were the rocks, the water, the ground below, the sky above. It reminded her of when she had seen her mother in Grimwold's gem, and everything had been crimson and scarlet.

Ivy Morris gestured to the bank of a stream. "Sit

with me," she said. Spectral though it was, her human form was startlingly clear against the green world that stretched around them.

Cara settled beside her. She thrust one foot into the water but felt nothing. Nor, for that matter, could she feel the ground beneath her. Only her grandmother seemed real.

"Secrets are a heavy burden," said Ivy Morris quietly. "More of a burden than I wanted to place on a child. They want to be let out, struggle to be free, beat against the walls of your heart until you ache with the effort of holding them in. But some secrets *are* better left untold."

She turned her head away. When she spoke again, her voice was soft and filled with pain. "Luster is a big secret to carry — so big that more than once I *did* try to share it. But it also turned out to be too big to tell, too big for anyone to believe."

She turned back, looked directly into her granddaughter's eyes. "I have not been close to many people in my life, Cara. Something in me — the same thing that made me a Wanderer, I suppose — makes that hard for me. But a few, a very few, I loved and tried to tell. Their disbelief was painful. Their fear for me, their sense that I had lost my mind, stung my heart. I was even put in a hospital for it once, and had to pretend not to believe the truest thing in my life until I could finally convince the doctors that they had 'cured' me." She laughed ruefully. "I would have just fled to Luster and left them wondering how I had escaped, except that I had been taken without the amulet." She paused, then said thoughtfully, "Or maybe I wouldn't have. It wasn't time for me to return yet. Anyway, given what I knew about trying to tell this secret, what would I have told you, my darling — and how would you have dealt with it?"

Cara sat silent, uncertain how to answer. She remembered the playground teasing she had taken over things that, next to the reality of Luster, were like grains of sand compared to a boulder. "Why didn't you just take me to Luster with you?" she asked at last.

Her grandmother sighed. "And what would you have told your friends when we came back?"

"I mean, why didn't you take me there to live? I would have liked that."

Ivy Morris shook her head sadly. "I couldn't do that

until I was ready to return myself. You don't know how I longed to tell you, Cara. I thought about it almost every day, trying to find the right way, the right time. Then that man began following us — "

"You don't have to pretend. I know it was my father who chased us into St. Christopher's."

Ivy Morris looked startled, then nodded in acceptance. "Then came the night when your father began following us. Suddenly there was no time left to tell you, and I had to send you off unprepared. For that, you have my deepest apologies, my darling.

"After you jumped into Luster, I was left alone in the tower — alone, and lonely. That was a feeling I had not experienced for a long time." She smiled, but it was a tight, painful smile. "Wanderers cannot afford to be lonely. Of course, I was not merely lonely. I was frantic with concern for you — and for the unicorns. What did it mean that your father had discovered us? What did it mean that he had followed you into Luster?

"I should not have gone home after that. I should have moved on at once. I knew that. But there were things I did not want to leave. Foolish, foolish of me. Things tie you down, Cara, and I could not afford to be tied." She sighed. "It wasn't just things. I wanted to be there in case you returned. So I went home." She drew a deep breath. "Beloved was there, waiting for me."

"Did she hurt you?"

"A little. But when it became clear that I did not have the amulet and could not get it, she set my soul wandering free of my body — cast me into this green strangeness with little hope of ever finding my way back. I have roamed the greenness of this place, Cara, pressing at its edges, seeking a way out."

"I heard you calling once, I think," said Cara. "I was in the cave of the Geomancer — "

"M'Gama," whispered Ivy Morris, a strange note in her voice. "Yes, I'm not surprised if my voice reached you in that place. The magic is deep there, and surprising things can happen. Did she help you find your way back to Earth?"

"Yes."

The old woman chuckled dryly. "I'm sure she had mixed feeling about *that!*"

Cara held up her hand to display the band of green on her finger. "It was her ring that brought me to you.

451

It's keyed to the song, I think. It pulled me in, some-how, when you responded to my singing. Oh, I can't believe I found you, Gramma! I've been trying so hard to get back to Earth so I can bring you home to Luster. The Queen wants to see you, to say — "

Cara stopped, the words catching in her throat. What the Queen wanted to say was good-bye. How would her grandmother react to that news? Suddenly Cara began to understand how her grandmother had put off telling her painful truths for so long.

Her thoughts were interrupted by Ivy Morris's whisper. "The Queen," she said softly.

The strands of emotion in her voice — the love and regret, the joy and sorrow, and most of all the long-ing — were too thick, and far too tangled, for Cara to sort out. "I took her your message, Gramma. I told her, 'The Wanderer is weary.'"

"Truer words were never spoken," said Ivy Morris ruefully.

"She asked me to bring you back so . . ." Cara fal-tered a second time on the painful thought, then forced herself to go on. "She says she has to see you before she can rest."

Ivy Morris looked stricken. Her voice little more than a whisper, she asked, "Is she so close to fading, then?"

Cara nodded. "I think she might have been gone already if she had not wanted to see you so much. She says there is an old wound she has to heal."

Ivy Morris's hand stole toward her heart. "So many years," she murmured. "And what about the succession? Is that settled? Do they know who will take her place?"

"I'm not sure. Just a little while ago, when we were fighting with Beloved — "

Her grandmother's eyes widened. "What are you talking about? What has happened?"

Cara sighed. "I have a million things to tell you. But we've got to get back."

"Ah, a jailbreak! Well, I'm all for that. Do you have any ideas?"

# CHAPTER TWENTY-FOUR

# FLICKERFOOT

Cara felt a twinge of uncertainty. "I was hoping the ring would carry us back."

Her grandmother smiled. "Maybe it will. I suppose the best thing we can do is try."

Joining hands, they began to sing. But though they went twice through "Song of the Wanderer," the ring remained lifeless and dark.

Cara felt a new twist of fear. Had she come so far to find her grandmother only to end up trapped herself?

Then, on its own, the ring began to glow again.

A moment later they saw a form running toward them out of the green distance.

Cara cried out in joy.

It was Arabella Skydancer, Queen of the Unicorns.

Suddenly Cara felt fear begin to tangle with her joy.

The Queen looked free and strong in a way she had not seen her before, and though it was beautiful to see, she wasn't sure what it meant.

"I heard you," said the Queen when she reached them. "I heard you singing, your two voices calling me with your need."

"We hoped the song would take us back to our bodies," said Cara. "I had no idea it would call you to us." She reached toward the Queen, then drew her hand back. "Are you . . . are you all right?"

"That is hard to say. My body is nearly used up. But that makes it all the easier for me to run free of it when I need to — makes it all the easier to enter the light that flows between the worlds." She turned toward Cara's grandmother. The two gazed at each other for a long time without speaking.

It was the Queen who finally broke the silence. "Greetings, Wanderer. It has been a long time."

"Too long," said Ivy Morris softly, joy and sorrow mingling in her voice. She gestured to Cara. "I see you have met my granddaughter."

"She is a fine young woman. But then, that is no surprise."

Cara's pleasure at the compliment gave way to her

sense of urgency. "What did you mean about 'the light that flows between the worlds'? Where are we? What is this place?"

The Queen glanced around, as if assuring herself that she was where she had expected to be, then said, "Earth and Luster — and other worlds, as well, I suppose — are connected by light. In some places that light is splintered, broken into shafts, just as a rainbow is. Such places can be reached only by deep magic, and those who have mastered that magic sometimes use it as a means to exile their enemies. That is where we are now, in a place between the worlds, a place that is neither here nor there, not in one world or the other, but reflects bits and pieces of both of them. Taken together, these places are sometimes called the Rainbow Prison." She smiled. "Obviously, at the moment we are in the green shaft."

"Is there a red shaft, too?" asked Cara eagerly.

"Of course," said the Queen.

"I think my mother is there!"

"What do you mean?" asked the Wanderer.

Quickly, Cara told them of her experience with Grimwold's gem.

"It sounds, indeed, as if your mother is also somewhere in the Rainbow Prison," said the Queen. "Whether we can reach her is another matter altogether. Our first task is to get you and your grandmother out of *this* part of the prison."

"Can you do that?" asked Cara eagerly.

The Queen's face grew troubled. "I'm not sure. If your bodies were near my own, I could take you back with little problem. But I don't know where they are resting."

"They are still on Earth," said the Wanderer.

The Queen frowned. "This is worse than I feared."

Despite hours of trying, the Queen was not able to free them. Nor was she willing to leave them.

So they stayed together — the Old One, the Wanderer, and the girl who had traveled so far to reunite them — in the green shaft of the Rainbow Prison.

And, as the world shimmered around them, they talked.

Cara spoke first, telling the other two all of what had happened back on Earth.

The Old One and the Wanderer listened in silence until she described the way Beloved had fled after the fight in the living room.

"I do not like the sound of that," said the Queen. "Beloved does not give up so easily. I fear some deeper mischief is at work here."

Cara nodded. "I wondered about that, too. Only I couldn't figure out what. Beloved said something else that puzzled me — she said Lightfoot was next in line for the throne. Can that be true?"

The Queen sighed. "No. On that matter, Beloved is wrong. Lightfoot is not the heir to the throne."

"Then who is?" asked Ivy Morris, sounding startled.

The Queen looked away for a moment. When she looked back, her eyes were deep and strange and far-away looking. "I need to tell you a story. It is not one I am particularly eager to tell, for it does me little credit. But it is time it was known. It involves a young unicorn named Flickerfoot — possibly the most obstreperous, wayward, restless filly it has ever been my delight and exasperation to meet."

*She sounds like fun,* thought Cara.

"Flickerfoot was well named, for she was a Wanderer

at heart, and those feet took her far afield, carrying her into more danger and adventure than I care to tell you, or need to for this story. She was a source of great despair to her family — especially to her grandmother."

"Why her grandmother?" asked Cara, glancing sideways at her own grandmother.

"Because her grandmother had certain hopes and dreams for her, dreams that were endangered by Flickerfoot's wandering. I know this, because *I* was Flickerfoot's grandmother, and I tell you I loved her, as I had no other of my children, or my children's children — loved her in spite of her obstinate nature, or perhaps because of it. Loved her, and feared for her. Because Flickerfoot developed a passionate interest in the last place that I wanted her to wander."

"Earth," said Ivy Morris with quiet certainty.

"Earth," confirmed the Queen. "Our ancient home, which we love and fear, long for and mourn. By cajoling, spying, sneaking, exploring, and a dozen other means, Flickerfoot found the location of five of the seven gates that I have allowed to remain open. Despite my warning, my pleas, my threats, she began to travel back and forth between the two worlds. It was a forbidden trip — forbidden to all of us, and doubly forbidden to her because she was of the royal family. But she would not be restrained.

"Now, because of a promise made long ago by my own grandmother to a girl named Alma Leonetti, there is always one unicorn on Earth, one who remains to keep alive the memory of what we were, and what was lost when we left. That one, whom we call 'the Guardian of Memory,' is always in danger from Beloved and her children. Flickerfoot, whenever she crossed to Earth, shared that danger. Worse, she increased the danger by drawing more attention to our existence. But she insisted on going, and nothing I could do would stop her.

"Worse of all, she became attached — deeply attached — to a young tumbler named Jacques."

At these words both Cara and her grandmother drew in their breath.

"Finally I ordered Flickerfoot not to return to Earth anymore. It did no good. She was obsessed, and would return, despite any orders I might make.

"I lived in terror that she would be caught by Beloved and her Hunters, and finally hit on a plan to try to give her a measure of safety. I summoned the Geomancer and asked her if she could create for me a talisman that would carry a certain enchantment. M'Gama was uneasy with the idea, but agreed that it could be done — though it would certainly not be easy.

"I ordered her to do it.

"A year later — the most nerve-racking year of a very long life — the Geomancer returned with the item I had requested.

"I called Flickerfoot to me, and we affixed the talisman to her hoof. 'This is for use in only the most dire of emergencies,' I told her. 'But if the worst should happen, then strike your foot against stone as hard as you can and call on Earth itself to save you.' Then M'Gama gave her the specific words to activate the magic.

"Flickerfoot was wary of the talisman, and rightly so, but accepted it to calm my fears — or perhaps simply to silence me.

"For a year, all was well. Then — I know this because Jacques told me later — there came a day when Flickerfoot was visiting him on Earth and the Hunters found her trail. They began to pursue her. Flickerfoot and Jacques fled, but he soon realized that he was slowing her down, and so they separated. He was hoping to draw the pursuit in his direction. In this he failed, and the Hunters continued to trail her.

"That was the last time Jacques saw her — and the last I heard of my willful and beloved granddaughter for many years. But I was certain she had used M'Gama's talisman to save herself."

"How did you know?" asked Cara.

"Because I would have sensed it if she had been killed." The Queen shook her head in something like a shudder. "We all know, always and at once, when one of our kind is killed."

"But what did the talisman do?" persisted Cara.

The Queen hesitated. Her answer, when it came, was quiet, and laced with pain. "It transformed her into a human."

Ivy Morris cried out.

"It made her human," continued the Queen relentlessly, "and in so doing, saved her from the wrath of the Hunters — for how could they capture a unicorn where there was none? But the transformation had its price, as does all magic. When Flickerfoot lost her form, she lost, too, all memory of her past. Moreover, though she was several decades old, the magic translated those years into the much shorter life span of a human, leaving her but a girl."

"What happened next?" asked Cara eagerly.

"Much of what followed is a mystery. Where that girl went, lost and without memory, I do not know — though we do know, now, where she finally ended up. As for Jacques, my granddaughter had given him enough clues that he finally made his way to the gate she had been using to visit him." Arabella Skydancer sighed and shook her head. "It might have been better for all of us if I had simply closed those gates long ago. Anyway, Jacques found me and, in great despair, told me what little he knew. I assured him that though I did not know Flickerfoot's present location, she had indeed survived the Hunt. Then I invited him to remain in Luster, for I feared Earth was no longer safe for him, that Beloved and her children might now be seeking him as well. And, to be truthful, I also hoped his presence might somehow draw Flickerfoot back.

"Jacques did not accept my offer at first, for he insisted on returning to Earth to look for Flickerfoot. He was not the only one seeking her. The unicorns do have friends on Earth, and I set them all to seek my grand-daughter. But it was her brother who finally found her."

"Her brother?" asked Ivy, her voice strained, intense.

"Moonheart," said the Queen. Now she turned her face full on Ivy and said, "Though I never told him, though he does not know to this day who you truly are, my Wanderer, the answer to his often asked question, 'Why was I able to sense Ivy's need all the way from her world to ours, when none of the others could?', is simple. You are his sister, my darling granddaughter Flickerfoot."

Ivy Morris was weeping now, though whether the tears were of joy or sorrow, Cara could not tell. The Queen, too, was shedding tears.

"Why didn't you ever tell me this?" asked the Wanderer.

"For a long time I didn't know myself. When you arrived in Luster I took you for just another human who had stumbled through our gates — though from the first I felt my heart reaching out to you in a way it never had to any other human. It was M'Gama who finally worked it all out. But it took her years, and it was only shortly before you and Jacques had decided to marry that she deciphered the puzzle."

"That was why you tried to stop the wedding!" said Ivy with sudden understanding.

The Queen bowed her head in acknowledgment. "I have always regretted the bitter words that passed between us at that time, granddaughter, and wished that I could have dealt with the situation with more wisdom and grace. But even a queen, and a very old one at that, can bungle situations of the heart far too easily.

"Part of the problem was that by that time, you had lived so long as a human I did not know how you would react to the truth — especially since there was nothing I could do to return you to your form at that time."

"At that time?" asked Cara. "Does that mean you can turn her back now?"

"It means it is *possible* now. The spell was an act of desperation, and as such had desperate consequences, one of which was that there was no reversing it for fifty years. Now those years have passed. Even so, the task will not be easy. But it is time to begin. At last, it is time to begin. For the Wanderer is weary, as she well has a right to be, and her own true shape will bring her renewed strength and joy. Though she is old in human years, she is young as a unicorn, and will have that youth restored if we can make the transformation. And she is the rightful heir to the throne — which will be an enormous relief to poor Lightfoot."

Suddenly Cara caught her breath. Looking at the Queen and at her grandmother, she asked in a fearful whisper, "If Gramma is really a unicorn . . . *what am I?*"

The Queen smiled. "You are, like your mother, one of the strangest children ever born on two worlds. But more than that, you are, I hope, the one born to bring an end to the Hunt. Within your soul is merged not merely human and unicorn, but unicorn and Hunter. It all comes together in you, child."

Before Cara could answer, M'Gama's ring began to glow again.

# CHAPTER TWENTY-FIVE

# THE JOURNEY HOME

A voice came drifting through the green:

*Oh, where's the thread that binds me,*
*The voice that calls me back?*

"It's Jacques!" cried Cara. "He's singing us home!"

"How would he know to do that?" asked her grandmother, who looked distinctly nervous.

"Maybe he doesn't know. Maybe he's just doing the same thing I did — singing it to you, to your body, because . . . well, because it just seemed like the right thing to do. Come on — we have to sing with him if we're going to get back to our bodies."

Cara raised her voice to join the song. As she did, the green strand appeared again, stretching from

M'Gama's ring into the distance, back toward the song that Jacques was singing for them.

"Go," said the Queen urgently. "Don't lose this chance to escape, for you may not get another. I can get back to Luster on my own. Your amulet will bring you to me when you're ready, Flickerfoot. Come as soon as you can. Please."

Cara slipped her arm around her grandmother's waist. "Sing, Gramma," she pleaded. "I think we both have to be singing to make it work."

Indeed, the strand of green was clear but not solid, and Cara could not close her hand over it.

Reluctantly at first, then with increased strength and clarity, Ivy Morris joined the song.

Cara began to pull them along the green strand.

"I'll be waiting for you!" called the Queen. Then she turned and galloped in the opposite direction. Leaping into the swirling green, she disappeared from sight.

Cara felt the strand of green grow wispy beneath her hand. "Don't stop now, Jacques!" she cried. "Keep singing until we're home!"

"Jacques, you old fool, keep singing!" shouted Ivy. Then she took up the song again herself.

Whether he heard them, or it was mere luck, Jacques began to sing again. Cara and Ivy faltered for a moment, trying to match their voices to his. Then they began to move, slowly at first, then faster, and faster, until the greens blurred into a single color.

Cara gasped and opened her eyes. She was in her own body, back on Earth, back in her grandmother's bedroom. On the bed in front of her, the body of her grandmother, which had been so still and lifeless, was stirring too.

"You're back!" cried Jacques. The words tore from him like a sob. "*You're back!*"

Ivy Morris reached a hand toward him. "This is the last place I would have expected to see you, old friend."

"You're not the only one who can wander," he said, trying to force the corners of his drooping mouth into a smile.

"I wandered a little too far for comfort that time," said Ivy Morris. She drew in a deep breath. "Well. Rescued by my granddaughter and my former husband." She stopped, and her face twisted in a way that was unreadable. "And coming home with a story that suddenly makes sense of my life and also changes it utterly."

"What do you mean?" asked Jacques.

"Later," said Ivy Morris, her voice vague and troubled. "I'll explain everything later. Right now, based on the things Cara has told me, we have to move fast."

"Faster than she realizes," said Jacques.

Dread and fear were so heavy in his voice that it frightened Cara. "What do you mean?" she cried.

Jacques wrung his hands and looked away without speaking. Though his face was always lined and care-worn, Cara had come to see that at least part of that was a mask, a pose. Now his features carried a look of pain that pierced her heart. She felt cold, wondering what new sorrow was in store.

"I should have stayed in Luster," he said dismally.

Cara put her hand on his arm. "You saved me! If you hadn't come through, Beloved would have had me."

He shook his head. "Thomas could have done that. It was his amulet that brought me through."

"Thomas has an amulet?" cried Cara in surprise.

Jacques nodded. "He let me take it so Lightfoot and

I could come after you. He wanted to come himself, but the amulet would only bring two of us, and I insisted that it be me, because . . . because I was hoping to find Ivy."

He turned his head away, and a racking sob tore from him.

"What's wrong?" asked Cara in alarm.

"The Hunters took it from me," moaned Jacques. "They took Thomas's amulet!"

She cried out, stunned by the horror of his words. Now she understood what Marcus must have been whispering just before the end, and why Beloved had made such a sudden retreat. Of course she had wanted to get away. She had what she was after. She had an amulet.

Cara's mind reeled at the thought of Beloved having a key to enter Luster.

Ivy Morris sprang to her feet. "We have to get this information to the Queen at once. Cara, may I have my . . . *our* amulet?"

Cara lifted the amulet from her neck and passed it to her grandmother. "What are you going to do?" she asked.

"Return to Luster. But only for a moment. I'll come back for you."

Closing her eyes at the same moment she closed her fingers over the crystal lid of the amulet, Ivy Morris whispered, "Luster, bring me home." In the words Cara heard a longing deeper than she would have imagined possible.

A moment later her grandmother was gone. The disappearance was silent, mysterious. She watched it but somehow could not see it. One moment her grandmother was there. Then Cara felt as if her vision had blurred, and when she looked again, her grandmother was gone.

Cara looked at Jacques. "Where will she end up?" she asked nervously.

"With the Queen," said Jacques, and Cara suddenly remembered what Grimwold had told them: that for her grandmother, the amulet was a direct route not only to Luster, but to the Queen herself.

She took Jacques' hand, wondering what, if anything, she should say to him of the things she had learned in the Rainbow Prison. But before she could speak, her grandmother reappeared at the edge of the bed. "Message delivered," she said grimly.

472

"Is the Queen angry?" asked Jacques, his voice trembling.

"'Angry' is not the word," said Ivy. She stretched out her hand to him. "This is not a good way for either of us to meet again, old friend. We will talk later, and if you have half as much to tell me as I have to tell you, it will be a long conversation indeed. For now, be at ease. The Queen sends her forgiveness, and bids you remember that had you not come through to Earth, you would not have been here to call Cara and me back from the Rainbow Prison, something it is unlikely Thomas would have done. I owe you my life, dear fool, and not for the first time. But we must move now, and move fast, before the transit point shifts."

"What are we going to do?" asked Cara.

Her grandmother smiled. "Set up a relay system. Right now, and for a little while longer, the amulet will take *you* back to Ebillan's cave. I want you to return there and, one by one, bring back your friends — at least those who wish to go to Autumngrove with us."

"Autumngrove?" asked Cara, feeling confused. "What about Summerhaven?"

"Summer is ending," said her grandmother. "The

473

court is already on the move. Now, come along; let's check on the others."

Ian Hunter was lying where Cara had left him. But he was awake now, and when his daughter, Jacques, and the Wanderer came down the stairs and entered the living room, he cried out in astonishment. He sprang to his feet, then staggered and sank to the couch again. Despite Lightfoot's healing work, he was still weak from the wound Beloved had inflicted on him.

His cry roused Lightfoot, who pushed himself to his feet more slowly. "Welcome, Wanderer," he said, bowing his horn to Ivy Morris. "We have traveled a long way to find you."

"Indeed you have," said Ivy Morris. "I understand you have been a good friend to my granddaughter. For that, you have my thanks, and the thanks of the Queen as well."

Ian Hunter stood again, more slowly now, and took a step toward them. His face was unreadable.

Ivy Morris reached out to him. "We have much to speak of," she whispered. "And much that needs to be forgiven on both sides. But Cara has told me what happened in this room last night, and if you are willing to set aside the past, then I am as well."

Cara stared at her family, or what there was of it here, confused by the tangle of joy and sorrow that bound her to the grandmother who was so much more than she seemed; to the father whom she had lost and found and lost and found yet again; and to the man who might be her grandfather.

But the time for talking, for understanding, for healing, would have to come later. Now she had to travel again.

Taking the amulet from her grandmother, Cara asked Luster to bring her home.

She returned to the crystal cave from which she had left. Moving quickly, but cautiously, she followed the dark tunnel that led to the larger cave that Ebillan called home.

She found them, her "family of the road," waiting at the front of the cave. The Squijum was the first to notice her. "Girl back!" he cried, bounding to her side and scrambling up to her shoulder. "Girl back!"

Ebillan turned his massive head in her direction.

"So, the little Wanderer returns, having slipped away while I was distracted."

"I apologize for my ungracious departure," she said, speaking in the courtly language of the dragons.

"No matter. Your friend was as good as his word, and for the mending he did of my wedding cup, I am willing to forgive perhaps more than I should. I notice, however, that you are alone. What of the friends who followed you to Earth?"

"Safe, and waiting for us to join them," said Cara.

Then, speaking quickly and telling only a fraction of what had happened since she'd left the cave, she explained the plan for returning to the Queen's court.

"Perhaps I should install a tollgate," said Ebillan testily.

"What's to complain about?" snapped Moonheart. "You'll be rid of us all sooner than you expected. I should think you would be relieved."

Ebillan grumbled his annoyance, but said no more.

"Earth?" growled the Dimblethum uneasily. "Then to court? The Dimblethum does not like this idea."

"It's either that or walk back the long way, you drad-blatted fool," said Medafil, stretching his wings behind him. "As for me, I plan to fly, and not to any court. It's time I headed for home."

Cara hurried to the gryphon's side. "I shall miss you," she said, stroking the feathers on his neck.

"Gaah! I'll miss you, too. But I notice you didn't bring the Wanderer back with you. Never will get that gutbumbled kiss, I suppose."

"Here's one from me until you see her," said Cara, stretching up to kiss his yellow beak.

"Gaah!" he said. But from lower in his body came a deep rumble. It took Cara a second to realize he was purring.

"We don't have time for long good-byes," said Moonheart. "The day will be over soon. If we're going to make this crossing, we need to start *now*."

Cara glanced out of the cave. The sun was appallingly close to the horizon. She turned to Ebillan. "With your permission, we will depart," she said, speaking once more in the guttural, fiery language of dragons.

"Permission granted — on the condition you do not return to my cave. Our dealings with each other are at an end."

"Terms accepted," said Cara.

She gave Medafil a final hug, then led her friends to the crystal cave where, one by one, she ferried them through to Earth.

The Dimblethum hung back with the clear intent of being the last to go. But when she came back for him, he shook his head sadly and said, "The Dimblethum will miss Cara. The Dimblethum will miss Lightfoot. But the Dimblethum will not go to court."

Cara felt her heart clench with sorrow. "Where will you go instead?"

"The Dimblethum goes to his own home, back to where you first met him."

"But how will you get across the wasteland?" she cried. "I can't stand to think of you crossing that all alone."

"I'm going to fly the fitbingled creature," said Medafil crossly. "don't know why. Stupid idea. But I offered, and there it is. Probably break my back. I'll guide him through the forest, too."

Cara laughed, despite the tears that were rolling down her cheeks. Then she flung herself against the Dimblethum and held him as tightly as she could.

"Go," he said at last, pushing her away from him. "Go now, while you can."

She looked up. The sun was almost gone.

She raced to the crystal cave, and let the amulet carry her back to Earth.

CHAPTER TWENTY-SIX

# THE BROKEN
# HORN

With five humans, four unicorns, and the Squijum inside it, the living room of the little house Cara had shared with her grandmother was more crowded than she had ever seen it.

What made it feel even more crowded was the tension that crackled from the unicorns' barely-contained anger at finding themselves sharing the space with a Hunter.

The sharing was not going to last long because soon they would be leaving for Luster.

Ian Hunter took his daughter aside to talk with her. They sat in the kitchen, looking at each other across the shabby little table where she used to sit to eat her breakfast. Neither spoke for several minutes.

480

It was her father who finally broke the silence. "You are a miracle," he said.

"I'm a wanderer," whispered Cara.

"And the most precious thing in the world to me," he answered, reaching out to take her hand. She slipped her hands forward. He folded them into his own, which were callused and hard with muscle. "We have to make a decision now," he said at last.

Though he did not speak it aloud, they both knew what that decision was.

Cara sat staring at him, at the lean, dark-eyed face, nearly haggard now, the face that had hunted her and haunted her and that meant so much to her heart. Stared at it, and with pain choking her throat finally whispered, "I have to go back to Luster."

He closed his eyes and nodded in acceptance. "You do understand that I cannot go with you."

"Why not? I bet the Queen would forgive you. I bet it would be —"

He shook his head. "I have to find your mother first."

Warm relief flooded her heart. "How will you do it?"

He looked away for a moment. "I am a Hunter," he

said at last. Then he turned back. "I must stay for another reason, Cara. The danger to Luster is growing now that Beloved has an amulet. I will do what I can to discover her plans, to help warn the unicorns of when and where the attack will come, as come it must. It won't be easy; I'm marked as a traitor now to the Hunters, and it is unlikely any unicorn will trust me either. But I may be able to help somehow."

"Every time I find you, I lose you again," said Cara, trying not to let her sorrow overwhelm her.

"I could say the same thing," he replied gently. "But it's different this time, Cara. Long ago you were taken from me, and I still carry a wound from that loss that no unicorn can heal. When we met in Firethroat's cave, I lost you in a different way." He smiled. "Your friend the dragon dropped me about as far from civilization as was possible. On the journey back I had a great deal of time to think — and what I thought about most was how amazing you are. And how the things that had been drilled into me by Beloved and the Hunters, the things I believed utterly, no longer seemed quite so certain."

He shook his head. "And now we part again, but not

in the same way. Because this time each of us knows the other's heart — knows that as soon as it can be managed, we'll be together again."

She slipped from her chair, went to him, and put her arms around his neck. When she pulled away again, her cheeks were wet with his tears.

Autumngrove was even more beautiful than Summerhaven, but the beauty was little balm for the sorrow that enfolded the unicorns.

The Queen was fading, and would not last much longer.

A glory was gathering, unicorns streaming into Autumngrove from all directions to bid farewell to their queen — and not only unicorns. Those humans who had gotten the word were traveling to pay their respects, too — as were many of the other creatures of Luster.

The gathering had started two weeks earlier, when the court was still in Summerhaven and concern about the Queen had reached the point that the unicorns put out a call for the farewells to begin. There had been a great deal of discussion about whether the Queen should make the trip to Autumngrove. She was the one who had insisted on going, and had succeeded in forcing the others to accept her decision.

Behind the sorrow was enormous concern, for the matter of who would take the Queen's place was still uncertain. Though the rules of succession had left Lightfoot in line for the throne, it was well known that he did not want the position.

And strange rumors had begun to circulate that there was someone else — someone unexpected — who might take the Queen's place. Other rumors were spreading, too — rumors of a growing danger from Beloved, and the possibility of a fierce, final battle that would decide the ancient struggle between the unicorns and the Hunters once and for all.

This was the state of things two days after Cara returned to Luster, and it was causing Lightfoot terrible anxiety. "I thought she would live forever," he said miserably to Cara as they walked in the woods of Autumngrove one afternoon. "I can't do this. I don't want to do this!"

"I don't want you to have to," she said sympathetically.

"You're nicer about it than my uncle. When I said this to him, he told me to stop whining. Then he went on about how when the Queen was well my shirking of responsibility was merely annoying, but now that she is going to leave us, it becomes" — and here he lowered his voice to imitate Moonheart — "'something deeper — something we cannot afford.' As if this was simply some chore I didn't want to take on."

"Why don't you want to do it?" asked Cara.

"Because I'm wrong for it! I'd make a mess of it! I can't believe they even want me to try. Any fool can see I'd be horrible at it."

"So why do they want you to? I could never quite figure out how it works here."

"Oh, it's nothing as simple as it is on Earth where the King's firstborn son follows him onto the throne and everyone else can just go off and play."

"Actually, it does sometimes get more complicated than that," said Cara gently.

"Well, at least there are some sort of predetermined rules. Here we have a ceremony where a group of unicorns read signs from the water, the sky, and the forest. You wouldn't believe how surprised everyone was when they announced that I was next in line for the throne.

They were as upset about it as I was. The only difference was, they kept saying, 'You have to accept your destiny,' and *I* kept saying, 'There's been some sort of horrible mistake!'"

He paused, then added more calmly, "To tell you the truth, I think there are times when Moonheart believes we should just ignore the signs; after all, they were less clear than they should have been. We both know that he would make a better king than I would. But when I tell him that, he gets more upset than ever. And to make things worse, now we're facing the possibility of an invasion by the Hunters. And who knows what the delvers might be getting up to. The last thing we need at the moment is me as the King!"

He shook his head and sighed. "Given how hard I worked to get away from the court, the fact that I ended up back here at this time is almost enough to make me believe that the Greater Powers really do want me to be the King — which, in my opinion, would mean that Moonheart is wrong. *I'm* not the silliest and most irresponsible thing in the kingdom. They are!"

♦   ♦   ♦

M'Gama arrived in Autumngrove two days after Cara and her group had returned, announcing that she had come to observe the passing of the Queen. Cara sought her out and told her all that had happened since they had last been together.

"I'm glad the ring was of use," said M'Gama.

Cara and her grandmother shared a grove much like the one Cara had been given at Summerhaven — a private place surrounded by a thick wall of shrubbery that was turning silvery with the autumn. But despite sharing this sleeping space, Cara did not see much of her grandmother, for Ivy Morris spent most of her time with the Queen.

When they did have time together, the two of them talked long and deeply.

But what neither of them brought up was the startling story that the Queen had told them while they were in the Rainbow Prison. It seemed to be fearful territory somehow, and Ivy was either unwilling or unable to discuss it.

One night they were called to the Queen's grove, a beautiful spot beside a silvery stream. Many unicorns were gathered there already. Their horns were dim, their heads hung low.

The Queen lay at the edge of the swiftly flowing water, so weary she could not lift her head.

Cara felt hot grief overwhelm her, and struggled to keep from disturbing the sacred moment with a wail of despair.

She saw a handful of humans scattered about the grove; Jacques and Thomas were there, as was — to her surprise — Armando. She saw others as well, humans she did not recognize, including a cloaked woman who gave an impression of great age.

The unicorns began to sing, a song that seemed to be made as much of light as of sound.

One by one the unicorns approached their Queen, knelt, nuzzled her neck, or laid their horns across her shoulder. Cara knew they were speaking to her in private, mind to mind, a last exchange of words and wishes, blessings and sorrows.

Occasionally the Queen would raise her head or nicker softly. Mostly she lay without moving.

One of the unicorns — her face so mournful, it took Cara a moment to recognize her as Laughing Stream — came to her and said, "It is your turn now."

Swallowing hard, Cara went to the Queen. Kneeling, she placed her hand gently on the frail, white curve of her neck.

"Greetings, Great-great-granddaughter," thought the Queen. "I must apologize for leaving so soon after you have come to stay with us. I owe you many thanks, for you have given me my heart's desire — you returned my wandering granddaughter."

"My heart has a desire, too," thought Cara, "and that is for you to stay with us."

"Don't be cruel," replied the Queen gently. "My time has come, and I must move on. I welcome it, for I am more weary than you can imagine. I have given instructions that you are to be allowed to drink from the Queen's pool. Think carefully before you accept this boon. It will add many years to your life, which can be a blessing, or a burden, depending on how you spend them."

"What about . . . about Flickerfoot?"

"Keep watching," replied the Queen, and Cara actually sensed a note of amusement in the thought. "With luck, all will be resolved. Now you must leave me, for there are others I need to speak to, and my time is short. I wish I had had more time to know you."

489

"And I you, Great-great-grandmother," whispered Cara with her mind and her lips.

When she lifted her hand from the Queen's neck her fingers tingled, as if she had been holding light and it had soaked into them.

Other humans were summoned to approach the Queen. Each knelt, and Cara saw that while they were with her their faces were transformed by a look of bliss, but that when they stood to leave, grief overwrote it and tears spilled down their cheeks.

Ivy Morris was last to be called. She knelt by the Queen, then fell forward across her neck, weeping with despair. This impropriety brought a gasp from the assembled unicorns — a gasp quickly replaced by a cry of mingled sorrow and joy as the Queen, the Old One, vanished.

Thomas, who had come to stand behind Cara, tightened his hands on her shoulders, and she wondered if he saw what she had seen: the Queen rise from the ground, looking as young and as strong as when she had been in the Rainbow Prison, though no more substantial than a beam of light. She had stood, staring down at the Wanderer for a moment, then turned to look around the circle of loved ones, bowing and smiling to each of them. Then she stepped onto the stream and, laughing herself, let the laughing water carry her away.

Now there was nothing left of her body except the horn, which lay glowing in pearly perfection beneath the stricken form of the Wanderer.

M'Gama stepped forward and slid the horn from beneath Ivy Morris's body. Holding it in both hands, she raised it above her head. Deep silence filled the clearing, as if the stream itself were holding its breath.

"What I do now, I do at the Queen's bidding," said M'Gama, her voice low but powerful. "The Queen's council knows this to be true."

She turned in a slow circle so that all could see the horn. Then, with one swift movement, she raised her knee, brought the horn down sharply against it, and snapped it in half. The unicorns cried out in horror, then fell silent as a rush of wind swept through the clearing, clean, clear, and ripe with magic. The leaves swirled up in dancing patterns, and silver stars seemed to rain about them. Cara thought, for just a moment, that she heard the Queen herself, singing.

491

And then Ivy Morris stood, and cried out in joy and in pain as she shed the false form that had imprisoned her for so many decades, and returned at last to her own true shape and name.

"Behold!" cried M'Gama, pointing to the beautiful young unicorn. "I give you Amalia Flickerfoot, long-lost granddaughter of Arabella Skydancer, returned at last from wandering and exile in time to bid her grandmother farewell. Amalia Flickerfoot, rightful Queen of the unicorns!"

A cry, a song, a shout rose from the clearing.

*The queen is gone. Long live the queen!*


And that is the story of how the one who was lost was found, of how one who wandered at last made her way back home.

What happened next, how Beloved made her attempt on Luster, and the battle that followed, is another story altogether.

It is recorded, like all such tales, in the Unicorn Chronicles.